Praise for *The Erra*

"Kate Innes's glorious first
the best of Pat Bracewell and Elizabeth Chadwick, it offers
utter immersion in an intricate, plausible world. A must read."
Manda Scott, author of the *Boudica* series and *Into the Fire*

"A skilful mix of stories and an intricate and very gripping
narrative. I enjoyed it immensely."
Dr Henrietta Leyser – University of Oxford, author of
Medieval Women – A Social History of Women in England

'*The Errant Hours* is a beautifully crafted epic tale of adventure,
love and courage, worthy of the greatest Medieval Minstrels. A
perfect read around a crackling fire."
Karen Maitland, author of *Company of Liars*

Editor's Choice – Historical Novel Society "an utterly
delightful novel that kept me reading into the small hours.
Very Enjoyable." **Helen Hollick, Historical Novel Society**

"Immaculately researched and beautifully written, this is also a
rollicking historical adventure which will grip you to the last
page. Kate Innes is a natural storyteller with an instinctive
sense of pace. Thoroughly recommended."
Sarah Vincent, author of *The Testament of Vida Tremayne*

"An evocative tale with completely believable characters and
inspiring landscapes … The author herself describes *The Errant
Hours* as 'a headlong journey through the dangers of
Plantagenet Britain' but that doesn't even tell half the story. It's
also about childbirth and parenthood, passion and longing, and
life's rich tapestry. I look forward to reading the next novel by
this talented writer."
Janet Soden for *County Woman Magazine*

The Errant Hours has been placed on a Reading List in the
Medieval Studies Department at **Bangor University, Wales**

Having lived and worked on three continents, Kate Innes has settled with her family near Wenlock Edge in England, and it is this landscape which inspires much of her writing.

Trained as an archaeologist, teacher and museologist, Kate now writes novels, leads writing workshops, and performs her poetry with the acoustic band *Whalebone*. Her first novel, *The Errant Hours*, is one of Book Riot's One Hundred Must-Read Medieval Novels.

www.kateinneswriter.com

All the Winding World

KATE INNES

TO Jo and Mark
with all good wishes

Kate Innes

Mindforest Press

Published in Great Britain by Mindforest Press
www.kateinneswriter.com

Copyright © Kate Innes 2018

ISBN 978-0-9934837-4-5
A catalogue record for this book is available from the British
Library.

Set in Garamond
Cover design by MA Creative http://www.macreative.co.uk
Maps by James Wade http://jameswade.webs.com

Kate Innes asserts her moral right to be identified as the
author of this work.

This is a work of fiction. The characters are products of the
author's imagination.

Printed and bound in Great Britain by Imprint Digital.com

For
Michael

Summary of the family of Illesa Arrowsmith told in *The Errant Hours*:

Illesa is born to Guiliane of Dax (Aquitaine) at Acton Burnel, Shropshire on the 12th September 1266 during an outbreak of the flux. She is the illegitimate daughter of Robert Burnel, at the time a clerk to Prince Edward (later King Edward I) and in Holy Orders. Later he became Bishop of Bath and Wells and Chancellor of England.

Guiliane, Robert's mistress, dies in childbirth attended by Ursula, the village midwife. Ursula had a stillborn daughter the day before and is full of grief. She takes Illesa as her own daughter. Illesa is raised alongside Ursula's elder son, Christopher (known as Kit).

When Illesa is seventeen, Ursula dies. Over a period of several weeks detailed in *The Errant Hours*, Illesa discovers the secret of her real family. Kit is killed on Bardsey Island. With no members of her adoptive family left alive, Illesa must rely on her newly discovered birth father, but she is angry and ambivalent towards him.

Over the course of her adventures, Illesa has fallen in love with Sir Richard Burnel (a cousin to her father, Robert Burnel) and she rejects her new father's attempts to marry her off to anyone other than him.

Events in the Burnel family between *The Errant Hours* **and** *All the Winding World*

By the end of 1284, the year in which Illesa was reunited with her father, Chancellor Robert Burnel had bought the barony of Holdgate – the overlordship of the village where she used to live. After recovering from his serious leg injury in King Edward's Round Table Tournament, Sir Richard Burnel marries Illesa on the 6th October 1284.*

On the 27th August 1285* their first son is born, named for Illesa's brother Christopher (Kit) who was killed on the orders of Giles, the Lord Forester.* In April 1286, Chancellor Robert Burnel visits Langley before setting off with King Edward for an extended administrative tour of France and Gascony on the 13th May. On the 26th February 1288, Illesa gives birth to her second son, Robert, named after her father the Chancellor. He is known as Little Robert. *

On the 12th August 1289, Chancellor Robert Burnel finally returns to England with the King after several years of challenging diplomacy in Gascony. He visits Langley again in July 1290. In December 1291 aged three, Little Robert develops a fever and dies.*

Chancellor Robert Burnel and the King arrive in Berwick-upon-Tweed on the 15th October 1292 to hear the cases of the various contenders for Scotland's throne. Chancellor Robert Burnel dies at Berwick on the 25th October. No cause is officially recorded for his death. (See the *Notes* section at the end of the book for more information.) His body travels from Berwick, heading for his Bishop's seat at Wells Cathedral where it will be buried.

* indicates fictional name or event

The Hours

Matins	one or two hours before dawn
Prime (first hour)	daybreak
Tierce (third hour)	approximately 9:00 am
Sext (sixth hour)	approximately midday
Nones (ninth hour)	approximately 3:00 pm
Vespers	early evening, approximately 6:00 pm
Compline	darkness/sleep, approximately 9:00pm

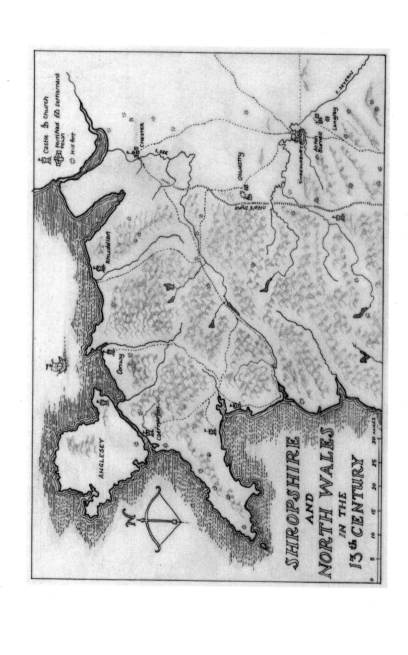

SHROPSHIRE
AND
NORTH WALES
IN THE
13th CENTURY

Castle ♜   Church ⛪   Fortified ⌂ Settlement
House
Hill fort ✳

ANGLESEY

Conway

Caernarvon

Rhuddlan

CHESTER

R. DEE

OSWESTRY

OFFA'S DYKE

SHREWSBURY

Acton
Burnell

Langley

R. SEVERN

0 5 10 15 20 25 30 MILES

AQUITAINE
IN THE
13TH CENTURY

church · Fortified Town
Fortified monastery · Settlement

MILES
0   10   20   30   40   50

Thursday the 6th November AD 1292
The 20th year of the reign of King Edward I
Langley Manor
Vespers

The rooks were flying back to Hawksley wood. Their harsh calls would alert her if the bier and its attendants came down the hill from the north. It was time to leave the churchyard. Illesa had prayed and wept, but not for her father. Old men die. Chancellor Robert would have said just enough prayers to ensure he spent the shortest term in Purgatory. In his will, there would be provision for Masses to be said for his soul for many years to come. Her father might, through all his careful preparation, already be among the blessed.

Whereas her young son, named after him, had only the prayers of his parents. Sometimes Cecily came with Illesa to the churchyard, but she had her own griefs and her own family to mourn. Little Robert had been unencumbered by adult sin. If he couldn't be here singing his tuneless, joyous songs, then, by God's grace, he should be with the joyful in Heaven.

Illesa touched the chapel wall below the statue of the Virgin and Child and looked once more down the empty lane. The slow progress of the funeral procession had allowed word to travel ahead. They would be quite close by now. Her father's body crawling home to Acton on a cart, eviscerated, his heart and entrails preserved, or perhaps buried at Berwick where he died. Someone would have laid him out, washing and anointing him. He would be clothed, wrapped and coffined for the journey.

Since word of his death arrived during the Feast of All Saints, Illesa had imagined it all. But she'd felt relief, not sadness, because the Chancellor's death meant Richard would be accompanying the corpse. He had been away for many weeks, and she had been dreading spending the winter alone.

But when the soul departed, it left the body open to evil use like an unguarded gate. The light was fading rapidly. It would not be good to meet an unburied corpse on the road after dark, even if he was her father and a bishop. She almost ran the rest of the way home. Above the western wood, the sky was painted red and gold like a reliquary.

Illesa quickly crossed the moat bridge, which had been lowered and waiting all day. From the manor came a high-pitched, wailing cry interspersed with snatches of a song praising the Virgin. Cecily's baby had been suffering with knots in the stomach since prime, but it would not be long before she slept. Even the most disconsolate child submitted to Cecily's stroking and crooning in the end.

Illesa's own stomach was twisted with anxiety and had not allowed her to eat all day. She plucked a leaf of mint from the herbs growing by the gate and chewed it as she walked through the yard. It was late and cold, and she had forgotten to wear her cloak. Perhaps Richard would not come tonight at all but stop at Acton Hall. If so, she would only see her husband the next day when she would have to go and pray with the others who had been summoned to Acton to mourn, but who would secretly be glad. Her father's heir, Philip Burnel, had arrived the day before with a train of attendants and baggage as large as the King's. It was his duty to accompany the body on its continuing journey to Wells Cathedral for burial, and, no doubt, he would do it in comfort.

There was no sense standing out in the cold waiting as the last light left the sky. William, the groom, was in the stable giving the horses their evening feed. Now she must see what the cook had prepared in case Richard arrived with company. And she must get Christopher out of the orchard and see that he was dressed decently.

Illesa went through the wicket gate amongst the pear and apple trees. The fruit had been taken in already, but the smell lingered where the fallen fruit had rotted before being gathered for the pigs. Pelta sat at the foot of a spreading apple tree, a slim grey shadow in the twilight. She licked at the smell on Illesa's fingers. By the gate a robin was singing the last song before dark.

"Come down now, my poppet. It's time to go in."

She heard the child move along a branch that grew out flat from the main trunk. He dropped onto the wet leaves and earth, straightened up and reached for her hand. She took his, rubbing the cold fingers. His brown tunic was smeared with green from the tree trunk. Christopher had always been quiet, and quieter still since his brother's death. But he liked watching the work of the manor, standing silently by the wheelwright, smith or wood-turner until they gave him a chore to do. And wherever he was, the dog would always be at his heel. Pelta should have been trained for the hunt, but she was far too docile.

They walked through the twilit orchard together. As they reached the gate, Christopher's hand gripped hers, tight and sudden. Horses were crossing the moat bridge. The boy slipped his hand free and ran. Illesa called after him, but he did not stop. She hurried into the yard towards the dark shapes of two riders.

The men dismounted together. The horses were both unfamiliar black palfreys with funereal harness, but she knew one of the profiles visible against the dark blue of the sky. Richard handed the reins to his squire, took off his gloves and came towards her. Hugh, barely recognisable in the shadow of his hooded cape, bowed wordlessly and took the horses to the stable. He had been with Richard for several months and was still almost as shy as Christopher. The sound of shod hooves moved away across the yard.

Richard put his arms out, and she went to him. His hands were warm and rough with callouses from the long ride, his lips cracked and cold.

"You look tired." She ran her fingers down the scar on his cheek below his missing eye and was rewarded with a smile.

"There is nothing more tiring than going slowly when you are close to home. Today we have come from Haughmond at the pace of a snail. We've left the body of the Chancellor in the church at Acton. Where is that boy? I saw him with you, and now he hides from me."

She pulled him round to walk by her side.

"He will come. Give him some time."

She opened the door to the hall. The lamps had been lit, but the table was not yet laid for supper. Richard looked around and unslung a leather pouch from his shoulder.

"I thought I'd find you here, not over at Acton Hall with that nest of vipers. Have you had many visitations?"

"No, but the messengers have been kept busy riding to and fro. Cecily has been over there and she says –"

"I can imagine. But you can spare me the details for a while."

"Go and change out of your travelling clothes. We will eat soon," Illesa said, smiling as she began to smooth a cloth over the long dining table.

He stayed where he was, looking around the hall for a moment and sighed.

"I give thanks I am at the end of my journey," he said. "Have you been well, wife?"

Tears started in her eyes at his question.

"Well enough. And better from now on," she said, not looking up.

"You are too pale. Hasn't Cecily been looking after you?"

"It's not surprising I look pale. I've been waiting for you in the cold all day, and then when you arrive you're nothing but a ghost of yourself. Any woman would look shocked."

"Ha!" he barked. "It's the dreadful food I've been eating. Mouldy bread and over-salted fish for a whole week. It's surprising there weren't two corpses to bury." He began to mount the stairs to their chamber.

Illesa watched his progress. His limp was worse, perhaps just from riding all day. She finished placing the cups on the table and went out to the kitchen.

They were all very hungry and ate without much conversation. But when Cecily, William and Hugh left the table to finish their duties before bed, the question Christopher had been hatching all week burst out.

"How did Chancellor Robert die, Father? Was he ill, like Little Robert?"

Richard stopped chewing and turned to his son.

"No, he wasn't ill," Richard said, swallowing. "He was an old man but in good health. He really was nothing like Little Robert except in name." Richard pushed his plate away and leant forward over the table. "Little Robert died from a fever. You know the prayers you must say to prevent it from coming back?" Christopher nodded solemnly and pulled the chewed edge of his tunic. His father gazed at him, fingering the pendant cross hanging from his neck. "I will tell you how Robert the Chancellor died if you can keep it to yourself," he said softly.

"I will, Father."

"I know you will, Christopher. You keep everything to yourself," he said, sighing. "But I am telling you this so that you understand Death is always near, and we cannot tell when he will come for us." A muscle by his mouth twitched, and Richard rubbed his week's growth of beard. "Chancellor Robert was with King Edward in Berwick, speaking to the Scots about the succession to the throne. He had been receiving representations from all the contenders with their very complicated legal arguments. But the Chancellor was the best man in the Kingdom to deal with that."

"Did you see the throne, Father?"

"No, Christopher. I was in Berwick, not in Scotland. Do you want to hear this tale?"

Christopher nodded, looking wary.

"The Chancellor went out of his lodging to clear his mind. Breathing fresh air helps a man think. He was walking along the coast with his clerk when he suddenly fell to the ground." Richard leant closer to Christopher. "An idiot lad amongst the Scots had slung a beach pebble in a fit of temper. The Chancellor was wearing simple robes that day, so he probably didn't know he was aiming at a bishop," he whispered. "That pebble hit him on the back of the head, and the King's most trusted friend died immediately, without a chance to confess."

Christopher opened his mouth to speak, but Illesa put her hand on his arm as Richard continued.

"The things we cannot do before death, those who love us do for us after death through God's grace. Mass will be said for his soul tomorrow, and he will soon meet his saviour."

"Was he like Goliath, killed by the boy David?" Christopher asked. He was looking up at his father, excited, waiting for more.

"Except that the good was on the side of the Bishop, not the stupid lad who threw the stone," Richard declared, bringing his hand down hard on the table. "So you should learn this lesson and never sling stones at people."

Illesa shivered suddenly in a cold draught.

"Little Robert had the remedies of the Church before he died," she added, putting her hand on the crown of Christopher's head and stroking his hair. "We also had Masses said for him. We pray every day for his soul, don't we, darling?"

Her son's eyes were large and shining in the firelight, searching her face, wanting the promise that his brother was in Heaven.

"Christopher, go and find Cecily. She will put you to bed. You look tired."

The boy wrapped his thin arms around her neck for a moment and then went, closing the hall door behind him.

"Is that true?" Illesa asked, turning to face Richard. "My father was killed by a sling-stone? You said none of this in your message."

"No, and nor should you to anyone. It must remain a secret and never be written down. If word got out that the Chancellor was killed by the Scots, it would throw the negotiations into confusion. There would be violent clashes. That's why his body was taken away so quickly while the other bishops have all stayed in Berwick. His death has not been widely proclaimed."

"But surely they didn't kill him on purpose? They would know that they would go straight to Hell for such a grave sin."

"No, it was just a lad barely older than Christopher. He's had his whipping," Richard said, running his hand through his lank hair. "A lad slings a stone, and now the world changes."

Things would certainly change at Acton. The ravens had already landed for their share of the Chancellor, dividing up the goods and chattels at Acton Hall without thought of his will. If she'd thought she could face the FitzAlans, Illesa would have gone there and at least rescued some of the books and the bed hangings. But she was not yet strong enough to argue with them or even look at their haughty faces.

"I have something for you from your father," Richard said. "He intended it for both of you, but I think the boy is too young to read it yet." He got up stiffly and went to the leather pouch slung over the chair.

"Your leg is worse," Illesa said to his back.

12

"Ack, not so bad. It doesn't like riding. And walking by a cart even less."

He slumped back in the chair, pushed the platter to the side and opened the pouch. The object was wrapped first in cerecloth then in silk. She lifted the fine blue fabric away. The book was quite large, its brown leather binding ornamented only by a simple tooled border of repeated waves, like a stormy sea. Illesa pulled the tight leather strap off its pin. The spine creaked as she smoothed the first stiff page of the book flat with her palm.

"The Romance of Troy. In French."

"Yes, the boy must begin to read French, not just Latin as you did as a child. There are lots of words and not very many pictures."

"One of the Stories of Antiquity," she said, lightly brushing her finger over an image of the Golden Fleece.

"You could read it to Christopher for now. It will give him something else to think about."

"Whose idea was this, Richard? Yours or my father's?"

He sat back in his chair and stretched, smiling at the ceiling.

"You know us well."

"I know that he would have bought me a jewel, but you told him I'd rather have this."

"I know you well also."

"You should by now. Where is it from?"

"France. Maybe Normandy. He bought it from a merchant in Aquitaine. The family who commissioned it fell into poverty."

Illesa turned the pages slowly, seeing word upon word of combat and death, and stopped at a page with a small illustration showing knights jousting.

"King Menelaus jousted with Paris, striking him, I believe, so that he split his shield. Paris would certainly have been slain on the spot, but his hauberk was so strong that his opponent could not undo the mail. But Menelaus made him slip off his horse from the blow, and Paris fell over his horse's crupper. He was very much ashamed of this because Helen was watching him."

"It seems much blood will be shed before the end," she said and turned the page.

"Illesa, I'm afraid you must come to the church tomorrow for the Mass."

She looked up from the procession of words.

"And be condescended to and muttered about. Of course I will be there. And when it's finished, I'm taking the books out of Acton Hall and bringing them here before they can be sold off like this one was," she snapped.

He smiled.

"You must be feeling a bit better. Perhaps even well enough to read this?"

He pulled a folded piece of parchment from the pouch. The wax vesica seal showed a striding elephant with the name 'Roberti Burneli' in the border.

Illesa put it down on the table and folded her hands in her lap.

"Just tell me what it says and save me the trouble of reading his scribe's dreadful script." A tear spilt onto her cheek, her first for him.

"I do not know what it says," Richard said, softly. "But I do know that he was very concerned about you. He did not like quarrelling. It upset his digestion."

She looked at the tiny elephant, a strange creature, long-legged with a nose like a snake. Not at all like her rotund and infuriating second father who had come to her so late and could never publicly be her father because he was a bishop. Who was now lying in the church he'd built next to the hall he would never eat in again.

She carefully opened the letter, sliding her finger under the wax to leave the seal intact.

Lady Illesa
Greetings to you in Christ's name —

I pray this finds you well. I am detained here in the North for some time, preventing me from visiting my beloved natal place, as I hoped to do. If this business is completed satisfactorily, I hope to visit you at Christmastide.

It has been made known to me that I was not thoughtful about the death of your son Robert, and that your grief was worsened by my seemed indifference. Dear Illesa, I also grieve for him and keep him in my prayers. He is listed on the roll of the Chapel at Wells. Despite the many demands on my time, I always pray that you will be blessed with another son, or a daughter. For they are also gifts from the Lord.

I was gladdened to have word from your Aunt in Guyenne after I visited her during the King's sojourn in Gascony. I beg of you to write to her inviting your cousin Azalais to visit you. She sings most wonderfully, better than many men. Some may disapprove of this, but it is the custom in the demesne of your mother's family and further east, I am told. Azalais has recently been widowed, and I believe it would relieve the rest of the family if she went away for some time.

May Saint Margaret and all the saints protect you and your son Christopher, keeping you safe from the attacks of Satan.
In Christ's love
Roberti

Illesa read it twice and turned to Richard. He was cradling his head in his hands, barely awake. She gave him the letter. When he looked up from it, he raised his eyebrows at her.

"A noble widow of Gascony." He sucked his breath between his teeth. "She sounds like trouble."

Chapter I

Tuesday the 24th August 1294
Langley Manor
Vespers

Illesa had been expecting William to return with the stockmen, so she did not look up at the sound of hooves until the horses were already over the bridge. Three men, all strangers. Two of them on good rounceys, bearing the arms of the King. The last man, a servant, on an inadequately broken palfrey that kept turning its head.

The older man-at-arms turned his horse to assess the hall. The other was blond and tall. He stilled his horse and sat motionless, waiting. The servant with the bad palfrey was weighed down with several packs, red-faced and hot from heaving his mount's head up from the grazing.

"Christ preserve us." Richard limped angrily towards the gate where the men were waiting. "Coming at the end of the day and expecting a bed for the night."

Illesa stood up from where she'd been squatting by the herb beds, wiped her hands on her worst surcote and followed him, reaching the gate as the older man was dismounting from the roan mare. He smelled of leather and drink, and a long journey.

"Burnel?"

"Indeed. Your name, sir, and that of your companion?"

The blond rider had dismounted quickly and stood, his face expressionless, attentive at the first man's side.

"You must be getting old if you don't remember a fellow soldier who fought alongside you at Rhuddlan and Conwy. Eh? You've started to grow soft in your Garden of Eden?" He waved dismissively at the carefully planted beds of herbs and vegetables between the hall and the moat.

"Clement." Richard's mouth stiffened around the name. "It's been many years, and you have changed. Grown a beard, and some girth."

The man laughed, sudden and loud, and the servant behind him started as if stung by a bee. Jumpy from too much beating.

"This here is Walter de Penderton, my lieutenant," he said, indicating the blond man. Walter stepped forward, his head slightly inclined, his eyes fixed on Richard.

"My wife, Lady Burnel," Richard said without turning to her. His hand was fidgeting with his belt where his scabbard would be if he were not at home and at rest after a long season with the court.

Peter, the stable boy, had finally noticed that there were three unknown horses in his yard and was inching towards them. William was still in the forest. Azalais was in London, spending her inheritance and enjoying herself. Cecily was indoors with baby Joyce. And Christopher would be reading behind their bed on the floor, where the light came through the window, with Pelta's grey head resting on the small of his back. That's why there was never any warning of strangers. The blessed dog was too content to have a boy as a cushion.

Clement was unstrapping his pack from the skittish horse, making himself at home and shouting at Peter as well as at his own servant. Illesa turned to Richard and opened her mouth, but he shook his head very slightly at her as Clement strode towards them. Richard stood a little straighter.

"You are welcome here, Clement, but, as you see we have a simple home. Our repast may disappoint you."

Clement's smile was knowing.

"Our business is brief, Burnel. We will not drain your casks in one night. I see you are as careful with your money as your cousin was wasteful." Clement put his hand on Richard's shoulder. "It can't cost much to live here with so few servants and no town nearby. Took a lot of trouble to find you, so best you make an effort."

He steered Richard towards the door, and they went into the hall while Walter de Penderton followed the servants and the horses into the stable.

Illesa stayed by the garden, where she had been cutting comfrey and putting it into a cloth bag. She could hear the red-faced servant complaining loudly to Peter. There was no sound from the blond man with the strange, empty eyes. He looked capable of anything.

"Lessa!" Richard hissed from the doorway.

She went quickly into the dark hall, shutting the door softly behind her. The negligent dog was leaning her narrow head against Richard's bad leg. Richard pulled Illesa across to the corner by the pantry door.

"Who are they? Why are they here?" she whispered.

"Agents of the King sent to recruit for the war."

"I thought the next visit would be to appropriate treasure for his war chest. They won't find many soldiers here."

"Shhhh," he said, raising his hand.

Footsteps sounded on the flags outside, getting louder.

Illesa ran to the door and pulled, just as Walter pushed it open.

"Come in, Master," she said as he tripped forward into the sudden absence of door. "Oh, I am sorry."

He righted himself without a word. There was no anger in his face; it was simply the look one saw on a fox stalking hens.

Richard was quickly there beside her, apologising and showing the man to the stairs and up to the best chamber with the view of the fields and livestock, the fishponds and watermill. Everything they relied on.

Illesa turned and went through to the pantry to store the herbs. Outside in the kitchen, Adam was banging and clattering, preparing what meat they had already slaughtered. He would have to kill at least two ducks, but he didn't need telling. She stayed out of his sight. He would only become more anxious and ask questions.

Upstairs baby Joyce was crying. Cecily must be preparing the chambers for the guests or running after her own two girls. Joyce was swaddled and couldn't come to harm, but when she was hungry she was as loud as the trumpets of Hell. Illesa took the stairs two at a time, arriving breathless in their chamber lit by the golden evening light. Richard was rocking the cradle and trying to offer Joyce his finger to suck.

"Here, I'm here. What a noise. Enough to wake the dead." She held out her arms, and Richard placed Joyce in the curve of her body. She sat down on the edge of the bed and put her to the breast. The sudden silence was filled with the small noises of a baby feeding.

Richard was not smiling as he usually did when Joyce was quiet and content. He stood by the window, running his hand through his hair.

"Who is that blond man Penderton? Have you met before?"

"No, never." Richard shook his head quickly. "But he's seen service somewhere."

"I don't like him being in the house," she whispered. "Where are William and the other men? They should be back by now."

"They won't be back today. I told them to go to Shrewsbury."

"What?" Illesa cried. "Why?"

"Better if you don't know."

"Richard!"

"We mustn't antagonise them, Illesa. It will only make matters worse. They have great power. We need to placate them and move them out quickly. It's the best chance."

"But what do they want? They aren't really thinking of taking our men on a fool's errand to France are they?"

He shook his head again and walked to the door.

"Probably," he sighed. "But we will try to persuade them otherwise. A bribe might be needed. Change your clothes and tell Cecily to prepare the table. Perhaps they will be willing to negotiate after a good meal," he said, shutting the door behind him.

When Illesa entered the hall in her best kirtle with her hair freshly arranged under a fine cotton veil, the men were already seated, and the meat was steaming in the centre of the table. Peter's brother, Crispin, had been brought in to serve at table. He was offering the cloth to dry the visitor's newly washed hands. He looked terrified.

Richard frowned at her as she approached, holding the baby. He did not like Joyce in the hall while they were eating, but she cried if she was put down alone in the evening, and Cecily was busy helping Adam. Richard, seemingly, had sent everyone away who could be of any help. Cecily walked behind her with the cradle and put it down near Illesa's chair. Illesa placed Joyce carefully inside and pulled it towards her so she could rock it with her foot.

Cecily curtseyed slightly, first to Richard then to the visitors.

"My lords, my lady," she drawled and left through the door to the buttery.

Clement watched her go, his mouth already full. He continued helping himself from the platter of meat with a fine sharp knife.

"I was just saying to Sir Richard that we have found the lands here most agreeable. So fertile, so sheltered," he said through his food. "I expect it was a hovel before the blessed Chancellor got hold of it. But haven't you done well with his money? Or should I say the *Crown's* money."

Richard kept eating, his eyes fixed on his wine, but Walter had stopped chewing and was completely still. Waiting for something.

"Comfortable for you, isn't it? We've been almost the length of Wales. Started in Carmarthen. What a shit hole," he said, grinning. "Nothing there. You'd think the Welsh lived in sties; that's all we saw, just a few pigs!"

Richard stopped eating. He lifted his cup and sipped from it. Clement chewed thoughtfully in the cold silence.

"But yes, this is a nice place. I can see why you haven't wanted to leave for a while, Sir Richard. And why the summons have found it hard to reach you."

"What is the purpose of this unpleasant journey, my lords? You seem heartily sick of your travels," Illesa asked.

Clement looked at her and smiled slowly, showing the meat stuck between his teeth. He turned back to Richard.

"There's nothing like hearth and home – and a wife, eh, Sir Richard? Nothing quite like the warm bed and the feel of your chair beneath your arse. You've been keeping quiet and looking after your line of succession ever since the death of the Chancellor. That's what's been keeping you awake at night. Not the service you promised. Not the duty you owe your King."

"Clement, you have come to board and there is good meat to eat. Let's discuss this later when we have had our fill. When

20

my wife has retired with the babe, we can speak of these things plainly."

Clement laughed and picked up his cup.

"It won't matter when we discuss it, the outcome will be the same."

Under the table, Pelta darted forward to retrieve a piece of bread that had dropped on the floor. And that meant Christopher was nearby even though he had been strictly told to stay out of the hall and to eat with Cecily and Adam. Illesa glanced quickly around. Yes, he was behind the screen that blocked the view of the buttery, given away by the chewed end of his old brown tunic.

Clement was draining his wine, but Walter remained as still and alert as before.

"Good. Yes, quite good. From Gascony, I expect. I did hear that the Chancellor had several tonnes sent back. He shared everything with you, didn't he? And provided for that boy too, I heard." He pointed to where Christopher hid. "Though I've never understood a fondness for whelps myself." He held his knife as if to throw it at the figure behind the screen.

He laughed as Richard surged to his feet, his chair clattering behind him.

"Ha! The rabbit is out of his hole. Don't worry, Sir Richard, I won't kill the boy even though he is spying. I have a boy of my own, but he's a proper squire. Going with me to France."

Richard took Christopher by the arm and pulled him out.

"How old is he, eh?"

"I am nearly nine years, sir," Christopher said.

"Nearly nine are you? You are too young, my lad. Too small and weak to join the knights. And not fit for the conversation of your elders either. Nearly nine," he scoffed. "Well, skin and bones, keep spying and you will never reach the age you seek."

Richard put his arm around Christopher's narrow shoulders and whispered in his ear.

"Yes, Father." He bowed slightly to Clement, who was eating again, snapped his fingers and left the hall. The dog followed, her claws clicking on the hard floor.

Illesa could hear Christopher running up the stairs and across to the small room where there was a little gap in the wall, to listen there. He was as stubborn as both his parents.

Walter had got up and was walking around the hall, looking behind the screen into the buttery. Joyce grizzled at the lack of attention. Illesa tapped the cradle with her foot and glared at Clement.

"What is this mission of yours, Clement, that gives you such licence in our home? What brings you here?"

"You would know that already, Lady Burnel, if your husband had thought it right to tell you." Richard cleared his throat, but Clement did not wait. "Your husband has been summoned to serve in Gascony, to fight against the treacherous French who have invaded the Duchy. King Edward has demanded Sir Richard's service, and all we have had is excuses. Excuses and no men. We need at least twenty from this place."

"I wrote to the King explaining why I cannot serve him overseas," Richard said in the flat tone that masked his anger. "We have lost much since the Chancellor's death. His heir, Sir Philip, has also died. The inquisition into his debts will take months." Richard pointed at the hall window. "The men of this demesne are not soldiers. They have no experience and no training. And I am no longer fit to lead them into battle."

"You seem virile enough," Clement said, glancing towards the cradle.

Richard leant forward, pushing a platter out of the way.

"The King knows my faithful service over many years. The Burnel family has always been loyal, but I am no longer a soldier. My wounds trouble me and prevent me from the physical duties of a knight. Surely you can see that?"

Clement placed his large stained hands, palm down, on the table and stuck out his chin.

"If I listened to every excuse, we'd have no army," he grunted. "Do you know what I had to do to encourage the Welsh to enlist? It was like a scene from the Feast of the Innocents. Walter here makes a good Herod's man. He never baulks from his duty. I didn't let him massacre the children, but the screams of their women when he threatened the babes with his sword had the men coming forward in large numbers."

At the mention of his name, Walter stopped his tour of the hall and turned towards his master.

"But we don't want a useless cripple on our expedition," Clement continued. "You say that your wounds pain you? Well, of course you cannot come if you suffer so much and can hardly move. And if you cannot serve, how can your men?" He straightened up and waved his arms in the air. "These imaginary men who barely exist."

Illesa was so horrified by Clement's speech that she did not notice Walter moving to stand near the cradle. He picked up the swaddled baby and held Joyce high over his head. Illesa pushed herself out of her chair, saw Richard lunging at the man.

Clement smiled.

"But it is remarkable what a man will do when he must," he said.

Walter threw Joyce high and far down the length of the table towards the bare floor, her mouth open, eyes suddenly wide. Illesa stumbled over the upturned chair as she ran.

The blur of movement at the end of the table was Richard, his arms in the air, reaching Joyce as she fell. He landed heavily on his side with the baby clutched to his chest. She began to gulp air, her face turning red as if she were choking.

Illesa fell down next to him, took Joyce in her arms, put her cheek to her lips to feel her breath, ran her fingers over the dome of her head. The baby gasped and began crying loudly. And from above, Illesa could hear Christopher screaming through the small hole where he had been watching.

"You devil!" she shouted at Clement. "You damned devil!"

Richard was breathing painfully, hunched over his bad leg, white and shaking.

"It seems to me, Sir Richard, that you still have the speed and reactions of a knight and will be entirely fit to serve," Clement said with satisfaction.

Chapter II

Monday the 13th September 1294
Langley Manor
Tierce

"Have you been to the chapel?" Illesa asked as Richard came into the hall. He nodded, closed the door and came to the table where she sat with Joyce asleep on her breast. "With the candles I laid out for you? Do you think the quality was good enough? I had them from a new stall, and – "

"Yes Illesa, they were good strong candles. It was the work of two men to stand them up before the altar."

She had measured him, had the candles made to his length and dedicated them to Saint Christopher. But the offering was more powerful if Richard lit the candles himself. The silk she had used to measure him was in her purse, wound and knotted in the special way. She would keep the length of him near her while he was gone.

"And I went to Little Robert's grave and prayed for his soul," Richard said quietly as he sat down on the bench on her left side, so he could see her with his one eye. He put his hand to Joyce's forehead. But there was no point waking her so that he could hold her before he left. She would only scream.

"Have you got the special salt-meat that Cecily put aside?"

Richard raised his eyebrows at her.

"Illesa, you have asked me twice already. You watched William pack the satchels. I have all the comforts you have made, all the fortifications that a woman can provide."

"Tell me again the names of the men who are going with you. I forgot the ones from Pitchford."

Richard scratched the back of his head beneath his old cap.

"Almost all of them seem to glory in the name of John. We have three Johns, so we shall have to have John the lesser, John the greater and plain John. The others you know: Hugh, Reginald and Alan."

"And William."

"Of course."

William, of all the men, was the one who reassured her. He was always alert and had no scruples when it came to enemies.

"Illesa, I must speak of a few things before I leave."

She drew breath. This happened each time he went away. Richard was meticulous in matters regarding the stock, the planting and the necessity of keeping the drawbridge maintained. It would be a long list. They had new cattle that were not easy to handle, and the war would not end quickly enough for the winter slaughter.

Richard turned so that his legs were on either side of the bench, and the faint light of a dull morning showed dark swollen shadows under his eyes. He'd been sleepless for many days.

"I'm glad you have Azalais here, when she *is* here. I wish you'd let Cecily nurse Joyce, but you will not listen to that, I expect," he said ruefully. "You will have your hands full with the manor while I'm gone, so don't try to be with Joyce all the time. Cecily is a very able nurse."

Illesa nodded, staring ahead with blurring eyes.

"I've told the herdsmen to sleep in the stable while I'm gone. They will be at least a first warning of trouble."

She said nothing. Interruptions and questions only stopped his thoughts, and he had to chase them back to their source. It made him cross.

"I trust what you do with the stock. Matthew of Hanley will help you. He has a good head on his shoulders, although it's not a quick one. The Chancery men will come to take the tax in a few weeks, so there are things that will need to be hidden. You know the usual places. I think it would be best to put the citole away, as well as the books. Valuable and portable objects will be just what the men are looking for. When I come home, we will dig them all out again and dance in the hall as we used to."

Joyce seemed to agree in her sleep, sighing and burping at the same time, her open mouth falling away from the breast.

Richard smiled.

Illesa sat Joyce up and stroked her back.

"There is one more important thing I must tell you before I go." He straightened his leg and flexed it under the bench again, the old boots scraping on the flags. He had not let her get him new ones, said it was a waste wearing good leather in war as they were likely to be stolen, probably by the supposed friends on your own side.

"Illesa, are you listening?"

She nodded. Joyce had started to complain and rub her face on Illesa's tunic, but once she was back on the breast her wide blue eyes closed.

"When your cousin William came to visit in June –"

"I'd rather you didn't call him that."

"I know, but there are so many Williams it is sometimes necessary. In any event, when the Dean of Wells arrived in June, I'm sure you noticed his baggage."

William, the arrogant nephew of the Chancellor, never travelled anywhere without at least two packhorses and three grooms. He didn't speak to Illesa if he could help it. As far as he was concerned, Richard had married beneath him. Her own parentage was a secret. That was the way it had to be, and Illesa was glad. She did not have to greet him as any relation of hers. His temperament did nothing to recommend him.

"Inside the larger chest there was an embroidered cope which your father had commissioned," Richard continued.

"One of the long capes he wore when he was in processions? Why on earth would William bring that here?"

A strong beat was thudding in her temple. The long hand of High Office was still reaching into her family, rifling through their lives, fingering every dish. Richard got up from the bench and looked through the window. He came back to her with his finger to his lips and sat down again on the bench.

"We need to speak quietly. All the men are in the yard." Richard took a deep breath, as if he were climbing a hill. "Three years before he died, when Bishop Robert was in Gascony, he had made a commitment to the Archbishop of Bordeaux to procure an embroidered cope of fine English work. The Archbishop made it clear that his loyalty to the English King would be improved by this gift. He wanted to be as magnificently clothed as a cardinal," Richard said scornfully. "But the work on it stopped because the King would not pay.

Edward insisted on spending all the Treasury's silver on preparations for his next Crusade." Richard looked over towards the window. "It seems there is little chance of that happening now."

Richard had spoken of this before. Since the death of Queen Eleanor, the King had been frustrated in his desire to take up the Cross in the East, and in many other ways.

"There was debate about what should be done with the unfinished vestment," Richard continued. "No one wanted to pay, and the embroiderers refused to complete it. It stayed like that for more than a year. But Robert must have wanted to keep his word to the Archbishop because he included the cost of finishing it in his will. I don't think King Edward liked the idea of pandering to Bordeaux, but Uncle Robert knew the value of flattery. The cope is exquisite," Richard said, his face brightening with the memory.

Outside in the yard, someone was hammering a shoe. Someone else was cursing as a pack split a seam. Soon they would all be mounted and gone, and Richard would not be sitting near her. Illesa put her free hand on his.

"This vestment is still here?"

Richard nodded.

"By the time it was finished last year, relations with the French King had soured, and all shipping was threatened. It could not be sent or taken to Bordeaux legitimately; that would look like appeasement. So it went to Wells, where the new Bishop took a liking to it. He wanted it for his Easter procession. William, as I think you know, does not like the new Bishop. He finds him unsympathetic and lacking in the appropriate attitude to his office. I think the feeling is mutual. In any event, William pointed out that the Chancellor had paid for its completion from his own funds, and so it was no longer the property of the Bishop's See." Richard smiled a little. "While the Bishop was away in London, he packed it up and brought it here. It is worth at least forty pounds," he concluded quietly. "If the tax men find it, it will certainly be taken. There is nothing they would like more."

In the yard the horses were being saddled. Greyboy whinnied. Hooves scraped the cobbles, and Cecily admonished William for taking all her beeswax for the harness.

"Where have you put it?" Illesa whispered.

"You won't like it."

"You have to tell me anyway," she said.

"It's in the cell with the Anchoress," Richard admitted. "We thought no one would willingly go in there."

A shiver crept down Illesa's spine. She could picture the stone tomb in which Richard's mother had been laid to rest; it was a shape of greater darkness just visible if you opened the shuttered, barred window of her cell. The smell of decay that hung there like smoke on a still day made people cross themselves when they passed. Not even the protection marks Illesa had carved on the wall with her shears made it feel any better.

"How have you stored it? The cell roof has lost some tiles; the rain might have got in."

"That is dealt with. It was one of the last things Sir Philip paid for. He didn't want the angry revenant of the Anchoress haunting him, demanding better housing. And the cope is well wrapped in cerecloth."

"What does it look like?"

She would love to see it and to run her hands over the fine needlework. Illesa had only ever seen one cope before, when she had been at Wells for the feast of Corpus Christi. It had been covered in pearls and gold thread on scarlet velvet. As bright as blood.

One of the men called from the yard, and Richard got up from the bench heavily.

"It is like looking at Heaven. The seraphim's wings flash as if lit by the glory of God. It shows the Creation of the World, with all its creatures, and the Garden of Eden. The Expulsion, Adam delving and Eve spinning." His hands moved up and down, as he pictured where the scenes appeared on the cope. "And in the centre – the Crucifixion and Resurrection of Our Lord. It makes you want to kneel. I have never seen a better vestment. It is a shame it lies in darkness."

Adam delving and Eve spinning, condemned to suffering along with all those who came after them. And all because of a moment beneath an apple tree, in between the sweetness of a bird singing and then growing silent. She shook the thought from her mind. Illesa laid the sleeping Joyce in the cradle, set it rocking and went to Richard's side. He took her hand.

"We must find Christopher," she said, her voice choked.

"I've seen him this morning. He followed us to the chapel with that dog. She is more present than his shadow."

"Pelta guards him like the angel at the gates of Paradise."

"May he be kept safe," Richard said, gripping both her hands. "May all be well while I am away. May the Lord protect you."

"And may you return safely." Illesa brought his hands to her lips. Then they went out into the bright sun in the yard.

"Ah, here he is," Richard said, letting go of her hand.

Christopher was standing by Greyboy, giving him a last brush. William was stroking Pelta, who was wriggling with excitement.

"What will you do while I'm gone, Christopher?" Richard asked him, pulling his riding gloves on.

"How long are you going for? I may be a grown man when you return," Christopher said. He put the brush down and looked up at his father.

"By God, why do you say that?" Richard asked. "I will be home very soon, maybe even before Christmastide."

"The knights who went to Troy were gone for ten years. And some for longer."

William straightened up laughing. He got Christopher round the neck with one arm and ruffled his hair.

"We're only going to Gascony, lad. Not to the Ancient lands. You live in a different world in that book of yours. By God, we'd better return soon, or I'll swim here myself!"

He released Christopher, who backed away from him grinning.

"And I've come and gone many times to war," Richard said, "and none of them lasted more than a year. This time I am to be one of the commanders. Hopefully I'll be out of the fray and keep my remaining eye." He winked at Christopher with it. "So you will still be a boy when I return, please God. Bear Christ, my son, and guard your home. And remember me when you pray."

Christopher lowered his head. His shoulders hunched.

"I will," he whispered.

"My good boy," Richard said softly, going to Christopher and holding him in the crook of his arm. "My good lad. I will pray for you." He looked around the yard. "Now, where is that woman, Azalais?" he asked, clearing his throat.

"There," Illesa said, pointing to the kitchen. Azalais, in a kirtle the colour of fresh straw, stood eating bread in the doorway. It was probably the bread intended for dinner. When she saw them looking at her, she came over, wiping the crumbs from her dress.

"You want me to look after your wife and your children, Richard?" She said it as if she was offering him a kiss. "But you know I like to be free. I am not used to staying in this quiet place. When I am here, I will be always concerned with their care, naturally. When I am not, I will pray. That is that," she said wiping her hands of the obligation, "and God will look after you and them, as you well know. Go now, before we all start weeping."

"That is a fine farewell, I must say," muttered William. He bowed to Azalais while Richard kissed Illesa.

"I will send word when we sail."

"I will remind him," William said.

William helped Richard mount Greyboy, who shone with his bright new harness fittings. His crupper had been adjusted to help Richard ride comfortably with his injured leg. The other men moved forward on palfreys, leading the two packhorses behind them. William had expertly balanced their loads. There would be no lame horses or falls into ditches because of their burdens. He mounted the skittish new riding horse they'd had to buy in Welshpool at huge expense. Illesa knew William would have her perfectly trained by the time they reached Portsmouth, if not before. William and horses understood each other.

"It's a fine day to start your journey," called Azalais. "May God bless you with fair weather."

Illesa gripped Christopher's hand. Her voice had dried up. She watched them ride away, waving as Richard crossed the bridge.

Chapter III

Thursday the 30th September 1294
Shrewsbury
Tierce

Azalais was quick with her purse at the town gate and treated the guard to one of her grateful looks as they walked through. It was always so expensive coming to town, finding a safe place to stable the horses and paying the tolls. Illesa was grateful that Azalais, who always seemed to have plenty of coin, had agreed to come with her, especially so early in the morning.

"I have some business nearby," Azalais said, holding her veil against a gust of wind. "You don't need me to come to the mews, do you? I will meet you at Saint Mary's, if we don't get blown to Heaven first."

Azalais tolerated most animals, but not birds. She avoided them and wished they would do the same to her. They reminded her of a hanged corpse she'd seen as a child in Dax. She had watched as its eyes were pecked out. If a crow landed near her, she turned as grey as a raincloud.

"Very well. At the hour of sext by the Lady Chapel?"

They parted at the top of the Wyle, and Illesa thought she knew where Azalais' business lay. There was a certain furrier on Candle Lane. Azalais always felt the cold, and she would want to be prepared for the English winter. Her cousin had been happy enough to accompany Illesa and Christopher, as long as they were back in time to go to the Michaelmas Fair at Acton. If they were delayed she would be sulky. Even sulkier than Christopher, who always looked forward to the fair but found it overwhelming.

Illesa took Christopher's hand in a firmer grip. He was not looking around him, just straight down at his feet. At least he was alert enough to avoid the puddles and piles of dung. Normally being in Shrewsbury would have felt like a treat. She enjoyed buying candles for the chapel, finding the kind of pie

Christopher liked, seeing the goods for sale. But there was an emptiness since Richard's departure that even the best pie could not fill.

It was still early, and the stalls and shop fronts were just opening. Ahead of them the square tower of Saint Mary's rose high into a patch of blue sky. The first time she had been inside was when Richard brought her to Shrewsbury as his new wife. He had coin in his purse and wanted to spend it. As well as arranging for new sheets and bed curtains, he had made a rather showy donation to the church and asked for a Mass to bless her unborn child. He had also bought wine, having sampled many kinds. It had been a hot day in April after the Feast of the Resurrection.

They rounded the back of the church heading for the Altus Vicus with its tall houses. In the distance she could hear heavy wheels grinding on stone and a low beat, like a drum, echoing on many walls. It was not the usual sound of Shrewsbury. Illesa looked down at Christopher, but he was still staring at his feet as if he had never seen them walking before.

"What do you think, my love, will it rain on us again?" she asked, smiling at him.

He looked up at her and nodded solemnly.

"When we get to the castle, you can come to choose the goshawk with me. And you can hold it while I speak to the man who is taking it to London."

"Why can't we keep it?" he asked, his eyes growing wide at the thought.

"I wish we could, but this hawk must go to the King's Mews at Stepney. If we do not send it, the King could take our home away." They were coming down the hill towards the wall of the bailey, and the wind was gusting up the wide street. "When old King Henry granted the land to the Burnels, he wanted a Welsh goshawk to fly every year because they are the fastest. That was the agreement in exchange for the land, and it has been ever since. So even now we must send the blessed bird across the whole country at some expense. I doubt that King Edward ever has a chance to fly them all. He must have countless hawks and falcons."

"He wouldn't miss this one then. We should take it home," Christopher said, his voice excited for the first time that day. They arrived at the wide bailey gate and stopped.

"He would miss it," Illesa said firmly. "The King doesn't allow anything to slip past him. Here we are. Keep quiet, as you always do, and only touch the bird when I say you can."

The guard looked at her parchment and its seal with an expression of deep distrust.

"We are here to see the Master Falconer as Sir Richard Burnel does every year. Please send word to him that Lady Burnel is here to conduct the usual business."

He gestured her through, and they stood just inside the gatehouse while a boy was dispatched to the mews. Christopher looked happier now that they were away from the street. A small cat was stalking a bird on the castle wall, and he watched it intently.

"Will Gilbert catch Robin?" Illesa sang.

"No, Robin will get away. You watch," he said confidently.

The pageboy came running back, and the robin flew up to the castle tower. The cat stared after it and then began to wash its paws. Christopher clapped his hands and laughed. The older boy gave him a pitying look and signalled for them to follow him.

Illesa had never done this duty. Richard had always swept it into one of his other errands in the town. But it was traditional that it was done at Michaelmas when the birds had fledged, and the falconer could see how things stood for the next year. Then he would set aside the goshawk for Langley. But for this Feast of the Archangel, Richard was in Gascony, and William, who would have done it in his absence, was with him.

They had passed all the buildings of the bailey and gone round the back under the wall of the keep to a long low building with a new thatched roof. The boy opened the door for them and ran back to the gatehouse.

The room was familiar and strange. The first time she had ever seen Richard had been in a mews. When she thought of it, she remembered it as full of light. But this building was in the most shaded part of the bailey and rather gloomy. There were several young men checking the condition of the tethered birds. She didn't want to call out and alarm them, so she coughed quietly. A man straightened up and came over to her. Christopher was trying to pull her towards a falcon on their left, but she tugged him back.

"Master Falconer? I am Lady Burnel. My husband has been sent overseas, and so I have come to arrange the delivery of a goshawk as is customary."

He nodded his head and looked at Christopher.

"Good day, Lady Burnel. That boy's eyes are as big as an owl's."

"My son, Christopher. He is very interested in birds."

The falconer nodded. He was a small, quick man. Not old, but very weathered.

"Well, you have chosen an interesting time to come," he said, looking out of the nearest window.

"Isn't this the customary time? I thought – "

"Yes, yes it is. Let's choose the bird and get you out of here before you are caught up in the other business."

"In what, Master?"

"You may find out all too soon. Come this way."

The goshawks were kept apart from the other birds at the back of the mews where the smell of meat and straw mingled. As the Master Falconer approached, the smallest bird tried to flee, beating its brown wings against the wooden partition and half-falling against its tether.

"You don't want to send this one, I warrant," he said, picking it up by the feet and replacing it on its perch. "No one would thank you for it. The calmest is this one over here," he said pointing to a hooded bird, white banded with speckles in neat rows.

Christopher was still watching the young hawk as it settled its feathers. Illesa squeezed his hand, so he would remember not to touch it.

"Very well. I understand that the costs are already agreed?"

"Yes, Lady Burnel, at least for the bird. But it's up to you to negotiate the price of the carriage. Sir Richard usually asked for Edmund to take it, and I know he has a wagon being readied to head south next week."

"I will speak to him."

The Master Falconer's head was cocked like one of his birds. He shook it suddenly.

"Now that's early. They are already here. You should leave straight away. I will speak to Edmund for you. He's not been engaged for the war, so it should be straightforward. Come now, pay me the money and let's get you both away."

All the questions that Illesa had been instructed to ask about the diet for the bird and the specifics of the breeding, which would all be enquired into by the King's falconer, left her. Outside the sound of voices and feet grew louder.

She took out her purse and gave him the silver, counting it into his hand.

"I will pay Edmund the Carter, and you will come and settle with me before the end of the month," the falconer said and placed the coins in the purse hanging from his belt.

"Who is it?" she asked as he led the way to the mews door. Christopher was still standing in front of the birds, and Illesa had to pull his arm hard. "Who is coming?"

"The Welsh. The conscripts for the war in Gascony are mustering here before they are sent to a southern port. It's going to be lively."

As they left the mews, the noise became angrier; the men were shouting and banging staves on the gate.

"They've been gathered from all of Powys, and I've heard there has been much resistance. But Clement and his men wanted to count them in before they went, so here they are. If you ask me, they should have sent them off in smaller groups," the falconer said in an undertone.

They came round the wall of the washhouse into the open space of the inner bailey, and the falconer stopped by the well.

"They are mustering out there." He pointed unnecessarily to the gatehouse. The noise of the men was so loud it was hard to hear his words. Christopher was rigid at her side. "And this is just the first contingent."

A man came through the door of the great hall, pulling on a pair of gloves, his scabbard loose and slapping at his side. It was Clement, the recruiter. Illesa seized Christopher and pulled him hard round behind her. She felt as if her chest was being pressed under a great door. And in her mind, the baby fell again towards the floor.

The falconer had begun to say something to her, but he stopped as Clement noticed him.

"Oi, Gaston, get that woman out of here," Clement roared. "Now's not the time for your pleasures! Get rid of her, get your sword and join me, you coward!" He strode towards the gatehouse, which was shaking with the hammer blows of staves.

"Come, come, both of you," the falconer said, "this way." He gave Illesa a push, and she breathed in a great gasp of air. "You can't stay here like an effigy. Whatever he did to you, there could be worse to come."

She didn't know she was running up the mound until she felt Christopher's grip sliding through her hand as he fell behind. The watchtower was only a little further, but the way was very steep. Ahead the falconer had reached the tower door, but he did not open it. He kept running round it to the left.

"Here," he called. A ladder was coming out of an upper door and being lowered to the ground. A head looked out of the opening. "See them up, John you lucky sod, and then bolt yourselves in," the falconer shouted. "Be ready to shoot on the Welsh if they try to storm the gate." He pulled Christopher onto the first rung of the ladder. "I hope Henry has thought to bolt the mews door, the dozy lad," he grumbled to himself, striding back down the slope into the bailey, now swarming with guards.

Christopher climbed the ladder like a squirrel and was pulled in. As Illesa reached the top, she heard Clement's voice rising up from the crowd.

"You are charged with service – now form the companies! Sergeants, call your men to order!"

Hands grabbed her and pulled her through the door into sudden darkness.

"Christopher!" she called.

"Your boy is over there, blocking the light from the window. Watch out; stay to the side." The guard pulled the ladder in through the door.

She joined Christopher at the window. Below her, the inner bailey had emptied, and all the men were crowded inside and just outside the gatehouse. She couldn't see Clement or his man, Walter de Penderton. But in front of the gate, a crowd of armed men stood like a close-planted forest of staves, some armed with spears, some with swords. Bareheaded, with short cropped hair and cloaks of Welsh pattern. Their voices rose as one, but she could not understand the words. Then the chanting broke up suddenly.

"Where is the Uchelwr Madog? I will speak with him, not with an ill-disciplined mob of dogs!"

It was Clement again, sounding less confident. He had gone through the gate to try to control the Welsh and was now trapped.

"He's not coming. He has other business to attend to in the north, the south-east and the west," a Welsh voice called, followed by a roar of approval. "You can't bribe him, and you can't have us!"

"You owe service in the King's name. Tomorrow we march for Portsmouth," Clement shouted, banging his sword hilt on the gate.

"We will march, but we march today and not in any name but our own. We have lost enough men and women and children, and we will not fight your foreign war against the French King. We would rather fight you and fight here."

"If you do not march and serve the King in Gascony, you are traitors and your land and families will be claimed for the Crown," Clement shouted. "Do we have to discipline you again?"

The crowd pushed forward, surrounding the area where Clement's voice rose, high and desperate.

"Guards, disarm these men, they are rebels! All of you stand your ground on pain of death; we have arrows aimed at your hearts."

"And we have something for your dark heart, Clement," a Welshman cried.

It was a sound that seemed to come from close at hand, almost a whisper, as if someone behind her had spoken. Illesa was thrust away from the window by a guard as she saw an arrow from the tower platform shoot down into the Welsh crowd, hitting a man in the throat.

"Get down, get down."

Illesa pulled Christopher far from the window to the back curving wall of the tower and hid his face in her cloak.

The sounds of fighting and screaming were very close. Illesa counted the number of arrows she could hear flying and striking. At eighteen there was a roar of delight from outside the gate and the crack of splintered wood. The Welsh were inside the bailey. One man's voice rose above the tumult.

"Cymerwch eu harfau ac yn dychwelyd i'r Trallwng, byddwn yn march yfory i'r gogledd."

The shouting subsided, replaced by the sound of many boots running through the bailey into the castle buildings.

The servant who was crouching against the back wall with them went forward tentatively to see what was happening.

"Do they have bows?" Illesa whispered.

"No archers that I can see," he replied. "Spears and swords. They just want to pillage the arms and go. Stay there."

But she had to see.

"Stay low by the wall," she whispered to Christopher.

Illesa went on hands and knees to peer through the narrow gap. She had seen a man who'd lost his eye to an arrow flying through a window. It was an excruciating injury.

The Welsh were ransacking the castle. It seemed that the Town Guard would simply let the Welsh leave rather than force a battle they could not hope to win. Welsh soldiers were carrying the dead English through to the inner bailey and dropping them on the ground. There were eight, including one that was only just alive. The Master Falconer was not among them, but Clement was. He lay like a butchered pig, his throat and chest red with blood. The injured man began to cry out, trying to get up, bleeding heavily from his side. They pushed him down, crowding around him. One of the Welsh lifted his spear, and the cries choked and stopped.

At her side, Christopher began to whimper. She put her hand over his mouth and held him close.

"You must be quiet!"

The Welsh began gathering their own dead. There were three, all shot with arrows through the neck or chest. A crowd of men assembled round them, coming out of the castle holding new bows and pikes. Quickly they lifted the dead onto their cloaks, cleared a way through the debris and marched out, the wounded supported by armed men.

One of the tower guards came down the stairs breathing hard.

"Ran out of arrows," he said, approaching the window. "Clement's dead. There, look," he pointed. "The Town Guard have finally arrived." Four men in the Shrewsbury livery were picking their way through the remains of the gate. "We have a rebellion on our border. Good thing there's no one else here they wanted, just that bastard Clement."

Christopher was trembling at her side.

"Is this what it is like in France where Daddy is fighting?" he asked, gripping her hand. "Would they spear him like that if he was wounded?"

Illesa gathered him inside the folds of her cloak.

"No, my darling. He is a true knight, not just a man-at-arms. They would take him hostage, not kill him. But he is strong and prepared. He will come back soon."

Christopher was vibrating like a bird caught in the hand.

"But at the siege of Troy, they killed knights," he said, his face pressed against her side. "When Hector was wounded he was speared through and through. Patroclus was killed."

Illesa held Christopher out in front of her. The guards were lowering the ladder and climbing down to assess the damage. She could hear the chaplain already praying for the dead and ordering the guards to take the bodies to the chapel of Saint Nicholas in the outer bailey.

"Christopher. We do not live at the time of Troy. The Ancients were heathen and savage. Now the knights fight with the benefit of the true religion and the love of Jesus Christ. There is mercy even on the field of battle. Besides which, they would rather get a big ransom for a high-born knight than kill him." She tried to smile, shaking his shoulders slightly. "Come, my darling," she said, pulling him towards the door. "Let's go and find Azalais."

But he was wracked with sobs, his face red and wet. Illesa sat down with her back to the wall of the tower and pulled

Christopher to her lap. He buried his face in the fabric of her tunic.

"We will pray, darling. Pray for those poor souls who died, that they will swiftly find the path to Heaven. Here, put your hands inside mine."

But even with the bodies so near and having witnessed the moment of their death, Illesa could only pray for one man.

Chapter IV

Saturday the 9th October 1294
Portsmouth Harbour
Tierce

"Rather foolish, isn't it?"

Master Geoffrey was standing on the quay, looking at Richard accusingly and pulling fretfully at a loose thread on the sleeve of his elaborate tunic.

"What is foolish, Master?" Richard asked, turning away and coiling a rope so as not to invite a long answer.

"Embarking today of all days. By Christ, if I were one of the commanders I would have chosen any other day," Master Geoffrey said, crossing himself.

"The weather is fine today. That is surely why. You can't ask them just to pluck a day unknown to sail a fleet into the winter sea." Richard had only recently met Master Geoffrey, but the man seemed to be a pedantic bore. Apparently, he was a skilled diplomat much regarded by Edmund, Earl of Lancaster, and would be one of the principal negotiators if there came a time to sue for peace. Richard could not imagine him having success with the French when the men on his own side would happily throttle him. "Besides, what is so very wrong about today?"

He should not ask, should walk off and leave Geoffrey waiting there by the partially loaded cog and go to help the other men. There would be so many more conversations on the long sea voyage. But Richard had been given charge of Master Geoffrey until they landed, when he would presumably begin to use his expertise. He certainly had no military training – or manners.

"I know because I went to church, as I should, to pray before a voyage. What were you doing that prevented you from worship?"

"Overseeing the loading of all the horses and fodder," Richard said. "They didn't walk on of their own accord." And nor would he.

"It's the feast of Saint Denys! The French King's own patron saint. What sort of omen is that? I tell you, I was praying to Saint Michael, who killed Satan, not to that French Bishop. Christ preserve us, what a day to set off to kill the French!"

"Christ," Richard muttered under his breath. It couldn't get much worse. The army that was meant to return Gascony to the hands of King Edward was made up of convicts, elderly soldiers and the injured; every single knight, to the man, reluctant to go. Half the able army had been redirected back to Wales to fight an uprising there. And on the very day of departure they still had only half the rations they would need.

The whole journey had been like this. Nothing but bad weather and trouble. You don't arm groups of convicts and expect them to behave like saints. They could be controlled given enough, but only just enough, ale and plenty of rations. The constables in charge of the companies of convicts were inexperienced, however, and the outlaws had already ransacked several taverns in the town. The sooner they set sail and started on the French the better.

Master Geoffrey was climbing stiffly aboard the cog. No doubt he would have some complaint about the way it was packed, but at least the sky was clear blue and there was a brisk wind. They needed to take advantage of the good weather now and not fall behind. Other ships were already setting off, the wind waving their banners as if at a fair. It did raise the spirits a little to see them. The men of the *Sainte Marie* were standing on the castle platform of their aft deck, sailing out of the harbour and singing the *Ballad of the Battle of Lewes*, which seemed provocative.

"Here they come at last, the lazy apes! Hurry up!" Master Geoffrey shouted at a group of men moving down the south quay, sun glinting off a pair of pikes that they must have taken from the Portsmouth Town Guard.

William and Hugh walked side by side. Hugh was the only one who was excited about leaving. He had not yet been to war. William would be doing his best to prepare him for the worst. Sir Thomas Turberville was at the front with his two sons, both acting as his squires. The similarity in their appearance was striking, except that the two lads had not inherited their father's thin nose. Behind them were the rest of the men and a few mule carts piled high with fodder and barrels.

"Where are we going to put all that?" shouted Master Geoffrey as the company came to a halt in front of *La Grâcedieu*.

"This man is an expert in packing." Richard pulled Vincent le Spicer out of the crowd. "His father is a spice merchant. He will pack it all in without a spare speck of space for a mouse, won't you Vincent?"

Master Geoffrey subsided, grumbling, to the foredeck to harass the captain. Vincent set about the work with the two Turberville sons, while the rest of the men tapped a barrel of beer. He knew he should tell them not to get comfortable, but the warm sun and the birds wheeling overhead were lulling him into a stupor.

"Sir Richard, let's drink to the success of our voyage and our swift return to England. And after that, we'll drink to the faithfulness of all our wives, which is a true miracle!" Reginald the archer said, grinning at him.

"By God, Reginald, you need to pray for that more than I do." He took the wooden cup, and the ale slopped over his fingers.

"My wife can scarcely move with her enormous belly. Nothing will get in there," Reginald said.

"You should keep planting in that field," Richard said, smiling. He drained the cup. Seven ships were plying the Solent now, with gulls behind them like small, fierce angels.

"Have you finished, Vincent, or is it going to take another year or two?" asked Reginald. "By then the war will be over, we'll have finished the ale and we can all go home again!"

"Just that barrel, if you lot haven't emptied it already," said Vincent. They poured him a tankard, put the bung in the barrel and rolled it up the gangplank. In the hold, the twelve horses whinnied and stamped, unsettled by the repacking. It would be a long time before they tasted grass again. William was in the hold with them, brushing and calming them, especially Greyboy who had never sailed before. Richard wished they had left Illesa's brother's horse behind. He had been dearly bought after Kit's death, rescued from the bandit who'd captured him. But they had no money to pay for a new warhorse, and Illesa had claimed she would be happier if they took him.

"Who will say a prayer?" someone called. "The chaplains have gone off on the bigger ships."

"Let it be Turberville; he keeps it short!" someone else replied.

Sir Thomas looked around, a smile on his usually melancholic face. He was tall, wiry and good on horseback. Richard had fought beside him in Wales and been glad of his cover. But now he seemed aged, almost stooped, next to his vigorous sons.

"Ah well, not to Saint Denys, eh men? I think we should neglect him today," Turberville said jovially. "We will appeal to a saint who does not favour the French! We raise this prayer to Saint Nicholas. Deliver us safely over the water, as you saved those three sailors long ago, and speed our journey with your power. Pray for us to Our Lord Jesus and have mercy on us now and at our return."

The captain and crew of *La Grâcedieu* began elbowing the military men aside to get the ship underway. Two lads loosed the ropes and pushed off with long thin oars. William came up from the hold and stood next to Richard, who was leaning over the side. They looked back to the town with its rising trails of smoke and sunlit church towers.

"Who's this fellow Geoffrey? Pain in the arse, isn't he?" William said in an undertone.

Master Geoffrey was standing near the steerboard, gesturing and muttering to the captain, his words, thankfully, whipped away by the wind.

Richard sighed.

"Yes. But he has travelled the world for the King. Went on Crusade with him. Was sent to the Khan with a gyrfalcon and brought back a leopard. He's meant to be wise and good at negotiation, but I think he's more concerned with soft beds and hot meals now. We just have to get him safely to port on the other side and leave him with the earls."

Turberville came over and stood on the other side of Richard. His face had returned to its usual frown.

"I vowed I would never return to Gascony after that long sojourn with the King years ago," he said, pulling his cap firmly down on his head. "He sent me into Aragon as a hostage for Charles of Salerno, and I nearly died of fever."

"God might listen to such oaths, but the King pays no attention," Richard said, wiping some spray from his forehead. "Let's hope that the French don't detain us long."

Turberville propped his elbows on the rail and looked over to where his boys were already playing dice with Vincent le Spicer.

"Did you hear the story of how the French King tricked Edward?"

Richard shook his head, although he'd heard one version of it. There were always others.

"They say that King Philip promised King Edward his daughter, Margaret, and set up this secret treaty for Edward to relinquish Aquitaine and regain it once the marriage took place. But Margaret would not have him. She thought he was too old."

William looked over, eyebrow raised.

"The King hasn't started a war over a woman, has he? Depriving the rest of us because he can't have the one he wants?"

"It may be," Turberville said, wrinkling his thin nose. "But I think it's just French lies. I met King Philip. He has wanted to claim Aquitaine ever since he came to the throne. The Earl of Lancaster was too trusting. He should never have believed Philip's promise that he would return the Duchy. If the Chancellor had not died, he would have seen through King Philip's plot."

"What's this French King like?" William asked.

Turberville sucked his teeth.

"Hard to say. Philip speaks little, but his eyes are always open. When we were taken as hostages, he had all the details of our families and estates noted down by his scribes so he could determine our worth. He would not believe anything the Chancellor or the King said. Instead he would send one of his men to listen at doors and steal documents. Philip had a stare just like an owl." Turberville fell silent. The slap of water on the ship's sides changed as they left the shelter of the harbour and entered open water. "He wanted to find the weakness in everyone," Turberville concluded gloomily.

"Well, we are not weak," said Richard grandly. "At least William isn't, are you?"

William gave him the long-suffering look he had perfected over many years.

"I am not a soldier. But if it comes to it, I'll cut the French King's head off with my knife. As long as I can then go home with my horses."

Turberville looked both impressed and worried.

"Philip is not a soldier either, but he is extremely well guarded. Don't expect to see him on the battlefield. He will send in his brother, Charles of Valois, who is an enthusiastic killer and far more basic in his instincts." He sighed. "Best thing for us to do is make a big impact as soon as we land so they regret starting this war. Then the suing for peace can begin, and we will all be free to go."

They passed some fishing boats returning to the port, having hauled in their morning nets. Off the bow, a brown head emerged from the dark water. The sea-dog eyed the men on the boat and then submerged, leaving only one bubble. The water was already deep and there were many miles of it ahead that would need to be calmed by prayer.

On the other side of the deck, Vincent le Spicer had taken some money from one of the Turberville sons. He threw the coin in the air, laughing.

The chances of their safe return were no better than for a game of dice. In fact, taking the convicts, poor rations and few numbers into account, they were probably considerably worse.

Chapter V

Monday the 22nd November 1294
Acton Burnel
Tierce

Illesa had been told to be at Acton Hall by prime to meet the Clerk of the Inquiry. He had taken a long time to reach the final conclusion about the scale of Philip Burnel's debts and what should be done with the remaining property, as Philip's son was still in his minority. The clerks on these assignments were paid for each day worked, and they took their time.

But Illesa made sure she was there much earlier. The tax collector, Walter de Hodinet, was apparently due to reach Acton and Langley within the week with his assistants trained in assessing the value of goods and chattels. He would be collecting a tenth for Edward's war chest, and no one who owned land was exempt. Certain things needed to be made safe, and, as there was no one in Acton who cared about these precious things, it was her duty to make sure they did not disappear into the wide mouth of the Treasury.

Now that there was no family in residence, the servants were lax about many things, one of which was bolting doors. Illesa went through a back entrance on the east side that led to the old part of the manor and climbed the spiral stairs in cold darkness. On the first floor, dust and cobwebs had collected in the corners of the corridor. A shutter was broken, and the loose piece of wood was streaked with bird droppings. It had been months since any servant had been through with a broom. Illesa would not be discovered by the Steward or the Reeve either. They liked their comforts and kept to the rooms where there was fire and food.

So much had been done to the manor in the last ten years, but this particular room had remained almost untouched. A new window had been made to fit with the rest of the east face, but that was all. God willing, no one would have thought to raid it yet.

47

As she came to the door, Illesa paused, the hair standing up on her arms even under her thick mantle. This was the room where her mother, Guiliane, had died and where she had been born. Illesa always said a prayer when she entered it.

She lifted the latch carefully. It was unlocked. The air inside was musty and stale. Even in the darkness, she could see swirls of dust. She crossed to the window to open the shutter a crack. In the shaft of light, she saw something small and dark lying on the floor by the bed: a dead bat, clawed wings outstretched, like one of the demons in the margins of her Book of Hours. Its chest was just a cavity, eaten out.

Illesa took a step away from it and put her hand to her lips. Demons entered the body in many ways, but the mouth was the most common. She stood very still and prayed the *Ave Maria* silently. The bat did not move. And suddenly she felt foolish for her fear. Even dark and ill-favoured animals died if they were trapped in a room without food or water, like prisoners forgotten in a tower.

Illesa stepped round it and went back to the door, closing it carefully. The bed was a bare shell without mattress or curtains, but the prie-dieu still stood by the window. And in the shadow by the north wall was the cabinet that had always held the family books. She crossed to it, peering in the half-darkness, her hands feeling for the protective grille. It was still locked, but she could see nothing inside.

Quickly she went to the prie-dieu and ran her hand down the inside of the stand until she felt the hook. The key still hung there, small and cold. She twisted it off and ran back to the cabinet. She didn't dare open the shutter any further. Someone outside might see it was open and come to investigate.

It wasn't easy to fit the key in the lock with so little light. When it finally turned, sweat was crawling down her back despite the cold. She pulled the grille open and swept her hands along the top shelf. The books that had been kept there were gone. That was not a particular surprise. Richard had brought the red book of *The Knight with the Lion* to Langley years before. It was now hidden with the rest of their books in a special lined hole under the woodpile.

Maud, Philip's widow, had briefly stayed in this room. She would have seen the books here as hers for the taking. The highly illustrated and boring *Decretals of Gregory IX*, the *Apocalypse* that the Anchoress had read so thoroughly, and the small *Psalter* with the paintings of beautiful musical instruments would all be in her possession at Arundel. Maud knew how much things were worth in coin. And she was welcome to those books as long as she had not taken anything else.

Illesa put her hands on the smaller lower shelf.

Maud had been told that the book of Saint Margaret was not to leave Acton. It was there to serve the women of the manor when they were in childbirth. And for once, the spoiled woman had done as she was asked and left it alone.

Illesa knew the binding as she knew her own flesh. It fit into her palm like the hand of a friend. The last time she had held it was at Joyce's birth, so much easier than either of the boys had been. At Christopher's birth, she'd bled and bled, coming close to death. She had been weak and ill for many days. They'd had a wet nurse from the village, but Christopher had fed badly. When, at last, they found another nurse who was not a drunkard, he began to grow.

Little Robert had come out cleanly, but blue and listless with the cord around his neck. She had blown into his little mouth, crying and reciting the prayer of Saint Margaret while Cecily rubbed his chest with a cloth. When he began to breathe, it felt like the creation of a new Adam.

He had escaped Death once. But the next time, Death had not listened to any prayer.

Joyce had come out like a lamb, bleating for milk and immediately quietened by it. Whole and well, she'd seemed untouched by the struggle that brought her into the world.

Illesa pushed the book under her surcote and her tunic, where her breast straps would hold it close to her body. She ran her hands over the rest of the shelf and felt another book there, larger than the book of Saint Margaret. Her fingers felt a tear in the leather of the binding. It was not familiar. She took it to the window, opening it carefully to a middle page.

There was a painting of a fierce animal, a wolf, facing a frightened flock of sheep, its nose pointing, and its foot raised

49

to strike. The words were Latin. She ran her finger over them as she read.

> *"If it has to hunt its prey by night, it slinks up to the sheepfold like a lame dog, and, so that the dogs do not catch its scent and wake the shepherds, it goes upwind."*

Illesa turned a few pages. They were all descriptions of beasts: of the air, the land and the sea. Her eye was caught by a picture of a small, thin animal biting a fierce serpent.

> *"The weasel, 'mustela', is a sort of long mouse; 'telon' means long in Greek. It is very cunning; when it gives birth to its young in a house, it carries them from one place to another and puts them somewhere different each time. It attacks serpents and mice. They are said to be skilled in healing, so that if they find that their young have been killed, they can bring them to life again. The weasel signifies a thief, as in Leviticus."*

The Steward was calling in the yard, demanding that a servant called Benedict get off his lazy arse and bank up the fire in his chamber. She would have to go down before the manor came fully awake. Illesa closed the book, running her fingers over the brown leather binding. It was an old Bestiary. She had heard of them but never seen one before, certainly not in all the times she had come and gone from this room.

Had her father bought it and left it there on his last visit to the manor? He often acquired things and then forgot about them. Perhaps he had intended it as a present for Christopher.

Illesa stowed it next to the book of Saint Margaret, making sure they were hidden by the thick fabric of her lined mantle. She locked the cabinet, put the key back in its place and closed the shutter. The room was abruptly dark, and she had to step carefully to avoid treading on the bat. At the door, she listened for footsteps in the corridor before opening it and retracing her steps down the stairs and out into the grey morning.

She needn't have hurried. For the next three or more hours she was left in the cold hall with an inadequate, smoking fire, hungry, thirsty and cold. Her appeals to the servants for food and drink eventually produced a cup of ale and some old maslin. It seemed that the servants had as little respect for her as the Clerk, who had called Lady Burnel for an audience at prime and kept her waiting until tierce.

When the Clerk eventually came into the hall, he did not apologise.

"Lady Burnel, another person has arrived who has precedence on my time," he said pulling his cap straight with ink-stained fingers. "Walter de Hodinet, the tax collector, is within, and is at this moment deciding on the tenth that will be collected from Acton." The Clerk looked cross and anxious. Someone was going through his carefully prepared figures and scratching them all out. "There is no point in our meeting to discuss the small remnants of the Burnel estate until the tax collector has finished his deductions."

Illesa nodded, very aware of the pressure of the books against her chest.

"I understand. Will he be visiting our manor next?"

"He expects to be here all day," the Clerk said, looking rather desperate. "Presumably he will alight at Langley tomorrow with his assistants. My advice to you is to go home and prepare."

Chapter VI

Monday the 6th December 1294
Feast of Saint Nicholas
Bordeaux

It had been a trial for the young men on board, the slow, careful, sick-making crawl down the French coast with little action to take their minds off the constant swell. They tried relieving their feelings by hitting birds with slingshots until they had their ears boxed for wasting shot. The raid on the Île de Ré had excited some, but little had been gained from it. Some meat, wine and a few sacks of skins, but the real treasure was packed into the church chest, and none of the more experienced knights wanted to enrage Saint Martin by stealing it.

It was a relief when they entered the Gironde and the swell died, although they knew the fishing skiffs skimming along the banks would carry word of their arrival up-river. Nevertheless, the conquest of Macau took less than a day. It dropped into their hand like a ripe piece of fruit from the tree. One of the commanders, John de Saint John, had been the Seneschal of Gascony and was popular with the people, so he had little trouble gathering information about the French army.

Their victories had continued at Bourg and Blaye. These smaller towns along the Gironde were tired of being caught in the disputes between the French and English Crown and glad to re-establish their old partnerships and trading routes.

But Bordeaux was another matter. The city sat like a king on a throne, ruling the curve of the river.

"Bloody bastards," said Turberville, looking out on the granite walls morosely.

"Looks impressive," Richard said.

"Of course. You don't think King Philip has been idle? He will have been buttressing the coffers of Bordeaux against us since last year when he hatched his plan of lies."

Bordeaux's stone walls were higher than a castle mount. The quays were protected by several large crossbows, and, set inside the city itself, a trebuchet had been erected on one of the towers that faced the river. Moored on the northernmost quay were two warships. There would be even more to the south.

John de Saint John had been informed of new fortifications at Bordeaux and wanted to wait for reinforcements from England to arrive before attempting to take the city. But John of Brittany, the King's lieutenant, insisted on an attack before Christmas, and he had the overarching authority despite his lack of experience. Master Geoffrey had moved to the flagship once they had reached the Gironde and was probably encouraging him in his recklessness.

All twenty English ships were within sight of the city's towers, strung along the Gironde like beads on a necklace, when the flagship raised the signal to anchor.

"We either dock and attempt an attack on land, or we sail on. Staying here within range of their engines is sheer stupidity. Can't they see that?" Turberville complained. "We must move up-river immediately or go back to Blaye. We don't have a chance here."

The archers and the younger men-at-arms were climbing on to the timber towers set at either end of the ship. As if that would do any good against a whole city with untold amounts of weaponry behind its thick walls. The English had large crossbows on two of the ships manned by three engineers, but they were no match for the Bordeaux defenses.

"Go to the King's Lieutenant, Richard. If anyone can talk him out of this, it's you." Turberville pushed Richard towards the rope ladder. "I can't abide that man."

Richard glanced at *The Trinity* with its bright, jaunty flags in the midst of the fleet, looking as if it were dressed for May Day.

"For the love of Christ, I should not have to tell the commander when he is putting the whole fleet at risk," Richard muttered. "Vincent, I'll need your strong arms to get there quickly. Come."

The young man smiled, showing his big white teeth. He descended the rope ladder quickly and pulled the skiff in. Richard followed, one-legged. He fell more than jumped into the small boat and pulled himself up on the thwart. At least they would be rowing with the current.

Across the water, the rest of the fleet stood unnaturally still as the strong grey water flowed past. Vincent rowed straight for the black hull of *The Trinity*. John of Brittany stood on the stern deck in an elaborate coat of plates that made his small head look ridiculous. In the distant north-west, a black cloud sat heavy on the land. There was an onshore wind and the rain would soon be upon them.

"There are soldiers on the trebuchet tower," Vincent shouted.

Richard turned around. Spider-like men were moving over the large engine. On the city walls, crossbowmen were taking up positions.

"Turn around, Vincent. Quickly, back to *La Grâcedieu*!" If they were going to die, he would die with William, Hugh and the others, not with the likes of Master Geoffrey and John of Brittany.

Vincent had efficiently turned about and was rowing with the long smooth motion of a young man with no aches and pains. Richard looked away across to the city, just visible between the bulk of the *Sainte Marie* and the *Sainte Cruz*.

"The flagship has given the signal to weigh anchor," Vincent said, sounding disappointed.

"Good. We would have been mown down by the crossbowmen if we'd attempted an attack on foot. With that trebuchet, any action by daylight from the river is simply foolish." Richard shielded his eye from the glare. "Look," he said pointing.

The mechanism on the tower moved, and the huge sling was hurled upward, flinging out its stone. As it flew high towards the river, the sound of the chain whipping back reached them just before the stone hit the water fifty paces away from their ship.

"They will adjust the reach and start again," said Richard, as the waves from the stone rocked the boat, wetting him even more. "We have only a few moments."

Vincent rowed even faster, reached *La Grâcedieu* and pushed Richard up the pitching ladder. The crew were already heaving up the anchor. The English fleet looked like mice at the bottom of a barrel, running frantically from one side to the other. Richard sat against the side of the ship with his legs out in front of him, trying to ease the spasms of paralysis.

If he were thrown in the river, he would not be able to swim the short distance to shore, and even if he got there, he would be arrowshot before he put a foot on land. William was below deck with the horses. He couldn't swim at all, but Richard would not be surprised if he rode Greyboy to shore like a centaur. That horse did whatever he ordered.

Again, the trebuchet was being ratcheted into position. Richard could hear the clicks of the mechanism, more than a hundred times the power of the sling that killed the Chancellor.

There were three ships between *La Grâcedieu* and the shore, and they were already moving north with the current. Richard heaved himself to his feet and hobbled towards the captain manning the steerboard.

"Run her to the far shore; they have the trebuchet set for mid-current!"

His words flew away in the wind. The captain was pulling the ship to the near shore instead, more concerned about damage to his ship from the large stones than the bolts of the crossbowmen on the crew and passengers.

"Or drive her back down the river!" Richard said pointing north. "We must retreat or at least find somewhere out of its reach."

But the captain was paying no attention to anyone. The wind was bringing the rain, and his crew fought to turn the vessel about. The distant crack of the counterweight being loosed cut the air. The stone flew in an arc across the sky before smacking into the water close to the flagship. It rocked alarmingly, and a figure pitched off the deck. His shouts rose above the water, but only briefly. On the quays, figures were swarming on the warships, readying them to sail.

Vincent and Hugh stumbled towards the stern, bows at the ready.

They obviously had strong men at work on the giant catapult, as they were already ratcheting it up again. The fleet was scattering across the dull water of the Garonne, like a bag of jewels cast on grey flagstones. A horn from the flagship sounded the retreat, and the ships that could quickly right themselves for down river began moving off into the onshore wind.

"Praise God, they have seen sense," muttered Richard. The retreating ships were running fast with the current, barely avoiding each other.

The sound of the trebuchet chain made him turn. The stone was no bigger than a bird at first, one that appeared to be flying directly at them.

"Hold!"

It flew over their mast and smashed into the hull of the *Four Winds*, which was thrown port and then steerboard, men falling from it like nuts shaken from a tree. One of Turberville's sons, leaning over the side next to Richard, watched as the men started swimming or drowning.

"Will it stay afloat?" he asked, his eyes glassy with shock.

"Lower the ropes!" roared Turberville from the aft deck.

Four ship lengths separated them from the nearest French warship bearing down on them.

"Archers ready," Richard called. He tightened his helm and drew his sword, lowering it to signal the release. Most of the arrows fell short into the waves like diving birds.

There were at least twenty men swimming for *La Grâcedieu* from the sinking *Four Winds*. The rest clung to it, unable to swim. The first of the swimmers reached the rope ladder and started climbing. Richard signalled another volley of arrows onto the French ship, and these found marks on the deck.

"If you still have a weapon, draw it and make room for the next man," Turberville said as he pulled the dripping man over the side of the ship.

The rest of the English fleet was well downstream and out of danger, but three French vessels were homing in on *La Grâcedieu* and the stricken *Four Winds*. The crew finally pulled the sail about, and the ship kicked forward with the wind. The rope ladder swung violently, knocking the clinging men into each other.

"Climb, climb, we are about to be boarded!" Turberville shouted at them.

The water streamed from their clothes as they fell on the deck.

A volley of French arrows struck in a wave across the ship, and Vincent crashed over the side of the platform.

Richard was pitched backwards and lost his footing. Around him the noise of groaning, splintering wood, then water rained over the ship in a torrent.

He pulled himself up and leant against the deck rail. A flying stone had clipped the side of the stern, shattering the platform and sending men into the river.

At the bow Turberville was directing the archers to take up positions in the wreckage. Vincent le Spicer lay amongst it, an arrow through his stomach, gasping, blood seeping from his mouth like a great sea fish, speared and caught. All his promise and strength leaving him slowly with his breath.

The captain stood grimly at the miraculously intact steerboard. The force of the stone had propelled the ship forward, and it was now out of reach of the French archers. The men it had struck floated, still and broken, drifting in the current towards the sea.

Chapter VII

Friday the 24th December 1294
Langley Manor
Vespers

The wind had almost succeeded in knocking Edith over, burdened as she was with a large basket. The old cotter looked emaciated. Her skirts did not reach the ground. They blew around the threadbare hose on her bony ankles.

"Edith, what a time to come out; it's nearly dark!" Illesa said, pulling her through the doorway. "We thought you would bring the pastries tomorrow." Illesa took the basket, covered with several cloths tied over the corners, and Edith jolted backward as the weight was lifted away. Her thin nose was red and dripping, her stringy hair coming out of the coarse wimple.

Illesa put the basket on the table in the hall and turned back to the old woman, who was steadying herself against a chair.

"Didn't Christopher tell you to come tomorrow? I told him to say that." The old woman was rubbing her raw hands together and shaking her head.

"I know what he said," she managed, "but you must have these by dawn. That is what we have always done, and this year should be no different. In the morning it will be snowing, and they would be ruined on the way."

Somehow in the small cottage she shared with her sisters, both nearly as old as she, Edith produced miraculous things. With the fine ground flour, butter, honey and chopped nuts Illesa gave her, she made these feathery pastry cribs for them each Christmas.

"I wouldn't want that boy to be disappointed in the morning. I could see it in his eyes that he wanted them tonight."

"Come and sit down by the fire," Illesa insisted, taking the old woman's hand.

"My, my, what's this?" cried Cecily, walking through from the buttery and peeking under the cloths. "Now it feels more like a feast! Bless you, Mother Edith." Cecily went over and embraced her, covering her frame completely. "Now we must give you your treats for the Feast!"

"No, no." Edith shook her head. "I'll just take some hot wine. We three will come tomorrow, just as always, snow or no snow. But I'll take one or two loaves, if you can spare them, for the dog. He's been keeping the fox from our hens all year, and so he can have a reward, poor cold lad."

"What nonsense! You will have a good meal now that you are here and no arguing. Isn't the sun down already, and the fast only one darkness from being over? You look like a puppet made of bones! And we will fill that tray for you and your sisters and send one of the lads back with you to carry it, with some logs strapped to his back." She looked at Illesa who was motionless by the table. "Goodness, the pair of you look as pale as each other. Sit down by the fire, and I'll bring you wine. Mistress, sit!"

Illesa sat down, her body numb. As soon as she had uncovered the tray of cribs and smelt the honey, she had remembered Little Robert eating his first, crumbs all around his mouth. The way his bright pink tongue had sought them out, and how he had cried for more, his hands strong and chubby then, pulling on Richard's cloak as he'd held the tray out of his reach. And Richard had laughed as he gave Little Robert another and saw his eyes grow big with pleasure.

Edith was looking at her.

"Where is your son?"

Illesa paused. Outside the wind blew hard over the churchyard where Little Robert lay buried in the white shroud that she had sewn.

"Christopher was asked to help Adam with the preparations, and I think he will have a nice warm place putting the bread in the oven and taking it out," she said, trying to keep her voice light. Edith didn't usually ask questions. She would generally start her litany of complaint and worry as soon as she saw another person. But the old woman was sitting there staring at her, her nose still dripping, chafing her hands, the skin of her uncovered legs dry, cracked and weeping. "You need some more of that ointment, Mother. Let me find some for you."

"Not yet, Lady Burnel." Now Edith was holding out her hand, palm down, not quite touching her, as she perhaps wouldn't dare to do, but detaining her with her urgency. "I wanted to speak with him."

"Oh, what has he done? I hope he has not broken your tree boughs?"

This had been one of the frequent dire predictions. The boy would break the boughs of the best fruit and nut trees with his frequent climbing. To her knowledge, he did not go as far as the three sisters' cottage, but he had been much absent since their visit to the castle in Shrewsbury. She often didn't know where to find him.

"No, no. Nothing like that. I will speak of it when he comes."

Cecily entered again with a jug of wine, cups, a bowl and a loaf on a tray.

"I know you won't touch meat until the morning, Mother, so I've brought you the leek pottage you like. Eat it all before you go anywhere."

"Cecily, can you find Christopher? And get some comfrey ointment from the store."

"He's not in the kitchen. Do you really need him? I have all the doles for the workers to prepare."

"I know. I will come and help you, but Mother Edith would like to speak to Christopher."

"No, I don't want you to help me, for the love of God's Holy Mother," Cecily looked up to Heaven. "Haven't you done enough, sewing all those new cloaks? Did you know that, Mother? Lady Burnel has made new cloaks to be given out at Epiphany."

"Cecily," Illesa frowned.

"I wasn't meant to say anything, I know. But people should know how hard you are working for their good."

"Thank you, Cecily. That will do. I will find Christopher. Will you ask Peter to walk back with Mother Edith?"

"I didn't mean anything by it," Cecily muttered as she left. "If that Azalais was here more often, you'd not have to work so hard."

60

Mother Edith had retreated under her wimple, huddled and shivering in her poor cloak, her eyes shut.

Illesa got to her feet. The basket on the table held the promise of happiness, at least briefly, for her son. She began to climb the stairs, reached halfway and nearly fell down with shock as Christopher's head appeared on the top step.

"Come down!" she whispered urgently. He had been crouching by the railing where he couldn't be seen. "You are too old to be listening in to conversations."

He got up, Pelta at his heel, wagging her tail hopefully. Illesa's anger subsided. He would have heard the old lady arrive and known what she would bring. He had been waiting since the Feast of the Resurrection for these pastries.

"Mother Edith wants to talk to us," she whispered in his ear.

He nodded and followed her to the hearth. The old woman opened her red-rimmed eyes.

"Good tidings for Christ's birth," he whispered and bowed slightly. He never could remember who to bow to. Mother Edith smiled, and her teeth stood out white against her weathered face.

"Young man, I watch you as you go through the forest. You look more like your father and less like your mother. This is a sign."

Christopher stood up a bit straighter. He wound the threads at the end of his sleeve round his finger, as he did when he was thinking.

"I thank you, Mother."

"It is a sign that you need to take on the responsibilities of your father. You are not a child any more. I have something for you." She frowned at him and reached inside her cloak. "When your father was your age, he used to come into the woods like you, dreaming, cutting branches, gathering nuts. I tell you, the Forester's men chased him daily."

"You knew him when he was a boy?" Christopher looked astonished.

"I still had my son Jacob then. Three years younger than your father, he was," she said, pulling her purse out of the fitchet in her surcote. "I would send him to do chores, and your father would help him. You see, Jacob struggled to do the

61

work with his withered arm, and I was busy nursing my husband." She loosened the leather thong of her purse and took something out. "The year before Jacob died, Richard came at Christmas and gave this to my son."

It was a small wooden figure of a bearded man holding a long staff. On his shoulder was a lumpy child.

"He'd carved it himself. Said it was Saint Christopher and it would protect my son from drowning." Edith shook her head. "Your father was afraid that Jacob would fall into the river or the moat, and because of his arm he wouldn't be able to get out. But Jacob died of fever in the end, and ever since then I have carried it."

She looked up at Christopher, her green eyes suddenly sharp and intent.

"But it is your Saint, and you should have it. It will protect you and remind you to look after your home for your father and not to go wandering." She held out the little wooden carving. "You need to look after your mother and your sister now."

Christopher held the figure tentatively in the palm of his hand.

"Yes, Mother."

"You pray to Saint Christopher for your father, child. And soon he will be coming back over the waves to us." She clapped her hands together. "Now go and eat a pastry; it gives me joy to see people eating them. And if you wait until the morning, I will miss it."

Edith stood up, only a little taller than the boy, and took him by the arm over to the table. Behind them, there was a commotion at the door. The wind was blowing a light fall of snow into the hall, and many voices were all speaking at once. Into the light of the candles and hearth came Azalais, bundled in a great grey cloak trimmed in fur, the tall Jean Fracinaut behind her. And behind him a blond head of hair, worn long, in the fashion of the court. Gaspar, the player. Illesa had missed him for more than a year.

They came in with wafts of cold air. Azalais embraced Illesa thoroughly, then held her arm and pointed at Gaspar, who was stamping his boots free of snow.

"Look, just look, who we found on the way. By the light of Christ, he was travelling well. Walking beside an old mare with a terrible limp. He would never have made it before the cock crowed tomorrow if we hadn't found him on the road from Shrewsbury. I swear he would have spent the night in a ditch! What a blessing we were on our horses!"

Gaspar wore an expression of amused interest, as he did when he played Satan in *The Fall of Man*. He had aged, but his smile was the same: full-lipped and knowing. She ran to embrace him. With Azalais and Gaspar for Christmas, it would be a proper feast.

"I'm so glad to see you! You were not needed by the Earl?" she began, her face suddenly hot.

Gaspar held her at arm's length, his hands icy cold.

"No indeed, he is busy fighting the Welsh with the King, and, as you know, the King cannot abide me. God knows why." Gaspar looked sanctimonious for a moment, then leered evilly. "No doubt, a thug with a spear would have killed me as I rode to Conwy anyway. So I made my excuses at Chester, put up with the company of a Chancery clerk on his way to Shrewsbuy for two whole days," Gaspar imitated the clerk's supercilious expression, "and here I am." He winked at Illesa and went to warm himself in front of the fire.

Christopher was finishing off the last of his pastry, his hopeful eyes on Gaspar. The player had a vast hoard of amusing stories, anecdotes, gossip, funny voices and rude noises. Even though Christopher had not seen Gaspar for a long time, he had forgotten none of his benefits. Mother Edith was fumbling with the basket, taking the pastries off, putting them on the tray and looking around.

"Now where is that Cecily? If I don't leave now, my sisters will think I've been eaten by the wolf."

"No wolf would bother, dear lady. They would consider you too close to Heaven to make a good meal," Gaspar said, gliding over to the pastries. He picked one up and ate half in one mouthful, his eyes closed.

"Get away, you ruffian. They are for tomorrow," Edith said, slapping his hand.

"I've been dodging Welsh spears and trudging next to a lame horse for hours, and I'm close to starvation. Besides, he's had one, I can see the crumbs!" Gaspar said, pointing at Christopher's messy mouth. The boy started laughing, spraying bits of pastry.

Pelta barked and bounced up at Christopher, her grey ears flapping. Jean Fracinaut and Azalais were conversing by the fire in very rapid dialect and paying no attention to anyone else. The room was bursting with noise, and when Cecily came in with a crying Joyce, Illesa nearly laughed herself with the suddenness of her happiness.

Eventually they packed Edith off with food, fuel and Peter, who was instructed to get a blazing fire on the hearth before he returned. Joyce was settled in her cradle, and Illesa, Christopher, Azalais, Jean and Gaspar sat at the table. The fish was seethed in a stew of herbs. The bread was light and crusty. Adam had had a good day in the kitchen, thanks be to all the saints.

"Tell us what is going to be on the table tomorrow. Let us imagine we are eating it right now," Gaspar said, winking at Christopher.

"Oh, I didn't say!" Azalais exclaimed. "We've brought you three woodcocks we saw in the market. I hope they are enough as I didn't know this glutton was coming along." She tipped her head at Gaspar.

Gaspar was not the slim youth Illesa had first met in Wales, but the extra flesh suited him.

"It's hungry work, travelling," he said simply and continued to put food in his mouth.

"I hope you brought something with you for the household," Azalais continued, imperiously. "Perhaps a bridle for your tongue."

"Woah! I'll bridle you if you're not careful!" cried Gaspar. "Of course I brought something, but it will have to wait for the Feast of the Holy Innocents," and he pulled a furious face at Christopher as he held up and swung an imaginary whip.

"Over my dead body will you touch the child! What a barbaric custom to beat children to remember the dead innocents. They never do this in Aquitaine!"

"No, they're too busy killing their neighbours."

Illesa let them argue. When they had first met, early the previous year, they had spent most of the time quarrelling, and

64

they seemed to enjoy it. It was Jean Fracinaut she wished to speak to.

Jean was from Bordeaux, and it was his ship, *La Mariote,* that had brought Azalais to Conwy the previous spring. Azalais was a widow and had her own money. She did as she pleased, and the thing that pleased her most was being with Jean. He had been given letters of protection from the King to victual the English army in Wales with Gascon wine and grain, while most foreigners had been moved away from the coast for the defence of the realm. He was proud, both of his commission and his ship.

"How was your crossing from Bayonne?" she asked.

Jean chewed thoughtfully and took a sip of wine before he spoke.

"I could tell you about the crossing, my lady, but it was not out of the ordinary. And I know what you want me to tell you. That I saw your Richard and that he is well." He shook his head. "I cannot tell you that, not even for a celebration of Christ's birth. But there is some news."

There was something about the way his jaw was working that made Illesa's heart sink deep in her chest.

"Tell me quietly so the boy doesn't hear," she said in an undertone. At the other end of the table, Christopher was listening to one of Gaspar's many comedic tales, probably one about a speaking dog, judging by the sounds he was making.

"When did you last hear from him?"

"We had a message in November, but it was dated only a week after he sailed. We've had nothing since. But we heard from the Constable of Shrewsbury that the English force had conquered Blaye."

Jean nodded.

"I have no direct knowledge of Sir Richard, but I've heard something about the attack on Bordeaux earlier this month." Jean set his cup of wine carefully on the table and leant towards her. "The men of Bordeaux were shocked by the idiocy of the English fleet. They arrived at the port and were anchoring up in front of the walls, in plain view."

"They should have sent scouts," Azalais put in. "It was stupid to trap themselves there on the curve of the river."

She'd obviously already heard the story on the way to Langley and had formed her own strong opinions.

"Have you finished?" asked Jean, tapping the back of her hand with his rough finger.

"I'm never finished!" said Azalais, but she indicated that he should continue.

"Perhaps the commanders thought they would frighten Bordeaux with their little fleet of old ships," Jean said scornfully.

"When was this?" Illesa asked, her heart beating hard against her chest.

"The feast of Saint Nicholas. The French have not been idle this past year. The new trebuchet can hit the other side of the Garonne if it needs to. The English ships were easy targets. They were milling around in confusion, one sailor said, as if they were roosting hens when the fox gets in. So then the French guards decided to rig their own ships and chase them."

Azalais looked disgusted but held her tongue.

"That is when the English sailed back down the river and went to hide at their stronghold at Blaye with the rest of the fleet. One of the ships was holed by a stone and sunk, but some of the men were able to swim to another ship and survived."

"Which ship?"

"The *Four Winds*."

"Not *La Grâcedieu*," Illesa breathed. So he was not drowned, at least not on the feast of Saint Nicholas. But by now anything may have happened.

Azalais snorted.

"I don't know what the *commanders*," she spat the word, "think they are doing. They should not take Bordeaux lightly. It is the strongest city in France, even more than Paris because our walls are made of granite!"

"And so are your breasts," called Gaspar from the other end of the table.

Illesa looked down the table anxiously. The talk of war should end before Christopher heard anything to upset him.

"And the English King is not blessed by the sea in his own waters either," Azalais continued. "He sent all that wool and silver to Flanders – you heard of this, didn't you, Gaspar?"

Gaspar nodded knowingly. "And do you know what happened, Jean? They sent off the Ludlows and the King's Clerk to go and bribe King Philip's enemy in Flanders, and a storm drowned them!" She looked around the table. "It is an ill omen. This war will not go well for the English. Edward has chosen to crush the Welsh rebels, but he lets the Gascons suffer under the French. He ignores the danger of the French King at his peril!"

"Don't exaggerate, woman," Gaspar admonished. "Only two of the ships sank. The rest were still intact with the coin, and they will still go to Flanders. In fact they are already there, no doubt. God bless the souls of John and Lawrence Ludlow, and their fat purses that will now go to some lucky men who marry their widows," Gaspar prayed. "Perhaps you could introduce me to a lovely Ludlow wife?"

John de Ludlow's wife was not lovely, but she was certainly good with money.

"She would throw you out of her upstairs window," Illesa told him. "This is not a laughing matter. Those men are only ten days dead. Thank God their bodies were found and can be given proper burial." It would not be that way if Richard died in the Gironde or at sea. His body would be taken down to the deep to be fed on by fish.

"But if we didn't laugh we would cry, would we not, my lady?" Gaspar said and picked up Joyce, who had started to make little hungry gasps. "War to the west, and war to the south, and hungry mouths all around your table." He rocked her in time to his words. "Here you are, this must be your wailing infant," he said passing her on to Illesa. "Now, I suggest we all retire to bed because in the morning we want to start eating our way through the stores early, isn't that so, Christopher?"

"Certainly, let's go to bed before you two begin your caterwauling competition," commented Jean, getting to his feet. Azalais, who took it as a point of pride to match anything Gaspar could sing, hit him on the shoulder.

Eventually the others rose and went to their rooms, the dog trotting behind Christopher.

Cecily looked round the door at her.

"Do you want me?"

Illesa shook her head. Joyce was almost fully asleep, only sucking from time to time, and she was warm and peaceful by the fire.

"No. I will put her to bed. You go and get some rest with your girls."

Cecily flicked her cloth across the table, which was completely bare and ready to receive the feast.

"I will just make sure that silly man is in his room. Last time I found him curled up in front of the fire the next morning, and God knows where he had spent the night!"

"Don't worry about him, Cecily. Gaspar keeps his own hours."

Perhaps he would come down now that it was quiet and tell her what he really knew about the war from the Earl of Lincoln. Or perhaps the news was too bad, and Gaspar would keep it to himself until the end of the feast, thinking to spare her. Gaspar was a secretive person and told her little of his life. But ever since they had both been caught up in that disastrous Round Table Tournament, she had thought of him as a brother. She had no idea how he thought of her, but he had become a regular guest at Langley and a friend to Richard on his travels with the court.

Illesa looked down at the head pressed against her breast, the profile so like Richard's. She should take Joyce up to bed before the ghosts returned to the empty hall. But the darkness pressed her close to the fire, and the wind outside seemed to bind her to the chair.

She stared at the undulating flames, forming the words of the prayer to Saint Christopher in her mind, picturing the ships sailing and sinking, the saint carrying the man, not the boy. Eventually, holding Joyce firmly to her chest, Illesa got to her feet, blew out all the candles except one and let the room settle to fire glow.

And by that warm light, she climbed the stairs.

Chapter VIII

Wednesday the 6th April 1295
Podensac – Aquitaine
Sext

It was like waiting for a handful of tinder to catch light in your palm. The day was warm, and the heat from the blaze had not dissipated. Above the roofs the smoke of the burnt-out house hung and swayed, snakelike in the unnatural calm.

The crowd were watching the Baron, Sir John Giffard, as he sat down on an elaborate chair set up on a market table that only two days before had been covered in vegetables. His squire and the guards of his household held the table steady. It looked as if he was about to be dunked rather than address the townsfolk as the commander of the liberating force.

The people of the town had been out of their houses since dawn when the challoner's shop had been set alight. Water wasn't scarce in the town, but even so, the pitch arrows set fire to the thatch, and there was little anyone could do to save it.

Giffard was coughing, maybe preparing to speak. At his side, Turberville was whispering urgently in his ear. Since he'd arrived in March at the head of his own company with a letter of protection from the King, Giffard had increasingly cut himself off from the other knights. He distrusted everyone except his Welsh household guards and Turberville, who had fought with him during the Baron's revolt.

According to his sergeant, Baron Giffard had been part of the suppression of the Welsh rebellion in Builth and received great favour from the King in Conwy. Something must have happened to him between his victory in November and his arrival in Aquitaine, because he was now a confused and irritating old man.

Across the river in Rions, John of Brittany should know about the French assault. The two towns were within easy signalling distance, but there was no sign of help arriving.

The previous week, Richard had tried to speak of his concerns about Giffard to the King's lieutenant. "Want the command for yourself, do you?" was all he'd said. Of course Richard didn't. But neither did he want unnecessary deaths because no one would believe that Giffard was incapable.

The French were gathered close under the walls outside, so close that they were almost impossible to shoot. Two nights before, they had rowed up from Bordeaux in unlit galleys and tied them up out of sight of the town. Now they were right under the gate, where they might even be able to hear the shouts of the unhappy crowd.

"Sir Giffard has spoken to the French invaders who are threatening your town. Hear him now," Turberville cried.

Giffard held out his hands, waiting for quiet.

"As you know, food supplies are very low," he said in his thick English accent. "We won't be able to bring in stores of grain if the French are controlling the river. They have an army of thousands and have promised to trample your fields, causing starvation. We will not let this happen!"

The crowd jostled and shouted insults at the French leader, Charles of Valois.

"You are subject to the rightful Duke of Aquitaine, King Edward. But, to save your homes, your crops and your lives, our force must leave you now. People of Podensac, we will return to restore your town to its proper ruler. Gascon soldiers, remain here and protect your people," Giffard ordered, waving his gauntlet at the armed men. "You will be paid once the conflict has ended in King Edward's victory!"

The crowd muttered, uncertain of the meaning of his garbled French. But as the message spread through the crowd, they began to shout angrily, drowning out Giffard's weak voice. Some of the Gascon men drew their weapons. The townspeople pressed forward.

A strong arm took Richard by the elbow, pulling him behind one of the market pillars.

"What in God's name is Giffard doing?" William shouted in his ear. "We haven't even tested the French yet, and at the first sight of them he surrenders? The people of Podensac will be killed if we leave now."

"Quiet, William," Richard said, scanning the square for the other English knights. "The Welsh guard might hear you. We must seek an assurance of safety from the French. Look, Turberville is trying to speak again." Turberville had jumped on the table which was pitching alarmingly. His bright surcoat looked clean despite months of campaigning.

"Listen! There is nothing to fear. Sir Giffard has negotiated your safety. The French have agreed that they will tax you, but no one will be harmed. Your town will remain standing. As long as all the English leave now, all will be well."

The crowd passed this news under their breath, testing out its truth.

"Why didn't he say that before? The French are as reliable as the devil! You leave us to our deaths!" someone shouted.

Turberville got Giffard under the arm and hoisted him to his feet, so his guards could lift him off the table.

"We will return with renewed forces and free you from the French yoke as soon as the promised men arrive. We had word they were gathering in Southampton last week." Turberville produced a silver coin from his purse. He jumped down from the table and gave it to a woman holding a baby. "For the tax!" he shouted. "Knights, do as I do and contribute from your purses to the people of Podensac who have welcomed us and fought for our King."

The crowd expectantly turned to the nearest English knight, hands out.

"These are alms for the Feast of the Resurrection. May God bless the souls of these faithful people," Turberville shouted, warming to his story. He walked through the tamed crowd, giving silver to those near him. Somehow he had managed to turn a riot into something like a festival.

"That was well dodged," muttered Richard, handing a penny to a small boy who stood in his way as he tried to push towards the circle of guards protecting Giffard from the crowd.

A horn sounded, calling the companies to assemble.

"He means us to leave straight away. William, get the horses. Meet me by the main gate. I must speak to Turberville."

Squires and men-at-arms were rushing across the square. The townspeople were milling about in confusion. Richard limped into the circle of knights by the gate.

"Sir Thomas, I must speak with you."

Turberville glanced at him from his place at Giffard's side. One of the guards was holding Giffard's helm as he pulled on his gauntlets.

"We will speak while we cross the river. Have you rallied your men? Leave none behind."

Richard lurched forward and grabbed Turberville by his mail sleeve.

"I do not believe that Charles of Valois has given any such merciful undertaking," he hissed.

Thomas pushed Richard's hand away and took the rein of his courser from his squire.

"That is a dangerous opinion, Sir Burnel," he said, his eyes assessing the crowd over Richard's shoulder. "Once we are gone, this town will be no worse off than when we arrived here a few weeks ago." He half smiled. "Here is the rest of your retinue. You want to live to return home, don't you? You have talked of little else since you arrived."

Behind him, William, Hugh, and Reginald had arrived, already mounted.

Richard turned to his men, starting to explain, but the gate opened and the horses moved forward around him.

"Mount, Sir Richard. You are in the way!"

At his back, Giffard's guards stood ready to shut the gates behind them. He was pushed outwards, crushed through the barbican, clutching Greyboy's halter. William came up behind him, reached down and pulled him halfway onto the saddle. He swung his good leg over as the English force was called into formation by the horn.

The French soldiers were ranged along the side of the road, laughing and mocking as they rode past.

"Cowards!"

They picked up clods of earth and pretended to throw them at the retreating men.

"By God, I'd like to pick them off one by one," said Reginald, his face twitching, his free hand on the strap of his bow.

But instead of meeting their obligation to defend their territory, the English were scuttling away like frightened boys, leaving the sheepfold to the wolves. At the base of the hill, a group of expensively armoured knights waited, watching their descent.

Giffard and Turberville stopped before the French commanders. Richard urged Greyboy forward to join them, and William, bearing his pennant, followed. The highest-ranked noble was un-helmed, his pennant of arms the bright blue of the Royal House of France. King Philip's brother, Charles of Valois, regarded the English in front of him with amused interest.

"Small fish," he said, and laughed, turning to his companions. "Don't worry, men, we will catch bigger ones soon. But these poor ones are too small to keep and eat!" He laughed again. "Go now, English. You are free to find shelter where you will."

But something caught his eye amongst the twenty knights. He stared up at Richard's pennant of arms, unfurled in the quickening breeze.

"I am familiar with part of these arms," he said pointing. "Who bears them?"

"I am Sir Richard Burnel."

"Burnel. The Burnel who once spoke for King Edward at such length? No, that isn't you," the Count scoffed. "He was a large man, in every way. You are scrawny and one-eyed. So you must be a poor relative of the cunning Chancellor?"

Robert Burnel had been proud of his reputation in France for long and exacting speeches, often wishing to recount the content of them to Richard when they travelled together.

"I am the cousin of Chancellor Burnel, Bishop of Bath and Wells, my lord. And you, I take it, are the Count of Valois," Richard said, bowing his head. "I would expect more courtesy from a man of your breeding."

Charles of Valois stared at him while his overdressed charger stamped and scraped the ground, impatient in the heat.

"I see that you lack the benefit of your cousin's diplomacy as well as his form," he said finally. "We have granted you English a boon. Do you wish to renounce it?"

73

"I wish to plead for the town. It has been loyal to all its lords. You may, by kindness and mercy, gain its loyalty today and a good foothold in Gascony. The people of Podensac have no respect for the English any longer, but you may win them to your cause."

"We have no need of a foothold! We have plenty of men from King Philip's lands ready to fight for him. The same cannot be said of your poor King, who lacks the loyalty of his subjects and cannot raise an army to defend his territory. You might need Gascons alive, but we do not."

Richard drew breath and moved Greyboy a little nearer.

"So my good lord, as you are unthreatened by them in either way, alive or dead, you may show mercy and grant them their lives. Our merciful Lord Jesus in Heaven gives you this power. As a Christian lord, you may strike or stay your hand from striking and thereby gain your subject's love and the good of your soul."

The Count's lip curled. He shook his head.

"Perhaps you are also a cleric and therefore can presume to tell me of my duty? Look at these people you plead for. They are ranged on the walls of the town aiming arrows at our hearts. They do not ask for mercy. You are telling me a story as if I were a child. Now go." At a signal Richard didn't see, all Charles' men drew their swords. "Unless you wish to engage in battle with the river."

He and five other mounted knights spurred their horses towards the town gate while the remaining French pressed the English knights towards the water.

Richard turned to start up the hill after the Count, but William got hold of the reins and yanked Greyboy's head round.

"Oh no you don't. Your lady would never forgive me."

Greyboy was ignoring Richard's spurs and doing just as William instructed, going to the ramp of the nearest ship and walking on, as docile as a pony, smelling out his old stall.

Through the glaring sun and smoke, Richard saw the French commander reach the gate of Podensac.

"Wake up, Richard! You are on board now. Look to the lives of those who serve you." William was gripping his saddle. "Dismount!" he shouted.

The ramp was pulled in, and the ship set adrift on the water. Richard looked around for his men. They were all there, armed and angry. Reginald had his bow aimed at the group of soldiers on the bank.

"Row! Don't shoot!" shouted Turberville. "We will be sitting targets if we don't put some distance between us."

On the far bank down-river, another force was gathering; the English and Gascon men from Rions were ready to embark. But that battle would never happen because they had surrendered Podensac and left it to its fate.

"What a packet of pricks," William muttered to himself as he led Greyboy below.

Chapter IX

Friday the 8th April 1295
Rions – Aquitaine
Tierce

Ralph Gorges, the Lord Marshal of the English army, sat with his back to the altar, two guards on either side of him, and regarded the men in front of him with dismay.

"It is very unfortunate. Very unfortunate indeed. I can only reiterate what I said earlier; the French are unreliable. That is how this war started. We are hard pressed and cannot defend all the towns without further troops and supplies from England."

"No this is not right!" said the merchant, La Megge. "You have much support here. We are giving you money and men to fight against the northern King. But we are repaid by slaughter! My sister is in Podensac. Do you have any idea what they are doing to her?"

Next to Richard, Turberville moved uncomfortably, and next to him, Giffard leant against the nave wall in the attitude of someone listening to a boring sermon.

Another merchant had started speaking very loudly, as if he were hailing a ship on the other side of the river.

"If the English King cannot find the men to fight for his lands, what sort of king is he? We need a man of iron to fight this Philip! We thought he was the hammer, but now he seems to be the anvil, and we the people of Aquitaine are the nails that are being bent in half!"

"Arnaldus, this is not true. King Edward has commissioned warships up and down the coast. We are soon going to win this war, and Aquitaine will overflow with wine and prosperity once again."

La Megge snorted.

"It's overflowing with blood; blood and bile against your treacherous knights." He pointed a finger at Giffard, who stared back malevolently.

"Let's hear from Giffard now," Gorges said placatingly. "He will explain how this happened."

"Let the rest of the town come in to hear him," shouted Arnaldus. "Let them in! Open the doors!" Outside there was a roar of approval as the listening crowds heard the demand.

Richard hurried up to the Marshal as fast as he could, leaving William to stand with the two older men. Giffard's guards had not been allowed into the church, and he seemed diminished without them.

"Lord Marshal, wouldn't it be better to hold such proceedings at another time and in another place?" Richard whispered. "We must prepare for battle against the French."

"No, Sir Richard. If we don't address this issue, the Gascons won't fight for us. I just don't understand it," muttered Gorges, tilting his head towards Giffard. "They told me he was a strategist. Why didn't he call for aid from Rions, rather than surrendering so quickly?"

"Giffard is not what he was," said Richard. "If I were you, I'd remove his command. But you will need to do it formally. Those loyal to him will fall in line if it is handled correctly."

"We don't want the Gascons to desert us and give us up to the French. We must give them justice."

"What do you mean, Lord Marshal?"

"Put Giffard on trial," Gorges said, leaning close. "What part did Sir Turberville play in all of this?"

Richard looked back at Giffard and Turberville, commanders of at least twenty good men between them.

"The matter can be looked into later. The French will move against Rions within the day. The town must be prepared for siege."

Gorges shook his head and waved his finger at Giffard.

"It will not take long. Then the Gascons will know we are here to defend them. Otherwise they may betray us as, it seems, Giffard betrayed the people of Podensac." He looked gloomily around the noisy church. The west doors had been opened, and the whole of the town was crowding into the nave. "We need to have John of Brittany here to formally strip him of his command. Send for him, will you? I think he is on the south wall."

"Lord Marshal, please reconsider. Give the merchants an assurance that justice will be done, but only once the immediate threat of the French army is defeated. Giffard is not going to escape. He can barely climb the stairs."

"Burnel, I've made my decision. Send for Brittany; he can take over the proceedings. This isn't really my duty." He got up and stretched. "You should stand as a witness."

Gorges spoke to his guards, and they moved to surround Giffard and Turberville. Then the Lord Marshal called the two Gascon merchants to his chair. Richard beckoned William, who came quickly to his side, frowning.

"What is happening? Now is not the time for a town meeting."

"No indeed, but that is what we are having, and a trial, and then who knows." Richard shook his head. Turberville and Giffard were hidden behind a wall of guards. Richard was glad; he did not want to see their faces.

"Go to the south wall, William, and beg John of Brittany to come here with all haste. Let's hope that his good sense is in evidence today. You stay there and keep your eye on the river. Come to me if anything changes."

It did not take long to set up the trial after Brittany arrived. The large crowd had grown quieter with anticipation. More English knights were ranged around the church. A few who had been in Podensac, but mostly those stationed in Rions from other ships. Giffard's Welsh Guards had pushed their way in and were approaching the chancel.

The nasal voice of John of Brittany cut through the noise of the crowd.

"Turberville, what explanation do you have for the events? I understand that you spoke to the people of Podensac and assured them of their safety."

Turberville stood, slightly hunched, on the steps of the chancel.

"My lord, someone needed to reassure them or we all would have died," he said. "I was certain that a good man, such as Sir Giffard, would not have left without some agreement of mercy."

"Who decided to treat with the French to vouchsafe the English?"

78

"What did you want, a long siege and half the remaining army dead?" shouted Giffard. "I got us out, and now we can return home. If no more companies are going to be sent to Gascony, it is a lost war. We have been left to die here by this cursed river!"

"Be careful what you say, Giffard," warned Brittany, his soft face uncharacteristically stern.

Giffard pulled at his surcoat, which displayed his arms.

"I have served King Edward all my life. He sends me here and there, and I go. But there are lords in England who will not step forward to serve him. They are too comfortable in their estates. Too fond of their own skins! This leaves the rest of us exposed."

"Enough," John of Brittany barked. "Ships are gathering on the far side of the river. Let us conclude this business. I've had the boy witness sent for."

The boy, supported by a Gascon woman, was already coming up the nave. His head and hands were bandaged, and he was dressed in a new tunic. When he'd arrived in Rions, he had been naked. He moved unsteadily, tentatively.

"Bring him up here where we can all see him," Brittany ordered.

The crowd in the church hushed. Now they would hear the bloody story from the boy's own mouth.

He was lowered onto a stool at the top of the steps in front of the nave. His face was very pale, except for the scrapes and cuts around his mouth. He licked his lips, shivering.

"Your name?"

"Henri."

"Your age?"

"Thirteen years."

"Your father?"

"Henri the joiner."

"Alive?"

"No sir," Henri the younger whispered. "He was hanged this morning."

"God save him. Now you must tell us of the events in Podensac. Mind you keep to the truth for we have other witnesses to call upon, boy," John of Brittany said, gesturing vaguely at the crowd.

"The French launched burning arrows at our town. We spent hours putting out fires. There were new French companies arriving all the time." The boy looked around the church and then straight at John of Brittany. "You must have seen them coming up the river."

"Yes we did, and we prepared for our own defence! I am not asking you for advice."

The boy turned away from him, head lowered, clutching his hands between his knees.

"They brought a battering ram down the river at nones and dragged it up the hill," he said very quietly. "But they didn't use the ram because Sir Giffard sent word that he would speak to Charles of Valois."

"How did you know that?"

"They spoke from the tower above the gate, and I stood there with my father ready to brace the door."

"Where did they go?"

"Sir Giffard went out through the small door in the tower with two guards. When Sir Giffard came back through the gate, he told everyone to gather in the market square. Then he told us that the English were leaving. And the other man told us that the French had guaranteed our safety and would only take a tax. But that man had not been out to meet with the French. He stayed inside the gate."

"Which man was that?"

The boy pointed to Sir Thomas Turberville.

"And then they all gave us some coins and left like a dog that's been kicked," the boy said. He had shaken off some of his stupor. "Then the French came in and rounded up the fifty men who looked like the burgesses. They kept them in the church overnight. They had a Mass." The boy's voice tailed off again, his head bowed.

The sound of the crowd's anger grew louder. The boy looked up.

"At first light they led them out and hanged them in the square," he said. "My father was one of the last. I tried to tell them that he was a fine carpenter with four children to feed. They just beat me and then hanged him next to the miller."

The boy pushed himself to his feet. "All our men are dead. They sent me here to tell you that they will do the same in Rions! And I hope they get you," he shouted, pointing at Giffard, "and all the rest of you English. You are lying cowards!" The boy's face twisted with grief and fury.

The crowd of people in the nave surged forward.

"This matter will be dealt with by a court," shouted Brittany. "Sir John Giffard and Sir Thomas Turberville will stand before the court to be tried for this act of treachery."

Richard felt a hand on his shoulder. William stood behind him looking disgusted.

"The French are landing. Already three ships have arrived. Tell them!"

"By Christ," Richard said. On the nave steps, Turberville and his men were surrounding John of Brittany, hands on their sword hilts. The boy, Henri, was being bundled away through the church by a band of Gascon women.

"Bring that boy back here," Giffard ordered.

Giffard's loyal guards advanced on the crowd, swords raised, with Turberville's sons on either side.

"For the love of Christ!" Richard shouted. "The French are knocking at the gate. This will hand the victory to them! Brittany, rally the English. Bring them under control!"

But John of Brittany was hidden behind a knot of fighting knights and guards. People were streaming out of the church into the town square. Everywhere he looked, the English were fighting their allies. Several bodies already lay bleeding in the church. A Priest ran from the chancel, down the steps and into the vestry.

Reginald was being pressed into a corner by one of Giffard's men. The Lord Marshal was at the west door, ordering his guards to block it, but the riot had already spread to the square. Richard grabbed William's hand.

"William, you must get out to raise the alarm. I trust your skills. Make your way to Blaye and have them send help. I doubt we will escape this, but if we do we will need Tibetot's force to break the siege."

"You should come too." William said, his eyes quick around the church, assessing the best route of escape. "I'll bring the horses, and we can ride swiftly out of the gate."

"No, I must fight with the men here. Besides, I will only slow you down. Now, go quickly. You know the way out through the back wall."

William looked unhappy.

"I should stay and fight, not leave you alone."

"No, I order you to go. Before long the French attack will block all escape, and no word will get out except by bird," Richard said, looking out of the church door. "Besides I have Hugh to help me."

"You know how I feel about Hugh," said William with barely concealed anger. "Why isn't he here?"

"I gave him another post by the gate. He'll get better. You did. Remember?"

William scowled.

"I will only go because you order it," William said, not looking at Richard. "God save you."

And he was gone, further into the church, finding a forgotten door, turning into the shadow that he always held inside. Perhaps he would even make it to the stable and take one of the horses. He was a master of disappearance.

Reginald was injured, but he was still keeping Giffard's guard at a distance with desperate sword slashing.

"Save it for the French! Get away! He is with me!" Richard shouted at the guard, parrying his falchion.

Reginald rallied a little, and the Welsh guard backed away from the pair. He looked around for his fellows, saw a bigger fight outside and ran into the light of the square.

Reginald was breathing heavily, fighting to stay upright.

"What was that about?" he wheezed.

"Come here, to the wall. I will look at your wound." The young man was ashen, and there was a seeping red patch on the left of his chest.

"Why did they turn on us, Sir Richard? We are all on the same side."

"Those guards only obey Giffard. He keeps them loyal like dogs."

Richard lowered Reginald to sit on the floor by the wall. The archer's face was shining with sweat. His eyes darted across Richard's face.

"He got in between my ribs," he gasped.

"No, just a scratch I think," Richard said, but he didn't pull back the fabric. He could feel the blood seeping down the side of the strong torso. "I will bandage it tight. You lie down. Soon your strength will return."

Reginald slumped down on the flagstones.

Outside women were screaming. Arrows thunked into wood. The French had arrived.

"Reginald." Richard touched his cheek. "I am going to get the physician for you."

The archer did not open his eyes, but breath still moved on his lips.

Richard stumbled to his feet and ran limping to the vestry. It was locked.

"Father, there is a man dying. Come out and give him the sacrament." There was a long pause. "Do not deny him the last rites because of your cowardice, Priest!"

"I am no coward," the priest replied, opening the door. "I was arming myself." He wore the habit of the Templar Priests, and held a sword and shield. They ran to the prostrate figure by the north wall. The patch of darkness on Reginald's left side was pooling on the flagstone.

"What is his name?" the Templar asked, holding his hand above Reginald's mouth to feel his breath.

"Reginald of Pitchford."

The priest touched Reginald's smooth forehead with the unction.

"Through this holy unction and His own most tender mercy may the Lord pardon thee whatever sins or faults thou hast committed by sight, by hearing, smell, taste, touch, walking, and carnal delectation."

Richard knelt next to him, but his eyes were on the church door; his lips repeated "Amen" without thought or prayer. Soon French soldiers would be pouring through it. They would stroll through the unmanned gates of the town because everyone inside would have already killed each other. Hugh might be already dead. By Christ, he felt like killing Gorges, Brittany and Giffard himself for betraying their allies and provoking their troops. They seemed to believe that no one would dare revolt. But men treated as badly as that would go up like dry brush struck by lightning.

"He is gone," the priest said, rolling back onto his feet and standing up. Richard looked down at Reginald, suddenly aware of his dereliction. The Templar stowed his vial of holy oil in a pouch at his waist. "We must pray for him later. There is much to do outside."

"He came with me," Richard said and crossed Reginald's hands on his chest, pressing them together. He struggled to his feet and faced the priest.

The Templar drew his sword.

"Stay by me," he said. "We can guard each other's backs." He made the sign of the cross in between them and led the way.

Chapter X

Rions
Vespers

"Sir!" Hugh shouted, nearly running into Richard on the threshold of the church. "The French are bringing a ram up to the gate."

The lad was breathing heavily, struggling under his coat of mail. He wasn't yet strong enough for battle, despite what his father had said the previous summer. His father, with his large, hopeful face, had spent a fortune equipping him, but this trip to France was revealing Hugh's weaknesses. It would be a miracle if he survived.

"Go back up to the tower and wait for me there," Richard ordered. "They will try to scale the walls with ladders. Use the pikes. I will bring some archers up with me if any are left alive."

Hugh looked across the frenzied square where at least thirty men were still fighting. It was hard to tell if he was relieved or disappointed not to be at Richard's side.

"Yes, Sir Richard," he said and ran through the mêlée, sword and pennant in his gangling arms.

A small group of knights and guards were putting the posts in position to brace the gate. A boy was chasing a panicked horse around the square in between the brawling men until it galloped down an alley, scattering birds and dogs. They may as well open the gate and let the French stroll in and save the timber.

"Let's remind these men of their duties," said the Templar, setting off towards the largest group of fighters.

Richard and the priest did manage to bring some of the men to their senses. The Templar intervened bodily in several fights, knowing they would not want to kill him and suffer in Hell for it. An English outlaw thrust at the priest's back with a falchion, but Richard blocked it and pushed the robber away. The man had been on *La Grâcedieu*. Richard got hold of his thick jerkin, shouted in his ear and shoved him towards the cracked and groaning gate. The Templar was already taking a group of Gascons across the square to prepare for the breach.

Richard gathered the archers he could find and led them to the tower, limping up the steps behind them. The sun was setting, and the moon was low on the horizon. Below them the French ram had nearly broken through. With every thrust, the stones shivered. Hugh stood by the far parapet, holding a pike ready to push off the ladders.

"Sir, there are mounted knights leaving the town," he said in his high voice, pointing. Richard went to the arrow loop that faced east.

A group of eight knights were riding a sortie behind the main body of French. Even at that distance, Richard could recognise the arms of John of Brittany, Gorges and Giffard with their remaining men, including the short figure of Master Geoffrey, charging down the hill towards the river. The few soldiers guarding the French ships were not prepared to take on the cavalry and fled after a volley of arrows.

The English commanders halted at the largest ship, lowered the plank, rode aboard and cast off. They flowed quickly down-river with a late evening breeze behind them, their banners flying in the golden sky.

Richard redirected the archers to try to hit Charles of Valois as he galloped in, but it was no use. A bank of French crossbowmen rained bolts on the towers, and they had to take cover behind the parapet. The French infantry didn't need the ladders. They could ascend the stairs from the inside. The tower guards were either prisoners or dead. From their trapped position above the town, Richard, Hugh and the remaining archers could hear the hooves of mounted French knights rounding up the townspeople in the square and boots climbing the stairs.

Richard lunged, engaging the first guard to reach the top step, but soon the fighting platform was thick with French soldiers. A large man caught Richard's left arm as he parried with his right and swung him towards the wall. Two men held him, and one slammed his hand against the tower wall until he released his sword. On his left, Hugh dropped the pike, unable to use it in the crowd. The French soldiers drove them down the stairs into the torch-lit square.

Most of the townsfolk were sheltering under the market roof, clustered around the columns. Mounted knights were riding slowly around it, swords drawn.

On the side nearest the gate, the remains of the English force were gathered: Turberville and his two sons, Fulk son of Warin, Elias de Hauvill, de Mubray, Fulburn and a few others. All had been disarmed; all were bareheaded.

At the gate Charles of Valois, still on his charger, was conversing with another mounted man who was just as richly attired. Another bloody French Count. Just visible in the growing dark, soldiers on the far side of the square were dragging bodies to the church. There was no sign of the Templar Priest. He could be in the church, praying for the dead. More likely he was dead himself, without the benefit of the sacrament he carried.

Two towns surrendered in two days, and the English command had galloped away, leaving others to fight and die.

"Thomas!" Richard whispered.

Turberville turned his head. He was sweating freely and looking angrier than Richard had ever seen him before.

"The command has left!" Richard said.

"I know. My men have been slaughtered, and now we will be taken hostage thanks to them."

"Did you hear that Reginald was killed?"

Turberville turned away, shaking his head. The flickering torchlight made his profile twitch and warp. The French soldiers were moving the English knights into a tight group in front of Charles. The other Count came forward, mounted on an exquisite white stallion.

"Ah a small piece of good fortune!" Turberville said. "Boys, stand close to me. We might be taken hostage by the Count of Artois, God willing."

"Robert of Artois?" Hugh asked. "I've heard that he is a bad man."

Turberville turned on him haughtily.

"How would you know of him? He is a man of courtesy, a great noble. I visited his home with King Edward. It was full of wonders: fountains and devices of great ingenuity, a head made of bronze with a moving mouth," he explained, gesturing in the air. "The Count also keeps a menagerie of many beasts," Turberville said, turning to his sons.

"I hope he doesn't cage us with the lions," said one of them under his breath.

"He is the nephew of Louis, a great French Saint!" his father reprimanded.

"But he is not going to take us to his palace, Turberville. We are not his guests," Richard whispered in his ear. "What's that animal he's holding?"

"I can't see."

"It looks like a dog," Richard said, leaning round the pillar for a better view of the large animal.

"He has given it to his servant now," Turberville said. "It is a dog, pulling on a long chain."

The French infantry were still coming through the shattered gate and lining the square, pikes held aloft.

"There are too many spits for my liking," said Richard. "Come, let us try some diplomacy with this Count of Artois."

"That is no dog," said Hugh who had gone forward a pace, peering through the press of armed men. "It's a wolf. Look at its teeth."

The animal was ranging near the townspeople on the west side of the square, restrained by a short, thickset man who held the chain by a leather handle. The wolf strained towards the frightened people, its mouth open, panting and foaming with the effort. The horses nearby wheeled unhappily.

"Artois, keep that beast away from our horses!" one of the mounted French knights shouted. "If they injure each other in a stampede to get away from your pet, you will pay damages!"

The Count of Artois turned his horse and ostentatiously brought it within a foot of the wolf.

"Guillot! Restrain the beast. Do not let her near those terrified men and their poor horses. Use her to keep the common people docile. There will be some sport for her later, perhaps." He nodded at the other knights and walked his white destrier back to where Charles of Valois was commanding the last of the arriving infantry.

"Are you sure he is Saint Louis' nephew, Father?" said one of Turberville's sons.

Richard leant against a column, suddenly exhausted, his bad leg weak and useless under him. Escape was impossible. The only option was to try to negotiate a decent imprisonment. His mind was empty, drained. He tried to take off his glove, aware of new pain in his hand, but it was swollen, and he could not remove the gauntlet.

"Hugh!" he hissed. "Get this off my hand."

He wished he'd left it alone. Pain burned its way down his gut as the squire tugged the gauntlet free. His knuckles were no longer discernible, and the fingers were swollen. His sword hand was badly bruised, maybe broken. He needed a leech to set it. He needed Illesa, who would bandage it with her valerian salve.

Richard looked up to the sky where the moon was rising towards the figure of Orion. A flock of doves swerved above the market in the last of the light. He took a deep breath of cool air. Was there anything else that would be taken from him? Any other part of his body or soul that would be broken?

Hugh put his arm under Richard's shoulder.

"You should come forward with the other knights," he said, helping Richard to move a few paces. "Put your arm up on your other shoulder, so it doesn't get knocked. I will tie it with my belt."

Turberville was at the head of the group with his sons as they approached the mounted nobles. Four guards stopped them ten paces from the men. The Counts of Valois and Artois were not to be interrupted. They carried on a loud conversation about the hunting along the Gironde while the English knights stood, an injured ragged company, in front of them.

"What a remarkably easy task this has been. I do believe we have lost only a dozen men to conquer both of these fortified towns. Like women who scream at first, but soon submit."

The Count of Artois laughed loudly. He clapped Valois on the back and turned to Turberville and the other knights.

"Well good sirs, it is a rout, you must agree. You have not shown your mettle. I expected more from you!"

"My lord, Count of Artois," Turberville began, bowing slightly. "Perhaps you remember the visit I made to your delightful palace in the company of King Edward only a few years ago?"

"I remember the visit of the Duke of Aquitaine, when he held that title," remarked the Count, amused. "But I do not know your arms. You cannot have been someone I spoke to."

"Sir Thomas de Turberville, my lord. I was with you when you were building the first of the wonders in your garden at Hesdin," Thomas said in his most charming tone. "What a splendid sight it must be now."

"My man, I cannot remember you at all, but what you say is true. It is one of the most splendid and amusing places in the whole world. I expect you must have been dreaming of it ever since."

Charles of Valois made a snorting laugh.

"Charles," the Count of Artois said, turning to him, "this Turberville is one of the knights who accompanied Edward. I suppose someone had to detain us with courteous remarks while the command fled. He could prove profitable."

The Count of Valois moved his horse a bit nearer to inspect the group of prisoners. He met Richard's eye.

"You," he said, pointing his sword. "You took me for a fool yesterday, but today I take you." He smiled briefly. "Although we won't gain much for you, crippled and half-blind as you are, unless some of the wealth of the Chancellor still clings to your family."

Robert of Artois had lost interest and was whistling for his wolf.

"Put them in the gaol for now," Charles told the guard at his side. "In a few days we will take them somewhere more suitable."

"Most kind of you, my lord," said Richard, bowing. "There was trouble over the deaths at Podensac. The men of Rions rioted against Giffard. Dozens were killed. It would be best if we were not imprisoned together, or the Gascon and English nobles might leave you with nothing to ransom."

Charles stared at Richard, expressionless, then turned to the men beside him.

"Guards, make sure the Gascons are gaoled separately," he ordered.

Behind him there was a disturbance among the infantry. Two men were pushing a small, hunched figure forward. One of the soldiers goaded it with the sharp end of his pike.

"Look what we found behind the barrels in the cellar!"

"What? Oh, that boy we sent here yesterday?" Charles said, looking across briefly. "Put him with the rest of the commoners. He can be used later. Now we should hear Mass. Find the priest!" he shouted. He regarded the group of defeated knights standing before him. "Let's have one of you at supper, and you can tell us about the habits of the English King." He gestured to Turberville. "You, *Monsieur Courtoisie*. Are these your squires?"

"My sons," Turberville said, drawing them both forward beside him.

"Ah, I see," Charles smiled. "They will go to the cells. But you can remind us of the Duke of Aquitaine's famous reputation for military strategy," he said, mockingly.

The Count dismounted at last, and the other lesser knights who had been waiting for this signal also dismounted and started talking loudly.

Turberville gripped each of his sons on the shoulder and then walked into the midst of the French knights who were making for the church doors. Inside they would find Reginald's corpse in a pool of blood. They may look for the priest, but Richard doubted they would find him. Templars had no loyalty to towns or Kings, only to their order.

The Mayor was brought forward, and six guards escorted the knights and their men through the empty streets to his hall, which housed the gaol. The Mayor took out a large key and unlocked the door, his face slack with shock. He did not know whether his town would be burned or used as a base, whether he would keep his life or lose it along with his family at first light. Only the wealthy knights could rest easy. They were worth more alive than dead.

"English in here," a guard said thickly, opening one of several studded doors. There was a bench, a bucket, and a smoking, guttering lamp. One of the outlaws who had joined the fleet in Portsmouth was lying insensible on the damp floor, but otherwise the cell was empty. They entered without a word, and the key turned in the lock behind them. Through one high window slit, they could hear the doves settling in the dovecote and, in the distance, the cries of a baby.

In the semi-darkness they agreed who would get the bench first, and the rest sat on the floor. The outlaw had a rattle in his chest. At any moment they thought he would cough and wake.

"Do you think they will bring any meat or drink?" asked one of Turberville's sons, pushing up his sleeve to look at a cut on his arm. His voice was unsteady, and he cleared his throat.

"We can pray that they do," sighed Richard, shifting on the bench. There was barely room for him to stretch out his bad leg. "Perhaps your father will be able to remind them of our needs." He looked down at the two lads sitting close together like frightened puppies taken from their dam. "It must be the first time you have been imprisoned."

"Yes, but Father was held by the French when he was last in Gascony," the other son said. "They treated him well."

"They would have done as he was a hostage exchange for Charles of Salerno, and we were not at war with the French then, merely negotiating. I would not hope for good treatment this time," Richard concluded, trying not to sound as angry as he felt. Anger had no place in a small room.

"But the King will send ransom for us, won't he? We won't be left here for long?" the first boy asked. They took turns to speak as if rigidly trained.

"The King has the uprising in Wales to fight, and he has to muster more troops for Gascony. We are not so important to him. I think we will have to find our own way out of this."

The boys glanced at each other silently, their eyes wide in the light of the single flame.

Richard almost regretted his words. But hope was a costly guest and hard to banish once it lodged inside your heart. It would be better if they expected the worst.

Chapter XI

Sunday the 10th April 1295
Bordeaux
Vespers

Hugh sat next to Richard in the barge, staring at the city shimmering on the water. There was no sound of missiles or arrows on this journey, just church bells and the distant cries of traders on the docks.

The sun was setting beyond the city, gilding the towers, flags and the wings of the gulls flying above it. In the east, a gibbous moon rose above the fields and forests of the Gironde. Soon they would disembark, walk through the gates of Bordeaux and be locked in, out of sight of sun and moon.

Turberville stood by the rail, his tied hands fiddling with his tunic, the end of a rope, the beard growing prickly on his chin. That morning he had appeared at the quay with a guard, already bound, and been loaded on the barge with the rest of them. His hopes of being taken to the Count's garden of wonders had come to nothing.

Richard had tried to talk to him, but Turberville was terse and distant. He did not meet his eye and would not tell him what had happened to the townspeople or the boy from Podensac.

"It's best not to talk about such things in front of the young," he muttered and went to stand beside his two sons.

Richard had finally found out their names. Payne was the elder, always at his father's side wanting to talk or help or plan, while Henry kept his own company. His preoccupation reminded Richard of Christopher, who often seemed to be living in another world, absent and unattainable.

What had happened to the town while he and the other knights had been in the gaol worried Richard. He had been awake and in pain most of the night. When his mind snatched at dreams they were terrible and bloody. But he remembered the sound of screaming and frantic running, the laughter of the men who watched.

They had not seen Reginald buried, nor any of the other dead who had set off from the Marches, travelled to the South Coast and sailed with them from Portsmouth. Men they had lived with for six months or more. The French should provide Christian burial, but a commander who could set a wolf on an injured boy for sport might have little concern for anyone's soul. The stench of corpses had hung in the air over Rions that morning. Perhaps the French had already set the pile of bodies alight.

The barge was pulling up to the jetty by the largest and most fortified of Bordeaux's gates. Guards moved on its towers, black as crows in the fading light. At least they would not be paraded through the streets in the middle of the day to be subjected to stones and rotten fruit. Curious late traders carrying baskets and bales stared at the English prisoners as the barge was tied to the posts.

There were eight guards in all, half-pushing, half-guiding the bound men onto shore. If their hands had not been tied, the fifteen prisoners would have had a chance. Even now, Hugh, who could swim well, might have slipped away and made it to the other shore. But he spoke no French and had little independence. Why hadn't they arranged a plan? Hugh could have joined the rest of the army at Blaye.

Instead they would all be sleeping in cells tonight.

A sudden longing overwhelmed Richard: the hearth at Langley, the short climb up the stairs to the soft bed, the shared pleasure. At least the French had not found his silk pouch when they removed his scabbard and his armour. It hung around his shoulder on a soft cord, almost weightless with Illesa's fine stitches. He would not dare look at it or even touch it until he was alone. Inside were a few dry herbs she had insisted on him carrying and something folded up by Christopher that he'd not yet opened. God willing, it had not been ruined by seawater or sweat.

The guards marched them through the gate into Bordeaux in the very last of the light, and soon the smell of fish was replaced by the stench of the tannery ditches. It might be years before he smelled fresh earth rising behind a plough again.

They turned into a wide square. A nearby church was still ringing with the hours of prayer. Turberville, who was walking a few paces in front of Richard, crossed himself. At the other side of the square was the Palais de l'Ombrière. To the right of the gatehouse, a tall white tower rose into the dark sky, the crenellations on its roof standing out like large teeth in a huge mouth.

As they were brought through the gate, Hugh's breathing changed, becoming harsh and wheezing. There was an acrid smell inside the castle walls, as if they were burning lime. Richard's eye began watering, and he stumbled limping into Turberville. Hugh caught him by the arms before he fell badly. He would not have been able to save himself with his arms bound together and his hand still swollen.

Turberville turned, his face full of dark shadows.

"Richard, can you walk? Do you want my boys to help you?"

"Thank you, but Hugh is here," said Richard. "He can use his long arms."

Hugh adjusted his grip on Richard.

"What a stink," he complained.

"They must be building," Turberville concluded.

They had stopped inside the antechamber, while one of the guards went through to the hall to learn where the hostages would be housed.

It was only moments before he was back.

"The Constable is dining with the Mayor. They wish to see the knights before you are taken to your cells. We will enter through the courtyard." He pushed the squires to the back.

Two of the guards led the knights out into the dark. This was where the smell was strongest, although there was no fire to be seen. It must have recently been doused. There was a flight of steps leading to the upper level of the hall.

"Here Richard, you will need my help now," said Turberville, putting his tied arms out so that Richard could lean on him, perhaps trying to apologise for his rudeness on the barge.

After the darkness of the yard, the hall seemed as bright as daylight with many candles glinting on glass and silver. Large tapestries hung on the walls. There were three long tables running lengthways down the room, but only the head table was occupied. Six men sat there enjoying a variety of meat and bread.

The Constable, seated in the middle, was busy cutting from a roast haunch with a long knife and did not look up. The man next to him, wearing the dress of a prosperous merchant, frowned at the group, his thick hands playing with his knife. The Constable's hair was almost white under a deep blue cap. The embroidered supertunic he wore matched it. He looked up from his food.

"The English have arrived," the Constable said, regarding the line of knights, "and yet we are unafraid," he smiled.

A few of the lesser men at the table laughed. The aroma of roast venison was thick in the air.

"You were hardly Hector and the Trojans. From what I've heard, you allowed Rions to fall with barely a fight." The Constable mused for a moment. "But what is to be done with you now? That is the question." He wiped his mouth with a small white napkin. "We hope you can earn some coin for us through ransom, although considering the poor situation of the former Duke of Aquitaine, that seems unlikely."

Turberville stepped forward and bowed.

"My lord Constable and my lord Mayor, noble men of Bordeaux. We greet you and appeal for your mercy. As you know, Edward remains the Duke of Aquitaine, so we are within our rights to be in this Duchy. We are glad to be in your custody as we know you will treat us fairly and understand that the disagreement between England and France will not last long. Soon we will return to trading and making wealth, particularly here with the merchants of Bordeaux."

The Mayor looked uncomfortable.

"A fine speech," the Constable smirked. "But you are sadly misinformed about the citizens of Bordeaux. They do not support the former Duke of Aquitaine. All those who held that loyalty have been taken hostage and are being held at the rightful King's pleasure. Now who is this that speaks so pragmatically about the making of wealth? There may be other ways to go about it."

"Sir Thomas de Turberville, my lord. My sons accompanied me and are waiting with the other squires. We have no animosity to the nobles and burgesses of Bordeaux. We have always had a profitable friendship up to now. So I appeal for myself, my sons and these other good men here, that we are accommodated with mercy and comfort after several nights on hard stone. Then we can begin to plan how to turn this situation to your advantage and ours."

"Sir Thomas de Turberville." The Constable tried the name in his mouth. "You are familiar with our concerns. But this is a late appeal. Perhaps you did not get our message loud and clear when we sent it flying over your bow in December?"

"Perhaps we did appear a bit threatening," Turberville said with a diplomatic grimace.

"And the English fleet have been busy taking towns all along the Garonne."

"But most have simply surrendered to us as their rightful lords," Turberville said apologetically.

"That was fortunate for you. But I understand you have come to the end of that spin of Fortune's wheel. The Counts of Valois and Artois have rooted you out of your little towns. Now you are not the lords of anything," said the Constable, twirling a lock of his white hair.

The Mayor continued to eat, staring belligerently at the men.

"My lords, you speak the truth. We have been humbled before you," said Richard holding out his bound hands. "But, in the name of the Lord of Heaven we both worship, we beg you to house us with Christian mercy and feed us. We will be worth nothing to you dead."

"You are almost there already," said the Mayor suddenly. "What a sight! What desperation there must be in England that they send even the one-eyed cripples to fight."

The Constable silenced him with a movement of his finger.

"What is your name?" he asked, turning his pale eyes back to Richard.

"Sir Burnel. I am a cousin to Chancellor Robert Burnel."

"Ah." A long silence grew between them. The pale eyes blinked. "A very wealthy cleric. I remember him well. He was infinite in his pragmatism. You seem to have been rather unlucky, considering the privilege of your family. I hear the bankers have called in almost all of his property."

"The merchants of Lucca are quick to reclaim their debts," said Richard evenly.

The Constable leant back in his chair and looked thoughtful.

"There may yet be some profit to be made. Some fine garments might be sewn from this pile of skins. We will see. That is enough for now." The Constable got to his feet. His eyes rested on each of the prisoners in turn.

"There will be no negotiation between us. You have nothing to gain from appealing to me about loyalty or the plight of your families. My concern is France, and, for France to prosper in this matter, I need gold and silver. Silver for defence and gold for offence. Perhaps some of you will be able to help me with this, while others will simply eat and drink up our stores. What you have cost me in lives and lost revenue, I need you to make back for me. I do not give anything away for free."

He signalled the guards by the wall to come forward.

"For now you will be well housed and given food and drink. Tomorrow you will be allowed to attend Mass in the Palace Chapel. But soon we will reckon the loss, and those who cannot bring profit – " he shrugged. "Let us say that your bodies will not be given the comforts they are used to."

The guards moved them back down the great hall. Once more, Turberville took Richard's arm when they came to the stairs into the yard.

"What kind of business are you hoping to do with these men, Thomas?" Richard whispered. "The only profit they want is profit for the French Crown."

"Don't be naïve, Richard. I am speaking to them in the way they understand. Through deals and negotiating, we may get ourselves out of captivity and back to our rightful positions."

They were nearly at the bottom of the steps. Richard stopped and turned to face his friend.

"Through deals like the one at Podensac that cost fifty men their lives?" he asked.

Turberville's grip on his arm tightened painfully.

"If I had not said what I said, we would all have died there, either killed by the French or by the good people of Podensac. Is that what you want?" he demanded, his thin nose flaring. "We all die, humbled and dirty in our cells? I have sons here, and they are not going to die like that because their father cannot come up with a plan to escape this living death."

Richard shook his head.

"Thomas, if you negotiate with them they will soon demand everything of you. Look at how Philip fooled the Earl of Lancaster. They cannot be trusted."

"We trusted our King to equip us, feed us and send more forces," Turberville whispered, "and he has not. Yet he demands everything of us."

He strode away, leaving Richard in the courtyard to be prodded on by the last guard.

Chapter XII

Tuesday the 12th April 1295
Palais de l'Ombrière, Bordeaux

The hostages had been divided into two groups. One, about half-way up the tower, had the majority of the men including Richard, Elias de Hauvill, and Roger de Mubray with their squires. The other, on a lower floor, was for Turberville and his men. Richard wondered if it was a better-equipped room.

In this large cell, they each had a bed, but the straw was old. They fed, although not on meat. They had a bucket for water and another for their shit. It was a prison but not the worst. The Constable would not spend unnecessary money on their comfort, but he would keep them alive for their potential ransoms if nothing else. This was what Richard repeated to his men when they began to worry. None of them had been imprisoned before. They did not know how to school their minds away from the future.

When they had been taken to the chapel, Richard had hoped to make peace with Turberville. He should not have started an argument, should have preserved the trust between them. But the guards kept the two groups of prisoners separate, and after Mass they were immediately marched back to the locked room with no chance of speaking. While they had been in the chapel someone had searched their few remaining belongings.

After a bad night, Richard lay on his bed throughout the morning, hoping his leg would improve with rest, fingering the silk pouch inside his tunic. The other men spoke in undertones, uncertain whether a guard had been set on the other side of the door to listen to their conversations. They were listless, as if drugged.

The slit of a window had a narrow view over the grey thatched roofs and the dripping tavern poles. Heavy rain was falling directly down, filling up the river. Perhaps this was the start of the next flood.

At home, spring would be greening the fields, and the young animals would be calling for milk. Joyce would be walking and maybe speaking as well. And Christopher? Perhaps he would have come down from the trees by now, and begun to be a man.

At tierce the guards began taking the knights out, one by one. They were not returned. By sext, everyone had been called except Richard. Hugh had become as jumpy as a rabbit, expecting the guards at any moment.

Eventually they were led out by three guards, who shouted at each other in guttural northern French all the way down the narrow stairs to the courtyard. This time they were taken into a small room off the gatehouse – the Constable's private office.

The Constable was dressed in black and red. His shocking white hair shone like a bright fire. At the table in front of him, a clerk sat, cutting his quill. There was a sheet in front of him already half-full of notation, perhaps about the other knights. The Constable nodded for Richard to sit in the one free chair before the table. Hugh stood just behind him.

"I had the chair brought in for you. My guards report that you cannot stand for long."

"My thanks for your courtesy, my lord," said Richard.

"Thus far you English have not given us much trouble. It seems to me that you make good prisoners."

Richard ignored the slight.

"We are certainly grateful for the food and beds. The Counts of Valois and Artois were not so considerate."

"No they are not. It is their business to bring you to submission. It is my business to make some money out of you, or, if that is not possible, to make some other use of you. If neither of these things is forthcoming, then the conditions may harden." He smiled briefly. "But we all hope this will not happen. After all, one day the alliance between our Kings may be rekindled. Then we will be allies again and no longer enemies. At the word of the Kings, we must all change sides, eh?"

"Yes, my lord. It is wise to take the long view of these matters. We have often enjoyed the hospitality and blessings of the Kingdom of France and hope to offer the same in return, in better times."

"Better times," the Constable paused. "It is hard to imagine their arrival when our sailors massacre each other and the citizens of towns are harried by dogs and hanged in the streets for speaking French. There must be recompense for these atrocities. And the English King is slow in delivering. He caused the war we now suffer. But I suppose you disagree?"

"Of course."

"Yes. I have found that there are always these two opposing points of view." The Constable smiled thinly. "There is no point debating it any further. My scribe will take your details, and then we will talk about how you can help us."

Hugh opened his mouth to speak, but Richard elbowed him. It did not escape the Constable.

"The younger soldiers are often disappointed by real war," he said, conversationally. "I see your squire believes that you should never help your enemy. He has not yet understood that if you don't you might be tortured and die. You see, we are not far apart, and yet we are not close together. The same would happen and has happened to French soldiers and sailors at the hands of the English," he said laying his hands flat on the table and leaning forward slightly. "So you *will* help us. It simply remains to see how."

He got up and went to the window behind him. In the yard beyond, the crossbowmen were practising. They could hear the sound of ratchets and bolts slamming into their targets.

"I often think about Saint Sebastian when I watch them practise," the Constable remarked, his back to them. "He was particularly uncooperative to his captors, I believe."

Hugh gripped the back of Richard's chair, making it rock, but the Constable laughed and turned to face them.

"I do like to frighten the young ones," he said. "What do you take me for? I am a Christian. I will not kill you, at least not in that way." He shook his head slightly, and the hair moved around his face as if it had its own animal life.

"He is playing with you," Richard murmured, placing a hand on Hugh's wrist. "Let us continue our discussion," he said aloud.

102

"You must forgive me. It is tedious work questioning the English," the Constable said, sitting down carefully on his elaborate chair. "They are so straight. I've only had one little scrap of joy this whole day."

"Who was that from?" Richard said, rather too quickly.

"No, no, I will not tell you. That is my secret." The Constable smiled at the clerk. "Now, what I need from you is the amount that you think you will be ransomed for. Has this happened to you before so you know the price? No?"

"Lord Constable, time has changed my situation as you know. Chancellor Burnel is dead and there is little wealth left. There may be a chance that the King will meet the obligation for the love of his old friend. If you can provide me with a scribe, I will write a letter which asks for his help."

The Constable raised his pale eyebrows and blinked.

"We are not that simple, Sir Burnel, and I sincerely hope that you are not. Your King will not ransom anyone. He is holding tight to what little coin he has for making ships, and he certainly will not send any money to the French until the peace treaty is signed and sealed. No, it is your family to whom we must appeal. They may provide enough, don't you think?"

"All our wealth is in livestock. And I don't think you want my wife to sail up the Garonne with our English sheep. Even their fleeces would not bring you much."

The Constable stared at him silently, pressing his thin lips together.

"You are painting a sweet picture of a simple country knight," the Constable mimed the movements of an artist with a paintbrush. "But I am not convinced. No. I do not think that the knight who was a favourite of the Chancellor lives the life you describe." He shook his head slowly and the white blaze of hair caught the sunlight through the window. "Your family must have things they can sell. If they really thought your life was in danger, they would get enough silver."

Richard stretched his legs and winced.

"They are quite used to that. Every day it is a surprise to them that I wake up."

The Constable raised his eyebrows even higher and tilted his head.

"Now you are trying to imply that they are indifferent to you. Well, let us leave it there. You may think about it in the upper rooms of the tower for a while. Then we will talk again. I am sure you will find that your memory and your love of home are a little bit sharper after that."

And the guard hoisted him out of the chair and led him away.

Chapter XIII

Saturday the 30th April 1295
Langley Manor
Tierce

The crops were growing, pushing their bright green fingers out of the soil. A lark was singing above the long meadow where the newly freed cows were enjoying the fresh grass. Joyce pulled Illesa's hand, wanting to crawl off through the garden where she would grab the dark soil, pull out the seedlings and eat them no doubt. Illesa scooped her up and kissed her cold red fingers. She put the small handful of tansy into the pouch at her waist and opened the wicket gate into the yard.

She had been wrong to allow herself to hope that the message was word of Richard's return. When she had taken the parchment from the boy at the gate, her heart had risen like that lark. And then fallen to earth as if hit by a stone.

At least he wasn't dead, Cecily had said. Richard would be well looked after in Bordeaux, with all that wine and wheat. She made it sound like the fields of Heaven. It was William that worried Cecily. Ever since her husband had died, she had transferred all her spare anxiety to him. She worried that he might be ambushed on his way to Blaye, and they would never know, or that his clothes would wear out, and he would be taken for a vagrant. It was foolish of her. If anyone could look after himself, it was William.

But he had not kept his promise to stay and guard Richard. If he had brought the message to her in person, Illesa would have slapped him. How could he have left Richard there to be captured? And now they were here, waiting. Waiting for the crops to grow, for the tax collectors to come and relieve them of whatever they had left, waiting for word of life or death. It was Purgatory. Even bringing in the woodbine and hawthorn for May Day felt pointless.

She swung Joyce high in the air as they passed close to the moat. If she wasn't distracted, the little terror would try to jump into it. Christopher had already saved her once, but the cold water in her eyes and mouth had not put her off. Joyce leant, arching her back, reaching out for the water, not fooled. She had an instinct for trouble. It was almost as if she had inherited her spirit from Kit without the benefit of blood.

While Christopher, who was named after her reckless brother, was much more like Illesa in his habits: wary and anxious. And the things he had witnessed had made it so much worse. He had been using his bow and sword every day, raising his thin arms, swinging, pulling, and all in silence, with the intensity of a hawk that waits for the rabbit to bolt. Pelta would lie, flat by the wall, eyes shut until Christopher finished, puffing and wet with the effort.

But today he didn't seem to have the heart for it. He was sitting by the wall himself with Pelta's head in his lap and his eyes shut against the bright sun. The dog's tail wagged twice as they approached.

Illesa put Joyce down on the cobbles and held her hands as she ran at the boy and the dog, falling on top of them and laughing. Christopher caught her, smiling, and held her little fat hands for a moment. He barely spoke these days, not even to her. Joyce sat down on his lap and started patting the dog hard on the head.

"Christopher, come inside with me, darling."

He got up silently, pulling Joyce with him. They each held one of her hands and walked with her between them to the side door. In the pantry, Cecily was making a beeswax cake, and Joyce wanted to stay in the cool room, clinging to Cecily's skirts and be given tiny pieces of curd to chew.

Illesa led Christopher towards the stairs in the hall. He climbed ahead of her, head down, as if expecting a piece of the roof to fall. It was a long time since she had seen his face lightened with laughter or smiles. The last time was the day before Gaspar had left in January. And since then, she had been unable, for all these winter months, to find anything to cheer him.

They came to the door of the solar where they all now slept since the nightmares had returned. Christopher would not say much about them, but it seemed he watched people being killed, stabbed or shot with arrows. In the dream, he would try to pull the arrows out of the bodies and bring the men, sometimes his father, back to life.

The sun was slanting through the south window, lighting up the remaining coverlet on the bed.

"I thought we could read together, like we used to do. Would you like to read from the Bestiary?" she asked.

He shook his head and took his hand out of hers.

"I want to read about Troy," he said, looking at her gravely. It was all he would read these days. Although he had been interested in the book of beasts for a few days, he soon returned to the story of battle. She had tried to argue with him, sure that it made the nightmares worse, but today she had no strength left for fighting.

They both knew where the book was kept, but Christopher was the meticulous one. He made sure it was removed and replaced so as to leave no sign. The tax collectors had taken the tapestries from the walls, the fine glass jug and small silver ointment jars. To Illesa, the bare room seemed to cry out the presence of its remaining treasure.

The chest by the window had been covered in new iron straps, but underneath it was old. It was one of the few things she had recovered from her cottage in Holdgate after her father, Robert Burnel, had bought the barony. He had known that she would never live there, but he had bought it nonetheless and made an empty promise to leave it to her son. This legacy had never been recorded, and the Manor, like all of the Chancellor's estates, had been sold to pay off the debts of his wanton heir, Philip, who at least had had the good grace to die quickly.

The chest was the only thing she had really wanted from her childhood home, although it had conspired in the secret that destroyed her adoptive family. It was the chest where the book of Saint Margaret had been hidden, the chest she had lain in as a baby. Watching Christopher opening it and carefully tipping the false bottom always gave her a feeling of peace.

The garments in the chest were only there to hide its secret. Christopher lifted them out and placed them on the floor. When he was five years old and they had started reading together, his arms could barely reach into the chest to release the base. Now he could do it in the dark and almost silently, with only the merest whisper of wood.

He held the book in both hands, brought it to her and returned to the chest to put the clothes away. Only Richard, Illesa and Christopher knew about the secret place. Illesa could not explain her insistence on this, but it was one of the few things she would not share with Cecily, faithful as she was.

Christopher finished replacing the clothes and softly lowered and secured the lid before he came to sit next to her on the bed, his feet a little off the floor. He reached out for the book which she held, unopened, on her lap. He deftly unstrapped it but did not open the cover.

"What is your favourite part?" she asked.

"I like reckless King Ajax," he whispered, "in the twentieth battle."

"That is a very bloody scene," she said. "Are you sure?"

He nodded.

"Will you read it to me?" he asked, his voice nearly inaudible.

"Yes, darling. But you find the page."

It did not take long; the parchment fell open at the scene. He relaxed against her shoulder as she began.

"The Twentieth Battle. In the month of June, when the days are longer and the sun produces sweltering heat, they made ready once more with high pride and great anger. The Greek host's companies set out. King Ajax advanced in the forefront. He had become so reckless that he donned no armour, nor did he take any with him. He wanted to fight without any protection.

Then came the duke of Athens and Ulysses along with all the Greek princes and all their kings. Agamemnon accompanied them with more than thirty thousand armed troops, men who were strong, dependable and battle-hardened. Throughout the city all the Trojans armed themselves again. They feared the perilous day lying ahead of them. Paris sallied forth with his helmet laced on. His heart was heavy and distressed because of his brothers, who had been slain. He knew that it would be very difficult for him. I do not think he was far from the truth. Alas! What an awful destiny had been foreordained for him that day!"

Christopher wriggled next to her.

"Is that your favourite part?" Illesa asked. The dog had found her way up to the solar; they heard her whining at the closed door.

"No," he said, jumping down from the bed to let Pelta in. "I want to hear the part when Paris kills Ajax and Ajax kills Paris."

"That is a bit further," Illesa said, turning the page. "Here it is." Two pages along one of the few illustrations showed the knight Ajax, bareheaded on a large horse with a red caparison. Behind him Paris, in a golden helm, notched an arrow to his bow.

"Ajax roamed around the fighting without a hauberk or visor, and without a helmet laced on, or a shield hanging from his neck. He should have realised that he was a fool. It is a wonder he survived for so long. Hear now what misfortune befell him. He was inflicting great harm on the Trojans as he roamed to and fro through the lines of combat. When Paris caught sight of this madman, he had no desire to put up with it any longer. He notched an arrow that was strong, sharp and poisoned. Taking careful aim, he let the arrow fly with such force that it hit its mark precisely, penetrating both sides of Ajax's body and dislocating his spine. Ajax felt the deathly blow and spurred his horse. Out of his mind enraged and mean, he forced his way through the press, dealing and laying on perilous blows and killing more than twenty-two Trojans."

Illesa stopped and looked at her son. He was enraptured by the image of the half-dead knight, still fighting, still killing.

"He should have stopped killing and prayed for forgiveness for his own soul," she said.

Christopher looked up at her with wide eyes.

"No, you have to keep reading, please. This is the best part."

"I hope it gets better."

"They don't pray like we do," Christopher said, putting her hands back on the book. "It happened so long ago that they were heathens."

"I know, but they had their own gods to appeal to. And all they seem to want to do is slaughter each other."

Christopher sat silently waiting.

"Very well. I'll read some more." Illesa put her finger on the text below the image of the blood red horse.

"Ajax looked for Paris until he found him, and I assure you that before Paris moved, they dealt one another so many blows on the nape of their necks that their heads were bleeding. They attacked one another with brutal cruelty. Ajax shouted: 'My lord Paris, I believe you are now in a tight fix. Although you fired an arrow at me from afar, I have closed in on you and joined battle with you. You have killed me, I know and feel it. Nonetheless your soul will be in the underworld before mine; I want it to set out on its way there. You will never again shoot with a laburnum bow. Here your love is sundered from Helen's, the woman whose birth was so inauspicious that many have paid the ultimate price for it. You will die for her as I am doing now.'"

Illesa paused again.

Christopher fidgeted at the delay.

"That bit about the woman isn't important," he said, bouncing a little. "The next part is my favourite."

"Ajax seized Paris in both his arms that were stronger than those of a giant. He laid heavy blows on him right away. Ajax wanted Paris to pay for and settle with him for his own death. Paris could not escape from his grasp. Ajax drove the point of his burnished blade straight into Paris's face. Paris dropped dead on the spot, the sword still stuck in his face. For his part, Ajax was savagely mangled. Blood made him appear brighter red than crimson silk. Ajax's own troops bore him back to their tents, weeping and wailing on the way. As soon as they withdrew the poisoned arrow from him, his life ended. With great effort and pain, his soul took leave of his body. He almost chewed it with his teeth as it came out."

Christopher had his eyes screwed shut while he listened, and his small hands curled into tight fists, perhaps spearing his enemies through the face. He was young to have seen what he had. Some boys would have seen it and not thought about it again, but Christopher was making it happen again and again. Seeing it, hearing it, changing it.

"That is all we can read now," she said gently. "Can you hear Joyce crying?"

Christopher was looking at the page, tracing the outline of the spear and the back of the horse with his finger.

"Do you think that Daddy has been fighting like that?"

"I hope not."

"What's going to happen to him now?"

Illesa put her arm around his shoulders. Downstairs, there was silence again. Joyce had been bribed with some more food.

"He is out of the fighting for now and will wait in Bordeaux for the King to ransom him."

"So we should pray to the King and ask him to pay the ransom."

Illesa frowned.

"We can't pray to the King. He is a man, not a god. But we can appeal to him and ask him to help."

Christopher was quiet for a moment.

"Will Father be there a long time?"

"I don't know. But King Edward wanted your father in the war because he knew that he has lots of experience. He won't leave him to waste away in a French cell. I think there will be a peace treaty soon, and all the knights will be coming home once these men have stopped their foolishness."

"It's not foolish, Mummy. It is what knights and heroes do," Christopher said, and took the book out of her hands.

"It is what knights and heroes do. That is true," Illesa said. "But they do not always have the best advice. They don't always go to war for good reasons." She took the book out of his hands again. "Here, let me show you something."

As Illesa turned the pages looking for the part about the Greek commanders, she saw that one of the last pages was missing. Near the spine there was a clean cut across the parchment.

Christopher was watching as her finger traced the sharp edge. He looked up to see if there was anger in her face.

"Why did you cut this out of the book, Christopher? You know that this was the last gift – "

He hid his face in the curve of her arm.

"I gave it to Father."

She pulled him out from where he was hiding and held his face in her hands.

"Why did you give him that page?" He was turning pale. Tears were pooling in his eyes. Quickly, she kissed him on the forehead.

"I'm not angry with you. Tell me why you gave it to him."

"I wanted him to have the picture of the giant horse. He told me that was his favourite part. He said he liked Ulysses for his cunning."

Illesa put her arm around her son and held him close.

"Your father has his own cunning. Maybe he will find his own way out of the prison, riding on Greyboy all the way home," she said.

Christopher said nothing for a while. He turned back to stare at the absence of the page.

"What about William? Who is he like in the story?"

Illesa smoothed the pages, trying to remember all the people in the very long epic.

"I don't know, Christopher. There is no one else like William in the whole world. William doesn't like fighting, but he does it well when he has to. I think he is one of the faithful horses that save the knights when they are hard pressed and bring them home swiftly and safely."

"But what if they can't come back?"

Illesa got up from the bed and went to the window. Outside a field of ewes and lambs were noisily finding each other. The new fleeces shone bright in the sun; meat on the hoof.

"I don't think that will happen. The King will ransom him, or his friend the Earl of Lincoln, perhaps. He and William will return."

"But you don't really know," he said, accusingly.

"How should I know, Christopher? I am not a soothsayer," Illesa said, exasperated. "But I am trying to have faith because he has always returned before. He finds a way. God helps him."

"And Saint Christopher." Christopher took out the figurine of the saint from his waist pouch, jumped down from the bed and ran out of the room, leaving her there by the window.

Chapter XIV

Saturday the 30th April 1295
Palais de l'Ombrière, Bordeaux
Nones

There was no chair set out for Richard when he arrived in the Constable's office this time, otherwise the room was the same. The Constable was absorbed with a document on his desk; the clerk was ready to begin his notations. Richard noticed the sounds of the outside world, so much nearer than through his high cell window.

"Where have the Turbervilles been taken?" Richard asked, staring at the top of the Constable's head. Raoul de Nesle looked up at him, pushed the parchment over to the clerk and folded his hands on the table.

"Ah yes." The Constable smiled a little. "You have heard of his departure. We have sent Sir Thomas to a place where he is better able to provide the help we require," the Constable said, sliding back a bit in his chair.

"Sir Thomas would not agree to help you," Richard said. "You have taken him somewhere else to try to break him."

The Constable looked over at the clerk and smiled. The clerk raised his quill.

"Well, Sir Richard," the Constable said, leaning forward over the table, "I am sorry to have to tell you that you are entirely mistaken about your companion. He was falling over himself to offer us terms. And several of the other knights are also leaning this way." He gestured towards the pile of parchment in front of the clerk. "You do not seem to understand the level of dissatisfaction amongst the troops. Forced to serve with unreliable convicts, left with insufficient food," he counted these problems out on his fingers. "Not enough weapons, the idiot Giffard for a leader, the foolish John of Brittany who knows nothing of war," he sighed deeply. "They have been unburdening themselves, and it is sad to hear what a low point the once strong English chivalry has fallen to. King Edward may pretend to be Arthur of the Round Table, but he is falling far short. His knights are at the end of their patience."

The Constable got up from his chair suddenly.

"It has given me a powerful thirst."

He opened the door.

"Bring wine," he called. He shut the door, and turned back to Richard. "You look like death, Sir Burnel."

The sweat was standing out on Richard's forehead from the pain of standing.

He stared at the Constable and said nothing.

"Well, as I was saying," Raoul sat down carefully in the chair, "the thing that seems to be riling them most, is the stupid manner in which the King's brother, the Earl of Lancaster, gave up the whole Duchy!" He slammed his hands on the table, making the clerk grab his small inkpot. "He was easily led. It is a pity your relative the Chancellor was already dead. He would have been more circumspect. But the next generation are never as clever, are they?" he asked, cocking his head at Richard.

"We cannot all understand the crooked mind of Philip – the Fair," Richard replied.

"It is an adept mind that conceives of many ways to trap his enemies, while they whistle and stare at the lovely blue sky and fall in like deer in the wood," the Constable said, miming a man falling into a hole and looking over at the clerk who was smiling appreciatively.

The door opened and a boy wearing an apron came in bearing a tray.

"Here on the table."

The Constable poured the wine into a cup as soon as the boy put it down and drained it quickly.

"We are grateful for the hospitality you continue to provide," Richard remarked, "although it is very much like a hole in the ground." He pushed himself up on his stick. "We are overcrowded in the cell. There are only enough mattresses and blankets for half the men, and the food is insufficient. The men will sicken and die if you do not provide better for them. They will be no use to you then."

The Constable looked over at the clerk and shook his head slightly. The clerk put down his quill.

"I am sure you can understand that as soon as you start helping us your situation will materially improve." The Constable filled his cup again and another one for the clerk, sliding it over towards him. "The men you are housed with, let me see," he reached over for one of the rolls of parchment. "Elias de Hauvill, yes, and Roger de Mubray and all their men. They have wealthy families who are still, let us say, *thinking* about helping us. And so, until all is decided, it is not worth our while to spend more on you. When we have agreed the ransom, things will improve for them. But you," he waved his hand at Richard bent over his stick in the middle of the room, "you keep telling us what a poor knight you are and how little wealth remains from the Chancellor's great accumulation. Over ninety manors! You claim the bankers of Lucca have taken it all. It is a sorry tale." He looked at Richard over the rim of his cup. "And one that is hard to swallow."

"The truth is often hard to believe – and hard to live out. The Bishop's heir was inconsiderate in his life. Within the space of two years, he spent what had taken a lifetime to accumulate. We used our last coin on equipping this company to fight in Gascony for the King. You already have our mounts, our weapons and our arms, worth many pounds. There is nothing else, nor can we borrow against the debt already incurred."

The Lord Constable put his cup down carefully on the table.

"This may be true. Or a few more weeks in your cell may bring some other source of wealth to your mind. When I return from my visit with King Philip, we will speak again." He was moving to get out of his chair.

"Lord Constable, I would like an audience with the Archbishop of Bordeaux."

The Constable looked surprised for the first time. He straightened up and stood by the table.

"What do you want with that foolish old man?"

Hugh had not been allowed out of the cell to accompany Richard this time, and for a moment he was glad of it. With all the passion of his young age, Hugh hated the impious.

"Bishop Robert, the Chancellor, knew Archbishop Henri when he was installed at Bordeaux. I would like to tell him of his death and of his great respect for him. I would also appeal for his prayers."

The Constable stared at him suspiciously.

"The Archbishop is no friend to the French King. I will not enable you to plot with him against us."

Richard looked him in the eye.

"There is no plot, Lord Constable. I merely seek the comfort of being in his holy presence and his prayers for my cousin's soul, and my own."

"You have the palace chaplain. From now on, you can attend Mass once a week. That is all."

And he went to the door and called for the guard.

Chapter XV

Tuesday the 25th June 1295
Oswestry
Nones

The journey had been awful. The horse Illesa had borrowed in Shrewsbury was lame by the time she reached the red cliff. She had to share a horse with Jean, as it was a point of principle for Azalais that she never walked if she could ride. Progress was slow, even though the weather was fine. Two downpours of rain in the night had made parts of the road a quagmire. Azalais claimed she had not wanted to come in the first place and refused to speak. Jean gave up trying to talk to her and stomped along in gloomy silence.

They finally saw the town of Oswestry on a rise next to the hill of ramparts.

"What is that?" Azalais asked, with her interested but scornful tone for when she was just coming round to a better mood.

"An ancient place made by giants," muttered Illesa. "They used to roll people down the hills for sport."

"No, you are teasing me!" cried Azalais, happy now. "Tell me what it really is."

"I don't know, darling. I think ancient people built a castle there, but it is all gone. Only a few commoners live there now. Oh, but look. Can't you see the giants peeping out from behind the banks?"

"Stop it! You will make me have bad dreams. Look, there is the gate. It's such a long way still. I am starving. Jean, why didn't you tell me it was going to be so far? You come this way all the time."

"Because it *isn't* far," Jean said shortly.

Illesa stopped listening to their argument. If she was going to see the King or the Chancellor today, she must immediately find the right clerk. They would move on tomorrow at daybreak, with all the petitioners who had not yet been seen.

But the clerk who had served her father for so many years would make sure they were seen today, if she could find him.

The sun was beating down on the veil covering her neck. It was hot, and she longed to wash her face in a fountain, but that was a foolish dream. This border town was not a city of stone and water. The stakes of its walls were made from fresh new trees, repaired since the Welsh uprising. The guards were heavily armed. The worst of the fighting might be over, but here they were ready for more.

The sealed letter she had from the Constable of Shrewsbury impressed the guard very little. He kept them waiting for a long time without explanation.

Jean and Azalais were completely and uncharacteristically silent. They had found out what reaction their accents drew ever since the French attacks on the South Coast. It did not matter that they were Gascons, and victims themselves of a French invasion. It was useless trying to explain. And it was just possible that they would be taken into custody by an over-zealous guard.

Illesa missed the charm that Azalais used to employ on these occasions which had always eased their way, whether it was through a gate or to a better deal at the market. Illesa wished she could be the same, but, in her, charm was entirely absent for strangers.

The gate was eventually and reluctantly opened to let them in. It was obvious where they should go. The castle was on a high mound, and the land around it was sparsely built. One church with a tall, fortified tower pressed against the walls. Richard had visited Oswestry once four years or so before, but whatever he had told her of it was past remembering. There was too much threat in the air to notice anything else.

For whatever reason, the guards of the castle's outer bailey were much less rigorous, and they were allowed inside without delay. Whereas there had been few people outside in the town's streets, the bailey was jammed full. The requirements of the King's court must be many, as it was necessary almost to push through the people carrying baskets and trays, leading horses, leashing dogs who were fighting, and arriving with carts. She was surprised that they had heard none of the din from outside, but it was like a forest stream; the sound did not reach them until they were upon it.

"Where do we find this clerk of yours in all this mêlée?" shouted Azalais. "I did not think that the court would be like this. You told me it would be calm and beautiful," she said with an accusing look.

"I lied," Illesa said, handing the horse's lead rein to Jean. "Can you find the stables and see if you can mend the horse? Then find something for Azalais to eat, while I find the clerk?"

"Wait." Jean put his hand out to stop her as she moved towards the keep. "You will not start without me, will you? I need that licence for trade, or I will be left without cargo for the rest of the year."

That was why he had volunteered to accompany her to the Welsh border to intercept the court. She knew Jean cared for Azalais, but he was a businessman first and foremost. War was sometimes good for business, if you could keep the enemy off your ship and stay alive. And Jean had been fortunate to be charged with restocking the army in Wales. Now he wanted the same commission for Gascony.

"Of course. I will find you before I talk to anyone. Even myself," she muttered. The lack of food didn't worry her, but she didn't like the heat. It made her temper short and her tongue sharp.

She swallowed the remains of the water from a skin in her pack and wove her way towards the keep entrance. The door was wide open, and people were running in and out without hindrance. Inside the keep it was immediately much cooler like a cellar. The hall was broad. People were standing in a line at one end, and, on the near side, several old and infirm sat slumped on a bench.

At the west end next to the lord's table, a man sat at a sloping desk, writing. The scratch of the quill on parchment was just audible. The man at the table was dressed in simple clerical garb.

She took one step towards him, but the line of people, as if all pulled by a string, frowned at her. A merchant gestured her away. She looked around the room for someone more welcoming she could ask. There was an old man bent over a stick by the door, dressed in fine but filthy clothes, his face nodding and shaking uncontrollably. She turned away and, seeing a young priest who had just entered the hall, she ran after him.

"God be with you, Brother. Do you know where I can find the clerk, Anselm?"

He stopped walking and blinked at her, surprised to be interrupted in his thoughts, perhaps. He had very prominent, very blue eyes.

"Do you mean Brother Anselm of the Chancery?"

Illesa nodded.

"Does he know you?" he asked dubiously.

"No, Brother, but he is well acquainted with my husband, Sir Richard Burnel."

The name had the effect she had hoped for.

"Come this way."

He led her to the wall behind the main table, passing the line of frowning, muttering people. Out of the corner of her eye, she saw the profile of the old, shaking man, now at the back of the line. It was a familiar face although covered in an angry rash.

Giles, the Lord Forester. She had heard that he was out of favour and in debt, but not that he was ill. Her mouth was suddenly very dry, and she was conscious of her movements, her breath.

The priest was gesturing her towards a bench. She sat down only a few yards away from the man who'd had Kit murdered. Her hands were shaking almost as much as his.

"I will go and find Brother Anselm. Wait here," said the young priest, giving her a stern look.

Illesa nodded, her tongue incapable of speech.

She kept her eyes fixed on her lap or on the important official who spoke to each person in a murmured undertone. Everything was very hushed, but the beating of her heart was loud and insistent, demanding revenge.

This was foolish. Illesa stood up, intending to confront him. The line was still just as long, but there was no old man at the end of it. She looked across the hall, craning her neck, but he was not there. Had he gone out or fallen over? Or had he been a spirit, a devil there to provoke her to sin?

She sat down hard on the bench again, gripping her hands together and feeling the breath catching in her throat.

A fat monk was coming towards her, his hands full of a long parchment roll, his expression concerned.

"Lady Burnel?"

She nodded, stood and he led her to the other end of the table, away from the official and his business.

Brother Anselm sat down, indicating the seat opposite, noting her distraction.

"Is something wrong, Lady Burnel? You don't look well."

She shook her head and cleared her throat.

"No, Brother. It was just a long journey. I'm very grateful to see you."

"Yes," he nodded. "The roads here are not good. Much attention is needed, but what can be done when the soldiers and the carts roll over them every week or so? The list of things to be repaired after the war is long and costly." He pressed his lips together in what was meant to be a sympathetic grimace. "Now, you have come to see me about your husband? Or is it something about the estate of the blessed Bishop Robert Burnel?"

His eyes were examining her, while his fingers tightened the parchment on the roll, his fat fingers winding in the words. He had been her father's clerk for more than ten years. He had written the letters that her father had dictated to her. He might even know about the embroidered cope hidden at their Manor. But none of this could be said, and his expression was, if anything, unsympathetic.

"It regards my husband, as you guessed," Illesa said quietly. "He is a prisoner of the French in Bordeaux, and I have had no information about the state of his health which has been poor for many years."

Brother Anselm folded his hands and nodded.

"There are other knights from the King's household who are also imprisoned," she continued. "I would like to know how matters are progressing with the arranging of their ransom."

Brother Anselm pressed his lips together. Along his forehead a line deepened in regret.

"It may be best to think of this situation in a different way. You have much to be grateful for. Sir Richard Burnel has been taken away from the fighting. He will be able to sit out the rest of the war in a secure castle and will be returned in due course after the Duchy has been returned to the lordship of King Edward. This appears, in many ways, to be a great blessing."

"He should not have been sent to war at all," Illesa said firmly. "He has sustained several injuries in the service of the King, and I am afraid that he will not survive his imprisonment."

"Well, it is not my place to say," Brother Anselm said, pushing the suggestion away with his hands. "But I do know that the Treasury is under great pressure. Essential expenditure only. But I might be able to arrange a short audience with the Chancellor, and Bishop Robert's long service may still bring you favour." He didn't look or sound optimistic.

Jean Fracinaut's face came into view behind the monk's back. He was trying to get her attention and looked very angry. She beckoned to him, standing up.

"Brother, may I present Master Jean Fracinaut who has previously supplied grain to the forces in Wales on his ship *La Mariote*."

Brother Anselm's face lightened. At last a straightforward query from a man of business, not a woman on the verge of tears. He indicated that Jean should sit in the place Illesa had just vacated.

"Certainly. I believe I remember you, and last time it was all arranged quickly. Of course now that there has been such violence on the coasts we must take extra care with the shipping, but it should not be difficult to get a document today. Wait here while I speak to the Chancellor."

They watched him as he went through a door to the private room beyond the hall. All the people in the queue watched him too and looked accusingly at Illesa.

She pulled on Jean's sleeve.

"When you were in the bailey, did you see an old man with a stick whose head shook?" she whispered.

"What?" Jean said. "There are hundreds of men here!" He was still cross with her for starting to speak to the monk before he arrived.

"A man in fine cloth, but dirty and shaking badly," she said. "Grey hair and a short beard. Red complexion."

Jean shook his head.

"No, I was busy dealing with your horses and trying to please that woman. Azalais would not eat their bread. Said it tasted like shit."

Brother Anselm coughed behind them.

"You have an immediate audience with the Chancellor, Lady Burnel," he said, expressing the tremendous privilege this was with his very serious expression. "And he has given permission for me to write up your licence straight away," he said to Jean as if distributing eternal life.

"We thank you, Brother," Illesa said trying not to let her irritation show. "Through the door?"

The monk nodded with a small thin smile, and sat down with Jean.

Inside the room the Chancellor sat in familiar robes with his seal and the other symbols of his office in front of him. A guard stood against the back wall. A clerk sat at the end of the table. Illesa examined his face, but he was unfamiliar. The new Chancellor had new staff, and there would be no help from that quarter.

"Lady Burnel," the Chancellor said. They had never met before, but he did not do her the courtesy of standing up.

"Lord Chancellor."

Nor did he invite her to sit.

"Brother Anselm has told me the burden of your mind," he said, looking at her briefly, then dropping his gaze to the document in front of him, and back up to her face. "He has expressed our situation to you, I believe. There is no plan to negotiate a ransom for the men who have been taken hostage by the French. If we started such an exchange, the Treasury would very soon be empty. Do you know how many noble Gascons are prisoners? They also fought for our King. In war, regretfully, the rules of chivalry must change."

"But these are the King's own knights," Illesa insisted, taking a step forward. The Chancellor looked alarmed and the clerk scraped his chair on the flagstones, as if he would get up. The guard adjusted his pike.

"As knights they have a duty to take this risk for their liege, the King," the Chancellor admonished, looking at her with hooded eyes.

Illesa gripped her hands together.

"Lord Chancellor, as you know, Richard was a favoured relative of Chancellor Robert. It would please him to know that his successor was still helping his family after his untimely death."

The new Chancellor looked down at his hands and pulled the soft fur at his cuffs straight.

"I understand his wealth has been depleted. If his heir had been more careful, there would have been plenty of money for Sir Richard's ransom without a need to petition the court," he said severely.

"What you say is true. The idiocy of Chancellor Robert's nephew was not fully understood until it was too late," Illesa remarked blandly. "And now, may God save him, he has left us all in a precarious state." Illesa was glad to see the discomfort on the Chancellor's bulging, self-satisfied face. "Without Richard, all of Chancellor Burnel's beloved manor at Acton as well as his other holdings would already belong to the Italian bankers. I understand that is of no concern to the King, who has his own wars to fight, but we did hope that there would be mercy for those who had risked so much for the King and served him well for many years."

"Noble hostages will be treated nobly. That is what you need to remember. Many other wives would consider you very fortunate indeed," the Chancellor said, moving a document closer to him so that she would know she had outstayed her welcome.

"I know the difference between bad luck and terrible luck. Neither is anything to be thankful for."

There was a long pause.

"I am sorry that your journey has been wasted," the Chancellor said, standing up. "There would obviously have been a different outcome if Chancellor Burnel had still been alive and in possession of his fortune. But time is rolling us all along in its clutches," he said with resignation. "I will bless you before you leave." And the Chancellor who was also Bishop of Chichester held out his ring for her to kiss.

She bent her head and pretended to touch the jewel with her lips.

His hand rested firmly on her veil and seemed to press down into her neck. She didn't listen to his Latin. There were too many angry words waiting to escape from her own lips. But they would only worsen her chances, as would tears.

She straightened up.

"Lord Chancellor, I beg you to speak to the King. Chancellor Burnel was his faithful servant all his life. I am sure that he would want to alleviate the suffering of his kin."

The Chancellor sat down and turned to the clerk.

"There is no need to make a note of this meeting. God speed your journey home, Lady Burnel."

Back in the hall, she rubbed her clammy hands on her skirts. The tears that had pooled in her eyes as she turned away from the indifferent, ugly Chancellor fell on her cheeks and ran down. She wiped them away. When her father had been alive, his insistent generosity had irritated her. But his absence now was a cold dry well.

Jean was still at the table watching as Brother Anselm set out the terms of his licence in the book, pointing at particular terms, checking that all was correct. He was not keeping an eye out for the Forester, and the sick old man was still stubbornly not there.

She had lost her fear in her anger. It was even possible that she was mistaken. Her mind was prone to imaginings and living dreams because her sleep was so disrupted.

And what would she say to the Forester if she did find him again? He would not listen to her justified rage any more than the Chancellor had. If he was unrepentant, his soul was damned. And bodily he was cursed just as she had prayed he would be. She should be glad.

She went out into the bailey and saw Azalais almost immediately. A small group of men stood around her, and she was singing a nightingale's song. Their eyes were all turned to her, enraptured. There was no sign anywhere of the ugly old devil. And Illesa didn't care.

Chapter XVI

Saturday the 13th August 1295
Palais de l'Ombrière, Bordeaux
Vespers

The crossbowmen had marched into the town at sext, and they had not returned by sunset when the guard, Pierre, arrived.

"Where have they gone?" asked Hugh as soon as the guard came into the room. "We had a good time laughing at their terrible aim."

"Gone south to kill the English of course," Pierre said as he locked the door, put his back to it and crossed his legs. "Going to put a few on the spit!"

"No chance! Haven't you seen their target practice? They couldn't hit a barn door."

"South where?" asked Richard, casually.

"No, I can't tell you that. You aren't meant to know anything. Shut up and don't ask me," Pierre said, looking agitated. He was incredibly strong, a local farmer before being conscripted by the French, so no one tried to draw him away from the door. He stayed there every night as if he were bolted to it through his heart.

"We'll get the information out of you before morning," said Adam, an annoying man in the service of de Hauvill. He'd been left behind, for some reason, when the rest of de Hauvill's company had been moved to better quarters as his ransom was being arranged. Everyone hoped that de Hauvill would change his mind and take Adam with him, but he had probably insulted his lord profoundly and was being left to rot like the rest of them.

"Leave him alone," Richard said. "He did us all a favour yesterday, and if the Guard Commander thinks he is giving us special treatment he will soon get rid of Pierre and give us someone like that day guard who spits at us."

"Yeah, leave me alone," said Pierre. He seemed different, nervous. His hands jingled the dice in his pocket, although he didn't offer to play. "At least you smell less disgusting today," he said, trying to steer the conversation.

Pierre had brought them three buckets of hot water the day before, and they had argued almost until it was cold about who would go first. They all felt better for having taken the worst off, although the lice were as bad as ever. Their appeal for new clothes was laughed off.

"Is the Constable back? Is that why you're so jumpy?" asked Hugh. Being locked up for so many weeks had banished his reserve. Unfortunately, he seemed to think there was no point being careful any more. His eyes had a fevered look. The bones of his skull stood out, and when he had washed the day before, Richard had been able to count all his ribs. Richard was gradually weakening, but Hugh was a young man, still growing, and his body was wasting down to sinew and bone.

"No, I'm not telling you anything," Pierre insisted. "Anyway the Mayor is bad enough, and I've got myself in too much trouble already."

"What's happened to you, Pierre?" asked Richard. "Have they punished you for looking after the sick?"

In July the Mayor had decided that the best way of taking care of the seven prisoners with fever was to isolate them. Two had died, but as neither of them were nobles, the Lord Constable had not been informed. Pierre had been the only guard willing to go into the cell to bring them bread and water and take out their waste.

Pierre just shook his head and worried at a sore tooth with his tongue.

"Shut up," he said, eventually. "New guard outside."

They all subsided, looking at one another from where they lay on the poor straw mattresses or propped up by the wall. The men had come to look forward to Pierre's time as guard. Occasionally he would get angry and accuse them of having no respect for him, but mostly, as long as they did not try to trick him into leaving his post, he would join in with their gambling and their conversation. They knew he had been put there to listen to their conversations and to report back about potential sources of ransom. But he was so clearly on their side that they spoke freely in his presence. A new guard, however, was a problem. He might inform on Pierre and take his job if he saw how familiar they were with him.

When they had all been quiet for some time, Pierre gestured for Richard to come near. Richard got up from the floor with difficulty; his leg would no longer bend. Pierre beckoned him nearer and nearer until Richard was only inches from his face.

"The new guard will be coming in soon. They are moving me to the town walls," he breathed through his thick lips. "Don't know when, but they aren't going to be keeping you here much longer either. Those that won't cooperate are being sent away to another castle the next time the Constable comes."

Richard put his hand against the wall to steady himself. Pierre was fumbling inside his gambeson. He found what he was looking for and held it out towards Richard.

"Your man came yesterday. Read it quickly and reply," he whispered.

Everyone else in the room had their eyes fixed on the guard and the scrap of cloth and stick of charcoal he was putting in Richard's hand.

"He is waiting below for it. I must give it back at daybreak."

"Which man," whispered Richard, almost without breathing.

"William of Clun."

Chapter XVII

Friday the 9th September 1295
St Giles Fair, Winchester
Tierce

Sir Thomas Turberville was looking well. Even in the gloom of the Cathedral's north chapel, Illesa could see that his face had the sheen of a well-fed man. He had been enjoying his freedom since his flight from France, evidently.

Since she had heard of his escape and arrival in England, she had been appealing for a meeting, and Turberville had eventually agreed to see her on this day at the New Inn, Winchester. Illesa had taken a room there, despite the expense. His latest message had not explained why there was a need to change the meeting place, but the Cathedral *was* very quiet. The previous day it had been packed with worshippers for the Feast of the Birth of the Virgin, and she and Christopher had been wedged in between a large woman who smelled of fish and another who smelled of pastry. They had been very hungry by the end of the Mass.

This chapel seemed to be where Turberville was doing all his business. Illesa waited, her back against the opposite wall, while he instructed a messenger. In the middle of two stone columns behind him were carvings, one of a crude devil pushing up against the stone, his mouth wide open, and the other, a king, impassive and regal, his head adorned with gold and green leaves.

Illesa made the sign of the cross. The devil might be caught inside the stone, but he was not idle even in this sanctified place. Sir Thomas stood between the two figures, giving a bag of coins to the messenger. By the size of the bag, he was expecting him to go a long way. Much further than the Turberville seat in Glamorgan.

Finally, he turned to Illesa as the messenger walked off towards the west door.

"My dear Lady Burnel, it is good of you to come all this way to see me." He bowed slightly. "You must forgive me for keeping you waiting and changing the place of our meeting this morning. I am trying to pick up the pieces of my life, sadly neglected while I was at war." He smiled regretfully, and indicated she should stand close by the wall.

Perhaps he had asked the Dean's permission to conduct his business here today, but she didn't think so. He seemed tense. Illesa bowed her head.

"It is good of you to spare the time to see me, Sir Thomas. I am sure you have much business to attend to, for the court and your family. It is remarkable that you are here at all!" she said, trying to sound cheerful. "It gave me comfort all these months, knowing you were with Richard in France. I know you have been together in other wars."

"Yes, we have known each other for much of our lives. I'm sorry he is not here with me now."

Illesa looked down at his feet, clad in new embossed leather boots, struggling to remain composed.

"Sir Thomas, I hope I will not try your patience with my questions. I wonder if you can tell me where he is held and what condition he is in?"

"Well, good lady, I can only tell you what the situation was when I left. And that was some time ago now." His eyes flickered around the chapel. "The last time I saw or heard of him was in the Palais de l'Ombrière in Bordeaux, and he was being kept there under Raoul, the Lord Constable of France."

Illesa's mouth had turned very dry. She licked her lips.

"It sounds severe," she said.

"Not very luxurious, I grant you, but my company was housed in a pleasant chamber. I believe Richard and several other men were together at the top of the tower."

"When did you last see him?"

Turberville leant back against the column. A canon of the Cathedral was walking past the chapel entrance. He did not speak until the robed man had moved out of view.

"I think it was before the calends of May," he said sadly. "You see, I was taken to Paris," he said sadly. "The King of France wanted any of the prisoners who were in Edward's household brought to him, and they knew me from my time in Gascony. So they transported me to the Louvre."

"But they didn't take Richard or his retinue?"

"They were not close enough to King Edward," Turberville said with a slight shake of his head.

"So who is left in Bordeaux with Richard?"

"When I saw him he still had the squire Hugh with him. And there were a few other knights from the Marches."

"But no one else from his company?"

"We had a terrible time, Lady Burnel. Ill-equipped and alone, we were a small fleet against the might of the French. You should not be surprised that the inexperienced soldiers died. Some were no better than ploughboys. One of my best-trained retainers did not survive the attack at Rions. It was only God's grace that saved my sons."

"Thanks be to God for his mercies," Illesa said. "I do understand about the danger of war, sir. But my concern is for my husband's health. I must find out who is with him and whether he could make his own way home, as you did."

"No, I do not think he would be able to escape," Turberville rubbed his chin, looking melancholy. "His leg was almost useless even before the imprisonment. And the tower of Bordeaux is well guarded. It overlooks the place where the crossbowmen train." He glanced over her head towards the nave.

"Please, I do not wish to detain you, but do tell me how you escaped," she said, trying to bring some warm appeal into her voice.

"I'm not sure it is a fitting tale for a lady, particularly an unaccompanied one." His eyes slid over her plain travelling clothes. "You look more like a market woman than a noble lady," he remarked.

"I find it is much safer whilst travelling," she said firmly, but the colour rose in her cheeks.

"Indeed?" he said. "Well, I will tell you briefly. When they were taking me across the Seine for questioning, I managed to kill one of the guards on the boat. The other one attacked me, and I ended up in the water. But I was able to hide under a bridge. It took me a long time to reach the coast where I finally found a ship sailing for England." He was staring at the chapel altar, his face grave. "When I arrived I was as thin as a winter tree."

"You have made a good recovery," she said shortly.

"Yes, I have, God be thanked." But her expression had taken the smile from his lips. "I am afraid I must leave shortly. There is a merchant I've arranged to see before I leave for my estate."

"I am sorry to keep you from it. I imagine your wife is overjoyed to have you safely back. I won't detain you, but I want to arrange Richard's release. You know his injuries and the pain he suffers. He will not survive long if the conditions are bad. We have little money left, but if necessary we might borrow. I've been to the Chancellor and appealed to the King, but no one at court will help."

Turberville closed his eyes and tilted his head back, grimacing.

"Dear lady, I'm afraid you are being impatient. You see the war will be finished very soon, and the prisoners will be released before the end of the year. I was just with King Edward as he spoke with the cardinals sent by the Pope. They will be negotiating a peace treaty shortly. Once that is done, you can pay the ransom and go to whichever port is closest to your home. They won't want to hang on to expensive hostages. This is indeed what I am hoping for my two sons, still in Paris."

"You left your sons imprisoned in Paris?"

"They will be looked after there," Turberville said sharply. "And when the time comes, I will pay whatever is required to get them back."

"So you will be negotiating? I beg you to tell me when you begin, so that I may not be too late. Will you act on my behalf?"

He looked relieved.

"But of course. It would give me great pleasure to help you to be reunited." Turberville started straightening his supertunic, his belt and his purse. "Now please do not waste your money sending all these messengers to me every week. As soon as I know the best time and place to start the negotiations, I will send word to you, and then you can bring me your silver. That is best. Meanwhile, pray for all the prisoners, that their guards will show mercy," he said, his eyes fixed on the nave. "It won't be long," he said, almost under his breath. "I am sure of it."

"I will, Sir Thomas. And I will pray for your sons," she said, trying to meet his gaze. "It must be hard for them."

"They are strong and have each other," he said impatiently. "God speed your journey home." He nodded his head and walked out of the chapel.

"I thank you for your time, Sir Thomas," she said to his back.

Illesa felt queasy. It was like being at sea with a moving horizon. Why was he trying to convince her the war would end soon when he didn't believe it himself? She should have questioned him for longer, should have asked what recent injuries Richard had. But Turberville had wanted to steer her away from the conditions in the prison. Maybe he just wanted to protect her from the truth: that Richard was most likely dead already, or nearly dead, and a peace treaty in three months was not going to be of any use to him.

She had only met Turberville twice before, and that had been at court occasions when they had only exchanged pleasantries. But he was certainly different in some way, perhaps simply anxious. She could not remember if he had more than two sons, and his succession was assured with an heir kept safe at home. Or perhaps the battle horrors had changed him into this distant puppet-like man who described his escape in the words of a child.

Illesa began to walk slowly down the nave.

The Cathedral precinct was probably the quietest place in the town during the fair, which was surely why Turberville was doing his business there, in the quietest part of the Cathedral, not a room in an inn where most people would meet. And he'd said he was going to meet a merchant. She hoped she didn't see him at the fair while she was buying Christopher's late Saint's Day present. Her son would certainly ask him awkward questions, and Turberville, if he had ever intended to help her, might change his mind.

Christopher was waiting exactly where he should be, desperate that she would also keep her promise and desperate to know what the knight had told her. He was sitting cross-legged by the base of a statue of Saint Nicholas and jumped up as soon as he saw her, slipping his hand into hers.

"Did anyone question you?" she asked looking down at his pale, animated face.

"No," he shook his head. "A Priest came to look at me but decided I was not a vagrant because of my shoes."

"I'm glad you kept them clean!"

"What did Sir Turberville say?"

"He says we are not to worry. He thinks the war will be over soon and then we will be able to ransom your father."

He was silent, and they walked on through the square in front of the Cathedral and into the crowded street heading east towards the river.

"Do you think that's true?"

"I would like to believe it."

"Do you think the animal man will be at the fair today?"

"I would hope so."

"Mummy."

"Yes?"

"Why are you upset?"

"Because I want your father to be safe, and I don't know if he is or not. And I hoped his friend would help me, but he was no help at all." She blinked out the tears and wiped them away with her free hand. "But I will not worry about that now, because we have a very important bit of business to do. We must have all our wits working! And then, after that, we can go home."

Although there should be something else to do, having come all this way. Someone else to see who could actually help them. But she had no one to introduce her, even if she did know the right person. She squeezed Christopher's hand. At least he would leave the fair with something to make him happy.

The River Itchen was almost entirely hidden beneath all the different craft and flat-bottomed barges being unloaded and towed. There were carts and ponies, mules and men carrying loaded baskets on poles, all making their way up the steep track to Saint Giles Down. They joined the slow flowing lines of cursing tradesmen, arriving late, thanks to the useless men who plied the river from Southampton and asked a premium for their work. The smith they were following was voluble about it, despite being almost breathless from carrying his load up the steep slope. As they crested the hill, the sound of the crowd enveloped them, and Christopher gripped her hand more tightly.

"They will put the animal traders at the edge, not far from the stock," she shouted at Christopher. "We will walk round the outside until we find them."

This was easier said than done. There was a wheel of people swirling around the central stalls, like leaves in the wind. Eventually they found the animal dealer on the slope facing away from the town. There were plenty of people crowded around his stall, but the dealer looked anxious. No one was buying.

"Don't tell him what you want, darling. Tell me and I will negotiate the price. Remember, we cannot afford any of the big animals, or indeed most of the small ones. Just choose something that will be easy to train and not difficult to carry around."

Christopher nodded, but his eyes were fixed on the piles of cages, and he'd probably heard nothing. She let go of his hand, and he darted towards the stall.

The stallholder was wiry and brown-skinned. He had a girl, probably about nine years old, who held the leash of a badger and looked very pretty leading it around to meet the crowd. They hoped for the wealthy nobility, if they were offering tame badgers for pets. Tall poles were strapped up to the side of the stall, and cages hung down full of brightly coloured birds. If the noise had not been so great, there would have been new birdsong to hear.

Christopher came back to her with wide eyes. He pulled on her arm silently and led her to the piles of small cages, away from the brown ape that attracted most of the crowd. He squatted down by a cage of four sharp-nosed, white-breasted weasels. One was much smaller than the others.

"It's not too big," Christopher whispered. "I think it is tame. I put my finger in, and it didn't bite me. It's just the way it is described in the Bestiary. Look at how long and fast it is!"

Illesa knelt down on the soft, churned-up earth and held out her finger to the small weasel. One of the larger ones ran around the cage, agitated.

"Don't get too close, eh? When they get scared they let off a stink!"

Illesa sat back on her haunches and looked up at the merchant.

"Aren't they tame?"

"Two of them are. The other two are learning, I hope." His accent was unfamiliar. He spoke to the small girl in a strange tongue, gesturing her to come near.

"Where are you from?" asked Christopher.

"Castile," said the man, with a flourish of his hand. The black-haired girl opened the cage and took out two weasels, one in each hand.

"See, they like girls, young girls with soft hands!" He laughed and turned Illesa's hand over. "That is rough as a peasant's! Let your boy handle them. Come," and he took the little weasel from the girl's outstretched hand and placed it in his. "This is the baby. He has learnt to like people from his mother. She is a good mother."

"How much for the baby?"

"I sell them together. If I separate them now, they will both get sick. I can give you a good price for both."

Christopher was holding the baby close to his face, and it jumped on his head and ran down his neck to sit on his shoulder.

"Yes, he likes you! This is where he likes to ride. Put the mother on the other side."

"Can we afford them both?" Christopher pleaded almost inaudibly, feeling around on his shoulder for the quick furry body.

"What other small animals do you have?" Illesa asked the man.

"No, no. Look, these are meant for you. See, the mother will sit on your shoulder." He took the larger weasel from Christopher and put her on Illesa. Her strong claws gripped through her tunic but did not scratch. The weasel sniffed her ear and snuffled in the fabric of her veil. "You have not even heard the price yet! Come with me, we can leave the weasels

136

with the children," he said and plopped the mother weasel back in the girl's hand. Christopher was trying to stroke the baby, but it kept running from one shoulder to the other.

Illesa went, heavy-hearted, to the quiet inside of the stall where stacks of fruit, straw, and the cages of mice were piled up.

"You are worried. I can see it. The boy was promised one pet, and now you must have two. It is more than you can afford." The man did not look at her as he spoke; he was busy pulling one of the empty hanging cages made of very thin wood slats down from the back. He reached a leather belt off a hook and began weaving the belt through the slats.

"I cannot give them away, but I will give you a very good price. And they are already tamed!" he exclaimed, as if this were a miracle. "They like to eat mice, so I am putting some in the cage for you, for your journey. They must drink often. You can let them lick milk out of a dish. Keep them warm. See I am giving you straw. And they like to burrow in holes. Don't let them down on the ground for a few weeks."

"Wait, you haven't told me how much they are!" Illesa said, putting a restraining hand on his arm.

"They will cost five shillings. That is a fair price, and I have given you the cage and some food. You will go and show the weasels to the other people of the fair, riding on your shoulder, and we will sell more. I have twenty weasels to sell."

It had never been possible for Illesa to accept a price at the first time of asking before, but it was a price they could afford, and she was grateful. She had no strength to argue with this strange, charming man.

They walked with the weasels on their shoulders at first, but the crush of the crowd was too much. They had to put them in the cage and head straight back to the inn. Christopher kept looking at them swaying in the cage, running from side to side, his face intent.

"How on earth will we manage with them on the journey all the way home?" Illesa said. But she felt better watching these tiny pieces of life, as soft and quick as water, making Christopher glad.

"I will hold them," he said. "They can live inside my tunic if I tighten my belt around it so they don't slip down."

"They will scratch you to death."

"No, I'll put an extra tunic on, so they will be between the two. I will feed them and train them on the way."

"Maybe they are best travelling in the cage attached to the saddle," she mused out loud. But Christopher would probably get his way; his face was set in a stubborn frown.

The inn was groaning with people who had come in for their dinner. They squeezed through the crowd and up the dark stair to their small room. Illesa opened the door.

A man was standing by the window, his profile black against the midday light. It was a breathless moment before Illesa recognised him.

"William!"

He held open his arms and Christopher ran to him.

Chapter XVIII

Friday the 9th September 1295
St Giles Fair, Winchester
Sext

Christopher and Illesa sat side by side on the bed. William drew the stool up in front of them, and the weasels ran excitedly between them until Illesa insisted that Christopher put them back in their cage. He kept it on his lap, delighted to have something so exciting to share with William.

William was hardly changed. His face still alert and weathered, but no new scars, or not any that she could see. Just a haggard look around his eyes, as if from sleeplessness.

"How have you come here? You must tell us everything," Illesa said, hope welling in her heart.

"And how did you know where to find us?" asked Christopher bouncing on the edge of the bed. "We only arrived two days ago!"

"I asked around," William said shortly. He smiled at Christopher, a sudden flash of bad teeth. "I followed your smell!"

Christopher snorted.

"The weasels' more like. If you scare them, you get a terrible surprise."

"I won't scare them, but your face might," William commented. "No, I saw Jezebel, of course. She is being grazed by the Itchen, and I was being carried up on a barge from Southampton in exchange for helping unload. As soon as I saw that mare, I knew you'd be here somewhere. You can't mistake that horse for any other."

"Thank Christ you saw her! Do you have any news of Richard?"

William set his brown stained hands on his knees and leant forward.

"I have better than that. I have a message for you from him," and he brought out a piece of oilcloth from inside his gambeson. "I've kept a copy of it safe in here, in case the cloth message got wet on the crossing and all the charcoal letters washed away. I made sure the clerk was on our side first. But he was such a drunken sod, I don't think he'd remember anything to inform on Richard anyway."

Christopher giggled. William unwrapped the packet and held out a piece of folded parchment and a piece of linen.

Illesa opened the scrap of fabric with her fingertips. It was thin, almost feather-light. On the top was a message written in French obviously by a second-rate clerk:

"William of Clun sends to Sir Richard Burnel. What message should he take to his home?" And below was Richard's answer in smudged charcoal.

"Tell my wife to arrange for what is hidden to be given to the Archbishop in Bordeaux for ransom. Jean could do this. My prayers are answered by you."

Illesa read it through twice, with Christopher leaning over her shoulder, before she looked up at William.

"What does he mean, 'what is hidden'?" Christopher asked.

"Shhhh child. Let us talk," she said, pushing him off her shoulder. "Do you know what he means, William?"

"No. But you do, don't you?"

"Yes, I think so. Tell me how you got this? Did you see him?"

"No. The tower where they keep the hostages is well guarded." He mimed a tall tower and men with crossbows for Christopher, who grinned. "It was all I could do to get safely in and out of the city and find a man who would take the message."

"How in the name of all the saints did you do that?"

"I was careful who I spoke to. I listened. I watched the palace," he said in a whisper. "Also one of the leaders in Blaye, whose horse I trained, introduced me to his Bordeaux family, and they were able to tell me who to speak to," he said cheerfully. "I got a relative of theirs, who was one of the tower guards, to carry my message to Richard."

Christopher had to run round the room with excitement.

"Did you find out how he was?" Illesa said under her breath.

William shook his head.

"The guard would not talk to me, only take the message and return it. He was in terrible fear of discovery. They aren't shy of hanging in occupied Bordeaux."

"Thank you for going, William," Illesa said. Her hands were trembling, and she put the piece of linen and parchment in her belt pouch. "I was so disappointed after seeing Sir Turberville. I thought it would go on forever, the not knowing. But now it is clear what we must do."

"What must we do, Mummy?" Christopher had come to a halt in front of her again.

"I will tell you later, when I am sure. And when we are safe at home."

"What did you say about Turberville?" asked William. "Sir Thomas isn't here, is he?"

Illesa nodded and swallowed the sudden rush of relief that was threatening to make her cry again.

"I heard that he had escaped from France, so I sent a messenger to ask to meet him. I had tried at court, but they were no help. Sir Thomas has known Richard for so long." She shook her head slightly, remembering his false cheerfulness. "But he was strange. He kept telling me that the war would be over soon."

"Is that what he said?" William scratched his cheekbone where an old scar stood out white against his ruddy skin. "I heard he had been taken to Paris. And then there was talk of him being back in England."

"He escaped from his guards when he was being rowed across the river. He managed to reach the King's Court when it was in Kent and is now on his way to Glamorgan. But first he is doing business at the fair," Illesa said, rather bitterly.

William raised an eyebrow. Christopher got down from the bed with the weasels and sat on the floor to take out the baby.

"Go and ask for some milk from the innkeeper's wife, Christopher. Bring it up in a pitcher with a saucer. Go on. William will still be here when you get back."

He left, quietly shutting the door behind him. Illesa drew breath and turned back to William.

"His two sons are still imprisoned in Paris. He promised to tell me when he began the negotiations for their ransom. He said he would arrange Richard's release at the same time."

"But you did not believe him."

"No. He just seemed eager to get rid of me. He was busy sending a messenger off when I arrived. Paid him plenty of coin and didn't want to talk about any of it. He was just strange," she concluded.

"Maybe I should watch him for a while. Where did you say he was going?"

"No, William!" Tears started in her eyes. "Please don't leave. We have only just got you back. It's been so difficult without you and Richard. Everyone we rely on is either in Wales or Gascony, and we are left trying to fend off the tax collectors." She was babbling. The relief she had felt when she saw William was like a draught of strong wine, and she didn't want to go back to the anxious misery of the past months.

"By the saints," William said, sitting up straighter on his stool. "Don't take on so. I'll come back with you. Has the boy been troublesome while we've been away? What about my horses? Have you been looking after them?"

"Christopher has just been very quiet. He had an awful fright, but I won't talk about that now. Yes, we've looked after the horses. The stable boy has grown up a bit." She paused for a moment, caught by a sudden hope. "Did you manage to bring Greyboy back with you?"

"No." William looked down at his hands. "He was captured by the French."

The tears began flowing down Illesa's cheeks. She used her veil to wipe them away.

"No. I won't cry about that now," she said. "Richard is alive, and so are you. But you know how important that horse was to me."

William lowered his head. He had looked after Greyboy, her brother's horse, ever since Richard had rescued him from the bandits in the Long Forest. Richard had gathered a company of men and, one year after the death of her brother, just after the birth of Christopher, they went to Sir Perkyn's camp at night and took him by surprise. When they'd brought

Greyboy to the stables at Langley, she had wept into his mane until it was wet through.

Richard had not wanted to take him to France, but she had insisted. Greyboy was a horse trained for war and would be better than some unbroken, unreliable cob from the South they picked up on the way.

"He saved Richard's life many times."

Illesa wiped her eyes and sniffed.

"Please don't tell Christopher now. He is so happy today, with the weasels and you. I want it to last a little longer. Are you able to travel, are your legs up to it? Let's get you a horse and go home. I'm longing to see Cecily's face when she sees you."

Christopher came in through the door, the baby weasel on his head, while he held a pitcher topped with a saucer in his hand.

"Come, Christopher," Illesa called. "We will make it to Sarum before dark if we are quick about it."

"But I want to show William the fair!" He put the pitcher down and appealed to her with wide eyes.

William went over and poured out some milk into the saucer. They put the baby down next to it on the sideboard. But he just ran about and then tried to leap to the floor.

"Put the mother there. She will know what to do and show the baby," said William.

They watched them drinking milk for a few moments, and all the strength went out of Illesa.

"I know it would be a terrible rush to leave now. I just wanted to get home and show Cecily that our prayers are answered."

"It would be better to leave at first light," William said quietly. "I will take the boy into the fair. Then later I will do a bit of asking around about your friend."

"What friend?" asked Christopher. "What do you want to find out?"

"You are going to need all your questions when I take you to see the famous horses from Spain. Then you will need to ask who, when and why? I intend to get a good one, and you are going to help me."

William and Christopher left after eating and did not return until vespers. Christopher came into the room almost bursting with information about the horse they had bought. She went down with them to see it.

The mare was dark brown, almost black, and the size of a palfrey. A little patch of pale hair above one eye gave her a curious expression.

"She's intelligent," Christopher said. "Much cleverer than the others. She's a Spanish jennet. William took her out bareback, and she did just what he wanted." The horse was butting William's thigh with her head as he tried to look at her forelock.

"She's a bit older than I'd hoped for. Maybe fifteen," William said, smacking her lightly on the neck. "But she rides well. And she likes work."

"What are you calling her?" asked Illesa, running a hand down the horse's shoulder to the rough patch where the saddle would sit.

"Her Spanish name is Sancha. That seems to suit her."

Sancha nosed the pockets of William's tunic.

"She likes pies!" Christopher said. "She's already had two."

"You are not feeding that horse pies. You will make her sick!"

"Just apple pies. We need to teach her English words now." He held out a piece of honeyed apple he had been keeping up his sleeve somehow.

"Apple," he whispered as she took it in her soft mouth.

"You both ought to know better," Illesa said, stroking the horse's nose. "Let's go and get some food for ourselves. We need to have a good meal before our long journey."

"You go. I'm going to do a few things in the town. Christopher, make sure you come and check on Sancha before you go to sleep. I don't trust that boy to give her a proper mash," he said, jerking his head towards the next stall. "You were wise to stable Jezebel elsewhere."

Illesa put a hand on William's arm.

"Don't go too far."

"Stop fussing," he said, calmly. "I'll be back soon. And tomorrow I'll bring Jezebel up to the inn at first light."

She had first met William as a young orphan in Clun. He had surprised her then with his self-possession and ability with horses. She'd found out later that, as well as touting for trade for the White Hart Inn, William was working for a gang of horse-thieves against his will. He still had an uncanny ability to blend into the landscape, to listen and see, but not be seen.

"Just come back, preferably in one piece. Imagine what Cecily would do to me if I lost you after finding you."

At bedtime, Christopher was far too excited. He wanted to see William before he slept, to tell him what he had done for Sancha and how she had kissed his neck with her whiskery lips. Eventually after singing to him for a while, Illesa took the stool over to the sideboard and sat, watching the weasels licking and grooming each other until she heard his breathing change.

Then she also fell asleep with her head cradled in her arms.

William had not returned when the compline bell woke her up. But just as she was removing her shoes to get into the bed, there was a slight knock.

"William," he said as she approached the door.

She opened it, and he came in, carrying cold night air with him.

"Where did you go?"

"Around the stables. Found out a few things of interest."

They sat down. Christopher had not moved at all. His hair lay spread out on the pillow, his mouth slightly open.

"It seems your man, Turberville, has been sending messages to France. The messenger he paid today will sail from Southampton tomorrow. He's even been given extra coin because of the frequent French attacks on the coast."

"He must be trying to get a message to his sons," Illesa said.

"Possibly." William sounded tired and unconvinced. "I'm going to speak to someone who works with the messengers' horses. See if they can keep an eye on him."

"But it might be something completely unimportant, William," she insisted. "Perhaps he was helped to escape by someone, and he is sending word that he is well. Don't go to all that trouble."

William looked over at the bed.

"Maybe. Go to sleep. I'll be fine here on the floor. Is the door locked?"

"Yes. And Christopher has checked the horse. He will tell you the whole story in the morning, and then we will travel home with two weasels and a Spanish horse. We will look just like Alphonso the Wise," she said, suddenly happy.

"Who?"

"The late King of Castile, brother of Queen Eleanor. He wrote a song to the Virgin praising his pet weasel when it was saved from being trampled by a horse."

"Well, for the sake of the Virgin, don't sing it. Having to listen to that noisy Azalais at home is bad enough." And he lay down flat on the floor, his hands under his head, and was snoring in moments.

Chapter XIX

Thursday the 29th September 1295
The Mass of the Archangels
Acton Burnel

To remove the Archbishop's cope from the Anchorhold by the church at Acton was never going to be simple. Since Illesa had read the note from Richard, she had been trying to imagine how it could be done. Besides the problem of the cell having no door, only a narrow window and a ground level hole big enough for a small bucket, there was also the risk of being seen.

The manor was busy now that the energetic Malcolm of Harley, King's Clerk, had been given charge of it during the minority of Philip's heir. His Steward had evidently been charged with making as much profit for his master as possible. There was a never-ending stream of people arriving at the manor to account for their rent and their boon work. They left looking poorer.

Fortunately Cecily had an indiscreet friend amongst the servants. And on Wednesday Cecily had come back from her excursion to the mill with information from Sabinia that the Steward had gone to Ludlow to negotiate with the wool merchants, and he wouldn't be back until Friday at the earliest. The Reeve was taking on the Steward's duties in his absence, but he liked wine and always slept late. So it would be best to leave at matins and get there at prime.

Cecily had argued that she ought to go with William, that it would look rather suspicious if the Lady of the Manor was seen creeping around the church with a pick. Illesa would have dearly loved to leave the task to someone else, but Cecily was a large woman. She would never fit through the gap. Nor did she want to send the stable boy, or Christopher, to do it. There was a need to keep the number of people who knew about the cope to a small and silent few.

William and Illesa set off in the darkness with the donkey cart loaded with baskets and sacks, as if they were going to collect wood or acorns not an expensive embroidered vestment. Under the sacks were stones similar to those used for the Anchorhold walls. Illesa was dressed in her worst clothes. She pulled her cloak hood down to shadow her face, but they met no one as they left Langley heading north.

William whistled tunelessly as he led the donkey up the hill into the beech coppice that looked out over the manor and the church. The morning was clear, and the light rising behind them lit the tips of the young trees. Beech nuts cracked under the cart's wheels. The crowbar hidden in the sack clanged against the stones as they went over the wheel ruts.

"I hope we don't have to break through. The noise will draw attention," Illesa whispered. They were coming down the hill towards the shadowed manor buildings, the tower of the church dark against the sky.

"You told me that Richard went in and hid it there, so there must be a way to get it out. He's not the most agile."

"I don't think he would have managed it. It must have been someone else. The clerk, William of Wells, brought it here, and he is quite small."

But no, she couldn't imagine her haughty cousin soiling his hands for any reason. He had probably sent his young servant into the cell, poor lad.

Richard's mother had died there, bitter and angry with everyone. Even angry with God for allowing so much sin. She'd coughed her life away, refusing all offers of help and cursing anyone who tried to provide it. It was her vindictive spirit that made Illesa avoid the church. She always felt Mother Alianore's cold, judging eyes on her, although the shutters of the window had been closed on her coffin for eight years. They would go in, get the cope and get out again as quickly as they could. Perhaps they would even be home before Christopher woke up and wanted to know what they were doing.

William pulled the donkey to a halt at the track leading to the church and looped her reins over the fence. She began grazing on the scrubby grass that grew just outside the churchyard. The sun would soon rise over the hill and light up

148

the east face of the church. Luckily the Anchorhold would remain in shadow. William moved along the wall towards it. But Illesa wanted to make sure there was no one inside the church before they began.

The north door scraped a little as she pushed it open. There was one candle burning in the Lady Chapel, but it was unattended. Illesa moved through the dark nave to check the vestry. Cecily's friend did not pay attention to the movements of the priest who was new to the parish this year and had more regular habits than they had been accustomed to find among clerics. But it seemed that Geoffrey of Welleford was either still asleep or away. The vestry was locked and there was no hint of light under the door. Someone from the village must have come to say prayers to the blessed Virgin, in memory of a child perhaps, and had then gone to the fields.

Illesa dashed back out of the church. William was on his hands and knees by the cell, tapping on the wooden cover that blocked the small arched, ground level opening.

"The easiest thing to do is break through this," he whispered, "and you squeeze in, get the garment and hand it out to me." He looked up at her dismayed face. "I'm too big to do it, obviously, or I would," he said as an afterthought.

"Do you need the crowbar?" Illesa said, looking back to the cart. The lane was empty, but the sounds from the village were becoming more insistent. Women were calling in their yards, casting out scraps for pigs or poultry.

William shook his head. He took his knife out of its sheath and began to try the iron fittings that secured the cover to the wall. The wood was quite rotten after eight years in the rain.

"They really should have filled this in with stone," William said as he levered the iron away and pushed the creaking board to the side. "That was much too easy."

The cell let out a stale breath of damp earth, decay and mice. They hadn't even thought to bring a lamp to frighten the vermin away.

"In you go quickly before the whole village turns out to watch," William said, stepping aside to give her room.

Illesa had to lie flat down and put her arms in first then push herself along the damp and slimy floor. Her oldest

149

clothes would probably never be the same. If anyone saw her, they'd think she had fallen in the tar pits at Pitchford.

Once her shoulders were in, she pulled the rest of her body through and got to her knees. Her breath was loud inside the stone tomb. It was completely dark in front of her. She put out her hands to get her bearings. There was something scuttling along the wall. Perhaps the mice had eaten through the cope and scattered the seed pearls into the dirt of the floor.

She was beginning to make out the shape of the coffin in the thin line of light from the gap in the shutters. To her left was the altar with the plain wooden crucifix, just as it had been when the Anchoress was alive.

Illesa got to her feet and pointlessly brushed the dirt from her clothes. The cope was hidden inside the cell, but Richard had not been specific about where. He would not have permitted his mother's coffin to be opened or moved. No one would wish to disturb his mother's spirit; she had been frightening enough when alive.

Illesa moved around the tiny room, trying not to let her clothes touch the coffin. It would have been foolish to leave the wrapped cope where a person doing real repairs to the cell could easily see it. And if it wasn't in the coffin, there was only one other place it could be, unless Malcolm of Harley or the banker's agent had already found it.

She stood in front of the altar and bowed.

The cell felt like a pit, like the opening mouth of Hell. But here before the sanctified altar, she should be safe. The words of a half-remembered Psalm spoke in her mind.

"Out of the deep, have I called unto thee, O Lord."

Illesa knelt down and reached round the back of the altar behind the facing stone where there was a gap of about a hand's width in front of the wall.

"Have you found it?" The whisper echoed and multiplied around the stone walls, making her whole body jerk in fright.

"Not yet," she whispered back.

She gingerly put her arm through the gap and felt a piece of rope and under that, cerecloth. She tugged on it. It was wedged in behind the stones, and it was heavy. The smell of mice was strong. They had probably made a nest in it, and she would find a parcel full of pink babies covered in gold thread.

Illesa pulled at the rope and had managed to shift it slightly when she heard footsteps.

"God give you Good Morning," William said.

"Morning, Master William. Back from Gascony?" The voice was familiar, but her mind would not tell her who it was. She sat on her haunches, barely breathing in the cold darkness.

"Aye," William said. "Got away with my life."

"More than many. Did you hear what happened in Wales while you were gone? We've lost another five from Acton in the infantry at Cardigan, and now I hear that the men who went to Gascony from Pitchford are dead as well. There'll be no one left to bring in the harvest."

"Hugh the squire is still alive," William said, knocking the iron fittings out with his hammer, "but locked up in Bordeaux with Sir Richard."

"Hugh's not from round here though, is he? Anyway we won't see Sir Richard for a long time, I wager. There's no money left to pay those French bastards. Everyone knows that. Lady Burnel looks worse by the day, with all these tax collectors coming every week and the Italians wanting their debts repaid. She will have to marry again as soon as she can just to keep the place from being mortgaged like the rest."

William grunted discouragingly.

"Why are you here so early, eh?"

"The Steward told me to come and fix this. The wood of the cover was rotting. Thought I'd get an early start on it. Brought some new stone to fill it in properly."

"I didn't notice that," said Stephen, the fence maker.

"It was the wet weather," William said, bending to his job and blocking any view the man could have inside the cell. "Steward told me about it as soon as I got back. The church has been neglected since the war started."

"Oh well, I'll let you get on. I've got to be down by the river today to help them make a new trap."

"Right, oh." William returned to his hammering. He had done well to get rid of the fence maker so quickly, who was notorious for leaning against his day's work and talking until dark.

By pulling and pushing it up and down, she eventually got the packet out from behind the altar. It was almost as long as a

151

man and must have been folded somehow to fit inside the altar. It would have to go through the door diagonally. She propped it against the altar and whispered to William.

"Is there anyone nearby? We need to get this to the cart."

"Wait, I'll go and see," his feet moved away from the hole.

Illesa waited in the dark room with the rotting presence of the Anchoress, her heart beating out the time. She turned to the altar.

"Archangels Michael and Gabriel, accept the soul of Alianore into Heaven in the name of the Father, Son and Holy Spirit," she breathed. There was no sound, just her ragged breaths and her heart hammering as if she were a thief.

William's tuneless whistle was coming back.

"Give me the end of it, and I'll pull," he whispered.

Illesa heaved the end to the faint light of the opening and pushed the other end as William pulled it out. She knelt down and looked into the new day where the cope lay in its shroud on the grass.

"I'll take it to the cart," William said, picking it up and flinging it onto his shoulder like a sack of wool. "Do you want to hide in the cart or inside that tomb while I make this look like I've done some work?"

"In the cart!" she hissed. He checked the lane again and then helped pull her out of the hole.

Illesa got to her feet and walked behind William to the cart. There was just room for her to lie down next to the packet, and he draped the dusty sacks over them.

"I'll just put this new stone in to show we've done something, then we'll go."

Illesa stank of decay and mice. It was all over her clothes and under her fingernails. But the packet looked intact, at least the part she could see. The donkey grazed restlessly, jerking the cart to and fro. Several people called out to William on their way to the fields. She could hear the birds gathering in the trees above her, waiting to swoop down on the fallen grain. Under the sack, Illesa shut her eyes and imagined the scythes cutting through the stems of the barley. She had nearly fallen asleep when William came back to the cart and turned it towards home.

She only sat up to survey the damage when they were through the coppice and coming down into their valley, the long meadows stretching out before them in the autumn sun. Her hands were brown with dirt, her skirt smeared, her veil streaked with cobweb. She knew her face was even worse.

William was walking by the donkey. He doffed his cap to her.

"That fence maker was right. You *do* look worse every day."

"That was the most horrible place I have ever been. Be grateful you didn't have to go in." Her skin crawled with the thought of it.

William grunted and shook his head.

"War is worse. The way the injured beg to be killed, the screams of horses in pain. I'd rather stay in that tomb for the rest of my life than be a soldier."

He was looking at their manor, the smoke rising from it and the shining water of the fishponds.

Illesa's heart sank. She had hoped he would go with her to France and help her free Richard. But the William who had returned was different, and afraid. She could not force him to go back. She looked down at her filthy hands that would somehow have to do this impossible thing without his help.

"Is that what they are all saying? That Richard is as good as dead, and I will have to remarry?"

They were on the lane coming past the chapel, and to either side she could see the cows cropping the last of the summer meadows, the half-harvested barley and the water mill turning slowly through the stream. A comfortable home, but one that could be swiftly taken away if they accumulated debt, and if Richard remained locked up in France for years.

"They are anxious because of what has happened at Acton. All was well while the Chancellor was alive, but since he died they don't know what to expect. They want another strong man to take over, but one that will look after the place, not an absentee lord."

"They should be a bit more loyal to Sir Richard, who has worked so hard to endow this place," she grumbled, "rather than giving him up for dead and looking for some stranger to take over."

William drove the donkey over the moat bridge and up to the manor door.

"Where do you want it?" he asked, taking the sacks off the package.

"In my chamber. I will unwrap it there after I have washed and changed." She climbed off the cart and walked stiffly to the side door.

Azalais met her there with a critical eye.

"Sweet Marie, what has happened to you?"

"I've been in the grave. I feel as if I've been buried for months."

Azalais clicked her tongue and screwed up her nose.

"Christopher has taken the weasels to the granary to catch mice, and Cecily is minding Joyce, so we won't be disturbed." She backed away from Illesa as she began washing her hands in the nearest bucket. "I will wait for you upstairs."

It took several washes in water and hyssop before Illesa felt clean again. She put on new undergarments, although the others were not stained. It seemed that the smell of the grave had penetrated everywhere.

She and Azalais set to untying the thickly knotted cords. They worked silently as if they were laying out a body for burial.

When the cords were done, they began unfolding the cerecloth and laid it aside. At one end there was a nibbled hole. The thick sheet of linen underneath was water stained in the same place. They turned the linen over, then, holding it in both hands, unfurled it across the floor, revealing a half moon of damask – the inside of the cope.

They looked at each other. Azalais' dark eyes were wide. Illesa had never seen her face so intent and serious. They each took an end and turned it over.

The light that came through the window caught the silver threads and pearls so brightly that, for a while, they could not see the pattern but stood blinded as if before twenty candles.

A cloud covered the sun, and they knelt down next to the vestment, examining it with their eyes and fingers. On each side was the story of Creation. Between the scenes there were seraphim, the eyes embroidered on their wings in deep black, interwoven by dragon serpents with gaping mouths of gleaming white teeth. Eve was pulled out of Adam's chest and stood naked in the garden. Adam and Eve stood beneath the Tree of Knowledge, looking up at the snake that coiled through its branches around the golden apples. An angel with a long bright sword barred the gates of Eden. Eve sat with her spindle, winding the wool of their disobedience. In the centre, Christ hung on the Cross surrounded by those who mocked and those who mourned.

Azalaïs had not made a sound since they began unfolding it. Her face was screwed up with concentration as if she were learning a new song.

"It is miraculous," she said. "I have never seen anything so beautiful. Look at these angels, all playing instruments." She pointed to one blowing a pipe and another gracefully holding a gittern. Azalaïs' finger lightly rested on the golden strings as if she could feel them vibrate.

"Mistress, mistress – come here!"

It was William, calling from downstairs.

Illesa got up from her knees and went to the landing with her heart knocking against her chest. He was standing at the bottom of the stairs holding something, looking up, his face agitated.

When she reached the last step, he took her arm and led her to the window.

"This has just arrived." He held out the unfolded parchment with three lines of careful letters. "It is from one of the men of the stables, the messenger I instructed to watch Turberville. I paid him to inform me of what he discovered." William took a deep breath. "I can't read all of it. But I do know the words 'King of France'."

Illesa took the parchment from his hands and held it up to the light.

"Turberville has been sending information about the weaknesses of the English defences to the King of France in exchange for a promise of one hundred livres and the safe return of his sons," she read out, her voice trembling. "He has been captured and imprisoned in the Tower of London."

Chapter XX

Tuesday the 18th October 1295
Feast of Saint Luke, Shrewsbury

Illesa and Azalais stood hand-in-hand near the west door of Saint Mary's. The bells in the tower above rang the hour of sext. Illesa's chest had been tight, her heart hammering, ever since they had arrived in the town at tierce. It had been reassuring to have William with them on the journey, but now he was busy with the saddler near Roushill, and had left them near the church. Illesa had not thought that the bloody uprising of the Welsh a year before would seem so close in the press of the large noisy crowd. Her palms were sweating.

Illesa was glad she'd decided to leave Christopher at Langley. The sight of the castle would only have brought back his nightmares, and they had been mercifully few since William's return. Azalais was also nervous. She had not spoken out loud since they arrived in town, just whispered words in Illesa's ear. Since the French attacks on the coast and the killing of a monk in Dover, there was so much anger against anyone who might be French.

A large woman with a child on her back pushed against them, keen for a better view. People were being moved aside like water in front of a ship as someone was escorted through the crowd by two guards with pikes. At the blast of a horn, a man carrying a long stick jumped up on the small platform near the stocks at the end of the Altus Vicus, his tabard showing the King's arms. Another man in a faded red and blue emblazoned tunic climbed up next to him, and the crowd pressed in, jostling. Town Guards prodded them back with the end of their pikes. Illesa squeezed Azalais' hand, half-wishing she had brought Joyce. The minstrels that accompanied important messengers were usually very amusing.

The herald began with the official line, begging the audience to say an *Ave Maria* and pray for their King, to bless him in all his endeavours. The crowd rumbled through the prayer, sounding more like a cow's stomach than Christians appealing to their Lord. Afterwards, the herald looked rather sardonic, as if he had formed an opinion of the people of Shrewsbury by this one act. But he bowed and began his introduction. He had no need of a scroll, as he had already been through Oxford, Gloucester, Worcester and Ludlow, as well as every other worthy town on the way, he claimed, and knew it off by heart.

"Let it be known that King Edward had a certain knight, Sir Thomas Turberville by name, whom he loved like a son. This Thomas was in his household and served him faithfully in war, most lately in Gascony. This same Turberville was imprisoned by the cunning King of France after the Easter siege of Rions. And this same deceitful King put it to the knight that if he would serve him instead, he would give him great wealth and land. And also the freedom of his sons, locked in a cruel prison in Paris. And Sir Thomas agreed."

The herald drew breath and for a moment watched the minstrel who stood beside him acting out the action of the tale by making faces at the crowd, gesturing and creeping around on the small stage. When he showed how much money Turberville would get from the King of France, he looked exactly like Judas betraying Jesus for a bag of silver in the play of Holy Week.

"The traitorous knight was set free and travelled to England, there claiming that he had escaped. And this same Thomas Turberville listened in to the council of the King and heard his war preparations and planned to bring together the King's enemies in Wales, Scotland and France to invade and defeat our godly King. But through a simple messenger, this plot was discovered and the letter to the Provost of Paris, which contained these harmful words, was intercepted and this matter was communicated to the court. Then that Sir Thomas Turberville fled, knowing that his infamy was discovered, and he was arrested in Gloucester in the square before the Cathedral where he had gone to seek sanctuary."

The crowd took advantage of the herald's deep breath to cheer.

"Sir Thomas Turberville was taken by the King's men and imprisoned in the Tower of London. And on the ninth day of

October, he was brought out on a poor hack, hooded, with his feet bound under the horse's belly and his hands tied before him. Around him rode six torturers dressed as devils who insulted, goaded, and beat him as he was led by the hangman to Westminster. He was condemned on the dais in the Great Hall, and Sir Roger Brabazun, the Chief Justice of the King's Bench, saw the letters Sir Thomas had sent to the Provost of Paris, and the Judge pronounced him guilty of treason against his noble lord and King and pronounced sentence upon him that he should be drawn and hanged."

The crowd cheered even more loudly at this, eager for the details.

"And so he was tied to a fresh oxhide and taken from that place, and he was drawn all the way to the Conduit in Cheapside and then on to the gallows at Smithfield where he was hanged. His body will remain there as long as anything of him should remain. And the King has sent word to all the prelates of the land to meet with him at Westminster. There they will decide how to end these plots of the conniving French King once and for all!"

The herald had reached the climax of his speech and continued in a quieter tone.

"Let the decayed body of Sir Thomas Turberville be a sign of what will become of all those who are traitorous to their rightful lord, and may we all beg forgiveness of our Lord in Heaven."

Having finished, the herald bowed his head and obediently the crowd cheered loudly, shouting insults against the French and waving their arms in the air.

The herald appealed for quiet.

"Attend and lend your ears, and your coin, to this minstrel's clever tongue. Hear his newly composed ballad of the '*Treason of Turberville*!'"

The lad stepped to the front and began to beat time on the dais with his stick. His voice, when it came, was loud and a bit high.

"Lords and Ladies give me your ear
and of a bold traitor you will hear
who has gained a most evil fame.

Thomas Turberville was his name.
He had promised cunning King Philip
and sworn by holy Saint Denys
that he would listen and spy
so that English men would die
conquered by his treachery and treason.
And Philip promised him military protection
great reward, much coin and lands
if he would give England into his hands.
So Turberville arrived at King Edward's court,
his loyalty having been dearly bought."

Azalais pulled on Illesa's sleeve.

"Have you heard enough? It is just the same over and over. And that lad has a voice like a cat."

"Yes, we should go now," Illesa said, turning away from the travelling minstrel. It had made her feel sick at first, hearing of Turberville's treachery. The thought of his many lies, and all the people he had been willing to betray. But now it made her sad. The two sons left in Paris and their father's body hanging in London, brought to ruin, maybe for their sakes. The boys would be killed now they were of no use to the French King. And Lady Turberville, their mother, had lost them all.

Illesa realised they were already at the bottom of the Altus Vicus and looked around for Azalais.

"I must meet with the widow of John of Ludlow. It will be a long meeting. Where will you wait for me, Azalais?"

"No, I'm not leaving you," Azalais said, gripping Illesa's arm through her cloak. "Not with crowds of people looking for the French to beat with sticks and William nowhere to be found. I will come with you and be silent, I promise. She will not get a word out of me."

Illesa could see that there was no arguing with her. She led the way past her favourite apothecary's shop, where she had bought flaxseed for Richard's pain, and on through the thinning crowd until they reached a street behind the new market and turned left. The track led up a gentle hill where the orchards and gardens of the larger houses muffled the noise and smell of the town. It was only her second time coming to this house, but there would be no mistaking it. It was the largest in the row. Even Azalais looked admiring when they stopped in front of the door.

On the second floor, a wide window looked out over the plum and apple trees. A young girl sat at the base of the largest tree which was still heavy with apples. Her small ragged dog ran at them, barking. It stopped quickly as it picked up the smell of weasel on Illesa's clothes and began sniffing and scraping at her cloak with its claws.

The girl ran over.

"Come here, Mitchet." She grabbed the dog by the rough fur on its nape and picked it up in her arms. "You come to see Mistress Borrey?"

"Isabel de Ludlow?"

"Aye, but she doesn't go by that name any more," the girl said. "They've all fallen out with each other, and she uses her other name now."

"Who's fallen out, my poppet?" Azalais said, smiling. She brought out a small sweetmeat from her bag and held it out to the girl. "Share it with your little dog."

The girl ignored this advice and popped the whole thing quickly in her mouth.

She couldn't speak for a moment or two, and spent the time chewing and looking up at Azalais with open curiosity.

"You are very pretty. Where are you from?"

"Never you mind," said Illesa. "Tell us who has fallen out, and then back you go to minding the fruit. I saw a gang of lads coming down the road earlier. You will have to look sharp to keep them off the trees."

The girl glanced behind her.

"Mitchet bites," she said shortly. She turned back to them and pushed a last bit of sweetmeat out of her cheek with her tongue. "It's the Ludlow family don't want our mistress to have the inheritance. She will get it though. She is much more clever than them."

"And you should be cleverer than that," Illesa reprimanded. "What if we were part of the Ludlow family and heard you gossiping?"

"I don't care," said the girl, dropping Mitchet back on the path. She ran off to the centre of the orchard, the dog jumping and barking after her.

The door behind them opened. The manservant standing on the threshold inspected them silently for a moment.

"Come this way," he said, before Illesa could explain. "Mistress Borrey awaits you in the solar."

He led them up the stairs to a bright corridor lit by two windows overlooking the meadows that ran down to the river. An empty barge was tied up at a mooring directly below the house.

He knocked on the door on the right, opened it and held it for them to go in without introduction, shutting it behind them. Isabel Borrey sat at a table in the middle of the room, a man in a fine linen shirt by her side and a pile of coin and parchment on the table. She stood up and came round the table, holding out her hands. Mistress Borrey was a small woman with deep-set, dark eyes and broad cheekbones. Not conventionally pretty but with a look of intensity that was attractive. Her linen surcote was finely made and dyed in expensive scarlet.

"Lady Burnel."

Illesa took her hands and kissed her on both cheeks.

"Mistress Borrey, this is my dear cousin Azalais of Dax. She is staying with us for the duration of the war."

Isabel Borrey looked Azalais up and down.

"Welcome. I am admiring your gown. What is that fabric?"

They spoke of the special damask for a few moments.

"I was saddened to hear of the loss of your husband in the shipwreck, Mistress," Illesa said as they were led to the bench in front of the table.

"I thank you," she said without warmth. "I am over the worst of the shock after almost a year." Isabel Borrey tapped her finger on the table near the clerk's parchment. "Now tell me the nature of your business. It is a particularly full day, and I will not have time for the usual niceties."

"Of course. I have come to ask you to consider lending me a sum of money," Illesa said, mirroring the merchant's tone.

"I see." Isabel Borrey looked over at the clerk, who was continuing to write sums in a table on the parchment. "You have come at a good time. We are doing accounts and will be able to give you an answer directly."

"That is good news indeed."

"Why do you require a loan, lady?" Isabel Borrey asked, watching the man rule a new line on the parchment. Azalais shifted a little on the bench. Illesa was having difficulty remembering that she was the social superior in the room. She sat up straight and rested her own hand on the table.

"You may have heard that Sir Burnel was required to serve the King in Gascony with several men and had to equip them with weapons, clothing and mounts. This used up all our reserves last year. Now he has been captured and is not likely to return until the end of the war. I must pay off some of the family debt to certain Italian merchants and also make payments to the labourers. I will be able to pay the loan back with our wool yield in the summer. So we only require a few months grace."

"You are familiar with our terms?" Isabel Borrey asked, looking at the clerk whose pen was busy summarising her words.

"The extra wool. Yes, that is understood."

"What is the sum you are wanting?"

"Twenty pounds, if it please you."

Both Isabel Borrey and her clerk looked up.

"A considerable sum for a small manor like yours," Isabel Borrey accused.

"The manor is rather small, but it has been caught up in the larger affairs of the Burnel family at Acton. And we have dependants there who are in need."

Isabel held Illesa's gaze for several moments.

"You will assure me that you are not using this sum as a ransom payment for your husband. I will not put up money that will be thrown into the French King's coffers."

"Indeed no!" Illesa said and felt the blood rise quickly to her cheeks. "We are not able to ransom him. They would want a sum at least twice twenty pounds, and there is no negotiation possible at the moment." This was at least very close to the truth. It was not wise to be completely open with a creditor.

"My good lady, we have no loyalty to that bad King," Azalais added in her most dismissive tone. "I am a proud Gascon and serve Edward the Duke of Aquitaine. We will never help his enemies, unlike that traitor Turberville."

Isabel folded her hands in front of her.

"That is good to hear, but I will require a signed document to that effect before this business goes any further. We must be diligent. My husband died in the service of King Edward. It was an honourable way to meet Christ our Saviour. But to be bought out like a sack of wool must be dishonourable at a time of war."

Illesa hoped her face did not show her anger. John of Ludlow had never borne arms in defence of the King his whole life. He had sat safe in his large warehouses, stockpiling wool and underpaying the estates that produced it. Now his widow was claiming that this was the highest form of royal service.

Azalais opened her mouth, but Illesa put a restraining hand on her arm.

"Honour above all, Mistress Borrey," she said quietly. "My husband is of the same mind. We would have him come home to us, but not at the expense of his honour."

Isabel held her gaze for another moment before nodding.

"It is what I expected," she said enigmatically. "Ralph will draw up the agreement now. You will of course keep me informed about the repayment, Lady Burnel. I would advise you not to travel far in the company of your cousin. There are some who do not understand the difference between the Gascons and the French. Also I understand that the authorities are confiscating their property. You should keep a lower profile, Lady Azalais, and perhaps not show your wealth so obviously in your sumptuous gowns."

"I thank you for your kind advice," said Azalais. She was trying to sound humble, but it did not come easily.

"With the news of the betrayal of one of Edward's closest Knights, everyone must be looked on with suspicion. Now I must check the bales and oversee the loading of the barge. I will leave you with Ralph and bid you Good Day, good ladies." They all rose and kissed again, with even less warmth than before.

It took an hour of Ralph's precious time to complete the agreement. The clerk was not talkative, although Azalais, who was very bored, tried to engage him in numerous frivolous conversations. By the time they left and found William waiting with the horses, Illesa could tell that Azalais was bursting with unspoken opinions. She would hear all of them on the long ride home.

But even that would not dampen her mood. They now had the coin, carefully hidden in the saddlebags, to pay for the ship, the accommodation and the bribes that they would need to get them to Bordeaux and into the presence of the Archbishop. They would begin their preparations as soon as they reached Langley.

Chapter XXI

Tuesday the 1st November 1295
Palais de l'Ombrière, Bordeaux
Prime

A storm was blowing blasts of cold air off the Garonne straight into the tower cell. Richard had been alone for almost a month in a small room at the top of the tower, and from here he could see far up-river. If any English ships were coming, he might even be the first to see them before they were holed by the trebuchet. But no ships came and no word from William. After the Feast of Saint Luke, he had lost heart and slept and slept, trying to make the days pass. But there was no relief from the weariness of hunger.

The Constable had been absent for months, and the Mayor ignored all his requests. There was no guard near his cell. When waiting for food, he often wondered if they had forgotten him and had to restrain himself from shouting and pounding on the door. Perhaps Pierre was still guarding the other prisoners, or perhaps his sympathies had been discovered and he had been executed. Richard knew he should care, but it was hard to focus on anyone when his mind was so completely absorbed in waiting.

His fingers knew the exact movements needed to untie the gossamer thin string securing the silk pouch around his neck. He swept a space clean on the floor and gently pulled the treasures out, laying them, one by one, next to him. Now that he was alone, at least he could look at them as long as he liked.

Small pieces of wizened roots which he should know how to use; Illesa had told him often enough. He held them to his nose in turn and shut his eyes. There she was standing at the board in the pantry, grinding them in a mortar, her eyes streaming with tears, her face blotchy, as she prepared a tincture for their son. Another piece of something, more like a twig. This time he saw her standing by the bed rubbing infused

165

oil over his injured leg, her hands kneading his muscles as she smiled at his grimaces.

Of the five cloves she had packed, two were left. Before they had been separated, he had given one to Hugh for his cracked and painful back tooth. Their smell reminded him of Cecily who was forever having toothache. He laid them aside.

The parchment came next. He unfolded it, holding it with both hands, watching as the tears in his eyes made the Greek soldiers in the horse distort and move. Christopher had often asked him to make a wooden horse that he could crawl into. But he would be too big now that he was ten years old.

The last object was a length of silk thread, bright blue, wound into a complex knot that seemed to have no end. He had never untied it, but he knew it was the exact length of Illesa's body, from the point of her toe to the top of her head. She had measured him and had candles of his height dedicated to Saint Christopher. But the measurement of her own body she had knotted into this sign of protection which he was to wear close to his skin.

It was the sort of thing that she believed in. He had tried not to look askance at her village magic. It would have upset her just before he left. But now he found himself wondering if he could conjure her by untying the knot and laying out the length of his wife across the floor, to run his hands over her body and up to her lips, to enter her and feel the relief of love. Or if he untied it, perhaps his life would unwind like a wheel down a hill, and all the small protections it had offered would leave him, and he would die like the others, shitting and screaming with pain.

He held the silk between his thumb and index finger, feeling the softness of the inside of her, the stirrings of pleasure. It was not good to do this every day. Turning inwards and no longer thinking clearly of how to get out or help Hugh, who had seemed close to death even a month ago.

If Jean Fracinaut brought the cope to the Archbishop, perhaps they would both be able to board *La Mariote*, drink some wine and sleep on deck under the stars, knowing that they were sailing home. It was a waking dream. He held the knot in his palm for a moment. It was the colour of water on a bright, calm day. One day he would sink into that water and clean himself of this prisoner stink.

Richard folded the parchment and replaced everything in the pouch. He tucked it away inside his belt before he tried to get out of bed. It took time and usually left him cursing as his leg seized with cramp. As he was heaving himself up on his good leg, he heard footsteps coming up the stairs just outside the door. Two men. If it was a meal, they were early. The bolt shot back on the other side of the door.

"On your feet," the guard said from the threshold. "Mayor coming to inspect you."

The Mayor entered and immediately covered his nose and mouth with a cloth. The guard brought in a lit brazier. Sage was thrown on the flames, giving out a sharp clean scent.

The guard checked the room before going back out of the door to wait by the stairs.

"Sir Richard Burnel, isn't it?" the Mayor said, his thick neck wobbling. He waved his cloth through the smoke from the brazier and went to stand by the window. "I'm taking stock of the prisoners and the state they are in."

"Have there been more deaths?"

"Not since July, in *this* palace," the Mayor said, looking out of the window.

"I'd be grateful for any news, good or bad. How is my squire?"

"It's all bad news for you. But you don't have the worst of it," he said, turning back to Richard, his nose wrinkling. He waved his cloth in the air again.

"You speak like the Delphic Oracle."

"Is that an insult in English?" the Mayor complained, his eyes bulging a little.

"No. It's a compliment. I was just saying that I don't understand fully what you meant about people dying elsewhere."

"I'm not your messenger. But if you want some news, I'll tell you that the Pope's envoys have come and gone from Paris, and there is still no accord. Bloody war is going to carry on for a lot bloody longer." He stared at Richard belligerently. "And you keep telling the guards you want to see the Archbishop," he mimicked a whining voice, "you want a doctor, you want a piece of parchment to write a letter. You must think you are very important. But look at you. Stinking cripple. Sitting up here like a bird in a shitty nest." The Mayor licked his lips where the spittle had collected and looked thoughtful. "Yeah, you must think you are important. So tell me, why do you want to see the Archbishop so much?"

"My cousin knew him. He owed him a treasure that I can get for him, in exchange for my freedom."

The Mayor looked unimpressed.

"What treasure?"

"I need to speak to him in person."

"No, it won't work that way," the Mayor shook his head. "The Constable and Robert of Artois arrive tomorrow. They will get rid of me. The messenger let it slip. I'll be sent to Carcassonne with the other hostages, and they've got a new Norman bastard to be Mayor. So if I'm going to save my skin, I need the protection of the only other man with any power in Bordeaux: the Archbishop." He clapped his hands together, obviously feeling the cold despite the brazier. "So you tell me all about this treasure that will make the Archbishop happy, and I'll see what I can do about getting you an audience with him."

"You give me more information about the war and the other prisoners, and I will tell you about it," said Richard.

The Mayor held his gaze for a moment.

"By God, you are as good as dead already, so I can't see that it will make any difference what you know," he sighed. "It's one of your other knights. Turberville. Went to Paris with Artois and was locked up in the Louvre. Audience with the Provost of Paris. Set up a deal. Turberville is given money and land and his sons are released if he gets information for the King of France. So he pretends to escape from prison and is accepted back into the King of England's court with open arms. Then he sends the information to the Provost all about Wales and Scotland rising up against Edward and the unguarded parts of the coast, expecting to get paid. But the messenger, instead of going to Paris, turns the letter in to King Edward's Constable. Then they catch him, try him and execute him. His body is hanging on a gibbet in London right now."

The Mayor burst into laughter.

"Ah look at you! Just like fish pulled out of the river. You weren't expecting that, were you? And his sons will be dead soon. King Philip will make sure of that." The Mayor was looking out over the river where the early boats were coming in with the first catch. "I told the Lord Constable – release the bordelais hostages locked up in Carcassonne, and you will gain our trust. No. He's not interested in trust, only treasure. He will confiscate all the goods of all those families said to support the English, and you will be sent to Carcassonne along with the rest. Bordeaux is going to be the new residence for Robert of Artois for the next assault on Bourg and Blaye. They want you English out of the way. So we'll all be dead soon, if you don't have something we can take to the Archbishop," he said fixing Richard with his bloodshot, bulging eyes.

This was no stocktaking of prisoners. The Mayor was looking for any way to save his own skin. In the absence of Jean Fracinaut sailing up the Gironde with the cope, this might be the only way out.

"Send word to the Archbishop that you have news of a great gift for him. A vestment of English embroidery, finer than any seen before," Richard said quietly.

"A what?" the Mayor spluttered. "I thought this was going to be coin, a donation, or a vessel made of precious metal."

"It's better than those. It's a cope, a garment for the procession of a bishop. A prestigious gift of kings, even more so because none have been given for years because of the war."

The Mayor looked crestfallen.

"Fucking King of England. You sure you haven't gone mad in here on your own?"

"My cousin the Chancellor had it made for Archbishop Henri to celebrate his installation. I can have it brought here by ship," Richard said, trying to quell the desperation in his voice. "I will write a description of it for him, if you bring me ink and parchment."

But the Mayor was no longer paying attention. He was peering through the narrow window, his fat white fingers splayed against the bare stone wall.

"By God's blood. They are already here."

And he lumbered to the door without another word, the bolt sliding into place behind him.

Richard limped to the window. A fleet of ships was sailing down-river, shining like a rainbow, covered in the pennants of France.

Chapter XXII

Friday the 4th November 1295
Langley Manor
Vespers

Gaspar finally arrived as the sun's last light left the western clouds. As usual, he had travelled alone, and, as usual, his horse was in a sorry state. Before Illesa even saw him she heard William scolding him.

"If you don't rest a horse you ruin it as I've told you before. How far have you come on this horse, limping like that?"

"It's not so bad. You should have seen the last horse I had. Face like the Duke of Swabia's arse!"

"Give me that," William said, grabbing the horse's halter. He led her gently into the stable.

"I need those saddlebags," called Gaspar. "Don't you start looking in them!"

William did not reply. Gaspar turned round as Illesa ran the last few paces across the cobbled yard. He put his hands out to stop her.

"No, we must greet each other as our status dictates. It's good to practise."

He bowed with a wink and swung her outstretched arm as if she were a child.

"*You* look better. Not so wretched and wan." He started walking beside her to the hall. "Not so ghostly. I hope there is something to eat soon. And what is that Azalais woman doing? Might we have an evening of quiet without her?"

He hated the competition for attention.

"She is here, but you might not see as much of her. She is very busy making her garments ready for the journey." She turned to look at him, stopping him just before the door. "Why did you ruin your horse? You know I want to set off in a few days."

"Don't you start on me! I did my best to get here when you said. I had to travel for days and days and no one has compensated me with even a drink as yet."

He went on like this while she took him inside and found him some wine.

"We don't have very much left, you know," she said, as he drained the cup.

"We will bring a barrel of Bordeaux's finest back in triumph. Better than this." And he poured himself some more.

Joyce ran through the door from the pantry on the tips of her toes, her face covered in syrup, her mouth wide open in excitement. Gaspar chased her round the table and swept her up in his arms. She screamed happily and this brought Christopher. There were several moments of mayhem before they could sit down to eat.

After the meal, the reluctant children were put to bed. Adam and Cecily cleared and wiped the table, and William and Illesa laid the cope out on it for Gaspar to inspect.

He was silent and staring for several moments. Then he went to the table and pulled the hooded end toward him. Before they knew what he was doing, he had it over his shoulders and was sweeping forward as if in a procession.

"Yes I can see why the clerics like them," he said swirling it behind him as he turned back towards them.

Illesa rushed forward.

"Take it off, Gaspar! You will damage it. Look it's already dirty from the floor!" Rushes and bits of dust were caught on its hem.

"You don't look anything like a bishop, more like a fat little demon," called Azalais.

Gaspar looked offended, but he stopped parading. Illesa took the hem and, between them, they spread it out on the table again. They picked off the rushes and inspected it. The patch nibbled by mice was barely noticeable. Azalais and Illesa had spent many hours rewinding the remaining silk and tying up the stitches.

"It is very large," Gaspar commented critically. "How are we going to keep it hidden on the journey?"

"I was hoping you would tell us that."

From what I understand of your plan," Gaspar said, rubbing the end of his chin, "we are meant to be pilgrims travelling to Compostella. Pilgrims don't carry large trunks full of expensive vestments."

"I do," Azalais said proudly.

They ignored her.

"But sometimes they travel with merchants. And the merchants have sacks of wool," said Illesa. "It could be rolled up inside a sack with some wool covering it."

Gaspar and Azalais looked sceptical.

"Why would the merchant only have one sack of wool? They either had a whole ship full or nothing," said Azalais. "We won't find a wool merchant travelling now. It's not the season."

"What if it was draped over a horse like a caparison?"

"Bend your knees before Buskins, Bishop of the Horses," Gaspar said, leading an imaginary horse forward and bowing to it.

"I meant we would cover the cope with another cloth of course," said Illesa, crossly.

Azalais was frowning.

"I know. We are taking our very sick mother or someone on a stretcher to Compostella, so she can be cured by the saint. The sick person lies on top of the cope."

"I am not carrying anyone," Gaspar said. "I have a bad back."

William was standing in the doorway.

"All we need to do is take a cart with us. The cart can have a false bottom, and the cope will be packed inside very carefully. The sick person will ride on top." William walked over to the cope, eyeing it critically. "There is one in the barn that would do. Needs some work to enlarge the storage area," he said thoughtfully. "And maybe a new wheel, but it could be made ready quickly."

"We need some pilgrim clothes," said Azalais, "some well worn shoes, and we must have badges. All the pilgrims that travel through Aquitaine have badges from the shrines. I have several in my chest from Poitiers."

"Some of us already have well worn shoes," Illesa said pointedly. "I don't think it will be difficult to make most of us look humble."

"Where are we embarking from?" Gaspar asked, sitting down in the chair by the hearth. "I hope you are not going to drag me across the whole of the country. I've already come from London."

"Jean is going to sail us out of North Wales," Azalais said, leaning back and stretching her pretty shoes towards the fire. "He will send us a message when he lands. The garrisons in the castles have been keeping the peace, so it may be Conwy or Caernarfon."

"That means a longer journey on the seas at this time of year," Gaspar complained.

"We can't go from the South Coast," Illesa said. "You must have heard about the attacks on the Cinque Ports and the fleet of French ships patrolling the Channel?"

"The weather in the Irish Sea could be worse than a few ships full of French. I have liked Richard from time to time, but I am not willing to be drowned and eaten by fish for his benefit," Gaspar said, spreading his palms across his rather round stomach.

"You said you would come!" Illesa cried.

She didn't know why, but the addition of Gaspar to their company was crucial. He had a bewitching quality, and, like Azalais, he had the ability to charm people into doing what he wished. Also, he was familiar with the customs of the court. Illesa just hoped he wouldn't turn the journey into an excuse to meet lovers as he had when he was younger.

Azalais, with her Gascon accent, would be able to keep them safe and arrange for meetings with the Archbishop of Bordeaux without suspicion. Jean, a native of Bordeaux, would sail them there in his ship under the guise of trading and transporting pilgrims. She was the only one who was useless. But she could not send them on this journey and stay waiting at home. She had to see the cope delivered and see Richard when he came out of the cells. He would need her care.

"I will come, Lady Burnel, to repay some of the kindness you have shown me, but don't expect me to enjoy it," Gaspar said darkly.

"If you keep complaining, you will make us all wish you weren't," said Azalais. "Besides, you will be rewarded by Heaven for your help. Which you certainly need." Azalais had a very poor opinion of Gaspar's morals. Probably because her own were less than perfect.

"Since when did Richard have the ear of Heaven?" asked Gaspar, but he desisted when he saw Illesa's expression.

"You are all so ill-tempered," Gaspar said, getting up. "Let's speak more of it in the morning." He went off to find his pack and steal more food from the kitchen.

Illesa and Azalais exchanged looks. William was measuring the cope by hand widths and muttering to himself.

"William," Illesa said.

He looked up, frowning.

"I want you to stay here. To look after things and keep the children and the manor safe."

An expression of joy and relief spread over his face, but then it changed as if a cloud had covered the sun.

"No, I must come to protect you and look after Sancha. You don't know the situation there. You might walk right into a French army."

"This is my decision." Illesa leant forward, her hands on the table, putting every jot of borrowed authority into her voice. "There is no one else I trust. You know this manor. You will keep the animals safe, and make sure the officials of Malcolm of Harley do not take any more of our goods. And Cecily will feel happy and secure if you are here. When she is happy, she works well. When she is worried, she curdles the milk and breaks the eggs." And forgets to mind the children. Illesa would have to speak very firmly to Cecily before she left. Joyce must be kept away from the moat and the fishponds, no matter if this meant there was no butter made until they returned.

William was scratching his arm. When he was worried by something, his skin became raw and red.

"But what if you are attacked? Gaspar is no soldier."

"The more men we have, the more likely we are to be attacked. If we look just like a few women travelling to the Shrine of Saint Jacques, then no one will bother us."

"You want Gaspar to dress as a woman?"

"Maybe," Illesa said, sitting down on the bench and surveying the cope which glowed in the candlelight. "He's very experienced at it. I will see."

She wanted to sound confident in her plan, but the doubt kept creeping into her voice.

"If he spends the whole journey whining, I will strangle him with my own hands," said Azalais. "There will be no need of robbers."

"I don't like to think of you going without some protection," William said.

"What is Jean?" Azalais said with scorn. "He is a strong man, a very experienced traveller and he knows the area. He will be with us."

"Not if your plans interfere with his business," said William in an undertone.

"I heard that! He looks after his business, it is true. But he would not leave me in danger."

"Not you maybe, but what of the others?"

"He will do what I tell him," Azalais replied heatedly.

William shook his head. He so wanted to stay, but he had to dispel his many misgivings.

"We will speak more about it tomorrow, William. But I will not change my mind. I charge you to keep this manor and my family safe. That is all."

"I hope we don't regret your decision," William said and went out into the yard, shutting the door firmly behind him.

"Are you sure that was wise? William is much more reliable than that Gaspar," Azalais said, beginning to fold the cope. Working together they quickly flattened it inside out.

"He wasn't always. But you are right; he is reliable. And that is why he must stay here with the most vulnerable ones. You will see that Gaspar is good in times of need, even though he is rather useless in times of plenty."

"My Jean will be more use," said Azalais. "He has a courageous heart." She looked fiercely at Illesa, daring her to disagree.

Illesa touched Azalais' soft hand.

"I know that. We are grateful for all his help. But when he is back in Bordeaux, where will his loyalties lie?"

"You believe the same for me?" Azalais said, her cheeks flushed.

"Of course not. We are family and I trust you with my life. But you are a true Gascon, and Jean is bordelais. They have never wanted Edward as lord over them, and I don't think Jean will take sides with us against the rulers of his own city."

"He doesn't have to. He is bringing them something that will honour the city. The exchange of expensive goods as ransom for a man is quite normal."

Illesa put her arm around Azalais' slim waist.

"I hope you are right. But if he wants to drop us at the first port, I won't be surprised."

"He would not abandon me that way," Azalais promised. "I will not have you saying those things about him."

Illesa kissed her angry face.

"I'm sorry."

She left her cousin and went round the room snuffing out the lamps. Azalais was waiting for her at the bottom of the stairs, and they went up together like sisters.

Chapter XXIII

Saturday the 12th November 1295
Rhuddlan
Tierce

Illesa's enquires in Rhuddlan had informed her that the church had been demolished to build the castle. If she wanted to say prayers and make offerings for their journey, she would have to walk to the Dominican Friary to the south. The castle stood above the town. Its guards were visible on the towers, watching the valley and the river, but there were few other people in evidence. Rhuddlan was wounded, waiting for help to heal. Illesa made her way back to the inn past ruined buildings.

Jean Fracinaut had suggested it as a good place to embark as there was less scrutiny than at the larger northern ports. Conwy and Caernarfon had plenty of men who were paid to check all travellers in and out. Thankfully, no one had yet questioned their story. If this mad group of pilgrims wanted to brave the seas to Compostella in November, they were not being prevented.

There was no knowing how long it would be before Jean arrived to collect them. They might be trapped in Rhuddlan for many days, and the accommodation was appalling. But the Friary was full of pilgrims heading for Bardsey Island, so they'd had to put up with the slack, lice-infested beds at the only inn.

Gaspar had not yet threatened to abandon the journey, and that made Illesa all the more nervous. If they had been able to get straight on board a ship, he would not have had a chance to change his mind. But he'd become quieter and quieter as he sat at the sticky trestle table, drinking.

Azalais, who didn't usually mind spending days in bed, was on the quay, watching the weather and looking out for *La Mariote*. Illesa wished she would stay inside, but she could not insist. Azalais was doing her a very great favour by coming with her to Bordeaux, as she kept reminding her.

The mother weasel ran round in her cage, restlessly. She should have been firm with Christopher. It was foolish to have brought the pet, but there was a terror in her son's eyes that she could not bear. Christopher had convinced himself that the little animal would protect Illesa, that she had magical powers of healing. It was not in keeping with their disguise. Only a wealthy pilgrim would take such a pet on pilgrimage, so Illesa often hid the weasel in a large cloth pouch around her waist where she slept through most of the day.

South of the town, the bells in the Friary church were ringing the third hour, the sound being whipped here and there in the wind. And in Langley, William would be coming in from the cold for a rest by the fire after his morning chores with the livestock and the horses. Cecily would be washing. Joyce would be running after the geese and hens in the yard, her face still sticky from her breakfast. And Christopher? He might be reading with the little weasel curled up on his lap, or trying to train Pelta to stand on her hind legs or maybe using his bow. But not lying in bed worrying in silence, she hoped. William would not let him. He would get him out to trap rats, or they would be out with the weasel hunting mice or shooting birds for supper.

Cecily knew about girl children; there was no one better to look after Joyce. But other than feeding Christopher and keeping him from freezing in wet clothes, she did not even try to manage him.

Illesa got to her feet. Gaspar didn't look up. She went over and whispered in his ear.

"I think we should go and ask for accommodation at the Friary again."

He nodded.

"May God reward your effort," he said and returned to his tankard.

"Won't you come with me?"

"You might have more success without me. Anyway it is nearby."

"It is not very close. I'd feel better with you beside me."

Gaspar raised an eyebrow.

"I would follow you to Hell, my lady, and, in fact, that is what I am about to do, but not to a friary."

"What do you have against them?" she asked him impatiently.

"I have met a few Dominicans in my time. Best not to go into the details."

So she gave up and went out into the yard.

The innkeeper had been taciturn when they arrived, but when she had asked for a secure place to keep the cart, he had laughed.

"If thieves want something enough, they'll find a way in," he said. "But that old cart should be safe in the yard."

Which was where they'd had to leave it, with its load of priceless embroidery and pearls hidden inside. They'd left her horse, Jezebel, at home. She attracted far too much attention, as they had discovered on many occasions. So they had Sancha, the Spanish jennet, who was a good carthorse and seemed to have a more even temperament than any of the people on this journey.

Illesa wrapped her plain wool cloak tightly about her and opened the gate from the yard to the street. The Friary was a small house of Dominicans, also impoverished by the war, south-east along the river in the biting wind. If she didn't find a different bed for the night, she was sure Azalais and Gaspar would go home and she would have to travel to Bordeaux alone, assuming Jean would still take her. She'd already paid him almost a third of the sum she had borrowed. And he had hinted that even more would be needed.

The path by the river was quiet in the sunshine. The wind had died and there were gulls flying in straight lines in the high sky. Illesa looked back towards the river quay. Small boats were tied up along one side, and some scruffy boys sat on the wooden boards repairing nets. The sky over the sea in the distance was clear. The onshore wind had pushed the cloud inland, and a ship with a black hull and bright white sails was visible in the distance.

Illesa watched it for a moment before she started walking quickly back towards the town. A figure in a flowing blue veil was running to meet her.

180

"Go and get that lazy man, and get on board," Azalais called when she was within earshot. "We are leaving even if we only make it as far as Conwy. I can't stand another night in that lice nest!"

It took them an hour to be free of the inn. There were extra costs and an issue about the coin. Some of the ones they were paying with were clipped, the innkeeper claimed. Gaspar had to get up out of his seat and put on his deep voice.

But eventually they were pulling the horse and cart up the ramp, into the cog and tethering them in the hold. Sancha shook her head unhappily. She had been at sea before and didn't like it.

If William were there, he would have calmed her. Gaspar and Azalais were not interested in horses, only in how fast or slow they went, so it fell to Illesa to stand with Sancha. She missed the journey from the river to the wide bay, only coming up on deck when the waves began to make her feel sick below. She'd have to get used to the sea, as the horse would.

Illesa clung to the rail next to Azalais, who was watching Jean giving commands to his small crew. Her French cousin looked happier, prettier and younger than she had in a long while. The wind had almost torn off her veil, and it flapped around her like a frightened bird.

Gaspar was watching the crew from the port side. She could see his mouth moving, but couldn't hear the song he was singing. The mother weasel was agitated by the churning and noise and was turning upside down in her bag, but it was too rough to take her out and let her have some air. Before she had left, Christopher had decided to name her Eve.

"So your baby weasel must be either Cain or Abel. Bad or good," Illesa had said.

"No, his name is Edward."

"Why Edward?"

"He is the King of the Weasels. You will see how big he grows."

"I didn't know that weasels had kings."

"Everything has a king," Christopher had said confidently. "One day Eve will have to bow down before her son."

Illesa had put the mother weasel down next to the baby, and she had begun grooming it, holding its ears with her sharp paws and licking it with her small red tongue.

"Animals have their own ways, different from the laws of men," she'd said.

"They should be the same if they were created by God," Christopher had said sullenly, picking up the baby and putting it on his shoulder where it nibbled his ear.

Illesa had smiled and picked up the mother weasel, putting it on hers.

"One day, Christopher, you may carry more than the King of the Weasels on your shoulder. And that will be someone worth bowing down to."

Chapter XXIV

Tuesday the 22nd November 1295
Blaye – Aquitaine
Nones

They had not set foot on land for eight days. For three they had not slept because of the terrible waves and the cries of the horse. For two they were struggling against a wind that was determined to push them back towards English shores. One day it seemed another ship was pursuing them under an unknown flag. The wind died, and it disappeared.

Illesa felt as if she had been thrashed and winnowed by the sea. The wonders of it were a dream. Great fish that leapt at the bow. Birds with enormous wings diving towards them. A night when the sky was lit with a bright star, moving across the heavens.

But from then, there was calmer weather and a southerly wind that seemed to know where they needed to go. As if the Heavens willed it, Azalais had said. The rest of the crew were silent on the subject. Sailors did not wish to tempt the stars.

Small vessels were tacking up the coast, occasionally shouting a greeting or a warning. *La Mariote* was well known in these waters. Well known but not always well liked. Some of the boats came alongside and attempted to trade, but Jean sent them away, cursing. He wanted the best price for his goods, and that could only be achieved in the towns and cities.

When they eventually reached the mouth of the Gironde, they slipped into the river's flow and out of the Atlantic waves like a bird that flies into a wood. The river was busy, and they were constantly engaged in avoiding the small fishing boats and their nets, the ferries and the barges.

They got as far as Saint-Estèphe before they saw a French cog decked with war castles fore and aft. Jean ordered his crew to weigh anchor and pull down the sail.

"Get your story straight," he said to Gaspar and Illesa. "They inspect the ship and its cargo. They will want to know

183

your origin and your destination. Remember what I told you. Better that you are Welsh, not English; you share a common enemy."

The cog drew up alongside, throwing ropes over to tether the two ships together and lowering a ramp. The short, moustached official who boarded with his armed guard was the new Constable of the Gironde. Jean immediately began a private conversation with him. Evidently they were well acquainted.

The men climbed down into the hold and remained there for some time. On deck Gaspar and Illesa did not speak. They had already practised their story on the long voyage and knew how to play it. Azalais didn't have a part in it, as she was, with great conviction, pretending to be Jean's wife.

Illesa fingered the pendant of Saint Margaret she wore on her cloak and muttered a prayer. She had made offerings before leaving home, had prayed at every shrine she came across along the way although briefly, as the others were impatient with her delays. But if they were imprisoned now, the children might never see their mother or their father again.

The official emerged from the hold and gestured to them with his glove. Gaspar went ahead, putting on his best impression of a Welsh merchant accompanying his wife on Pilgrimage to Saint-Jacques de Compostella. No, he was not bringing anything with him except his wife and her small pet. Yes, the weasel did bite. They were planning to find another craft to take them south, but his wife had been sick for days and needed to spend some time on land to eat and recover. Yes, he was aware that Blaye was held by the English. It was only because of the illness of his wife that they were landing. They were grateful and would say a prayer for the official at the shrine of Saint Jacques when, God willing, they reached the blessed place.

Illesa stayed by Gaspar's side with lowered eyes and nodded when necessary. The official quickly lost interest in them and became fascinated by the amount of silver Jean should pay him. But he did keep an eye on Eve the weasel, who squealed on Illesa's shoulder and then dipped back into her pouch.

Azalais watched with amusement behind the Constable's back. Eventually he left, his guard weighed down by bags of coin. No wonder Jean had wanted so much of their loan. If that was the first bribe, the money would not go far.

The crew weighed anchor, and they continued up-river. The Gironde quickly narrowed and was split by long thin islands of mud and grass. Little boats floated near the shallows hauling up large grey fish for the Friday fast.

After the longest island, they came to the port of Blaye, a small outpost of the English Crown in hostile territory. Archers watched from the gate towers, aiming at the ship as it neared the harbour. All weapons had to be left on board while they disembarked for inspection.

"I've brought supplies for the English force," Jean told the sergeant-at-arms. "But we best unload after dark so the French don't see us. They believe I am only stopping here to let off these pilgrims," he said with disdain. The sergeant looked sharply at Gaspar, who was grinning broadly and lifting up one foot at a time.

"I feel as though I am still at sea," he said. "Thank the Archangel Raphael and his great fish that we are not!"

"You are English?" the sergeant asked, confused.

"Indeed. Wholeheartedly! But let's get inside the walls before we tell you our tale."

"What about the cart?" Illesa called.

"I will come back for it after I have settled you into the inn," he said shortly. "My wife is not able to walk far and has become attached to the cart. It is an affliction of her lower body. We have struggled to conceive children all these years," Gaspar went on, as he walked with the sergeant up the wooden jetty towards the town gate.

"Spare us," the sergeant muttered and quickened his pace.

Azalais came up behind Illesa and gave her an arm.

"You will feel unsteady at first, still rocking from side to side," she laughed. "The colour of your face when the French boarded the ship was very convincing. I think that French Constable feared both your vomit and your pet!"

"Do you know this town?" Illesa asked as they walked through the heavily guarded gate behind Gaspar. It seemed the English at Blaye also knew Jean Fracinaut. They barely glanced at the sealed letter of safe passage. Which was all for the best as Illesa had forged it.

Azalais sighed rather dramatically.

"Blaye was once a town of Gascon troubadours. I used to come here often. Now it is full of English voices, drawn swords, cocks and cocked arrows."

"Would you rather it was full of the French King's men?" asked Illesa, rather more sharply than she intended.

Azalais turned and gave her a condescending look.

"I'd rather you'd all go away and leave us to live our lives. Our Gascon land was good. Now it is overrun and many are dying. But you are obviously tired and weak or you would not speak to me like that in my own land. I will take you to the only inn here that has good rooms. And we will eat some decent food!"

Once Illesa had eaten a simple pottage and some fine bread, she was so tired that she fell almost immediately into a deep sleep on a straw mattress next to Azalais in the upper room. She woke up in a sweat. Night had nearly fallen. Her first thought was of the cart. It was still on the ship where any passing French vessel could confiscate it.

Gaspar would have forgotten. Jean may already be back at the ship, may already have left. She got out of bed and put on her boots. In the cage, Eve was eyeing her, starting to turn circles. Illesa put the cage next to where Azalais lay breathing loudly on the bed. It might calm the animal until she could get back with some milk. Illesa went quickly down the narrow stairs to the hall. Rush lights high on the walls showed a dozen or more drinkers. Unusually, Gaspar was not holding court. He and Jean were talking quietly, their bent heads together.

Gaspar saw her approaching and raised his head, smiling broadly.

"My lovely lady wife, how are you feeling?"

Illesa sat down by his side, ignoring his greeting.

"What are you two talking about?"

Jean looked suddenly angry.

"We can talk without the women having to hear! We talk about the business of the ship."

"It is my business if I have paid you to bring us here. It is the business of this journey to get Sir Richard out of prison," she whispered, "not to make more money for you. Have you taken the cart off the ship and found a safe place for it?"

"Now don't get all hot and bothered because you have just woken up," Gaspar said, pushing his cup towards her. "Have some ale."

She pushed it back at him.

"I want us to keep in mind what we are trying to do. There is nothing more important than that. Or would *you* like to tell Christopher that you could not get his father back, Gaspar, because you let the ransom be confiscated by the French?"

"For the love of Christ, his mother and all the saints, we do not need to be told," Jean said angrily.

"Then let's go now." She stood up and pulled on Gaspar's sleeve. "It is nearly the curfew."

"You make a shrewish wife," Jean remarked. But he got to his feet and went to the door.

"Gaspar, come with me," she said, pulling harder.

He pushed himself up, leaning on the table, and Illesa wondered how much he had already drunk.

"Come, wife. Let us go with the captain of the ship to see that all is well," he said loudly in his country accent, his face now alert. But as she walked behind him down the dark lane to the quay, he seemed unsteady on his feet.

The half-moon was bright on the water, making a shadow of *La Mariote's* mast pointing up-river to Bordeaux. The sailor on watch called out, and Jean returned the greeting before they boarded the ship.

Illesa and Gaspar took a lamp and went below. He examined the cart, secured to the side of the ship.

"Going to need some help with these knots," he said. He hated anything practical.

Illesa called up to the sailor. Sancha, still in her harness for sailing and still unhappy, whinnied at the sound of her voice.

"Take that horse off for the night," Jean said from the deck. "She is getting ill."

"But we are leaving tomorrow for Bordeaux aren't we? It is only one more night," Illesa called up. Sancha was snorting, and butting her head against Illesa's shoulder. She moved a bucket of water within reach.

Jean came down the ladder to the hold.

"I've seen many horses on ships. Look at her. She's stopped eating. If she doesn't have some time on land she will be useless for pulling anything, and you will have to buy an inferior beast. There are hardly any horses left in Gascony. The French have requisitioned them all. At least feed her up in the stables, then she will have some strength for the journey."

"Where are you going to land us tomorrow? It won't be far to the city will it?" Illesa ran her hands over Sancha's back and hocks.

"We will see where the French ships are," Jean said, untying Sancha's halter and unhooking the hammock that supported her belly.

Illesa watched as Sancha was led up the gangplank to the deck. Gaspar stood against the rail, looking across the river. The cart had already been landed and sat on the quay leaning on its shafts.

It took all of them to harness Sancha. She was uncharacteristically stubborn, wanting to pull away and find grazing, but they managed after they found a handful of grass to tempt her.

Jean turned to go back aboard, but Illesa put a hand on his shoulder.

"You have brought us safe here, and we are thankful. But you know we have paid you to take us further."

Jean shrugged her off, frowning.

"I hope to take you further, but war makes a nonsense of plans. And you should know by now that I think this is a fool's errand. All you are doing is endangering Azalais and yourself, so that your children will become orphans."

It was hard to see the merchant's face in the growing darkness.

"Don't you believe in prayer and grace?" she asked. "What we hope to do is what Christ does – release the imprisoned. With enough faith, we will succeed."

Jean snorted and raised his face to the night sky.

"Look, woman. The saints are not interested in fighting men. When knights go to war, they lose their lives, one after another. They go to Heaven or to Hell, mostly the latter. But they do not bother the saints with constant appeals for help.

188

They know they are at war and must help themselves. It is the women who think they can change the way the world is and always has been."

"The world is fallen. We are told to pray for its redemption."

"What I heard is that it will be redeemed only after the Apocalypse. Do you want to pray to hasten that?"

"No, that's not right. It can be redeemed piece by piece, repaired stitch by stitch. That is why we are told to fast and pray."

Jean shook his head.

"Fast and pray all you like. It won't get anyone out of a Bordeaux prison. They are the thickest and strongest in the world." He turned his back on her and climbed aboard with his long legs.

Illesa and Gaspar led the horse unsteadily into the inn yard. They found the stable boy nearly asleep. All the time they were sorting the horse and stowing the cart, Gaspar was silent.

"What is wrong with you?" Illesa asked as they left the stable boy filling a manger of hay.

"Nothing, dear wife. I am merely tired."

Illesa looked him in the eyes.

"You are not fooling me."

"I would never try," he said in his country accent, and bowed her ahead of him through the inn door.

When Illesa woke the next day, *La Mariote* was gone, and up and down the river all they could see were French warships, flying the banner of King Philip.

Chapter XXV

Wednesday the 23rd November 1295
Palais de l'Ombrière, Bordeaux
Tierce

Without warning two guards opened the door to his cell, and a waft of clean air blew in. Richard rolled onto his side and looked up.

"Count Robert requires you," one guard called, watching him struggle to his feet. "Can't you walk?"

"I use a stick, but it was taken away," Richard said, his voice cracking from thirst and lack of use.

"Here Jacques, hold the door. I have to support this old one," the guard called into the stairwell.

During the weeks alone, Richard had been letting his mind wander into sleep at all times of day, and he was no longer sure what was dream or waking. But the guard's hard leather jerkin felt real against his chest as he was helped out of the door. The guard's meaty breath likewise. Richard felt suddenly lightheaded at being out of his cell, next to people who might speak or touch him, anchoring him back to the earth that was so far away.

The other very real sensation was pain. He had to be almost dragged down the stone stairs.

"You are Sir Richard, eh?" the guard asked as they grunted their way down the third flight. "I don't want to have to drag you all the way up again if you are the wrong prisoner."

Richard could only nod, his teeth gritted. When they reached the ground, the guard ordered a stick to be found while Richard leant against the wall sweating and trembling. The stick was not found, and the guard watched his attempts to hop on his good leg with obvious amusement.

"Like a rabbit," he said, laughing. "Big frightened eyes. God, these English!"

They went through a small storage room smelling of wax and then through a door into a large chamber with several cupboards against one wall, to store the administrative rolls of the Duchy, presumably. There was one table and three empty chairs.

Outside the tall windows were all the sounds of the city: the cries of women selling, dogs barking at each other – one high, one low – a heavy cart rumbling on the stones. It was so near; it brought tears to his eyes.

Richard had hoped that other prisoners would be summoned, but no one else came until the door from the private chamber opened and Robert of Artois walked in followed by a butler. The Count sat down in the largest chair and smiled.

"Pull that chair forward for this man. I can't bear to see him tottering on his one leg like that. It is making me feel ill. Bring wine for us both."

The butler returned in a moment with two fine goblets and a ewer on a tray.

"I believe you are aware that I have taken command of the army here in Bordeaux while the Constable is engaged elsewhere." He smiled briefly. "You were in Rions when we broke your hold on the town, weren't you? So many died that day, but, somehow, not you, even with your obvious shortcomings." He gestured to Richard's missing eye and useless leg. "You must have some special abilities that are not obvious." He seemed to have amused himself and smiled at the butler who was still standing by the table.

"I remember you," Richard said, his voice still cracked.

"Sit down and drink. You certainly sound as if you have been in the desert fighting the Saracens," he said, waving at the chair. "I told the victualler to increase the rations for the prisoners, and I hope you have been finding the food to your taste."

Richard sat and stretched his leg out in front of him before he answered.

"The food has improved, I thank you. But I have been kept alone for weeks now. I do not know what has become of my companions, and I have not been allowed to see a priest."

"One thing at a time. Drink. This is one of the finest wines from this area. I think you've had it in England before, but not for some time." Robert of Artois put the glass to his lips and drank, swilling the wine around in his mouth before swallowing. "It will bring back your voice." He held the goblet to the light and swirled the wine slowly. "And I do need you to tell me a few things."

Richard took the goblet in the palm of his hand and raised it to his lips. The taste was so rich his mouth watered, and he swallowed quickly.

"It would be well for me to have bread with this wine," he said.

"Of course. Your stomach will not be used to it." The Count turned again to the butler. "Bring bread and tell my clerk that I require him."

When the bread came the loaves were small and white, and each one was as soft as a pillow. Richard ate three in quick succession, not caring that the butler looked disgusted.

The Count of Artois got out of his chair and went slowly to the window.

"You see it is time to make a decision. In Bordeaux there are people eating and drinking like this every hour of the day. And having pleasure with women. It is all happening, just out there." He turned back to Richard and rested the tips of his fingers on the table. "You could return to this world of plenty. If you go to Blaye and Bayonne and work for me in these towns, then you will be given much. Land and coin and wine and women," he counted out the benefits on his fingers. "You need only enter the towns as if you are loyal to the English, and open them up for us."

A black-cloaked clerk came through the door carrying an inkpot and a quill. He went to one of the cupboards, retrieved a sheaf of parchment and then sat down, staring at the implements in front of him. He had not even glanced at Richard.

"I wonder that you make this offer to me after how badly things went for Sir Turberville," said Richard quietly. "It implies a lack of confidence in the military prowess of the knights of France to rely on these dishonest stratagems."

Robert of Artois frowned slightly and stroked the fur of his cape.

"You are confusing the petty, internal struggles you have on your small island with real warfare. In France we have many ways to gain territory. But you are right about Turberville. He did not look like a prisoner. His escape was an obvious falsehood. His actions were suspicious. You, on the other hand, look very much like a prisoner, and you have learnt from his mistakes. You will be most convincing."

"So how am I meant to convincingly escape from the tower with one useless leg?"

The Count smiled widely, showing a gap in his lower front teeth.

"That is taken care of. We are moving all the remaining prisoners to Carcassonne next week. We need the space here for the prisoners we will take at the English outposts. Did you know that Macau fell two days ago?" he asked brightly. "Well, during this move to Carcassonne, you will disappear. It will be witnessed by the guards as a genuine escape. Then you will make your way to one of the English strongholds and speak to the commanders. I believe that Ralph Gorges and Barran de Sescas are in Bayonne, but there will be lesser nobles in Blaye. When you have news of the time to attack, you will report it back to me."

"And how would I do that?"

"You will be accompanied by one of my special men. He will be at your side as soon as you call him, but when he is watching you, he will be invisible." The Count flicked his fingers in the air.

Richard put the goblet to his lips and took another sip of wine.

"It seems an interesting proposal," he said.

"Good! I am glad you like the sound of it. Now before we discuss it any more, I need to ask you something." The Count sat down and leant forward, his elbow jogging the clerk's inkwell. "What do you want with the old Archbishop of Bordeaux? I hear you have been begging to speak to him for months. What is it? A great and terrible sin you must confess?"

"The Chancellor Bishop Robert Burnel, who is amongst the blessed in Heaven, was my cousin, and he was present when Henri became Archbishop. I hoped that he would arrange my release. But it seems that the two bishops were not as friendly as my cousin had implied."

Robert of Artois looked at Richard intently.

"And I heard there was talk of a great and precious gift that you could give him? What kind of treasure was this?"

Richard looked down and interlaced his hands.

"My cousin promised Archbishop Henri a vestment for the Cathedral. But when he died three years ago, it was buried. I hoped to be able to get my freedom by the promise of this gift."

"So it is no longer in this world?"

"No, it has been buried with the dead."

"That is a shame. I was hoping that you had something we could use as surety in your case. But, as it is, we will have to use your squire. Is his name Hugh?" Richard's grip on his goblet tightened. "If you enabled us to break Blaye, for example, then we would be able to let Hugh out into the world again. A young man needs this fresh air and good food. I understand his hair is falling out."

"The air may be healthier, until you are hanged as a traitor on a dewy morning," said Richard.

"This will not happen to you." The Count of Artois shook his head. "You are more, what do you say, clever, than Turberville. He was not careful, but I can see you are a very careful man. Yes." He turned to the clerk, his faced screwed up mockingly in concentration. "I can see that your mind is calculating all the various costs." He pushed the tray to the side of the table and clapped his hands loudly. The butler reappeared.

"Bring me Almaric," he ordered, then turned back and looked appraisingly at Richard. "The thing that concerns me most is your leg. As you say, we must make your escape convincing. For that we need some casualties, which is where Almaric comes in. Did you meet my pet wolf in Rions?"

He looked curiously at Richard, wanting a reply.

"I saw it from afar," said Richard warily.

"She is a magnificent hunting animal. If you see her charging over the fields of Normandy after a stag, you will understand my love for her. She does not give up but waits for exactly the right moment to begin the chase, and when she commits to it, she brings down the stag with a savage bite."

The door opened and a man dressed in brown and grey entered, clean-shaven, even to the top of his head. Around his waist, he kept two knives and a sword. He had no particular expression on his face, but, in some way, he reminded Richard of William.

"Almaric, this is Sir Richard Burnel. He is going to pass on messages after his staged escape. The messages will be brought straight to me. If you see anything that indicates that he is about to flee from France, you are to shoot him through the heart or cut his throat. Whichever is more convenient."

Richard straightened his back, ready to stand.

"I do not recall agreeing to your proposal. There has been no contract of benefits or costs," he said trying not to look at Almaric, who was staring at him, memorising his face.

"That can be arranged swiftly. The alternative to this proposal is the road to Carcassonne, where, with the remaining English and the bordelais hostages, you can languish for any number of years to suit yourself. Your King seems little inclined to come to battle to save his faithful knights. Perhaps he has been emasculated by the rejection of the French Princess?"

Almaric kept looking at Richard with unwavering attention while the Count smirked at his own joke.

"Almaric, it will be necessary for a guard to die during this man's escape to make it more convincing. Make sure it is a Gascon guard."

Richard's stomach twisted painfully.

"This man is going to kill a guard so that I can escape?"

"No, he will make it possible for you to kill the guard yourself. Don't be a shirker. You have to earn your freedom, after all. So are we agreed?"

Richard did not move.

The Count turned to the silent clerk.

"Draw up the documents! I will even put my seal to it, so you know it can be trusted."

Chapter XXVI

Wednesday the 23rd November 1295
Blaye – Aquitaine

"Azalais, Jean is not coming back. He never wanted to take us to Bordeaux. But he has brought us near enough," Illesa said, trying to take her cousin's hand. Azalais had been standing by the town gate watching the river since prime, and it was nearly sext. Her eyes were red, but her mouth was stubbornly set.

"He must have been threatened by the French boats in the night and has moved off. He will come back and join us soon."

But when evening came and there was still no Jean, Azalais took to her bed, alternating between rage and tears.

Illesa sat down next to Azalais on the edge of the mattress. They had lost a whole day. Whether Azalais came or not, she and Gaspar would have to go to Bordeaux in the morning.

"I'm sorry, but he isn't coming back, my darling." Azalais shifted in the bed and pulled the blanket close to hide her face. "He didn't want to risk having his boat seized."

"He is a coward," Azalais said into her blanket. "I told him he would never have to worry about that. All the time he was with me, it was just to please him. If I ever see him again, I will curse him to shipwreck."

"He may yet redeem himself, but we have to find a boat that can take us on. Two pilgrims arrived at the inn today from Pons. They travel to Bordeaux tomorrow. We can go with them."

"I want to go home," Azalais said in a muffled voice. Her face was pressed into the bed sheet.

Illesa shook her by the shoulder.

"We can't go home, we have to get Richard out."

Azalais looked up from the bed, her face red and angry.

"Not your home, my home. I want to go back to Dax. I don't care what scandal they think I caused. The only reason I stayed in England as long as I did was for Jean. He was the only thing that made that cursed climate bearable. Now I just want my own house, not your rain and cold and grey skies. Look out there. Do you see how beautiful it is? That is nothing compared to the South!"

Illesa got up.

"I'm sorry you didn't like it in England. We tried to make you welcome. But now if you aren't going to help me get Richard out of Bordeaux, I will have to say farewell. Gaspar and I are leaving at prime."

Illesa opened the door and stomped down the stairs.

She was too angry to go to bed when she grew tired, so she spent the evening listening to the two pilgrims who were natives of Rouen. It was not their first time on the pilgrimage route to Saint-Jacques, and they were not going to let the war stop them. Their caps were thick with badges and shells.

"Why should the ways of God be closed due to man's sin?" the older one said, well practised in this argument.

Gaspar came in at curfew and sat next to her in the attitude of the attentive husband.

"We are accompanying my dear cousin who is suffering from fits. We take her in the cart so she doesn't fall down as she walks," Illesa explained to the pilgrims. "Do you know about crossing the Gironde with a cart?"

They knew all about it. There were several ways, all with their relative merits. In the end the pilgrims suggested that they travel together.

"If this is your first time, you should not be alone," said the younger one, André. "The way is full of thieves. You may meet a seemingly pious man offering you a bed for the good of his soul in exchange for your prayers, and then he cuts your purse and maybe your throat in the night."

"You only heard that in the tavern, André," said his companion, Paul. "The worst that will happen is you will be overcharged. But if you stay with us, even that will not happen to you. We know all the best places to eat and stay."

"It is very kind of you to guide us as far as Bordeaux, and then we should go on at our slow pace," Illesa said, humbly.

"We must stop often to tend my cousin, and we would not want to detain you. But if you have any more tales to tell about the way from Bordeaux to Dax, we would be glad to hear them."

They did, and it was late when Illesa eventually slid into bed next to Azalais.

"Are you awake, my darling?"

Azalais made an indistinct sound.

"If you come with us, you can ride in the cart the whole way. We have two pilgrim guides to take us into Bordeaux."

Azalais turned over, looking nonplussed.

"I could have got you into Bordeaux well enough. Don't you remember? I told you that I spent a whole year there when I was newly married."

"Even better. You will quickly get us an audience with the Archbishop."

Azalais grunted.

"I hate that man."

"You don't have to like him," Illesa said crossly. "Just make up a story so that he will see us in private and we will show him the cope hood."

Azalais was silent.

"Why do you hate him?"

"He forbade the singing of the old songs, the ones that I was trained for. Trained by the best masters, who are all dead now. I might be the last of those who sing the courtly songs. *And* he threatened me with excommunication because he said that the songs were putting a woman in the place of the Lord Jesus."

"Will he remember you?" Illesa wondered.

"I have been told that I am very memorable," she said archly. "If he does, I will have to do a sickening show of repentance."

"But it was years ago," Illesa said hopefully.

"Four years since my husband died in Bordeaux. Not very long."

From what Illesa understood, it had not been a happy marriage. But Azalais was in a delicate frame of mind to speak of men, even though she had been a widow with her own means and pleasures after he had died.

198

"Could you pretend that you have seen the error of your ways and have come to him for a special blessing?"

"Knowing him, he will want me to join a convent. I will think about it. Now be quiet and let me sleep." She rolled onto her side. "We will have to get up soon."

Azalais was right. It was only a few hours to dawn.

Chapter XXVII

Thursday the 24th November 1295
La Garonne
Vespers

The five of them negotiated passage on a barge ferry large enough to take the cart and horse that sailed between Blaye and Macau. Azalais sat in the cart on top of sacks and below a large wool blanket, managing to look very delicate if somewhat too well dressed for a pilgrim of limited means.

Paul spent most of the journey describing a persistent blister and a hacking cough that he'd had during their journey to Compostella two years before. Both had been cured by Saint Jacques. Gaspar had a fixed expression by the time they came alongside the quay at Macau. It was hard work getting the cart off the barge on the slippery planks. It seemed it would all end up in the river.

"You are very worried about your cart," André noticed as they finally got it on to dry land. "It won't come to harm from a bit of water. There'll be worse when you cross the Pyrenees. The rivers there are so deep that sometimes you have to stand on each other's shoulders to see the other side. You hope for Saint Christopher to guide you across!"

"That's something to look forward to," muttered Azalais under her breath, clambering back into the cart once it was safely away from the riverbank.

The river track to Bordeaux was open. There were certainly signs of the work of the French knights, burnt buildings and burnt fields, but no armed men on the road. After three hours or more in the cold wind, they were glad to see a village with a tavern within sight of the walls of the city. And as André and Paul approved of it, they stopped.

Illesa had been hoping to have time to speak to Gaspar and Azalais alone before they reached Bordeaux. But now it was looming in front of them, its thick grey walls only half a league away, and as yet, they had not planned what story they would tell to get rid of Paul and André.

"Please forgive us that we are not coming straight in with you. We must pray together," said Illesa, bowing her head. "It is our habit to pray together outside before we eat and give thanks for a safe journey thus far."

"Well, we must join you in this," said Paul. "It sounds a most holy habit. Come, André, let's gather here with our friends."

Gaspar raised an eyebrow at her, and she waved her hand at him.

"Go on, husband, say the prayers like you usually do."

Gaspar kept them there a good while. Once he had warmed to his theme, he didn't want to stop. Throughout the simple meal, the two genuine pilgrims were very attentive, especially to Azalais.

"You are so patient with your infirmity," Paul beamed, after Azalais had described her sufferings. "I am sure that blessed Saint Jacques will heal you. Your inner goodness shines out of this broken body."

Azalais looked at him with a condescending smile.

"My body is not broken. No. It is all in working order."

"Come now," Illesa said, standing suddenly. "We should be getting inside the gates of Bordeaux before the day is too far gone and all the beds are taken."

"You don't need to worry about that," Paul began.

Gaspar stood up.

"I will go and ready the cart and the horse."

Illesa followed him out into the yard, leaving Azalais to listen to their copious advice. Gaspar was attempting to pay the stable boy from his purse and fumbling with the small coin.

"How are we going to lose these men?" she asked in a whisper as they stood at Sancha's head. "We need to be alone in Bordeaux to set up the meetings."

"Do not worry, wife," Gaspar said flatly. "You were not listening to them properly in Blaye. Whenever they stay in Bordeaux, they spend a whole night worshipping at the Cathedral of Saint André. It procures them a special blessing. We will go to the place they recommend tonight. Then

201

tomorrow, we will move accommodation." He began to lead Sancha around to the yard gate. Illesa put a hand on his arm.

"I am worried about you, Gaspar. You are so quiet. Usually it's impossible to make you shut up."

"In these circumstances it is better to be listening properly, and isn't it good that one of us is?" he said, trying to pull the tack tighter across Sancha's back, but his fingers slipped off.

"Here, do this, don't just stand there moaning at me." He was rubbing his fingers together. "This cold wind," he muttered.

The other three came out of the inn, Azalais leaning on Paul's arm. She smiled at him as he helped her into the cart, where she sat like the Queen of Sheba.

"Onwards to the blessed shrines of Bordeaux," said Gaspar, and he pulled Sancha into a slow walk.

Illesa fell back, watching him. He was hiding something from her. She could not find out what it was with these men around, but when they were alone she would get Gaspar drunk and trick it out of him.

She checked inside her padded tunic where she had sewn her coin. Richard was within reach. Just a few walls lay between them. A few walls and a few soldiers. But the saints were not constrained by walls or soldiers. And she had an offering that would surely please them.

There was a mass of thick grey cloud above the city as they joined a trickle of people coming from the harbour. A few pilgrims with their staffs and badges were amongst the fishermen and traders returning from a day's work. Five soldiers guarded the base of the gate, and there were three more on top of the postern facing the river. The guards were stopping people one by one. Some were quickly allowed through, others had their baskets and packs unloaded and fingered.

"Shall we explain for you, as we have been before?" Paul asked, going to the front.

Azalais smiled and lowered her eyes.

"How very kind you are. You know so well how these things work."

"Come to the side, you are blocking the way," a small guard said as they all stopped in front of him. "You have to pay to bring in a cart," he said, waving his gloved hand at the cavalcade.

Gaspar reversed Sancha and pulled her to a halt just outside the gate arch. Azalais was smiling beneficently from her seat on the back.

"Get down, Goodwife, we need to inspect the cart," another guard insisted.

"Sir, we are humble pilgrims, some from Rouen some from Wales, and this lady is going to Saint-Jacques to beg for a remission of her fits," Paul said, standing his ground. "She cannot walk far."

"Looks healthy enough to me," said the small guard, leering at her.

Illesa looked at Gaspar, but he was letting Paul do the talking and watching with an innocent and wondering expression. Playing dumb.

"The cart is only to transport this poor woman," continued Paul.

"Do not worry," said Azalais in her most proud Gascon accent. "I am well enough to stand for this guard as he does his duty. He must keep the city safe."

"You are Gascon, Madam?" he asked, pulling the coverings from the back of the cart and putting them back again.

"I am from Dax, but I have spent many happy years in Bordeaux, and my heart is glad to see it again."

"And it's glad to see you, I'm sure," muttered Gaspar, only loud enough for Illesa to hear.

"And who are these others?"

"They are my Welsh cousins. They are accompanying me to Compostella, and there they will pray to be blessed with a son."

"Very well, you may go in. But if you aren't gone from the city in three days, you will have to report to the Mayor's office to pay for your dole," the taller guard said, waving the pilgrims out of the way.

"Get going," said the short guard, swinging some keys on his belt. "We are locking up soon."

Azalais was helped back into the cart and settled under her blankets by both Paul and André, before Gaspar was even allowed to guide Sancha through the gate and into the crowds of the city.

"All the hospitals will say we look too wealthy," Azalais insisted. "We should make straight for the Moon Inn and hope they have enough beds." No one disagreed with her, although it would be costly. Keeping Azalais content was most important now, and several nights on hard boards in a hospital would certainly make her cross.

Most of the people they passed ignored them, except for some small boys touting for the taverns and inns. It reminded Illesa of how she had met William years ago, doing this same job, and more, for the horse thieves. But now he was the person keeping their home safe. She hoped. Fixing things and being alert, like these small, dirty boys with their knotted hair, wanting a last penny's worth of trade before the sun set completely.

Paul kicked out at one of them who came close to the cart.

"Get away, you!"

"Don't hurt him," Illesa said, before she could stop herself.

"They are like rats, running underfoot making the streets filthy," Paul said and shouted a curse at the boys who were watching him, just out of reach.

They laughed, shouted back and disappeared into the narrow alleys between the tall merchants' houses.

The inn was close to the city's south wall and its gate. They let Paul and André go in to find out about beds and fodder while they stood next to the cart in the wet road, watching the last light that had broken free of the cloud.

"At least from here we can get out of town easily," Gaspar said, "although it seems we will have company. You have bewitched those men, Azalais. We will have to go to Compostella, listening to their tongues wagging all the way. You have wound them up on your spindle," said Gaspar, not smiling.

"I can get rid of them soon enough," remarked Azalais sharply. "Look how quickly I lost Jean."

They said nothing else until the men came out, looking proud of themselves.

The inn had plenty of food and fodder, but it came at a high price. Illesa tried not to show her worry. Jean had already taken much of their money, and she didn't know how much they would need to get home.

Paul and André would not eat more than bread and thin ale before their watch in the Cathedral, but Azalais asked for meat and wine. She was happy now she was back in her country, where they cooked things properly, and barely looked up when Paul and André left.

Illesa leant in to talk to Gaspar and Azalais.

"When you have finished, let's go to the stable to check the cart. We can talk out there."

"It's cold outside, and the stable boy will be listening," said Azalais, wiping a fingertip along the edge of the platter and putting it in her mouth. "Talk here. No one will hear us. They are all drunk."

"And I, for one, plan to join them," said Gaspar, draining his second cup.

"You must be sober tomorrow, Gaspar."

"Oh yes, sober as a monk! When have I ever been incapable because of wine?" he asked, pouring more from the green clay jug. "I have many ideas of how to get the Archbishop's attention. Would you like me to tell you all of them or just the most amusing one?"

"You need to remember you are not at the silly English court with their strange sense of humour," said Azalais, pushing the empty platter to the side. "The people who live in Bordeaux are proud and serious. They like high art, not rude jokes. They appreciate beauty and music."

Gaspar raised an eyebrow.

"That is exactly why I have a plan which includes you, princess. Who can resist your seriousness after wine?"

They continued to bicker, so Illesa went out. The yard was fully dark now, with just a sliver of moon. One torch burned by the cart barn. She went over to it, allowing her eyes to accustom to the dark shadows. If they released Richard, he would need to ride in the cart, and he was heavier than Azalais. At least he had been before he was imprisoned. Perhaps he could ride Sancha and they could abandon the cart. It slowed them down and made them conspicuous. But to ride he would need the use of both legs.

Her fingers found the special hidden clasps that kept the board over the secret compartment. After some wiggling, they swung out and the board lifted slightly so she could get a fingernail underneath and lever it up. There was hardly any light, so no point unwrapping it. She put her hand on the tight cerecloth. It felt slightly damp but not wet. Inside the parcel, the saints and serpents would be glowing with gold thread.

Footsteps were coming across the cobbles, but it was an acrobat's tread, light and swift. She replaced the board as Gaspar came into the barn.

"Is there anyone in the yard?" she whispered.

He shook his head, his eyes just dark shadows under his cap.

"Where did you hide the monk's habit?"

He drew close to the cart and helped her to lift the board away again.

"Under the cerecloth, in the same parcel as the cope hood. I will need them both at the same time."

Sometimes Illesa had to stop herself from feeling surprised at Gaspar. He came across as so carefree and spontaneous that she was often shocked when she realised he had been planning carefully. But he had been a player since childhood and would have had to prepare the costumes to wear.

She felt around in the compartment near the shafts until she found the smaller packet and handed it to Gaspar. He put it under his arm as if it were of no importance. Illesa stopped the complaint before it left her lips. Gaspar was right, the less attention they paid to it the better.

"Do you think the Archbishop is here? He might be travelling." Illesa's heart was heavy at the thought. Bishops were rarely in their seat as they were so involved with the business of kings and cardinals.

"He's here. I asked in the inn. He is getting old and lazy. Doesn't want to go to Rome, the innkeeper said. Hates the Pope."

"Really? But – "

"For us this is very good. He feels the Pope disregards the needs of Gascony. He doesn't like King Edward either, but our gift does not represent him. Rather it represents the rewards of Heaven and the fellowship of the clergy to a faithful servant of Christ," he said in a quiet version of his royal stage voice. "This gift is a vow fulfilled from beyond the grave. It should be presented with many candles at vespers, so it has the most impact. And we must carry the cope as if it were a person. At least in his presence."

"It sounds like one of your plays," she said doubtfully.

"It *is* a play. A play that will show the Archbishop how glorious he will be when he is wearing the cope, but not until he has promised to release Richard. Otherwise he might seize it, and then we have nothing," he said mournfully. "I trust bishops no more than I trust kings."

"You are full of blasphemy," said Illesa, smiling. Gaspar's plan could work. All his plays made the audience feel exactly as he wanted them to. "What if he keeps us waiting for days before he will give us an audience?"

"He won't. Would you, if someone said they had a beautiful gift for you?"

"I would if I didn't trust them."

"He will trust me. I have just the right words for him."

"I remember when you made up words in a play. That didn't go very well." He had ended up without an ear, which was why he always kept his hair long.

"This is quite different, my dear," he said archly.

"What time will you go?"

"I must present myself to the Abbey of Sainte Croix first."

"Are you going to do this alone? The real Prior of Bath Abbey would have at least one monk to serve him."

"My servant, Brother Stephen, sadly died on the sea voyage. We have buried him near the shrine in Pons and said a Mass for his soul. I spent a shilling on candles, I loved that lad so."

"Gaspar!"

"Well, I am the Prior and I may love the monks under me as sons," he said, his eye glinting in the dark. "There must be an explanation, and that is as good as any. We thought it was sea-sickness, but it turned out to be much worse."

"Very well," said Illesa. "I feel like mourning the lad myself now."

"You might need to. I would have asked you to dress as a monk and serve me, but I don't think your womanly form will be as easily disguised as it used to be." Gaspar said, casting a critical eye over her. "So you will just have to come dressed as yourself."

Illesa's heart began to hammer.

"I thought that you were going to negotiate with the Archbishop."

"I had thought that would be enough, but from what I've heard about him, we will require more leverage. He is hard on the rich, but can be merciful to those who are humble. He loves people to abase themselves, then he can dispense his largesse." Gaspar and Azalais had obviously been talking about it without her, and decisions had already been made. They'd decided she could be that humble person, because of the way she had been raised. "I am merely there as your man," Gaspar was saying. "You don't have a father or husband to put the case for you, so I am there to do that. It is up to you to make him feel good about what he is going to do."

"I am not good at acting. You know that." He should remember. It had been a disaster when she'd tried it.

Gaspar shrugged.

"You can play this part, as it is no more and no less than the truth. Richard's wife is longing for his release in the face of the marauding Welsh. You are not threatening him, just doing the will of Bishop Robert Burnel."

"But what if he takes the cope and refuses to help us?"

"He can search for the cope as much as he likes, but he will not find it until we have Richard."

"I don't understand how that will work," she said.

Gaspar walked away into the wet yard. Light rain was falling and shining on the cobbles. She followed him, drawing her cloak close to her throat.

"Just do exactly what I say, or the French might lock us up in there." He gestured to the north where it was possible to see the Tour l'Arbalesteyre by the torches on its outside stair. Large and well guarded, the tower where Richard was imprisoned had many flaming eyes.

From the inn came a voice as pure as a songbird above the water.

> *"Let fools say that it's not right*
> *for a lady to court a man she likes,*
> *a man who's shapely and of good height.*
> *I will prove to all you here*
> *that courting brings me great relief*
> *when I scorn the man who's brought me grief."*

"She doesn't understand the concept of inconspicuousness, but you have to admit her voice could tame a wolf," Gaspar said brightly. "We could use it to our advantage, not just to seduce unworthy drunkards. Let's get her to bed before the word spreads." He opened the door to the hall, and they went into the light and noise. "You will have all the dogs howling soon if you carry on," he called to Azalais.

Chapter XXVIII

Friday the 25th November 1295
Bordeaux
Sext

Illesa knelt at the statue of the Virgin, but her mind was wound tight and would not pray. She should be saying prayers for her son, her daughter, for protection from drowning, from fever. It was too long since she had felt the blessing of a saint, and her mind was entirely consumed with this worldly exchange, this knot that must be untied. First to persuade the Archbishop to help them, then, somehow, to release Richard from under the nose of the French commander.

At the east end of the Cathedral, the cantor was practising his psalms and having trouble reaching the high note. It would have made Azalais groan. The candle in front of the statue guttered and swayed like a snake. Out of the corner of her eye, she saw Gaspar coming through the side door, his hands hidden in the long black sleeves of his habit, his head bowed to show his newly shaved tonsure. He looked so unlike himself, so pale and serious, she would not have known him, except that she had shaved his head that morning.

Illesa got up from where she had been kneeling and gave thanks under her breath for his safety thus far. Gaspar's Latin was not perfect, but he must have convinced them at the Abbey of Sainte Croix. Presumably they were used to strangers, being one of the principal stops on the road to Saint-Jacques.

Gaspar had paused to kneel, facing the altar. When he got up, he stumbled, and put out his hand to stop his fall. The wool sack holding the cope hood fell instead, out of his sleeve and onto the flagstone. Illesa moved to pick it up, handing it to him, her head lowered.

He blessed her, and they walked side by side up the nave towards the north door.

"You look tired," she whispered.

"No, I feel so refreshed. I found a fisherman to row me up the ditch outside the walls to save my strength, thanks be to God. The miracle of light on water has opened my eyes to the Lord's bounty. Now let us pray that the Archbishop has time to see us."

It was unnerving being with Gaspar when he would not step back into his normal character.

"How were the brothers at Sainte Croix?" she asked.

"Most holy and thoroughly disinterested. They were grateful that I had made arrangements to be lodged elsewhere. The Prior will see me tomorrow. He is up to his nose in French soldiers at the moment, requisitioning all his wine and cider. Not a happy man. Wishes the Archbishop would offer more protection. Wants me to mention it."

"Ah."

"The French soldiers were slightly more curious. They examined me minutely as to the reason for my visit to Bordeaux. I had to make some interesting inventions. I hope they aren't so trying every time I go in and out of the walls."

Gaspar's voice had taken on a sonorous and measured quality, as if he were reciting the Mass.

"Remember not to speak until I have introduced you. You should be humbled to be meeting him, almost unable to speak because of his holy being."

He was giving her directions for the play, which they had barely rehearsed. Her heart started pounding, and she laced her hands together inside her sleeves. They walked out of the north door towards the Archbishop's gatehouse. Beyond it was a wide hall with many tall glazed windows overlooking the Cathedral.

"I wonder who is guarding the Archbishop's palace," Gaspar whispered. "Hopefully not more French."

Strangely, the guard on duty was also a monk – a Templar Priest, tall and scarred, but unarmed.

"Your names, travellers," he demanded in a Gascon accent.

Another guard appeared from the inside of the gatehouse. This one had a helmet and crossbow. He looked at them briefly, before turning to watch a young priest being admonished by a canon for arriving late for the office.

Gaspar bowed briefly and smiled beneficently.

"Good Brother, we are travellers from Bath Abbey in England. We have come on the long journey to Bordeaux to give the Archbishop the fulfilment of a promise made to him years ago by the Bishop of Bath and Wells." He held out the parchment that Illesa had written in her best imitation of a clerk's hand and sealed with her father's seal.

The Templar glanced at it and then at them.

"Your name is Gerald, the Prior of Bath Abbey?"

"Indeed."

"And who is this?"

"A relative of the deceased Bishop who has come to see the promise fulfilled. We would be grateful if you could take this to the Archbishop and tell him that we wait upon him."

Gaspar held out the white wool sack and placed it carefully in the Templar's gloved hands. He looked at it with a curious expression, as if it were a serpent's egg.

"The Blessed Henri is in residence," he said, "but he has been ill. He may not wish to see you. Wait here." The Templar strode away towards the palace. The other guard came to stand close to Gaspar and pulled the strap of his crossbow down so that it was within reach.

"We pose no threat to the Archbishop," Gaspar said reproachfully. "What times are these when a Brother in Christ must be threatened?"

"Monks are not saints," the guard said briefly. He coughed and spat out phlegm on the path.

It seemed a long time before the Templar emerged from the door of the palace, empty-handed. He beckoned them forward, and the other guard closed the gate behind them, his crossbow returned to its resting position. They walked through the wide doorway into a bright hall furnished with a large table and an ornate chair. It was empty.

"Archbishop Henri will see you in this chamber."

He led them through a door in the east wall into a small hot room. A large fire burned in the hearth. The Archbishop sat with his back to the only window in shadow.

"Stay here, Father Raymond." The Archbishop's voice was soft and slurred, but there was still a tone of command.

The Templar stood by the door. There would be no way of leaving unless he allowed it.

"Come forward and stand where I can see you," the Archbishop said in his strange voice.

He stood up from his chair and held out his hand. Gaspar knelt and kissed the large ruby in the centre of his ring of office. He stayed kneeling for a moment as if transfixed.

Illesa followed Gaspar, then they both rose and stood where the winter light shone fully on them, facing the dark figure of the old man dressed in a surplice edged in gold. He sat down slowly in his cushioned chair. The fire crackled, and Illesa tensed. She turned her head slightly and caught the eye of the Templar.

"You have brought something I never thought to see," the Archbishop said. "A gift from England." The words seemed bitter in his mouth.

Illesa's eyes were adjusting to the shadow. The Archbishop was speaking out of only one side of his mouth. Half of his face was slumped and sunken, and the eye on that side was weeping. The other half of his face was rigid. The hood lay on the small, carved table by his side, the sheen of its pearls reflecting light from the window.

Gaspar opened his mouth to speak, but the Archbishop raised his hand and Gaspar subsided.

"You come from England with this English work. So I wish to know what you mean by bringing it to me. This is not a gift, it is a rag torn from a bishop's vestment."

Illesa dragged her eyes away from his palsied face and remembered she was meant to be humble. She pressed her hands together and stared at the floor.

"Your Grace, I bring to you just a small portion of what is yours," Gaspar said, holding his hands out reverently.

Archbishop Henri's face shook with the effort of speech.

"I have read the letter from your Abbot, Prior. But it explains nothing about this." He pointed to the hood as if it were alive.

"Your Grace, it was necessary to keep this quiet on our journey. Have I your leave to explain?"

The Archbishop lifted the palm of his hand in acceptance.

"I was the sacristan during the tenure of Robert Burnel, the Chancellor, as Bishop of Bath and Wells. He made arrangements through me with an embroiderer in London to complete a cope for the Archbishop of Bordeaux. I believe that when he was here several years ago with Edward, King of England and Duke of Aquitaine, he promised you this gift?"

"The Chancellor made many promises," the Archbishop said, his slack mouth spraying drops of spittle that caught the light. "So did Edward," he said scornfully. "And look where we are now. Invaded. Trapped inside these walls while the French soldiers drink our wine and eat our meat outside. And Edward remains safe on his little island."

"It is a terrible state of affairs," agreed Gaspar, placatingly. "There has been little to recommend either side, I hear."

"Well, it is the Gascons that are taken prisoner. Even the citizens of Bordeaux from the most important families are being sent off to Carcassonne to die. Our churches are plundered. The English King has sent one small army and accomplished nothing. He treats us with disdain. Meanwhile, the French King thinks we are his buttery and his pantry." Spittle was now dripping down his chin, but the Archbishop was unaware. He breathed heavily, exhausted by his anger.

"This is but a small gesture to make amends. At a time when all is being set ablaze, we bring you a gift, made for your Cathedral, to bring the light of Saint André to the people."

The Archbishop reached out a shaking hand and took his glass from the table. Pale wine spilt from one side of his mouth. He took a long time to find the white linen napkin on the table and lift it to his lips.

"So you say, but all I see is the head without the body. The Chancellor was a man of many stratagems. Always wanting agreements – land for new fortified towns, nunneries, pardons. He would not leave me alone for all the requests! I made only one of him – a new cope of this 'English Work' for the Cathedral processions. And this is all I have after nine years!" His stiff, claw-like hand rested on the hood.

"We have brought you the whole cope, Your Grace," Gaspar said, coming a step forward. "It is the finest work I have ever seen, with the surface completely covered in the most exquisite embroidery. The thread is of gold and silks of many colours set with seed pearls. It is far too large and grand to carry in a cart through the city to your palace."

The Templar coughed and shifted his position against the door. But Gaspar's gaze stayed fixed on the Archbishop. He spread out his arms, as if holding a great swathe of cloth.

"Your Grace, allow me to describe it to you," Gaspar said, risking a different, more confident tone.

"If it exists, which I doubt, I will see it with my own eyes," the Archbishop said, jutting his head forward.

"It exists indeed, just as the birds of the air and the great beasts of the plain do. It shows the Creation of the World, the Fall and Redemption of sinners through our Lord Jesus Christ in stitches so fine that they seem to be the work of angels." Gaspar lowered his voice. "Imagine the space between these scenes linked by dragons and seraphim, our worldly life lived out between Heaven and Hell, while the saints that gild the edges stand guard over our souls."

The Archbishop grunted and shifted in his chair.

"Did you request that Saint André was to be included? For he is there alongside other powerful saints on the cope. The city will rejoice in its holy saviour when you wear it for Mass on his feast day. It will be a sight that inspires the hearts of every burgess of Bordeaux."

"You are very talkative, for a monk," the Archbishop complained, wiping his weeping eye with the napkin.

"This is true," Gaspar smiled apologetically. "My Abbot remonstrates with me for this sin. My words have a beginning but not an ending, he says. It is like Heaven, I reply. He disagrees."

"Enough," the Archbishop said, leaning forward angrily. "I wish to know why you have brought this now. The Chancellor has been dead for years. You have not come all this way in the midst of war to please me."

"Your grace and favour is humbly sought. But you are most wise. There is more of the story to tell. If you will allow?"

"Keep to the point of the tale." The Archbishop sank back in his chair, his palsied face falling in rest.

"The cope was completed when the Chancellor died, but the cost had not been met. So the Chancellor left instructions in his will that the cope should be paid for out of his estate, with the intention of presenting it to you during a state visit to Gascony. Sadly a delegation could not be sent due to the hostilities with France," Gaspar said with a mournful smile. "The cope was stored safely at the Chancellor's birthplace near Wales. This brave woman protected it and has arranged for it to be brought here now, fulfilling the promise of the Chancellor, despite the danger to herself."

Silence filled the room. Illesa kept her eyes on the Archbishop's table. She felt light-headed, as if she were about to fly out of the window. She rocked on the soles of her feet. It would not be helpful if she fainted now.

"And who is this woman? Can she not speak?"

Illesa looked at Gaspar, and he nodded slightly.

"Your Grace," she cleared her throat, now looking at his ring of office. "I am the wife of Sir Richard Burnel, cousin of the blessed Robert. My husband was ever trusted by the Lord Chancellor to complete his affairs and to show due care for his obligations. We have been holding this precious pluviale for you for two years. Sir Richard was sent out to liberate the Duchy from French control, but the war in Wales prevented further men from coming to their aid and he was taken hostage." She glanced quickly up and wished she hadn't. The Archbishop appeared to have fallen asleep. "He has been held here in the tower since Easter," she said more loudly, "and we have little news of his health. When I appealed to the Abbot in Bath, he suggested that we fulfil this promise in the hope that, as I light candles to the saints, this great offering to Saint André and my earnest prayers will allow my husband to be set free."

Gaspar extended one of his fingers, and she stopped speaking. The Archbishop opened his eyes and reached for his wine.

"My Lord Archbishop, this beautiful cope is here in Bordeaux," Gaspar began, opening his palms and smiling. "We wish to bring it to you without the French soldiers procuring it and also to discuss how this poor lady's husband might be set free to enjoy the blessings of Christ again, so that two good deeds may come out of this darkness."

The Archbishop swallowed his mouthful, and fixed his eyes on Illesa.

216

"You have come here with false and corrupted expectations, lady. We live under occupation. I cannot do what you desire, even if I wished to."

"Your Grace is most merciful," Gaspar replied quickly. "We understand that the prisoners are not your responsibility, but your priests come and go from the Palais de l'Ombrière more freely than most. Perhaps we can discuss a stratagem whereby Sir Richard might be released?" He looked round at the Templar for support, but the monk stared back impassively.

"The prisoners are due to march to the French prison in Carcassonne any day. There will be no one left to save," the Archbishop said, slurring his words badly. He made a gesture of dismissal.

Illesa turned to Gaspar. His eyes shifted between her and the Archbishop, then he bowed and stepped back towards the door.

"Your Grace, we thank you for your time. The cope will be delivered to you, according to your will. We bid you God's grace and favour."

Gaspar took her elbow. It did not require much acting for Illesa to sway and for her legs to give way under her. The Templar opened the door, and she was half-dragged out of the room and lowered onto a bench in the enormous hall.

"Wait for me here," said the Templar, and he went back into the Archbishop's parlour.

"That was awful," whispered Illesa.

"We will see. The Archbishop will ask the Templar to follow us. He will want the cope brought to him immediately. But that Templar had a speaking eye. I think he knows something more."

Illesa looked dubious. The Templar had seemed completely silent to her. She wiped her forehead.

"As long as you are not interested in him," she said.

Gaspar looked affronted.

"I am a Benedictine! We do not consort with Templars," he hissed as the tall monk came back into the hall.

Chapter XXIX

Bordeaux

The Templar Priest followed them through the rain, saying nothing on the way, walking beside them with a stride that spoke of long distances travelled. Illesa still felt light-headed. Around every corner she looked for lines of prisoners being dragged to Carcassonne.

Gaspar had the hood of his scapular up, as if at prayer. She hoped he did pray for some holy helper to intervene because it seemed they were about to lose the only chance they had to release Richard.

Eventually they reached the inn. The cart stood just where they had left it in the barn.

"I will ask the innkeeper for a private room," the Templar said and went through the door to the hall, bending his head to avoid the low lintel.

"This is going to look interesting. A Templar, a Benedictine and a lady walk into an inn," Gaspar said. "All we need is Azalais, and we will have the full hurly-burly."

"She said she was going to visit the family who live near the Palais de l'Ombrière, to get news of the French." Azalais had not wished to say any more about this family, and Illesa suspected that there had been a liaison.

"May the good Lord let her stay there all day," Gaspar muttered.

The inn door opened and the Templar beckoned them from the doorway.

They went through the hall, which only held one old, wheezing man drinking a strong-smelling cider. There was no sign of Azalais.

The private chamber behind the hall was usually the sleeping quarters for the innkeeper's servants or children. They had quickly swept the mattresses to the side of the room, but there was still the smell of unwashed bodies. Illesa and Gaspar sat at the trestle table with their backs to the window, the Templar facing them, waiting while the innkeeper's wife put down a jug of wine and three cups, barely looking at her three guests. Her life was probably full of strangeness, and more than ever since the war. She closed the door behind her without a word, securing the latch.

Gaspar pulled the hood back from his head and put on the friendly and enquiring gaze that he used on anyone who frightened him.

The Templar took off his long gloves, gave thanks for the wine and they all brought the cups to their lips. The Templar set his down carefully in front of him and spread his hands out flat on the table.

"Now, I don't want to hear any more stories. What you tell me from now on must be the truth," he said, staring at his hands on the table as if they were animals that might scuttle off of their own accord. "The Archbishop has bad eyes. Even before the palsy, he could hardly see an arm in front of his face. So he did not notice your new tonsure or the faked seal on your letter of protection." He looked up and stared at Gaspar. "So you can start by telling me your real name."

Gaspar licked his lips and smiled again.

"May you do the courtesy of telling us yours so that we know how to address you?"

The man nodded slowly.

"Father Raymond of Sergeac."

"Gaspar of St Albans."

"Not a Benedictine," the Templar concluded.

"No. And I am very disappointed that you noticed. The tonsure will take ages to grow out," Gaspar said lightly. He folded his hands over one another on the table. "But I can assure you that this is indeed Lady Burnel, wife of Sir Richard."

The Templar nodded but did not look at her. Illesa felt anger rising to her cheeks. It was forbidden for Templars to touch women, but surely not to look at them.

"Father Raymond," she began. But he held up his hand.

"I will ask the questions, and you will provide the answers," he said simply and drank again from his cup, setting it down with great deliberation. "Beware of Greeks bearing gifts," he said soberly, "even if the gift is a holy offering. Isn't that what we are taught by the Ancients?" He touched his lips, hiding a slight smile. "But I would see this cope you speak so highly of, and then we will discuss the next step in this matter."

"It is outside hidden in a cart," Gaspar said. "Well wrapped in cerecloth."

"I see." The Templar cocked his head as if listening to the sounds of the hall. "We need more privacy than we have here at the inn. Do you have a horse?"

Gaspar and Illesa nodded in unison.

"We will go to the house of an associate of the Temple. They have a good room, and they are loyal. I suggest that you change out of your habit and put on your true clothes. We will look less conspicuous.

Gaspar got up silently and left the room.

"He will not run," Illesa said under her breath.

Father Raymond's eyes met hers briefly.

"There are just two of you travelling together?"

"No. I have a companion, a woman of Dax. My cousin. She went to visit her friend near the Palais."

"Her name?"

"Azalais."

"A good Occitan name. But you are not from here, I think, judging by your accent."

"My mother was also from Dax. She died in England, when I was born."

He nodded.

"We will wait for this Azalais. She will need to come with us."

Gaspar entered the room, back in his travelling clothes, his cap on his head.

"Only a player could change clothes so quickly," the Templar said.

Gaspar nodded. He looked completely unnerved. Illesa reached out her hand to him.

"Sit down, Gaspar. We must wait for Azalais."

"Must we? In that case, let's at least have some food. It has been a long day already and my stomach is paining me."

Gaspar's stomach rumbled on cue.

Father Raymond smiled.

"I am also hungry, but I've heard the food here is dreadful."

"It's not so bad, if you drink plenty at the same time." Gaspar went into the hall, and they heard him ordering a good frumenty and some fish. The Templar insisted on eating in silence, so it was an uncomfortable meal.

Just as they were finishing, Azalais' voice could be heard in the hall, loudly asking the innkeeper's wife where they were.

Illesa went to the door and beckoned to her, putting a finger to her lips as Azalais approached.

"Oh, you have a visitor!" she cried, sweeping into the room. "Father," she curtseyed, "I am sorry to interrupt you."

The Templar rose to his feet, frowning.

"We have been waiting for you. Gaspar and I will ready the cart while your cousin tells you what she must."

Azalais grabbed Illesa's hand as the men left and the innkeeper came to clear the table. They stood close by the window.

"What has happened? Who is that?"

"A Templar Priest, Father Raymond. He is acting for the Archbishop. He saw through Gaspar straight away. Didn't tell the Archbishop, but he has followed us here and wants the cope. I don't know what else he wants, but he wouldn't leave without you."

"You shouldn't have told him about me!"

"You wouldn't have wanted us to just disappear without you, would you? We must get our things quickly. He may not let us return."

"You could have found me again afterwards," Azalais said, angrily stamping the dirt from her boots. "Now we will all be locked up."

"Don't moan about it. He would have found out about you anyway from the innkeeper," Illesa said, pulling her across to the door.

They went into the upstairs chamber they shared, and Azalais agitatedly started gathering her extra clothes. Illesa began to do the same and then remembered the weasel, left shut in a cupboard with a small dish of milk.

"Whose side of the war do you think he is on? Is he spying on the Archbishop?" Azalais asked, folding her second veil into the pack.

"I don't know, but the Archbishop seemed to trust him. He is from Sergeac," Illesa said. She unlocked the cupboard, and the weasel ran straight up her arm to her shoulder.

"Then he is a Gascon, and he should help us," Azalais said, sounding satisfied.

Illesa wrinkled her nose. She didn't have time to clean the mess in the cupboard.

"Make a bundle inside the blanket. We can put it all in the cart," Illesa said.

They went quickly and quietly down the stairs. At the bottom, the innkeeper's wife was waiting but fortunately not Paul or André.

"You leaving?"

"No, we are going to visit someone with the Father."

"What about those other pilgrims you were with?"

"We aren't with anyone else, we just spoke to them on the road," Azalais said firmly.

"I want payment for the night and food," the woman said, rolling one of her sleeves up her muscled arm.

Illesa did not have enough in her small purse, and she had to snip open one of the hiding places in her cloak. The innkeeper's wife examined each coin carefully before putting it in the cloth bag she kept in her bosom.

Illesa turned to Azalais, who was standing quietly by the door. The sound of Sancha's hooves on the cobbles outside told her that the rain had strengthened while they packed. She put the chattering weasel into the pouch at her waist with steady hands. The fear she had felt in the presence of the Archbishop was gone. Father Raymond was severe, but there was something about him that inspired trust.

Sancha was indifferent to the rain and glad to be out of the stable. She shook her mane and stamped, ready to be off. Gaspar stood at her head, back in his simple pilgrim role with Father Raymond by his side. Azalais took up her place on the cart, sitting on her bundle of clothes, leaving Illesa to follow.

They went north towards the old part of the city, past shops sweeping out the dirt of the day and closing their shutters. Past the barracks, the guards and the old broken wall, turning west into the last of the light, past a dark, old church, and on towards the far wall of the city. The street narrowed. At the very end abutting the wall, was the outline of a Temple. The monk stopped them a stone's throw from it at a house with a cross on the door. The house belonged to a wine merchant, judging by the barrel above the door and the smell coming from the open cellar.

Father Raymond called down into the dark.

"In God's name I come, and for his glory."

"In God's name I answer," came a deep-throated reply.

A large man, almost bald but with an impressive beard, came slowly up the steep steps from the cellar. He embraced Father Raymond and looked at the group curiously.

"I beg your help, Master Monadey," the Templar said in an undertone. "We need a private room where we will not be disturbed in order to examine the goods these friends have brought for the Brothers."

The merchant put his hand inside his jerkin and pulled out a cloth, blowing his nose loudly before replying.

"Of course. Bring the horse through to the back yard." He went straight to the side gate and unlatched it.

"Bring light!" he shouted through the gate. "We have a holy visitor. Bring wine!"

They were led through to the yard, which was full of basins and baskets. The servants had been gathering reeds, and the bundles gave off a sweet smell. A lad came forward and took Sancha's halter.

"Should I take the harness off?"

"Yes," the Templar said. "Let her put down her burden."

Azalais raised an eyebrow at Illesa as she helped her down from the cart. They would be here for some time, it seemed.

"I know of this family," Azalais whispered in her ear. "They are good Gascons."

Gaspar followed them into the merchant's house, humming a tune Illesa didn't recognise. She was sure he was trying to tell her something by it. Inside, two women set down the boards for the table and pulled up the benches. Father Raymond stood in the middle of the room, watching.

"Just some wine, Marie. We have broken bread already. I hope not to keep you long away from your room. We need the doors closed, if you please."

Once the curious glances of the women were shut behind the hall door, Illesa and Gaspar returned to the cart and between them carried the parcel inside, laying it down on the table.

"Let us see," said Father Raymond.

And they all began to untie the rope, like children suddenly longing to see the beauty within and to impress this man who seemed so aloof. The back was revealed first, with the scenes of Adam and Eve. The ornate, pearled dalmatic was folded inside, for extra protection.

"Stop," the Templar said, bending close to the cope and examining the scene where Adam, Eve and the serpent gathered round the Tree of Knowledge. "I give thanks to God for these good eyes to see such a thing."

He did not speak as they gradually unfolded and spread out the garment until it was a half-circle, part of it hanging down over the edge of the wide table.

"You did not lie about this," he said, straightening up after he had carefully examined each quatrefoil. "These seraphim will begin to sing when this is worn," he remarked, touching them with the tip of his finger.

"It is the most magnificent cope ever to be made. And all we want in return is one man. Not an earl or a duke, just a knight. I cannot see why this should be a problem." It had been hard for Azalais to hold her tongue all this time, and her tone was petulant.

The monk sat down on one of the benches.

"Pour the wine, Gaspar of St Albans."

"With pleasure," Gaspar said. He picked up the jug and began pouring, but it sloshed over the side of the cups and down the sideboard.

"Careful," shouted Azalais. "Do you want to mark the silk?"

"These old, unsteady hands," he said mournfully. Illesa found a cloth by the bucket at the back door and wiped up the spilt wine. She poured it into the cups. Gaspar wouldn't meet her eye. She took the cups across to the others, and Gaspar sat down, his hands tucked away under his tunic.

"Who is it that makes the decisions in this group of people?" asked Father Raymond. Both Gaspar and Azalais looked at Illesa. She took a deep breath.

"My husband asked us to bring the cope and negotiate with the Archbishop for his release. My friend and my cousin have come to help accomplish this at their own risk. I am indebted to them, but the cost of the voyage is mine."

"Very well. I will speak with you in the presence of the others," he said reluctantly. "I see that the substance of your story was true and that the falsehood was used to avoid the seizure of the cope by French soldiers. Impersonating a monk is a sin, but I understand this is what you regularly do, Gaspar, and that you were playing the monk in order to open the door to the Archbishop. I need to ask if any monastic authorities know you are bringing this here."

"No, Father," Illesa said, glancing at Gaspar. "The cope was hidden in the Chancellor's estate to prevent it from falling into the hands of the current bishop. We are simply trying to carry out my – the Chancellor's will."

If the monk noticed the slip, he made no remark.

"So this is the cope made for the Archbishop as a diplomatic gift from the English King through his Chancellor. Worth at least forty livres. But worth so much more now, because there is little chance of a gift like this being made again, since the hostilities began between the two kings. And you decided to carry it in an old cart through the occupied city, hoping to release a hostage and escape back to England?" The Templar smiled, making the scar on his forehead stand out white against his weathered skin. "You have been reading some of the old tales, I think? But you should know from those stories that the fates of those who go to war are in God's hands."

"Sir Richard asked us to bring it, and that is what we have done. It is a suitable offering. Just because we haven't got a diplomatic mission with us does not lessen the gift," Illesa asserted.

"But I fear it does, Lady Burnel. It means that the gift has little status, if it is not presented by a person of high rank."

"It was willed to the Archbishop by the Chancellor himself. The delay should not be important. He wants it, doesn't he?"

The Templar sat back a little and looked straight at Illesa.

"He wants it, but he is afraid. He doesn't want to be on the wrong side of the war, so he is on neither side. He will only speak out for the people of Bordeaux, and even that has little effect since his palsy. It makes him seem weak and unable to stand up to the French."

"I heard of the death of Jean Colom at Carcassonne," Azalais broke in. "One of Bordeaux's most beloved sons. The whole city is ready to rebel against the French for it, but they need a leader."

The Templar shook his head.

"They are just as angry with the English who caused the war by their stupidity. They are angry, but they hope to survive with their city intact and not have it razed to the ground by the victorious army if they choose to back the wrong side. So you have little hope of help from the Archbishop or any of the city leaders."

"But might we have your help, for mercy's sake?" Gaspar asked quietly. He held out his cup gingerly, as if offering the Holy Grail.

The Templar looked down at the cope in front of them.

"I met Sir Richard at Rions. We fought on the same side against the invading army. He helped me when I was attacked."

Illesa let out a breath.

"Was he injured?"

"No more than he was already, as far as I saw," Father Raymond said. "But after the French broke through the walls, he was rounded up with the other English and put in the gaol. I did not see him again." He looked up at Gaspar. "It will be very difficult to get him out of the Tour l'Arbalesteyre. He can barely walk."

Tears began to fall down Illesa's cheeks, and she wiped them away impatiently.

"But you can help us? You will help us?"

Father Raymond spread his hands out over the cope as he seemed to do when thinking.

226

"It is a fair exchange you offer. And it is my duty to help pilgrims, when I can." He felt for the crucifix around his neck. "We can make an attempt to release him from the French, but if it goes ill, they will not be merciful. It may be better to wait for an end to the fighting. He might survive, even in Carcassonne."

"But Richard asked us to bring it," Illesa said, her heart pounding. "He must be kept in poor conditions. He would not risk his men otherwise."

"Or his wife?" asked Father Raymond.

"He does not know that I have come. He meant his groom to bring it."

She knew Richard would be angry with William, and with her. He would be angry with himself for suggesting it. But if all went well, the anger would not last long.

The weasel woke and began to make high-pitched hungry squeaks. Father Raymond leant forward as Illesa opened the pouch, and the weasel raced up to her shoulder where she sat washing her face.

"I thought I caught the smell of the wild. Is it tame?"

"Almost. I will feed her, and she will become calmer," Illesa said. "But we were speaking of how to help Richard. Do you know when he is going to be moved to Carcassonne?"

"It will be Monday," said Azalais. "I heard from the guards at the house of the Rostan family. The officials have requisitioned provisions for the journey to be delivered by Sunday. Then they will pack it on the barges."

"That is good," said Father Raymond. "We have a Sunday. The prisoners will hear Mass before they depart." He put his hands together as if in prayer. "If it pleases God, that is when we will do it." He was silent for a moment then he looked up at Gaspar. "We will create a distraction and an illusion. You know about these things, Gaspar the player of St Albans. We will need to plan it very carefully." He held Gaspar's gaze until Gaspar nodded warily.

Father Raymond turned to Illesa and pointed at the cope.

"You must make this ready for Sunday morning. I will take it in the cart and present it to the Archbishop. But it must not be seen in public until you are out of the city. Its arrival in the Cathedral will attract the attention of the Count of Artois, and that will be a good distraction from the disappearance of Sir Richard, if we achieve it." He stood in the midst of them, running his fingers over the representation of the creation of the beasts, like a seer while they waited for his vision.

"And there should be a story about its arrival that creates holy wonder. For haven't you brought it out of death and into life?" The Templar looked up to the roof beams. "Even a story that could help the English cause. To rally those left in the city who are loyal to Edward."

He cast his eyes around, and they came to rest on the weasel on Illesa's shoulder.

"All God's creatures are made for particular uses. It may be that this little fury has a skill that we can use. Let me see how you feed her."

Chapter XXX

Saturday the 26th November 1295
Palais de l'Ombrière, Bordeaux
Nones

Richard had been brought to the room and left there with a guard who was half-asleep against the wall and nothing to eat or drink. The shadows of the city's towers came across the window. It was a bright windy day, and from the water he heard the cursing of boatmen and shipmasters as their vessels were caught by a sudden gust.

Apparently one of Count Robert's mistresses had arrived from his grand estate in the north. His favourite mistress, the guard guessed. In any event, the Count must not be disturbed and had probably forgotten that he'd sent for Sir Richard. Was probably still at it, or asleep.

It had been more than a year since Richard had lain with his wife. It would be a long time yet, even if he survived. He shifted in his chair. All he desired now was to be at home and never to leave it. But getting there would either be short and brutal, or long and agonising. Perhaps it was better to seem to accept the offer of the Count, as that would at least allow him to make his way to the English enclave. And there surely someone could rid him of the Count's man.

The Count presented Almaric as a devil: ever-present, always watching. But this was only to frighten him into agreeing. Almaric would bleed like any other man. William would be a match for him, and William would surely be in Bayonne, not Blaye. Nothing was going in or out of Blaye, according to the guard, whereas Bayonne port was operating as usual.

So it was strange that the reinforcements had never arrived. The King was not busy fucking a mistress – that was not his weakness. Surely he had dealt with the Welsh by now, and Edward, with thousands of men, ought to be sailing up the Garonne to take back the towns, even to try Bordeaux. If they lost the last enclaves, they would have no chance of repossessing the Duchy.

The door opened, and a man came through carrying a large book. He set it down on the table and went out again, leaving the door open. Richard wondered how long it would take for the sleepy guard to realise he'd gone if he hobbled through the door. But another servant came in with a tray of wine and bread, and the first one returned, sat down at the table in front of the ledger, opened his ink pot and prepared his quill. It was the same clerk as before, and he still did not give Richard one glance.

He sat like that for a few moments, refusing to meet Richard's eye, before Count Robert came into the room.

"I see you are looking better," he said, smiling with his full mouth of wide-spaced teeth.

"And you also, Count Robert," Richard said before he could stop himself.

The Count stood still, regarding Richard, then laughed suddenly.

"You have heard of the arrival of my woman. You are thinking of those you have had and wondering if she is as good as them. Well, I tell you, she is better. You cannot imagine." He sat in his chair, resting his back against the carved wood with his legs out in front of him. "But you will soon be back on the road and will be able to take pleasure where you will."

"The greatest pleasure will be a comfortable bed."

Count Robert laughed. From the other side of the door came a high-pitched bark followed by the sound of paws running on floorboards.

"That is the only thing I hate about her. That fucking lap dog. Always yapping," Robert said. The sound was fading, but his face did not lose its disgust. "Food for wolves." Then his eyes lit on the tray. "Where is that boy? Tomas!" he shouted, and turned to the clerk. "Felix is here to take down the agreement between us." The clerk was still sitting, quill ready, head down.

A pageboy came in and poured the wine, giving one cup to Richard and one to the Count.

"A priest is here to see you, from the Archbishop," the page said, bowing to the Count.

Count Robert looked thoroughly annoyed. He took a swig of his wine.

"For Christ's sake, bring him in here then. Let's get it over with."

Tomas bowed again and went out.

"The Archbishop is like an old woman the way he keeps on pestering me. Constantly complaining about the bordelais hostages and the soldiers eating his carrots. As if he doesn't understand we are at war," the Count said loudly. "He wants Bordeaux to have all the privileges given to it by the English and to owe nothing to King Philip."

The door opened again and a Templar Priest came in, his face clean-shaven and familiar. He glanced briefly at Richard and away, with the slightest shake of the head.

"Count Robert," he said, bowing his head and making the sign of the cross in the air between them. "I bring you a message from Archbishop Henri."

"Yes, yes. What does he want?"

Richard stared at the Templar's profile. He was the same priest who had fought at Rions when the riot started. Alive, working for the Archbishop and unsurprised to see Richard. He missed the Templar's first words as he was so distracted by this coincidence.

"So His Grace would like to provide a priest to say Mass for the hostages before they are taken to Carcassonne. The people of Bordeaux are uneasy about this move. It would calm them to know that the prisoners heard Mass before they were taken away. There was great anger about the death of Jean Colom, especially as there is a rumour he died unshriven."

"Well, they don't want to anger me," Count Robert said, stabbing his finger on the table in time to his words. "I have no compunction at putting up some more scaffolds and hanging the troublemakers."

"No, my lord. That won't be necessary. If the people know that the prisoners are being treated well and receiving the comfort of the sacraments, they will be calmer. It is a question of balance. You allow them to take comfort in their faith, and they will not distract you from your battle with the English."

The Count drank the rest of his wine and straightened up in his chair.

"The Mass must take place in the Palais. I will not have prisoners parading into the Cathedral and causing a riot."

"In the chapel here, as you wish."

"Is the Archbishop himself coming? I don't think he's left his precinct for months."

"No, he will be in the Cathedral. He asked me to conduct Mass here later in the day, nearer the time when they depart. I am accustomed to prisons and battlefields."

"My guards must be present."

"Of course."

"What's that sound outside?"

Someone by the river was singing, in a clear, high voice. The notes rose and fell like a lark in its spring flight. A shiver ran down Richard's back.

"It sounds like a woman," said the Templar, disapprovingly.

"It is extraordinary." The Count got up and went to the window. "I have not heard that tune before. I want them to come and perform for me."

The Templar frowned.

"That is a lewd, old Occitan song from the South."

"Shut your own ears, then. The rest of us haven't taken a vow of chastity."

They were silent, listening to the song, which faded and swelled with the breeze while the rest of the life of the river seemed to be stilled. Finally the voice stopped.

"You are leaving now, Priest. Go and find out who they are, and tell them I demand they come and perform for me," the Count said, waving his finger at the Templar. "Tomorrow."

"My lord, I will get Tomas," said Felix the clerk, getting up. "It is more fitting for him to speak to them."

"No," the Count said with a little stubborn smile. "Father Raymond will do it. He has come to ask me a favour. Now he will do this for me."

"What if they are just peasants? You don't want a group of rough jongleurs by your table," said the Templar, his eyes fixed on the Count as if he were a Saracen.

232

"They are not. That voice has been trained in a court. And there is also a talented accompanist. You can hear it now; they've started up again. They must be a group of musicians with a boy singer. But he sounds so like a woman." The Count looked sidelong through the window.

"The song is fading," the Templar said, looking annoyed. "If I am to find them, I will have to leave now. I will return tomorrow for Mass." He bowed and left the room without a glance at Richard.

"Do you know that song?" the Count asked, still looking out of the window in vain. The towers were in the way of his view of the river. "La la, de da," he hummed along with the refrain.

"No," Richard lied. The song had faded away to almost nothing. The Count looked bereft, as if every good memory had left him.

"Well, let's get this done," he said, coming to himself and leaving the window. "You haven't eaten any bread. We must have increased the ration too much."

Richard bowed his head and reached for a small loaf.

"So we have agreed that upon your release, you are to send information that will help us to take Blaye and Bayonne." The clerk started writing, his quill carefully making each stroke.

Richard's mouth was full of bread. His stomach was churning. The clerk dipped his quill in the pot of ink to begin the second line.

"If you convince the English to surrender, all the better. We will have more prisoners and lose fewer of our men. Otherwise make a plan to let the French army in through the gates. Almaric can give you some useful powders. They will create panic, and the gate could easily be opened while the guards are dealing with the fire."

"And how would I send a signal to Almaric?" Richard asked. His mouth was dry, his hands damp. He had not agreed, but, nonetheless, the clerk wrote word after word. And somewhere near the river the familiar Templar was going to speak to Azalais. That voice could belong to no one else.

"You won't need to, as I explained last time." The Count smiled broadly. "He will always be with you. He was raised by wolves, did I tell you that?" He laughed at Richard's expression. "Other people believe it. But the bandits who captured him as a child certainly were wolves. They made him work for them, but he killed them all in the end. He came into my service quite recently."

The Count looked thoughtful for a moment and scratched his groin.

"So now we will swear to Saint André to seal this agreement. Then we will discuss your mount and your equipment."

There was sudden loud yapping nearby. The Count's Mistress was passing along the corridor.

"Come, let's hurry," said the Count, looking towards the door.

Richard swore the oath without thinking. His mind was floating down the river after that voice, hoping he had not imagined the singer.

Chapter XXXI

Saturday the 26th November 1295
Porte Cailhau, Bordeaux

Illesa got off the small boat and pulled Azalais after her. The quicker they got out of eyesight the better. The people on the quay were crowding round, curious, wanting to see the owner of that voice.

"More later," Gaspar promised, struggling out of the boat with the instrument in one hand. "Make way."

The boat owner was happy with his pay, but the Harbour Master was approaching, accompanied by several other sailors. There were going to be questions. An old woman who had been mending a net caught Azalais' arm.

"Sing again, angel. We haven't heard the old songs for so long."

"I thank you, Good Mother, but I must save my voice," Azalais said and pushed firmly on.

Ahead of them, and just behind the Harbour Master, was Father Raymond. They all came to a halt next to a woman selling mussels from a basket.

"Masters," Father Raymond began, "I have orders to take these players straight to the Count."

"She can't sing like that on a boat," the Harbour Master began, "she'll scare off the fish and distract the sailors from their tasks. There'll be accidents." The sailors were looking the three of them up and down as if they came from Ethiopia.

"It was a trick to get the Count's attention. Hoping for some coin, perhaps. But now you will meet him in person, and we will see what you get," said the Templar, looking at Azalais threateningly.

"But I was only singing," said Azalais in a very poor imitation of innocence. At the other end of the quay, French soldiers had gathered.

"The Count wishes to see you immediately. Come with me." Father Raymond grabbed Gaspar's arm, marched them up to the gate and was waved through by the guards.

They walked towards the gatehouse of the Palais de l'Ombrière but did not enter, instead going up a small lane near the church of Saint Julien, becoming just a Templar Priest with three nondescript pilgrims trailing after him. He turned by the church door and they gathered round him in a tight circle.

"I don't think we have been followed. Get back to the merchant's house and begin your preparations. You will be performing for him tomorrow." He turned to Illesa. "Your husband was in audience with the Count, but I did not hear what they were discussing."

"Were you able to tell him the plan?" Illesa asked, gripping Azalais' hand tightly in her excitement.

"No, we had no time alone. But he seems like a man who will react quickly to this chance. A man of imagination."

"Was he well?"

"I did not see him walk. He was lean, but not starving. Recently shaved. Perhaps they are giving him privileges in exchange for something."

"Privileges for what?" asked Illesa, her stomach turning uncomfortably.

"Any manner of things. The Count does not hesitate to ask for what he wants. But with God's help, we will release him tomorrow."

Gaspar had hidden the citole under his cape. He brought it out.

"What time tomorrow? I need to familiarise myself with this out-of-tune instrument."

The Templar bowed to someone he knew, calling out Good Day to him.

"We will not go until vespers. They will be hungry for entertainment by then, and the dark will help us afterwards. It is best for you to go that way, past Saint Christoly. I will return the way we came. There is much to do. I will be with you at prime."

The wind whipped their cloaks as they turned onto the busy street. They walked quickly without speaking until they could see the Temple, sitting squat under its arches at the end of the familiar street.

"This wind will have stopped by morning. Mark my words. I know this climate," said Azalais, clutching her veil.

Illesa didn't reply. The plan was parading around her head, as it had all night. Now that there was some news of Richard, she barely noticed the gusty weather. Father Raymond had told the merchant that they needed to stay for a few days, and a whole upstairs room had been given over to them. The servants had been moved downstairs to sleep by the fire. It seemed that the family paid money each year to the Templar Commandery, and for that they were able to put the Templar Cross on all their goods and ask for their protection in trade and travel. They were in awe of Father Raymond, and, by association, spoke very little to their visitors. Illesa heard one of the serving girls being slapped by the mistress for trying to peek through the slits of the door to their room.

There was indeed much to do. Azalais was not going to practise as it drew too much attention. But she hummed the tunes of several songs as she made adjustments to the garments they would wear.

Illesa needed to re-attach the hood to the cope, and that was a difficult job without the special needles and the stretchers that the embroiderers would have used. She would feed Eve and then complete the work quietly by the window looking out on the sheltered yard.

"Don't look so full of dread," Gaspar said to her as he tuned the citole. "It is an easy play for us. I've performed harder parts in front of worse audiences in my sleep."

But his finger work on the citole was less assured than usual. He practised for a while but eventually slipped out, promising to return before dark.

"I don't know if we can trust Gaspar to do it properly," remarked Azalais, threading a needle in the fading light. "He never seems to be concerned about his work."

"Don't worry, darling, you will see how magnificent he can be," Illesa said with a confidence she didn't feel.

She finished the hood before vespers and began to train the weasel to wind round her arm and onto her shoulder using small pieces of offal. She had several nips to her fingertips, but when the weasel was on her shoulder she sat and ate like a true little devil, her hands quick with the bloody meat. It would look very striking.

"I am so grateful that Father Raymond is helping us," Illesa said, putting the weasel back on her hand to start the trick again.

Azalais shrugged her shoulders.

"The Templars have sworn to protect pilgrims, and that is what he is doing, I suppose. What I don't understand is how he has come to be working for the Archbishop, unless he used to be a Priest for the diocese before he joined the Templars. But war makes all things strange," she said, pulling the last loose threads from the hem of her blue surcote. "Every village around Dax was thick with Templars when I was growing up. They're brave men, willing to stand up to the rest of Christendom if they don't approve of the Church." She stopped her work and looked up for a moment. "I wouldn't be surprised if Father Raymond had been in Acre on Crusade. His skin has that wrinkled look from screwing up your eyes against the strong sun," Azalais demonstrated. "I wonder if the Archbishop knows anything of what he is up to."

"He will get his cope, and that should keep him quiet," Illesa said, returning to the vestment to have a final look at the stitching. "He won't be paying attention to anything else. He can hardly see."

"It's interesting that the canons aren't looking after him more. I suppose they are busy competing to see who will be elevated once he dies," Azalais said, matter-of-factly.

"Azalais!"

Her cousin looked up, surprised. She laughed at Illesa.

"Silly you! Clerics are just as ambitious as lords and dukes. More so, in some cases."

It was probably true, but Illesa did not want to think about priests ruthlessly pursuing worldly power like pigs fighting over a trough.

"The day will be cold and clear tomorrow. I have seen plenty of Bordeaux winters," Azalais declared, going out to collect a jug of hot water. She used the pot and began to wash her face and hands.

Illesa returned her attention to the cope. It was in good condition now, glowing in the last light coming through the window. She rolled it back inside the cerecloth and let the weasel out to scamper after the mice in the rushes. A door opened downstairs.

"Is that Gaspar?"

"I certainly hope so," said Azalais, drying her face. "I don't want him staying out late, getting in a fight and looking like the cat's dinner for our performance."

"He learned his lesson. He is very careful these days," Illesa said, remembering the mess he'd been in when his former lover had cut his ear and cracked his skull.

The door opened, and Gaspar came in. He smelt different, of spices or scented wax.

"Where have you been?"

"Looking around."

He wore a new pair of very fine leather gloves and held them out for Illesa to admire.

"Very elegant. But why are you buying things now?"

"It quietens my nerves," he said and put his hands dramatically to his forehead.

"You should have been here practising," Azalais said. "You haven't got the part right in the song of Saint Denys."

"Did you wear out your first husband with your tongue?" said Gaspar wearily, sitting down on a stool.

"No, I used something else," she said, swirling the skirt she had finished repairing around her ankles. "I think this will be suitable. Don't you?"

"You look like Judith, ready to cut off a general's head," said Gaspar.

In fact Azalais looked very beautiful, although the clothes were modest. The two subsided into their own preparations.

The weasel came to Illesa's hand, and she gave it a tiny piece of meat and put it away in the pouch. She imagined it was like having a falcon. She had to be careful not to feed Eve too much. Tomorrow it would be best if she were hungry.

***

At first light, the gulls woke Illesa into a state of tension. Father Raymond would arrive soon, and they needed to be ready for him. Azalais grunted and turned over. She always needed a moment to wake up. Gaspar was lying on the straw pallet on the floor, still asleep, his breathing deep and long. She went over to kneel next to him. His hand was thrown back on the coarse blanket palm upward; his fingers were raw and bleeding. She held his hand up to examine it. He opened his eyes and looked at her.

"What have you done to your hand?" she whispered.

He put a finger to his lips.

"It wasn't me, it was the citole."

"But why is it so bad? And why didn't you tell me?"

"It isn't so bad," he said, pulling his hand back and putting on the gloves from under his pillow.

"But it is! How can you play with them like that? You won't be able to."

He took her hand in his gloved one.

"I will, my darling. I will. You see I cannot feel any pain in my fingers. Or my feet for that matter," he said, his expression rueful.

She sat back on her heels and put her hands to her mouth. Tears began to fall, unnoticed, from her eyes.

"No, Gaspar. No," she said, staring at him, feeling the warmth draining out of her. "That isn't true."

"It is true," he said, propping his head on his gloved hand. "I am not playing a part. Although I wish I was." His face was very still, and he was looking at her with bright wet eyes. "But it isn't as bad as you think. I will be able to perform today, and after that you will have your Richard back. That is my final part."

"No," she said again, gripping his sleeve. "There are things that will help. I know of some amulets."

But he shook his head solemnly.

"Not now, Illesa." His voice was stern. "There is no time for your village cures. We have much to do."

"Gaspar," she said desperately, wiping her eyes.

He sat up and squeezed her cheek between two gloved fingers, pursing his lips.

240

"We can't have you looking like that! What a tragedy to see your face all wrinkled with care. It's time to get up." He rolled over, pushed himself to his feet and went to use the pot.

Azalais was waking up, so Illesa had to swallow her tears and turn away to wash her face in the bowl of cold water.

A leper. That was why Gaspar had been un-talkative and distant, not wanting to touch anyone. How long had he known? Had his precautions been enough, or would she, Azalais and perhaps even Jean Fracinaut become lepers too? Had he embraced Christopher when he left? No, he had avoided it; she remembered wondering why. He had been careful, and she had not read the signs, had not seen what was clearly wrong with him. Azalais must not be allowed to guess. She was assiduous in avoiding the ill, and lepers were one of her greatest fears.

The door opened, and Father Raymond strode into the room. He was clean-shaven, but his eyes were shadowed.

Without a word he swiftly placed the boards on the trestle and pulled up a bench. From inside his habit, he took out a small piece of black wool cloth and unrolled it quickly.

Inside was a tiny, dead brown mouse, its tail as stiff as a twig.

"Sit down, all of you. I have an idea for a new trick," he said.

Chapter XXXII

Sunday the 27th November 1295
Palais de l'Ombrière, Bordeaux
Vespers

Through the dust and droppings in the cracks, Richard, with his ear to the floorboards, could hear the other prisoners being let out. Just a distant pounding of feet and raised voices that was too muffled to pick out any individuals.

They would fill up the chapel floor with the squires and the common soldiers, but the knights would be on the higher floor. He would have no chance to explain to Hugh what was likely to happen in the morning when they began their journey away from the city. Once they left the Palais de l'Ombrière, Almaric would be watching, expecting him to kill one of the guards.

But there were the two coincidences: the Templar and the singer on the water. If Azalais was there, singing to the Count and his mistress, then who else would be there, waiting in the hall? It was a ridiculous idea. He had swung between believing it a dream and reality since he'd left the Count's presence.

Richard was still lying on the floor when the guard opened the door.

"You're the last of them," the guard said. "Come on, the priest has already arrived."

They grumbled him down the three flights and then up the stairs to the hall. Servants were preparing the tables and sweeping the floor. The Count would arrive soon for a feast with his lover. The benches would be full of his retainers. There would be entertainment.

The guards hurried him past it all, through the door behind the dais and up a short flight of steps to the upper floor of the chapel. Only a handful of knights were gathered by the balustrade. They stared at him as he limped towards the front, looking like faded paintings of the men they used to be: duller, paler, thinner. Then all the knights turned towards the altar. The Templar Priest had begun the Mass.

The Templar's Gascon accent was even more pronounced in his use of Latin. Richard stood next to de Mubray as the familiar phrases came and went. The chapel was as old as the prison tower, with heavy columns and ancient flaking paint. The south wall showed the martyrdom of Saint Catherine, with her torture wheel breaking into pieces and wounding her guards. The Saint stood serene under her halo, but, on her left, a soldier was coming with a great sword to carry out the order to behead her.

The Last Judgement on the east wall above the altar was the most damaged. It seemed that the blessed were fragile, while the demons had retained all their vibrant colour and were happily dragging the damned into Hell's gaping mouth.

"Have you heard anything from home?" Richard whispered in de Mubray's ear.

He shook his head and winced, touching his swollen cheek. De Mubray had the toothache.

"They've abandoned us," he said thickly. "No one is coming now until next spring when the weather is better. If at all. I heard that Earl Edmund is ill, and none of the other earls will serve the King in France."

Richard rubbed his forehead. What Giffard had said all those months ago was turning out to be true. There would be no rescue.

"Mubray."

"What?" The gaunt knight looked over at him, annoyed. There were red flaking patches on his face. His eyes were sunken, angry.

"If I die on the way to Carcassonne, take the pouch hanging around my neck. Give it to my family when you return to England, for mercy's sake."

With a thin splinter of wood from the floorboard and his own blood, Richard had written words of explanation on the parchment next to the painting of the Greeks' gift to the Trojans. If she received it, Illesa would be able to decipher it, and she, at least, would know that he hadn't died a traitor.

"What are you talking about?" de Mubray said. "The guards are watching us, you know."

Richard turned back to the altar. They had reached the *Agnus Dei*. The Templar's eyes rested on Richard as he said *"miserere nobis"*. It lasted no longer than a breath, but maybe there was some significance.

"Nothing," Richard said. He rubbed his bad leg. He would have to sit down soon if the pain didn't subside. "Just give anything you find on my body to Hugh, my squire."

"At least you won't be expected to walk," de Mubray said bitterly. "I can't see them giving us our fine horses back, can you?"

Richard turned away. He had never liked de Mubray, and his imprisonment hadn't improved him.

"I know that Templar Priest," de Mubray muttered.

"Do you?"

"Mmm. I've seen him somewhere before."

The Body of Christ was being placed in a monstrance and held aloft for the men to see. All knelt except Richard, who had to bow instead.

"What's happening?" one of the other knights asked. "If he is going to give us the Body, he must believe we are on the road to death."

The Templar was breaking bread. They were going to have the Eucharist which they did not expect to taste until Easter. Being offered the Body of Christ upset the squires and men-at-arms below. Some cried out that they were not sufficiently clean to receive it. But the guards came forward, and then they all knelt before the altar one by one opening their mouths. Hugh was one of the last. His hair was patchy, and he visibly trembled as he knelt before the priest. But the better rations had helped him. His face had lost its skeletal quality.

"We will have to go down," de Mubray said. Richard watched the knights file out in front of him. De Mubray reluctantly helped him down the stairs. There was a pricking on the back of Richard's neck as he came into the small nave of the chapel.

The ordinary men had been moved to the side to allow the knights through, and they stood watching them like the gloomy damned on the wall above. But Hugh's face had taken on a brightness, maybe from the Eucharist or just the thought

244

of leaving this prison. Richard caught his eye, tried to make some sign.

The guard behind Richard gave him a shove. De Mubray rose from his knees in front of the altar and went back down the centre of the chapel. Richard limped forward. The deacon took his right arm and lowered him onto one knee. He opened his mouth.

The Templar Priest put the bread on his tongue.

"The Body of Christ," he declared and bent down to make the sign of the cross above his head.

"When you enter the hall, feign death," the Templar whispered. He straightened up slowly and gestured for the deacon to get Richard to his feet.

Richard stood for a moment, holding on to the deacon for balance. He met the Templar's eyes and bowed his head. When he looked up again, the priest had returned to the altar and was beginning the dismissal. Guards in the nave were already filing the men out. Richard limped forward, seeing the back of Hugh's head disappearing through the chapel door.

The guards behind him were complaining.

"The Count will be angry. He wanted them out of chapel and back in their cells straight away," one said.

"We didn't know that Templar was going to give them all the Body, did we? And then bless them all one by one? It's not our fault the prisoners will have to go through the hall during the feast," the other said in a loud whisper.

"Shhh," the first guard warned.

The front of the line of prisoners had reached the door to the great hall. On the other side, Richard could hear singing.

Chapter XXXIII

Sunday the 27th November 1295
Palais de l'Ombrière, Bordeaux
Vespers

The wind was bitter and the tall city walls provided little protection from it. The three of them huddled together just inside the gatehouse to the castle, waiting for the Steward to come. Gaspar had a new green cap to hide his tonsure. He pulled it over his missing ear and held the citole inside his cape. It would need retuning after being out in the cold. Azalais was very quiet, wrapped inside her cloak. The walls around them darkened quickly under the cloudy sky.

"If it comes to it," Gaspar remarked mildly, "leave me behind. I will take the blame if they realise what is happening. You two can feign ignorance and use your wiles to get out."

"Oh, you are so chivalrous," Azalais said, mockingly. "As if they would be satisfied with you."

"Be quiet, Azalais," Illesa said sharply. "We are all leaving together. The evening will go as planned. If it does not, Father Raymond will get us out."

Azalais gave her an affronted look and wrapped her cloak even more tightly around her body. Gaspar's face was serious, without a hint of his usual mischief.

"Let's hope so. But remember, Illesa, you must not show your feelings. You must be there only to entertain. Your face can give too much away."

The guardroom door opened, and they all pushed inside the small room.

The Steward looked them up and down, and they him. He took up most of the space. The belt around his waist did little to contain his sagging belly.

"So you are the new musicians who performed on the river. Very inventive. But don't try anything in here. You sing and you play, that's it. The Count will pay you if you please him. If you don't, you get nothing." He shook his jowls. "But then, you're not starving, are you?" he said, staring at Azalais as she removed her cloak.

"We are not common jongleurs," Azalais said in her most imperious tone. "We have been trained by the best troubadours in Aquitaine. We don't get paid in half-pennies."

The Steward licked his fat lips then shook his head.

"Best if you save your breath for your performance. This Occitan pride doesn't go down well with the Count. Not well at all. Doesn't matter how pretty you are."

He opened the door in the other wall of the guardroom, and they followed him to the inner court. To their right, the tower rose into the dark sky. Torches were being lit along the walls to their left. They followed the Steward and the torch lighter as he went up the outside stair leading to the great hall. At the far end of the castle wall, the chapel and its small bell tower was a black shape against the deep grey of sky.

"Are you coming in with the food or standing in the hall at the start?"

"We will stay in the hall," said Gaspar. "We don't do all that capering about."

The Steward nodded and opened the door.

The hall was rather barely furnished. There was only one tapestry, and it looked moth-eaten. Only four trestle tables were set, so it was not a great feast. There would be the Count's closest retainers and maybe some city officials.

Illesa put the tabor down on one of the benches and blew on her cold fingers. The fire smoked in the hearth, but there was little flame.

"Can the fire be encouraged? We are perished with cold, and it is hard to play when you can't feel your hands," said Gaspar, giving the Steward his most charming look.

The Steward grunted, dragging his eyes away from Azalais who was shivering and wrapping her cloak back around her body. He clapped his hands at one of the boys arranging the tables.

"More wood, and make sure it's dry." He turned back to Gaspar. "I'll bring you a jug of wine but only one, mind."

He went out through the far door that presumably lead to the pantry.

They rehearsed quietly by the inner wall of the hall and watched the room gradually filling with men. Illesa had only been introduced to the tabor that morning. It was larger than the one she sometimes played at home to accompany Azalais. She tightened the strap to bring it closer to her body and tapped out a quick beat. The noise and vibration made the weasel restless inside the pouch. It remained to be seen if Eve would perform as well as they hoped.

At a blast of a horn, the Count and his close courtiers entered wearing brightly coloured supertunics. A woman followed in a peacock gown trimmed in marten fur, holding a small fluffy white dog with a silver collar.

"Hold on to the weasel," muttered Azalais. "That's a rat catching dog if ever I saw one."

The woman was pretty, with a small, pursed mouth. She wore her hair in elaborate plaits under a fine silk veil that fell down the back of her neck. She swayed as she walked, very aware that she was the only noble lady in the room.

The Count sat down on the largest chair in the centre of the dais, making much of his long cape as he did so. The woman sat to his left with the dog on her lap. The Steward finished seating the other courtiers around the table according to their status. He spoke in the Count's ear and then beckoned to Azalais. She approached the table and curtseyed. Gaspar and Illesa stood behind her.

"I heard you through my window," the Count said in a high, excited voice. "Sybilla, this is the woman with the voice." His woman smiled thinly, glancing suspiciously at Azalais.

"What song were you singing?" the Count continued. "You must begin with that one; it has been in my mind ever since."

"Ah, my lord, that is a most beautiful song of love," Azalais said, treating him to one of her best smiles. "We will be most happy to perform it for you."

She curtseyed again, and Illesa and Gaspar moved back, leaving her to stand alone in front of the dais.

Would you have me sing for you
the song lovers alone can sing?
Only those whose hearts are true

taste the fruit that love can bring."

While Azalais sang the Count seemed stupefied, sitting forward in his chair completely still. His woman stared at Azalais with a poisonous expression but came to herself in the pause after the first verse. When the Count turned to her, she coyly turned away, stroking her lap dog.

> *"The lady I love is dressed in light,*
> *in fur of ermine and shift of silk.*
> *Her shoes are of flower petals white,*
> *and her skin is soft and pale as milk.*
>
> *Her father is the nightingale,*
> *who sings from high among the leaves.*
> *Her mother is the Siren, of ancient tale,*
> *who sings from the shore of the seas.*
>
> *Lovely lady, of fine family,*
> *would to God, our Father above,*
> *that you were wedded to me*
> *and joyously gave me your love."*

The song ended on a low, melancholy note that hung in the air like a wingbeat. As it faded, Azalais made a very deep curtsey.

"A song of desire! How appropriate. And indeed you must be the offspring of a Siren and a Nightingale. I have rarely heard such a voice." He turned to his woman, who was adjusting her veil. "Was it to your liking, lady?" he asked her. She smiled insincerely and nodded.

"But now we should have something to accompany our feasting," the Count ordered.

The Steward, standing by the table, clapped his hands, and it seemed that immediately the room was full of servants bearing bowls and platters. Azalais, Gaspar and Illesa backed against the wall, waiting for the crashing and shouting to subside. When it was quieter, Illesa bent down and cleared the rushes away from the floor in front of them as Gaspar began to play his introduction on the citole.

There was no tabor in this song, but the small dog was on the woman's lap, so Illesa took the weasel from her pouch and placed her on the floor, holding the thin thread of silk, so fine it was nearly invisible, which was attached to the dead mouse. In this way she could make the weasel dance in time to the music, a lively estampie.

Illesa couldn't look up to see what effect it was having. She had to keep the weasel enthralled, trying to catch the mouse, tying her lithe body almost in knots, turning and twisting across the floor. But out of the corner of her eye, Illesa saw movement behind the dais. A guard came through and spoke in the Steward's ear. He made an impatient gesture, and the guard went back and opened the door. Illesa let the weasel catch the mouse, and she bit its neck and began to shake it.

A thin man in poor clothes came in, looking around the hall hungrily. Another followed, more bearded but no less thin.

If Richard was one of them, she didn't recognise him. She tried not to look as the men filed through and were guarded across the room past Azalais, who continued to sing. The men sitting on the benches near them began to shout.

"Hey, English, you don't look so strong now!"

"No sign of your great army!"

"Enjoy the famous hospitality of Carcassonne!"

The English prisoners seemed not to hear them. They just stared at the food and drink spread out on the tables, walking unsteadily like lepers.

Twelve prisoners had shuffled through the hall towards the door that would lead them back to their cells, but Richard had not been among them. Surely she would still know him.

The door from the chapel opened again. A man with a useless, dragging leg limped in, his face almost unbearably vulnerable. His eyes sought hers, looked quickly away. He walked two more paces then seemed to convulse. He toppled over on his useless leg and lay choking on the floor.

Chapter XXXIV

The Great Hall
Palais de l'Ombrière, Bordeaux

Richard watched his footing, pulling himself along the wall at the back of the line of men. It had been a strange instruction. Soon there would be no need for feigning. Death was stalking him as soon as he left the Palais. But the Templar was certainly trying to help him. Perhaps he had some elaborate plan to defeat the French or some private reason.

The voice in the hall was unmistakable now. It was Azalais. The hair stood up on the back of Richard's neck as she sang. The singer and the Templar. Between them they had a plan. He hobbled through the door into the flickering light of many candles and lamps and the full sound of Azalais, her head thrown back in the joy of her song. Behind her, Gaspar was bent over an instrument. At Azalais' feet, looking up at him, was Illesa.

He looked away, the blood already draining from his head as he allowed himself to tip over and hit the boards without stopping his fall. He landed on his side, made a choking sound and slumped onto his back, mouth open and eyes open, as he had often seen Gaspar do when he played those struck down by God for their sins. The guard behind him dragged on his arm and tried to raise him to his feet. He allowed spit to drip from his mouth; it should be tinged with blood from his bitten tongue. Voices and queries turned to shouts.

Gaspar was leaning over him, slapping his face. Richard allowed his eyes to roll.

"A priest!" Gaspar shouted. "Send for the priest!"

A dog was barking, and then there was a sharp yelp followed by a scream. Benches scraped the floor and were knocked over.

He allowed his eyes to close. It would be too difficult to keep them open for a long period, and who knew how long it would take for Gaspar's plan to play itself out. Illesa was only paces away, watching him. This could have been her idea. It wouldn't surprise him. She was trying to get him out of prison, as she had tried to free her brother so many years before. It was ridiculous. He should just get up and try to pass it off as a faint. They would never escape. Illesa, Azalais and Gaspar would be in danger.

At his side, someone new bent over him. He touched Richard's temple and lifted his wrist.

"Who is this unfortunate?" the new man called in a Gascon accent. It was the Templar Priest.

"Is it Sir Richard Burnel?"

"Yes, the cripple."

"We must move him. He is close to death," the Templar said. "Only quick action will save him. Come, help this guard move him to the Seneschal's office. I will send for the Benedictine."

His arms were lifted then his legs. They heaved him onto a board, and he let his head roll from side to side. He felt a sudden desire to open his mouth and speak, to ask Gaspar if he was doing well. But the board was being lifted, and he had to concentrate on not moving.

"Doesn't weigh much," said one of the guards.

"I'll have his surcote if he dies. It just needs some stitching."

"Have you tried getting him up the stairs? Not so bad when he's dead."

They put the board down hard on a table in a dark room.

"We need light. Bring in lamps from the hall," the Templar demanded.

Two pairs of feet trudged out.

"Very impressive!" Gaspar breathed in his ear. "I almost believe it myself."

"Quiet. You have work to do," the Templar said.

"I know," Gaspar said. "I will return quickly."

"Be sure to cover up well."

A moment later the lamps arrived and were set about the room. Richard could see their warm glow through his eyelids.

"I will give the man extreme unction. You can wait outside the door. Let the citole player out of the gate. He is going to call for the Benedictine healer."

The door closed on the guards' footsteps. The board Richard lay on had been set down on a trestle. He felt the breath of the Templar as he bent over his body.

"You may open your eyes now," he murmured.

Richard did. The Templar put a finger to his lips.

"Do you remember me?"

Richard nodded.

"I am helping your wife. You must stay exactly as you are. If you do, we will get you out." He straightened up, looking at the door and listening, then he bent close to Richard's ear again. "I will not give you the holy oil of extreme unction. If I did, you would have to live as a dead man, and you would not enjoy that. But I will say the words and make the prayers. You must also pray."

Richard licked his lips, dry from his mouth being open. He nodded again. And put his head back against the hard board.

He did not sleep but felt a strange peace as he allowed his body to be still. He was no longer responsible for striving to stay alive; his body was dead. This priest would revive him, or not. His wife would embrace him now, or in the life to come. A long dream played before his eyes, of sailing into a distant harbour where the lamps were just being lit. When the door opened with a loud bang, he nearly cried out, but the Templar had his hand on his mouth.

"There is little breath left," he said to the person who had arrived. "It may be too late, but thank you for coming, Brother."

The sounds of singing and shouting came through the open door. They were still working, Azalais and Illesa, still keeping the Count of Artois busy and distracted.

The Benedictine Brother gave him a cursory examination.

"He must be brought to the infirmary, immediately," said Gaspar in the authoritative voice he used when he played judges or kings. "I have my barge ready. But I will need help to get him aboard. The Brothers will help me unload him when we arrive. Guards, this man must be brought to the Abbey of Sainte Croix now. "

"Is he dead?" the Steward's loud braying voice asked from the doorway.

"No, master, but he is gravely ill. We must take him to the Abbey to be treated and bled."

"This will need to be approved by the Count," the Steward said. He was still in the doorway, not wishing to be close to a dying man.

"Well, go now and ask. It cannot wait until morning!" Gaspar the Benedictine ordered.

Chapter XXXV

The Great Hall
Palais de l'Ombrière, Bordeaux

Initially, few people noticed Richard fall. The retainers had returned to their food, and Azalais continued to sing, finishing the phrase. But when the guard tried to pull Richard onto his feet, the men on the benches nearby began to shout abuse.

Gaspar bent over Richard's twitching body. He called for a priest. The Count raised his head to see what was happening. Out of the corner of Illesa's eye, there was a rush of white fur. It was too late for her to grab the weasel; Eve had already run to the nearest table and climbed on top. The dog followed, barking madly.

Father Raymond came through the door in his simple Templar robe, and the noise died down. The Count's woman tried to scoop up the dog, but it would not be caught.

"Catch the weasel," hissed Azalais, pulling on Illesa's sleeve.

Father Raymond was straightening up from his examination of Richard, speaking to the Steward.

"Illesa! Catch the weasel!" Azalais said again.

But Eve had jumped off the table, avoiding the hands on all sides that tried to grab her. She ran, but the dog was quick behind her. As the weasel reached the wall, she whipped round and there was a high-pitched squeal from the dog. Eve shot up the hanging tapestry.

"Dirty filthy rat!" cried the Count's woman, picking up the barking dog and examining it. "Trynket has been bitten by that rabid creature."

"Calm down, Sybilla. And keep that dog quiet, or I'll have its neck broken," said the Count.

The men had put Richard on a trestle board, and Gaspar was holding a corner, helping to carry it out of the hall.

Azalais and Illesa stood at the bottom of the tapestry.

"Don't forget my citole," Gaspar whispered as he passed them.

The Count's woman had put a silk lead on the silver collar, and the dog jumped and pulled against it.

"Keep hold of him," the woman ordered her maidservant. "It is not safe here with these common players and their wild animals." She glared at Azalais and Illesa and then sat down next to the Count, who was watching the weasel running along the top of the tapestry.

The men carrying Richard followed Father Raymond through the door to the service rooms, and the Count turned his attention to Azalais.

"Continue. It was only one of the prisoners. He was unlikely to survive the journey tomorrow anyway." He waved his arm at the tapestry. "Perhaps your pet will come down when you begin to sing and play again."

His woman snorted derisively.

"Begin!" the Count shouted.

The men sat back down on their benches, watching Eve chattering on top of the hanging.

Azalais took Illesa's hand and they returned to where she had left her tabor and the small, sorry-looking mouse.

"What will you sing next," Illesa whispered, her hands shaking.

"We will do 'When Violets Bloom'. I think our lady needs some flattery," she said with a bitter glance at the Count's woman, who was now refusing to eat.

> *"When violets and roses bloom*
> *and the parrots sing in the wood,*
> *that is when I compose a merry song*
> *about my loyal sweetheart*
> *and the love she has given me for so long."*

Azalais sang, directing the full force of her voice and its charm at the smirking Count and his simpering woman.

Once or twice, Illesa felt her rhythm slipping, and Azalais had to hold her note to keep time. Her eye was on the weasel, and her thoughts on what was happening, somewhere, to Richard who lay helpless in the midst of the French Army command. They had placed so much trust in Father Raymond, whom they barely knew.

> *"I know her pouting mouth and beautiful hair,*
> *her firm and pointing little breasts,*
> *her gleaming throat, like the lily in May.*
> *She fills me with such sweet joy*
> *that, I swear, my heart will never stray."*

Azalais finished the song on a high note and early, to avoid the verse about the spies that sought to tear the lovers apart.

They all glanced up at the tapestry, but the weasel had disappeared.

"If it please you, my lord," said Illesa quietly, "we will perform a song with the dancing mouse, and that should bring her down."

"It is a female?" he asked, and smiled meaningfully at Sybilla. "That does not surprise me. They are often fiercer than the male. My wolf is also female." He looked satisfied with himself and took a long drink from his goblet. "Yes. See if you can bring her down. Otherwise I will call in the crossbowmen to do their best. But it would be a shame to damage the tapestry."

Azalais began a sliding, serpentine song that she had composed while she stayed at Langley. She sang it to herself when she was feeling homesick or lovesick. Illesa brought out some meat from her pouch and held the mouse string ready.

> *"I take the flax, I take the wool*
> *and from the distaff, thread I pull.*
> *I take the yarn, I weave a cloth*
> *made of many lover's knots."*

The weasel's nose came out from halfway down the tapestry. She had been hiding between the hanging and the wall. She looked down at the mouse, moving warily.

"Around the spindle, I am bound.
My heart, around your heart, is curled.
Like the shuttle, up and down,
like the needle, in and out,"
I will seek you till you're found,
through all the winding world."

Eve came across the floor in a blur, batted at the mouse and caught it in her teeth. Illesa scooped her up and fed her a large piece of meat then pushed her into the pouch.

When she looked up, the Count was watching her intently.

"Fascinating creature."

Azalais tapped Illesa's shoulder.

"The Virgin Mary now," she whispered.

They performed two very humble and contrite songs about the Virgin, while everyone continued eating and drinking. The Count's woman accepted some small mouthfuls from his platter, but fed the rest to her dog, occasionally glancing at Azalais and Illesa with contempt.

They were having a short rest when the Steward came into the hall and spoke in the Count's ear.

"If he dies there, the Benedictines or the Templars must bear the cost of his burial and the cost of the medicine! I won't pay for any of it. All those monks want is more donations, more Masses," the Count shouted, slapping the table with his white linen napkin as if killing a fly. "Send one of the guards to help carry him to the Abbey, then it is the Templar's responsibility."

The Steward walked away stiffly, back to Richard who was going to be sent to the Benedictine Abbey with a guard.

"Now, I want to hear your first song again, not these sad, religious dirges. Where is that citole player?" the Count demanded.

"I don't know, my lord. Perhaps he is helping to carry the knight?" Azalais said innocently. "But I can sing it without him. It is more pure. We will sing it faster for you with the tabor, and it will quicken your desire."

Chapter XXXVI

The Seneschal's Office
Palais de l'Ombrière, Bordeaux

"A guard has been released to take him to the Abbey. But the Count won't pay. You will have to bear the cost," the Steward said impatiently. "Now let's get him out before he dies here. After the night I'm having, I wouldn't be surprised if we woke up to the Apocalypse."

"You should be more concerned for your soul," said the Templar shortly.

"I am concerned for my position. If the Count is displeased, just imagine what he can do. Hell is in the future, but the Count is in the next room."

"Go back to him then and try to save your skin. But do not stand between other souls and Paradise."

"I need no sermon from you, Gascon," said the Steward. "Everyone knows you are all heretics." He spat on the floor. "I'll send two guards to get him in the barge. Send one back." He paused for a moment. "What happened to that player, the blond with the citole? The Count wants him."

"Poor man," said Gaspar in his new Monk's voice. "He injured his foot on the way to the Abbey to get me. His ankle was swollen. I told him to wait there for my return. If I apply a poultice, he should be able to walk tomorrow."

"I will tell the Count," the Steward said, his voice receding. "You two, take the sick man to the Benedictine's barge."

The guards came in, and Richard felt himself lifted up and cool air on his damp forehead. Their loud breathing gave way to swearing when they caught their hands on the stones of the doorway. The stairway down into the gatehouse was narrow; they had to abandon the board and carry him by his shoulders and legs. He had pissed himself, which didn't please them.

"Open the fucking gate, Philip," the guard at his head called to the gatekeeper. "We have to carry out this stinking corpse."

"The knight is not dead," said the Templar.

"He feels dead to me," said the guard at his feet, setting down his legs on the ground, so he was only supported by the other guard under his shoulders.

"No, he's not dead. See his chest? He is still breathing," said the guard at his head.

"We don't want him dead here, anyway," said the other. "We'd have to have him buried. And pay the priest," he added resentfully.

The gate opened, and they were moving again, out into a bitter wind which froze his wet clothes. The guards struggled along the path for what seemed a long time before they reached the ditch that flowed into the Garonne.

"Here is the barge," said Gaspar the Monk. "Lay him down there on the thwart, where I can examine him. The rough movement may have harmed him."

"Don't blame us," said the guard at his feet.

He was laid down on the bench where the oarsman would sit, his head lowered onto the wood in Gaspar's hands. The false Monk felt his chest, his neck.

There was a long silence.

"He has gone to the Lord," Gaspar said solemnly. "Father, had he received extreme unction?"

"The sacrament was performed," the Templar said.

"Then we will pray for his departed soul."

The current knocked the tethered boat against the wooden jetty as Gaspar and the Templar prayed for his soul in Purgatory.

"He died outside the Palais," said one of the guards as soon as they had finished. "He's your responsibility now. I'll tell the Steward."

"But one of you was meant to come to the Abbey to help carry him," Father Raymond said crossly.

"No need now, is there? He's in the boat. He's hardly going to escape anywhere," the guard said, chuckling at his own wit.

"Tell the Steward we will give the knight appropriate Christian burial, and one day he may thank us for doing the same for him," Father Raymond said.

"More than the fucking English deserve," said one of the guards, making the barge rock violently as he got out. Richard would have fallen off the thwart if Gaspar hadn't grabbed his tunic.

For a few moments they could hear the guards complaining as they walked back to the Palais. Then there was silence, except for the sounds of the water and the distant bark of a dog.

"That worked well," said Gaspar beside him. "Didn't know how we were going to get rid of those guards, but there is nothing like the promise of work or expense to make men flee."

"Their failings become obvious in the face of Death," said the Templar more thoughtfully. He touched Richard's hand. "You must stay as you are until we come to a place of safety. The town gates are shut, so we have to row along the ditches. Remain very still until we say you may wake."

Richard raised one finger in agreement.

Chapter XXXVII

The Great Hall
Palais de l'Ombrière, Bordeaux

"This Archbishop's wine is the finest I've drunk since coming to this stinking place. I was beginning to think there was nothing good to be found in Gascony." The Count sat back while a page filled his glass. "But this jongleuse is something to be savoured," he said turning to the man on his right, who was still eating. "I will not thrive in this climate without that voice," the Count claimed, drunkenly.

"Count Robert, the men are getting restless, and I want to retire," his woman complained. He ignored her, continuing a one-sided conversation with the noble on his right, whose head nodded continuously.

The men had been drinking for hours. Azalais had run out of new songs and was simply repeating them. There had been calls from the men to bring the weasel out again, but Illesa shook her head and kept her eyes on the tabor. Some of the men had started a fight in the corner of the hall, a matter of hands and holds, not knives. The Count was absorbed in betting on the winner.

The Steward trundled into the hall and round the back of the dais to speak privately to the irritated Count. He was quickly dismissed.

"Bloody English," the Count said to no one in particular. "As soon as they become useful they die." He pointed a finger at one of his men sitting on a bench nearby. "You, eh, Almaric. You are a lucky bastard."

"How long will we have to stay?" murmured Illesa. She was no longer shaking, but she felt dizzy from lack of sleep and food and her head ached.

"I will have no voice if I continue," Azalais said, touching her long throat. "I will beg for leave to go. You just smile and say nothing, and maybe they will forget about the weasel. Here, take the citole and stop looking guilty!"

Azalais gathered herself and went, smiling shyly, up to the high table, stopping just at the foot of the dais.

"My good lord, I beg leave to depart as my voice is most tired." She cleared her throat, bringing out a hoarse quality in her tone. "If you have enjoyed the songs, allow us to rest so that my voice may praise you and the Holy Mother of God again another day." She curtseyed prettily, her head bowed.

"Would you leave?" said the Count. "You haven't been here long."

"They have been here entirely too long," his woman muttered.

"Where is that creature you had? It was most amusing. Where have you hidden it?"

"My lord, we are sorry for the antics of the weasel," Azalais said, putting her hands together as if begging for mercy. "She is quick in her own defence. But now she is safely away in her pouch."

"Bring her out. Put her here where I can have a good look at her."

"No my lord," screeched his woman. "It bites!"

"Stop your mouth, you slut! Its keeper will hold it." He turned back to Illesa, wiping the spit from his lips with the back of his hand. "Put the weasel here."

He slapped his palm on the table in front of him, and the platters rattled.

"My lord," said Azalais.

"Now!" he shouted.

Illesa put down the citole, opened the pouch and brought out the weasel. She quickly woke and became alert. Illesa climbed onto the dais. The hall had become quiet and still. All the nobles and retainers were watching. She held the weasel out in her shaking hands.

"You don't keep it on a chain?"

"No, my lord," she said. "It is trained to come to me, so it usually has no need for a chain."

"Better than most women then, isn't it, Sybilla? Always returns, always loyal. You should be like the weasel and not always fawning over your stupid dog!"

Illesa started to put the weasel back in the pouch.

"No, keep her out. Put her on the table. I want to see this properly. How do you call her back?"

Illesa held Eve to her chest, trying to still her own trembling.

"It will be difficult here as there is so much food for her to eat. But usually I call her name and offer her a little piece of meat." She held Eve out over the table for the Count to examine. He put his finger against one of her claws.

"Like a tiny dog! Better than a dog because at least she catches mice. Does she not?"

"Yes, my lord."

"And dances to music?"

"If she sees the toy mouse."

"And what do you call her?"

"Eve."

"Oh, very good," he clapped his hands. "I will keep her. Almaric, come and take this weasel, and we will add her to my collection of animals."

"No, please, my lord! She was given to me by my son," Illesa said before she could stop herself.

The Count looked up at her indignantly.

"I will pay you for her, if that is what you want?"

Azalais touched Illesa's shoulder.

"Give it to him, darling," she said softly.

A man came onto the dais and stood beside her. She had not noticed him before. He was not one of the wrestlers, or a drinker. His eyes were clear. He held out his gloved hands and looked at Illesa as if she were a rat in a trap.

Illesa put the weasel into his cupped hands, where she turned round and round, her whiskers twitching.

The man picked up Eve by the scruff of the neck and turned to face the Count.

"Good, excellent," said the Count. His woman had turned away and was kissing her dog on the head. "Once you have it caged, you can retire. But at prime I want you to go to Sainte Croix. We need to be sure that Sir Richard is truly dead."

The man bowed slightly.

"Yes, my lord," he said, a Gascon by his accent. Azalais gripped Illesa's hand as Almaric strode towards the steps and pulled her into a deep curtsey.

"Now, jongleuse, without doubt I will require you here tomorrow night," the Count said. "Steward, give these women some coin for now. I can't bear to see pretty women looking sad. And send a guard to accompany them. Then we will know where to find them." He got up from the chair, leaning heavily on the table, and looked round at Sybilla. "Leave that dratted dog alone, woman. I have need of you." He pulled her out of her chair and out of the room.

Chapter XXXVIII

Monday the 28ᵗʰ November 1295
Four hours before Matins

"Where are you taking us?" Gaspar asked.

"Same house," the Templar replied, "although you may not be sleeping in the same room."

"I don't care where I sleep as long as I am not required to get up at monk's hours."

The Templar did not reply. Gaspar was working hard with the oar against the current. Richard had his eye open, although it was little help. He could only see straight up into the night sky, splashed with stars. Orion and the Great Bear in their slow pursuit across the heavens. There was the sound of another oar and a greeting. Perhaps a man checking his eel traps.

"I never asked you how the Archbishop likes his cope," Gaspar remarked after the other boat was far off. "You should listen to this too, Sir Ghost."

"Not now," hissed the Templar. "There will be people we can't see on the bank who can hear *you*."

"I am sorry, Father," said Gaspar. He sounded tired. It must be the early hours of the morning. Richard felt as though he had been dead a long time, and it was going to be hard to rise to life again.

"Here, at this jetty," said the Templar. They tied up, and the priest got out. "We will walk from here. You support him, and I will go ahead to see where we are."

Gaspar took hold of Richard's arms and pulled him up to a sitting position.

"Come on, up you get. Back from the dead," he muttered.

At first he felt that he had been decapitated, then there was a wave of dizziness. Richard put his head down between his legs for a moment.

"Quickly, you must not be seen getting out of the barge," Gaspar whispered, putting his shoulder underneath Richard's and heaving. They struggled to get out of the boat, and the

Templar had to pull him over the side onto the thin planks of the platform as Gaspar held him upright.

They set off, saying nothing, and Richard tried not to make any noise of pain. There was almost no light. Often his foot dragged against a pile of something in the street that he would rather have missed. It seemed a long walk with the vague shadow of the Templar ahead of them and Gaspar cursing under his breath when they tripped.

Finally they stopped at a large house with a cellar and a barrel hanging above the door. Before the Templar had even put his lips to the door to call, it opened and the light from the room made the face of the person in the doorway impossible to see. It was a man, and he stepped immediately back into the room as the Templar pushed Richard through the door, followed by Gaspar. The priest looked down the dark street in both directions and then closed the door.

"God bless you, Jorge," he said, turning to the large man who was standing ready, wringing his hands. "May you be ever blessed like the watchful virgins who faithfully waited for their master. We are very grateful. Here is the man I spoke of," he said, with a hand on Richard's shoulder. "We must hide him and clothe him. The cost will be met, but I must ask for your patience for a little while."

"Of course, Father Raymond," the man said, embarrassed. "We are glad to be of help. Here, he doesn't look well. Bring him to the hearth, let him sit down."

"Those comforts will have to wait," the Templar said. "We cannot have him in this room where anyone coming to the door can see him. He must go down to the cellar for the night. Down the ladder."

"You jest," Richard said, finding his voice at last.

"Ah, you're not so dead now, are you?" said Gaspar, smiling wickedly. "Don't worry Sir Richard, I'll lower you carefully down on a rope."

"You will not, Gaspar." Richard turned to the wine merchant. "Master, I'm grateful for your kindness. Show me the ladder, and I will attempt it."

"Wait, I will go ahead with a lamp," the man said, pushing a rug to one side with his foot. "Marie, bring food for these men and a pallet of straw. And some wine. The cat is down there, so you should not be troubled by mice."

He lifted a ring in the floor and the smell of wine barrels rose up at once on a draught of cold air.

"And blankets, Marie," Jorge called.

With a lamp in one hand, he climbed down easily, despite his large belly.

The Templar looked at the people gathered around the hole in the floor.

"I must go. If the French find me here, they will make too many assumptions. I will come very early tomorrow, and then we will move you again," he said looking at Richard. "Stay in the cellar no matter what you hear above." He looked at the merchant's wife, whose arms were full of blankets. "Marie, bless you. The two women will be coming soon, God willing. Keep watch for them."

Marie nodded.

"God keep you, Father. Margery, come and let the Father out and lock up," she called to a servant in the kitchen.

"I owe you thanks," Richard said to the Templar as he went to the door.

The Templar said nothing, but made the sign of the cross in the air to bless all in the room and went out into the dark street.

Gaspar passed the wine to Jorge, who was waiting at the bottom of the ladder, then Marie brought the bowls of pottage and the bread, followed by the straw mattress and two wool blankets.

"Just you now," said Gaspar, taking Richard by the arm. "I'll help you at the top, and good Master Jorge can catch you at the bottom."

He felt as weak as a kitten when he reached the ground. Jorge's strong arms helped him around a line of large barrels at the far side of the cellar to a small empty space. The wall there was wet, but the floor was laid with stone and covered in wood planks. It was quite dry.

"Here, Master Player, you have the stool and the knight can have the pallet. Not fit for your nobility, but maybe a bit better than the Tour l'Arbalesteyre."

268

"Indeed it is. My thanks," said Richard and lowered himself onto the pallet.

"I will come down once the others are safely here to see that you are well," Jorge concluded and disappeared around the barrels. They heard the heavy tread of his feet on the ladder. The light from the hall was abruptly cut off when the board was replaced, and they were left in darkness but for one small lamp.

"Let's eat," said Gaspar. "I don't think I've ever been so hungry since I was a babe abandoned on the street."

The food was well-seasoned and tasted so fresh that Richard went round the bowl carefully with his bread several times to make sure he had not missed any. When he lifted the cup of wine to his lips, he gave thanks for all he had not lost.

Gaspar looked exhausted. But before going upstairs to sleep, he would, Richard insisted, answer some questions.

It seemed William was not in France after all. He had stayed in England to protect the children and the manor. The others were here, with a plan so foolish and brave that it could only have been hatched by Gaspar and Illesa. The cope had already been presented to the Archbishop, who was no help whatsoever. But somehow by God's mercy, Father Raymond the Templar had decided to save them all.

"Do you know why he is willing to help us?" Gaspar asked. "He said he fought with you at Rions. But he is a Templar Priest. They are not supposed to fight, are they?"

"They are allowed to in self-defence or defence of the vulnerable," Richard said. "He is well trained."

There was a distant knocking above, and they fell silent, listening. Richard imagined he could hear the door opening, but they were at the back of the cellar and all the noise from above was muffled and indistinguishable.

There was a heavy tread across the floor and quickly back again. Then the sound of the door being closed, followed by long moments of indistinct sounds and high voices.

Gaspar had put his head in his hands and was half-asleep on the stool, but Richard was as alert as when he hunted for deer or boar in the forest, when every noise must be examined and interpreted. He wondered if he should snuff out the lamp, if there were guards outside who would see the faint glow through the outer cellar door and know where he was hiding.

Above there was a loud creak and a scraping sound, followed by a faint light.

"Gaspar, go and see who it is," Richard said.

Gaspar groaned as he got to his feet. He was very changed. Perhaps he was ill or wounded. He certainly didn't move as he used to.

Light footsteps were coming down the ladder.

"Here you are at last," Gaspar said. "Give me that lamp, I'm off to bed. You don't want me here anyway. He's round the back."

"Richard?" It was Illesa's voice, but uncertain, wavering.

"Here," he called, holding the lamp up so she could find her way round the barrels to the small space by the wall. Her face was just dancing shadows until she came into the circle of light, her eyes small pinpoints of candle flame.

She caught his outstretched hand and sat down on the pallet, her arms round him, her face pressed on his shoulder.

He pushed the fabric of her veil away and kissed her hair.

"Wife."

Illesa was weeping, silently holding in the sobs that wracked her chest.

"We are here, we are here," he said meaninglessly, stroking her hair. The veil had fallen down her back onto her cloak.

They sat that way for a long time until she was breathing steadily. He moved his leg, and she sat up, wiping her cheeks with her sleeve.

"Here, put your legs back on the pallet. I'll sit on the stool."

Her voice was hoarse, but it was the voice she used with her children, and him, when she was sorting them out. She was back to herself. Illesa found the wine and poured two cups, drinking hers quickly.

"I am still shaking," she said, holding her hand out flat in front of her. "They sent guards to escort us here. The Count wants Azalais to return tomorrow." She put down the cup and rubbed her eyes with her fists.

"You should not have come here, Illesa," he said gently, touching her knee.

"No, we are not talking about that," she said. "We need to work out how to get home now. When we are aboard a ship bound for England, then you can tell me all about what I shouldn't have done. And how unwomanly I am."

She had obviously rehearsed this speech. He put his hand on hers, where it rested on her lap, and unfurled her fingers. They were very cold.

"We will get out. God has sent us help."

She nodded and wiped her eyes with her free hand.

"The Count took Christopher's weasel," she burst out. "He just decided he wanted her. So now she will be kept in a cage in his cellar."

"What were you doing with a weasel?"

"I hope she bites him on the nose and it becomes septic. I'd like to cut his throat and let her lick his blood," Illesa said. "When I get home, I will curse him. Curse him to a humiliating death." She drank deeply from the cup. "Is there any bread? I'm so hungry."

"No, we ate it all," Richard said. "Illesa, maybe we should sleep. We can wake at the matins bell to make a plan. Lie here next to me, and we will keep warm."

She reached over her back and took off the veil that was caught on her cape. The plaits of her hair were unfamiliar, coming sideways across the dome of her head before falling down her back. He touched them as she came to lie down in the curve of his body.

"Sometimes when I was in the tower, I used to imagine your hair covering me. I dreamed of it running through my fingers. Of plaiting it around myself."

"You always were strange," she said. But there was a smile in her voice.

He put his face against the back of her head and soon heard her breath deepen into sleep.

Chapter XXXIX

Monday the 28th November 1295
Bordeaux
Matins

Illesa woke suddenly as something brushed against her hand. The lamp was still alight, but guttering and making wild shadows.

She pushed herself up on one elbow. Behind her Richard was still asleep. He grunted and rolled onto his back.

The blackness came nearer her face and brushed against her head, meowing. A cat, black as coal, hungry and cold. She stroked its back and it flopped onto the floor, purring. It had a small patch of white fur on its tummy.

She peered into the dark, looking for some crack of light from outside, but their hiding place was far from the cellar door.

A cup had tipped on its side, and the cat batted it between its paws. It was just a lanky kitten.

"Come on, we can't lie here playing all day," she told it. She edged out of the blanket, pushing it back over Richard and stood up, gathering the fabric of her veil. The cat wanted to play with that too.

It followed her as she felt her way back to the ladder. At the top, she pushed at the board, edging it out. A dim shaft of light came through. Someone was up and perhaps preparing food.

She pushed the board all the way to the side and pulled herself out, followed by the cat, meowing loudly.

"Here, I'll put that back for you," said someone above her.

She got off her knees, freed her skirts and turned to see Marie replacing the board with the cat weaving round her legs.

"You'd best come to the back. I'll soon sort that out," she said, looking at the veil in Illesa's hands.

"Thank you, Goodwife. I'm so grateful for your help."

The woman didn't answer. She was already in the back room, pulling a stool out for Illesa to sit on.

"The others are still asleep. You can wake them up once you are covered," Marie said, quickly pinning the veil in place. "Here, you had nothing to eat last night, did you? That bread is from yesterday, but I dare say you won't mind."

The bread soaked in warm milk was just what she needed. The cat was lapping up her milk from a dish on the floor.

"I'm sorry for the trouble we are causing you," Illesa said.

"Better trouble in this life than trouble in the next," said Marie matter-of-factly. "Here, take that up with you when you wake the others." She gave her a tray covered in a linen cloth. "You have many things to arrange. If anyone comes to the door, I will say you are still sleeping. Except for Father Raymond, of course."

Marie opened the shutters in the hall as Illesa walked through to the stairs. The sky was turning pale. It was still murky and cold, but the wind had died and the birds were calling loudly from a rooftop across the street. The upper room was very dark, but she could just see the table to put the tray on and went carefully to the window to open the shutters. Gaspar was stretched out on a pallet on the floor with a blanket half-over his face. Azalais was curled on the bed, still wearing her veil and cape. Illesa touched her shoulder.

"There is food and drink, my darling. Wake up, and come down to the cellar when you are ready." Azalais opened one eye, groaned and turned over. She would rouse Gaspar; she never let him lie.

Illesa left the room and shut the door. She went down the stairs almost at a run, not wanting Richard to wake and find her gone.

"Here," Marie called from the kitchen. "I'll hand this down to you when you are near the bottom."

The merchant's wife had opened the trap door to the cellar and was coming through to the hall holding yet another tray. It seemed she didn't like to be thanked, so Illesa just nodded and went down into the dark, putting up her hands for the tray. There was some light now, coming through the gap between the large cellar doors, but Richard was still asleep.

She got him up, helped him to relieve himself into the bucket and sat him back down, this time on the stool, while she shook out the pallet. He scratched his head thoughtfully.

The scratching went on and on.

"You've picked up lice in that prison. We should cut your hair," Illesa said. "Why don't I cut it now, then you will already look different."

"It's my eye and my leg that give me away," he said ruefully. "There's nothing I can do about them."

"Well, we should do what we can, and pray for the rest."

After they had eaten and drunk, Illesa took the shears hanging from her waist. She'd last used them on the delicate threads of the cope, now exchanged for a precious head of greasy, lice-ridden hair.

She was still working on the top of his head when the board moved aside again, and Azalais came down, followed slowly by Gaspar.

Gaspar was unshaven, and there were swollen shadows under his eyes. Azalais, on the other hand, was the picture of health and satisfaction.

"Here you are," she cried. "What a performance to get you out. I don't think my voice will ever be the same. And look at the state of you. Why did we bother, I ask myself?" She quickly embraced him and called up for more stools, refusing to sit on the pallet.

Gaspar leant against a barrel, his arms folded, watching Illesa finish Richard's haircut.

"No time for pleasantries. We need to decide what to do," he said with uncharacteristic seriousness. "Azalais tells me that one of the Count's men has been sent to discover whether you are really dead. He will be at the Benedictines by now, or very soon. They will know nothing about you, of course, and suspicion will immediately fall upon everyone who was there yesterday."

"Even the Father," said Azalais darkly.

"Especially him," Father Raymond said, coming down the ladder. They had not heard him arrive.

"Sir Richard, Lady Illesa, Dame Azalais, Gaspar of St Albans, blessings be upon you," he said, turning to each of them. "I bring you greetings from the Archbishop. If he

274

understood the matter better, he might have provided you with a letter of protection. But in the absence of his wit and wisdom, I have prepared one for you."

A cloth bundle was flung down the hole. Father Raymond bent over and picked it up.

"These are the clothes you must wear," he said, indicating Gaspar and Richard. "There is little we can do for you, Lady Burnel. You must change into your plainest cloak and wimple. Be as swift as possible. I will take you, Dame, with me," he said pointing to Azalais. "You have been asked to sing to the Archbishop, who has heard about your angelic gift. The others will be less conspicuous without you when they leave the city."

"Father, are you sure he understands what I sing? I have heard that he does not approve of the old songs," Azalais said, looking dubious.

"The Archbishop now understands that the songs of the trobairitz will give courage to the Gascons. With the memory of their proud history, the people of the South will have courage against the invasion from the North."

Azalais smoothed her hands over her fine skirt and smiled smugly.

"I am very glad he has changed his mind."

"God has seen fit to place his will in my hands, at least for now," Father Raymond said solemnly. "There is a gate out of the city from the Archbishop's Palace. You will be able to meet up with the others at the Hospital this evening."

"Where are we going?" Richard asked. They had not expected a fully formed plan.

"South. You are heading for Bayonne. The horse and cart is being prepared. The French will expect you to go by boat to Blaye and then to England. You will be caught quickly if you go by river. But there are many roads south to the shrine of Saint-Jacques, and the alarm will not be raised for a while yet." The Templar smiled to himself. "And I have an invitation for the Count that should divert his attention."

Gaspar whistled.

"You would make a very good leader of plays, Father. Your mind encompasses every detail."

Father Raymond stopped smiling and wagged a finger at Gaspar.

"I have also asked Marie to shave your head. The tonsure will give you away otherwise. Ladies, go upstairs to change and pack, and you men, put these clothes on."

Within moments Illesa and Azalais were standing in their travelling clothes in the hall watching Gaspar, in the clothes of an ordinary merchant, having his head shaved with a razor. The long strands lay around him like feathers from a plucked bird.

When Marie had finished, he stood wearing a mournful face, making the sign of damnation with his gloved right hand while his other covered the hole where his ear used to be.

"What happened to the citole?" he asked.

"It is behind the bed upstairs," Azalais said, handing her clothes to one of the servants to hide in the cart.

"I will leave it here for you good people," Gaspar said looking at the wine merchant, who was just coming in through the door. "If you can sell it, it should repay some of this expense."

Jorge looked embarrassed. Marie brushed the hair from Gaspar's shoulders, tutting.

"You look dreadful. Put your cap on," she said. "Everyone will think you've had worms."

Richard's head came up through the gap in the floor. The Templar was pushing him up the ladder. Jorge reached in and hauled him the rest of the way.

"I have my old things here," Richard said, clutching the dirty clothes. "Perhaps you should burn them?"

"Nonsense," said Marie. "I will wash them and cut them up into clothes for the children."

Richard was now dressed in black and brown wool, with a wide-brimmed hat that made him look like a ploughman cleaned up for church. At least the hat would make his missing eye less obvious.

"In the cart now, quickly," Father Raymond said. "You must cross almost the whole city. Go to the gate near the Cathedral. It is the busiest, and you are less likely to be remembered. Then take the road to the Hôpital Saint Julien, where you should stay the night. But first stop at the church of Sainte Eulalie, like the pilgrims you are, to beg for help from Saint Jacques." He pulled a sealed letter from his tunic. "Here is the letter of protection for your pilgrimage. I have stated that you come from Brittany. They know nothing of that place here and will expect you to be strange. When you get outside the city, there is little chance of trouble, but if you need shelter, stop at the Commandery at Poms. It is a two-day journey from here." He stopped for breath, looking around to see if there was anything he had forgotten. "Dame Azalais, you and I will wait here a while," he concluded.

"Will you meet us at Saint Julien?" Illesa asked him hopefully. It was a great relief to be with someone so capable.

"I think not. From now I will be fully engaged in the Feast of Saint André with the Archbishop, when the cope will be worn in public with much spectacle. It may even help the bordelais to rally against the French. It will certainly be very distracting for the Count."

"What about the prisoners who leave this morning?" Illesa asked, imagining passing them at a crossroads and Richard being recognised.

"They travel by ship. They will sail up the Garonne as far as Agen, before they have to continue by foot."

Richard tried to get down on one knee.

"Come, everyone," he said. "We must pray. Father you blessed us with your help; please pray for us as we leave."

Everyone knelt, and Father Raymond stood with his hands stretched out over them, praying for their journeys with his deep voice.

When he had finished, Illesa went to Azalais.

"You will come back to us tonight, my darling?" she said, holding Azalais by the upper arms and kissing her.

"I might," said Azalais coyly. "But you look so poor! You are much lower company than I am used to," she laughed.

Richard was helped onto the cart. Gaspar led Sancha, and Illesa walked beside him out of the yard and into the street, leaving the Temple behind them as they headed for the city gate and the road south, away from Bordeaux.

Chapter XL

Monday the 28th November 1295
Hôpital Saint Julien
Vespers

After the excitement of leaving Bordeaux, the Hôpital Saint
Julien was crowded and mundane. There was nowhere they
could speak privately. Monks came and went through the
cloister, treating the patients sitting on the stone benches.
After eating the watery pottage and old bread, Gaspar had
gone, as usual. Illesa had looked in all the public rooms, but he
was not in the Hospital. She did not want to tell Richard what
she feared, so she sat in anxious silence next to him in the
cloister. He was resting his head on the wall and kept falling
asleep then waking when there was a noise amongst the
patients.

For most of the day, he had seemed his old self. They had
all been elated when they were allowed through the city gate
without question, having presented the Archbishop's letter. At
the church of Sainte Eulalie, they joined others saying prayers
at the statue of Saint Jacques. Gaspar had found a staff for
Richard, and he was able to walk from the cart into the church
without help. Illesa bought a cheap lead scallop badge from an
old man at the church door. It was not as elaborate as Azalais'
badges, but it was fitting for a poor pilgrim. She pinned it to
Richard's short cape. With that and his broad hat, he looked
more convincing.

One of the Brothers looked at Richard's leg, but was
dismissive about treatment. He could be given salves, but that
was all, and they had run out because of the war. His best
chance was to pray continually that, at the end of the journey,
Saint Jacques would perform a miracle. Illesa was not
impressed, but she held her tongue, not wishing to make them
any more conspicuous than they already were.

The Hospital felt very close to the dangers at Bordeaux.
They were only a mile from the city wall, and there were

constant departures and arrivals. Illesa was itching to get further away from the Count and his men. She had spent much of the day worrying about Gaspar, and Azalais. Had Father Raymond really brought her to sing for the Archbishop, or was she locked up in a cell in the tower, a payment for their release in some exchange they had not understood?

As the hours passed, they sat waiting close to the Hospital gate, expecting Azalais and Gaspar at any moment. Sometimes Illesa's hand would fall to Eve's pouch at her waist, now empty, her mind churning with thoughts of her children: Christopher and his terrifying, violent dreams, alone at night, Joyce, wanting the comfort of her mother's lap when she was tired. It was hard to feel that they had accomplished anything when they were still within sight of the Tour l'Arbalesteyre.

At the bell they should have gone with the other pilgrims to Vespers, but instead they lingered inside the gate while the moon rose over the west end of the chapel. It was Azalais who came first. Wrapped in her best cape, she presented a parchment to the gatekeeper.

As soon as Illesa saw her face, she knew.

"I don't have long," Azalais said, coming towards them and stowing the parchment up her sleeve. "I really must be back before they close the city gate."

Illesa felt sick to her stomach.

"Why, what is wrong, darling? You look so ill. Is the food bad?"

"You aren't coming with us," Illesa said.

"Well, no. I am not," said Azalais, apologetically. Richard grunted. Azalais gave him a look and took Illesa's hand. They all sat down in a corner of the cloister.

"Darling, it is much better if I stay here and keep the Count and the Archbishop happy for this feast. They want to hear me, and it would be foolish to disappoint them. I am too memorable; there it is!" she said, putting her palms out in front of her. "They so appreciate my talent here in Bordeaux. It has been years since they had anyone trained to sing the old songs. They are like thirsty camels!"

"But we thought you would guide us to Dax," Illesa said. "I hoped you would introduce me to my Aunt."

"Oh, she is an old cow, really, so demanding and so sanctimonious. You would be sorely disappointed," Azalais said, flicking her fingers over her sleeve. She looked up at Illesa's face. "Please, darling, don't look like that. Imagine if I came with you, and barely a day had gone by before the Count's men came looking for me, demanding I return. And, by my faith, there is the escaped prisoner. What a lucky find for the French."

"Shhhh, Azalais!" hissed Illesa.

"I am not being loud," she said, looking affronted. "Well, you see the problem. They heard my voice, and now they won't let it go. I must stay in Bordeaux for a while with my friends in the old quarter. They are happy to have me."

"I'm sure they are," said Richard.

Azalais turned on him like a hunting cat.

"You never appreciated my talent," she accused. "You were always wishing I'd leave your family. And now I am."

"No indeed, my lady," Richard said, softly. "Your voice is an exquisite gift. I am grateful for your help. But I am also sad for my wife. She loves you. And we both wish that you were travelling on with us. You must stay in Bordeaux if that is what is best for you. But we are sorry to say Farewell so quickly."

It was hard to hear Richard speaking about her. He understood, somehow, what Azalais had been to her while he was away.

"But now that Richard is free, you don't need me," Azalais said to Illesa. "Do you, my darling?"

Illesa shook her head.

"I do need you." She put her arms around her cousin and felt the strength and passion in that small body. Azalais kissed her on both cheeks, then held her away, looking into her eyes.

"You must go to the coastal road. Those pilgrims, Paul and André, are going in-land through Saint-Sever. You don't want to come across them again! And also the French won't expect you to go that way because it is a bit longer. Start tomorrow and aim for Sanguinet, then you will reach the Commandery at Poms on the third day. Father Raymond says they will protect you. From there it will take a week to reach Bayonne." Azalais paused, looking pleased with herself. "Here in Bordeaux, we will be very amused when the Count's men fail to find you. And we will be working on a special performance for the feast day of Saint André. The whole city is going to be amazed," she declared. "The Count wants something superior to impress the other commanders of the French Army. But the Archbishop, or should I say Father Raymond, hopes that the beauty of the cope will show miraculous favour for the Gascon and English army, reinforced by my songs. They are each determined to humiliate the other."

"Haven't they noticed that you have lost your citole and tabor players?" said Gaspar who had come silently out of the gloom and sat down next to Richard.

Azalais looked haughty.

"No, they have not missed you at all. I told them that you were just common jongleurs I had picked up, but if the Count would pay for proper musicians then it would sound even better."

Gaspar laughed.

"Good for you, Mistress Azalais. You are more than a match for that Count of Artois."

"Did you see Eve today?" Illesa asked.

Azalais suddenly lost her jollity. She shook her head.

"But I've seen that man who took her. He was coming out of the Count's room at sext. He set off for the quay with a group of guards."

"Just what Father Raymond said the Count would do," said Richard. "Did you hear the man's name?"

"Almaric, a Gascon traitor," said Azalais.

Richard rubbed his chin.

"Do you know him?" asked Gaspar.

"He knows me," said Richard. "We must leave before first light. I wouldn't be surprised if Almaric doesn't stop to sleep or eat."

"I saw him eating," said Azalais, "like a wolf. But yes, it is all very well for Father Raymond to hide you in full view, but you are distinctive, and he will not have trouble tracking you if you don't move quickly. Almaric will be on horseback, and you just at walking pace. But again that is your protection. If you go riding at top speed through the countryside, the French army will follow you like bees after the flowers."

"You could wear a cloth mask," suggested Gaspar. "Like the lepers who have lost their noses."

"But then he would have to stay with the lepers," said Illesa. She did not meet Gaspar's eye, hoping he would not choose this moment to speak of it. Richard might not forgive him for putting them at risk of leprosy, even though Gaspar had done so much to free him. She would have to speak to Richard and try to make him understand.

But Gaspar seemed subdued and sat rocking slightly, cross-legged on the bench. It was nearly fully dark. Azalais got to her feet.

"You must not make any spectacle of yourself," she said pointing at Gaspar.

"We will leave that to you," said Gaspar, looking up at her with the twisted face of a demon.

"For that you can see me back to the city gate, Gaspar. I'm not walking on that path in the dark by myself, even with Father Raymond's letter of protection nailed to my forehead."

"I thank you for your help, Azalais, and I hope you come back to England," Richard said solemnly, bowing his head in its comical hat.

"If that Jean Fracinaut ever begs for my pardon, I might. It will depend on the degree of his sorrow and contrition."

Illesa went with them to the gate, leaving Richard on the bench. The lay-brother gatekeeper was unsurprised. So close to the city, the mere absence of daylight stopped little of the activity. In the fields beyond, dim shadows of boys gathered cows from the meadows.

"God keep you, Azalais. I will miss you."

Azalais' tears were perfect shining pearls falling down her cheeks. She even looked beautiful when she cried. She turned and walked towards the smoke and light of the town, Gaspar limping at her heel.

Chapter XLI

Compline

Richard sat up suddenly. A hand had tapped his shoulder and woken him.

"What is it?"

"Shhhh," said Gaspar. "It's me." He was sitting cross-legged next to Richard's pallet on the floor of the men's dormitory.

Richard rubbed his eye. It seemed only a few minutes since he had finally managed to ignore the pain in his leg and fall asleep.

"Is it time to get up?" he asked. He felt so groggy as if he had been drinking all night.

"No. Stay there. Everyone is still asleep."

"Why did you wake me then?" Richard propped his head up on his hand and blinked several times. It was cold. There was some moonlight coming through the shutters, and Gaspar's breath hung in clouds in the air.

"I am bidding you farewell," Gaspar said, miming waving and weeping. "I have already told Illesa the sad and sorry tale of my infirmity. Now I must tell you. I cannot stay near you any longer. My name must be Lazarus from now on."

"What?" said Richard. "What do you mean?"

He looked at Gaspar who was neither smiling nor sad, who held up his hands to show Richard the weeping sores on his fingers.

"From now on it's a clapper or a bell for me."

"No," Richard said. "Gaspar, that can't be."

Gaspar put down his hands, and stretched out his legs.

"I won't show you the gruesome evidence of my feet," he said with a wink. "I have tried to be careful. But now that you are out of prison, I must not stay any longer. There is a good Lazar house very near here – Saint Nicolas. Perhaps Azalais might even come to visit me from time to time," he said rather wistfully.

"But, but how long have you known?" Richard said, stuttering. He had a sudden, shameful urge to back away from Gaspar.

"I thought it was just the cold last winter when I lost the feeling in my fingers and toes. But the sensation never came back in the summer. And now I cannot play my citole without bleeding; I cannot ride a horse without causing both of us injury. So I certainly can't walk with you to Bayonne."

"So take a boat home. Come and live near us!" said Richard. "You cannot stay here with the French army ransacking the land."

"I like it here," Gaspar said mildly. "I'm fond of Aquitaine. I prefer the food. And I want to be able to listen to their music from time to time. I think here it will be easier to be a leper. In England it is nothing but snow and suffering. Here, at least, I will enjoy the wine and the sunshine."

Richard sat up painfully.

"But what – "

"Besides which," said Gaspar, "King Edward and his army are supposed to be retaking Aquitaine. Then it will be easy for you to come here, buy wine and visit me."

Richard closed his eyes and shook his head again.

"What dreams you have, Gaspar. What glories you see in the future, where I see only blood. I picture you on the stage, as Moses about to enter the Promised Land." He sighed. "I hope you are right. I hope you are right. The Gascons don't deserve this mistreatment, from us or the French."

Gaspar leant in a little closer.

"I am leaving it to you to tell Illesa what I have decided to do. She is already upset. Imagine the tears, the tearing of hair, the rending of clothes, if I said Farewell in person," he said with a hint of satisfaction.

Richard put out his hand as Gaspar stood up. Gaspar did not take it, but bowed elaborately instead.

"You have been a good friend to me, Gaspar."

"I know. It is simply because you have been a good friend to me, Sir Richard. I expect I will see you again. In one world or another."

And he was gone. Still quick enough on his feet, when he wanted to be.

Chapter XLII

Tuesday the 29th November 1295
Hôpital Saint Jacques
Le Barb

The sun was close to its apex when Richard finally admitted that Gaspar was not catching them up after 'helping Azalais'. That he had stayed behind in the Saint Nicolas Lazar house with the other lepers, and that he had not wanted to say Farewell to her. Richard had decided to tell her only once they were so far from Bordeaux that it would have taken the rest of the day to return.

"How could you let him go?" Illesa shouted at him. "I would have convinced him to come with us. Sancha is a good enough horse to take two men in a cart. The only reason he left was to protect us from the disease. But I know the prayers and special amulets that would have warded it off!"

Richard didn't say anything. He knew, from years of experience, that her anger was unstoppable until it burnt itself out.

They paused by a stream to water the horse and let her graze and rest. It would be disastrous if she went lame. They watched her in silence, tearing bits of grass up from the side of the stream, standing at ease with her eyes closed. Untroubled.

When they returned to the road, Illesa banged the pilgrim's staff down on the ground with each step. She was glad Richard was in the cart and not able to see her face. When her tears had stopped, an angry pain had started behind her forehead. It seemed that to get her husband back she had to lose her friends. And now they had to make it all the way to Bayonne in winter, alone.

An answering voice inside her told her that people walked three times as far to the shrine of Saint Jacques. And hadn't she already received God's blessings in full when Father Raymond had helped them? Did she expect an angel to pick them up and put them down in their manor yard in Langley?

This journey was not hard, compared to many. The roads were boggy, but not difficult for Sancha. If worse came to worse and she couldn't pull the cart any more, they would leave it as an offering at a church shrine and Richard would ride Sancha at a walk to Bayonne.

Illesa breathed out slowly. There were buildings in the distance. She walked quickly when she was angry. It was the Hospital at Le Barb that a few of the other pilgrims were also aiming for tonight, but they were the first to arrive. Illesa had not wanted to walk with the others. They would all catch up sooner or later, but at least Richard would have a chance of a bed, and there would be stabling for Sancha.

She glanced back. Richard had fallen asleep, his head resting on a sack. What a smile that would put on Cecily's face. Her master reduced to the appearance of a ploughman in rustic clothes, sleeping in a cart.

If all went well, it would be less than a month before they were home. Her mind slid away from all the accidents that might have occurred while she was gone. William and Cecily would not let anything happen to the children. The winter sicknesses usually came after Christmas, and by then she would be back to nurse them if they fell ill.

The Hospital was built of well-carved, fresh stone. It obviously had wealthy patrons, so perhaps it was well managed. But there was no way of knowing until you entered. She had heard tales of many hospitals where the patients were relieved of their coin and then ignored or thrown out. But they would have been warned if it had that reputation.

She pulled Sancha to a halt in front of the gate. The horse shook her head and snorted loudly through her nose. Richard woke with a start.

"I will knock," Illesa said shortly.

She stomped up to the door in the gate and rapped on it.

Eventually it was opened by a lay sister with raw, red hands. She looked Illesa over before speaking.

"On the way to Saint-Jacques? We expect alms from the well."

"Yes. I know. This man is ill. He goes to the shrine for help. May we receive your hospitality and medicine to help us on the journey?"

The woman went over and looked at Richard in the cart as if she were inspecting a sheep she was buying in the market. The sister pulled down his hose and prodded his leg, then she examined his missing eye.

"An old wound, Sister."

"You a soldier?"

"Once, but no longer."

She turned to Illesa, rubbing her hands down her brown wool tunic.

"It's extra for the horse. I'll take the man. You lead her round the back to the stables. Vespers soon. Then you will have your supper. You can sleep on the floor next to his bed for the night."

The woman helped Richard down from the cart and let him lean on her as they went through the door. No extra talk, only what was strictly necessary.

Illesa looked back down the road. In the distance dark smudges that could be pilgrims stood out against the bright sky. The birds were calling from the few bushes, and the wind that had been absent for two days was just getting up, whipping her skirts and veil. She felt the weight of the road gathering on her mind, the long distance home. Her legs were suddenly sore and heavy and didn't want to move. She smacked Sancha's haunch.

"You've done well," she whispered in her twitching ear. "But we've much further to go. Come on. I'll rub you down."

She spent a long time in the stable, taking time with Sancha, making sure that the stable boy understood her needs until the vespers bell sounded. Then she washed the dust and smell of horse from her hands and face and went through the cloister towards the chapel.

The ill who were able to attend were sitting on benches, but Illesa made no effort to find Richard. She stood at the back with the other well pilgrims. This was a place where Gaspar would not be allowed. He would be spending his first night amongst the afflicted: misshapen, fingerless people, covered in sores and lumps, abhorred by all except the religious who cared for them. And God was allowing this to happen to gentle Gaspar, while powerful men who thought nothing of wounding and killing sat on their thrones and cushions, eating and drinking the finest food and wine, indulging themselves. They should be punished, but God seemed to let them live and kill to their heart's content.

When the Brothers of the Hospital began to sing the Psalm, Illesa wept into her cupped hands.

He hath scattered abroad, he hath given to the needy;
his righteousness endureth for ever, his horn shall be exalted.

The wicked shall see it, and be vexed. They will gnash their teeth
and melt away. The desire of the wicked shall perish.

At the end, Illesa waited at the door for Richard. Someone had given him his staff. She had forgotten to bring it to him. They had also given him a shave and washed his hair.

He stopped in front of her and smiled.

"The people here are kind. I haven't had such treatment since I left home."

She looked away.

"Good. It is not always the case with these hospitals. The ones away from the towns are better, I think."

"Illesa," he said, reaching out for her hand.

She tried to look at him but found she was crying again.

"No," she said. "Let's not speak now. I am so hungry. We must eat."

Richard began the slow progress towards the refectory, with Illesa walking silently beside him.

"We should leave early," he said.

"Yes, before first light again. I told the stable boy."

He nodded and they went in to the hall.

There was nothing to do after their simple meal except retire to bed. Only two lamps were lit at either end of the Infirmary. Illesa helped Richard relieve himself and lie down on the mattress. It was not particularly soft, but the bedding was clean. She pulled the coarse blanket over him and began to set out her own sleeping place. A lay sister was tending to one of the patients at the other end of the room nearer the altar. He shouted in pain as she tried to remove his bandages.

"Do you think my leg will improve when we get home?" Richard asked, turning on his side to face her. She continued

288

making a pillow for her head out of her pack. They had given her a pad to sleep on, but she would need her cape as a blanket.

"Yes, it will. If we can ease the pain so you can move it more, it will become less stiff and sore."

"I don't want to be useless for the rest of my life."

"I know," she said. She touched his hand, and he curled his fingers around hers.

"How did all this happen?" he asked looking up at the arches above them, the ribs of the vault dark against the whitewashed walls. "Did God will it so?"

"God knows we needed kindness, food and sleep. Tomorrow we will be able to go further."

"Did you pray for the children at Vespers?" Richard asked, squeezing her fingers.

"I pray for them every day and all the hours," Illesa said, pulling the cape onto her lap with one hand.

He released her fingers and reached inside his tunic, bringing out the silk pouch.

"And I prayed for you," Richard said. "Here is the length of you in silk, and here is the page from Christopher's book."

"I was angry with him for cutting it out."

"I can imagine," he said, smiling a little. "But you can sew it back in with your tiny stitches. These things were a comfort to me."

"Your thread is in my purse, here." She fumbled with it, and brought it out. "I will knot them together."

He watched her a while as she tried to make the pattern in the dim light. Then he put his hand over hers and closed his eyes.

She lay down and fell asleep with the silk still in her fist.

* * *

Illesa woke. Something was scuttling over her body, close to her waist. She gasped and pushed it away. There was a high-pitched squeal, and it landed on the floor next to her. Illesa knew that cry. She sat up. The lamps still shone a dim light over the hall with its rows of beds and the snoring, gasping patients.

"Eve," she whispered. "Eve!" Had she dreamt it? Surely it had been the weasel that had wakened her. She felt whiskers on the back of her hand and turned it over, holding her palm out. The trembling feet of the weasel stood on her palm. She cupped her in both hands and brought the creature up to her face.

"Eve, where have you come from?" Her stomach turned over as she looked up and down the room. But she saw no one out of bed. Between the lamps, the shadows were deep. The weasel squeaked for food. Illesa reached for her pouch, but knew there was nothing left inside. But the familiar smell of her bed might be enough to keep Eve quiet. The Count's man, Almaric, was somewhere in the room, waiting to see where the weasel went. He was there to watch the weasel betray her mistress.

Illesa lay her head down on her pack. At her waist, she still had her shears and a small knife. That was all. Richard had nothing. She tried to calm her breathing and the heart banging hard in her chest. A sheep bleated outside, and an uneasy horse stamped its foot. Almaric's horse.

There was a slight change in the air, a breath of cold, a scrape of wood on stone. He had left the room, had been standing in the shadow at the far end by the small door into the ablution room. From there he would climb out of the open windows and drop down only a few feet to the ground. He was light on his feet; she heard nothing of his landing. But the horse was not as good at being quiet. It shook its bridle as he mounted to go only a short distance. Obviously he would stay in sight and watch the Hospital, tracking them when they left.

He knew where they were, but now she knew where he was.

The weasel turned around in the pouch and settled into a ball. Illesa sat up and put on her boots. The fear had gone and been replaced with a cold burning rage. She checked the room quickly, the knife in her hand, looking quietly under every bed. Then she went into the ablution room and peered out of the window. The moon was waning, low on the horizon. The black forms of the houses squatted by the road. In the distance she heard an owl calling sadly.

He would be watching from the patch of scrub that bordered the road to the south. From there he could see all that came and went.

Illesa went back into the Infirmary and knelt by Richard's bed. She took his hand in one of hers and at the same time put her finger on his lips.

* * *

When Richard told her what the Count had ordered him to do, she was very angry, but she remained quiet. When he revealed what Almaric's role was, she was afraid.

"Does he still think that you are spying for them? Does he think this is part of the plan to make it a more realistic escape than Turberville's?" she whispered.

Richard did not answer for a while.

"If he thinks that I am trying to escape and that I am not spying for them, then he will kill me. That was the promise. By returning Eve, he has told us that he knows where we are, and that he is watching us. Now he will follow us until I provide the information that they want," Richard whispered.

"He will track us all the way to Bayonne and wait for you to speak to the remains of the English army?"

"I am not difficult to follow," Richard said bitterly.

"Neither are you a fit soldier," hissed Illesa. "You can't go back to the fight."

"They don't want me for that. They want the strategy. Both sides want information about the next movements of the armies."

"What if you just sailed home?"

"He would see us. There was a promise of a bolt through the heart."

"He must sleep! He can't watch us every minute of the day."

"He won't be here alone. He will share the watch with someone."

"Then we have to outwit him."

Richard shifted on the bed, moving his leg into a more comfortable position.

"We certainly aren't going to defeat him by force."

Illesa looked up at the ceiling, so like the ribs of a boat in its construction. That was what they needed: a ship and a decoy.

"Tomorrow, will we go the way we planned?" she whispered. "To the Templar Commandery at Poms?"

"I think so. I could be gathering information from the Templars about the movements of the English army in this area, so it shouldn't look suspicious," Richard said. "We must pray for a helper there, like Father Raymond, if that is within God's plan. What hour do you think it is now?"

"Nearly matins. There's no point going back to sleep. At least we know that Almaric is as tired as we are," Illesa said with feeling.

Chapter XLIII

Wednesday the 30th November 1295
The Feast of Saint André
Commandery Poms – Aquitaine
Vespers

As soon as they arrived at the Commandery and showed the gatekeeper the letter from Father Raymond, Illesa felt hope return. The journey from Le Barb had been long and gruelling. No matter how much she looked, she could see no sign of Almaric or any other guard. It was close to dark when they arrived. Her eyes were tired from the constant searching.

"He will have sent word to the Count that he found us," Richard said. "Even if he went himself, he'd be confident that he could ride back and catch us with no difficulty."

"If he is riding, we should be able to see or hear him," grumbled Illesa. The lack of sleep had given her another pain in her temple, and the strong cold wind made it worse. None of the other pilgrims were heading towards the coast from Le Barb. They weren't fools who wanted the full blast of sea wind and driving rain in their faces on their journey. Illesa had stopped worrying about being shot. All she wanted was a good bed and a good meal. And the strong walls of the Commandery around her, to keep out even a man like Almaric.

The Templar Sergeant who dealt with pilgrims had an intelligent look. When they told him that they needed to speak to the Master, he quickly ordered men to take their horse and brought them into the cloister.

"Women are not permitted in the main house, but you may speak to the Master in the parlour. First, would you care to eat something?"

They cared very much. When they finished their pottage, their bowls were refilled with seethed fish. After that and spring water mixed with the Templar's wine, Illesa's head began to clear and she felt ready for an audience with the Templar Master.

"How much should we tell him?" she whispered.

Richard looked thoughtful.

"I think we must trust him. Father Raymond sent us here, and we will not get help anywhere else within three days' ride. It might be best if I speak to him. Templars are very strict about their contact with women."

Illesa sighed impatiently.

"I promise I won't touch him, but if there is something important, I will speak."

"I don't doubt it," said Richard, eating the last of the bread.

The Master called for them soon after, and they were taken to a small room which contained a large iron-bound oak chest.

The Master entered without ceremony. He was a small man, very neat in his appearance but with a full beard. He sat behind a bare table and indicated that they should sit on the bench against the wall.

"I hear that you have been in the care of Father Raymond in Bordeaux." Richard nodded and opened his mouth to speak but the Master continued. "And you have come down this route hoping to be mistaken for a pilgrim and not to be discovered as the knight who recently escaped from the tower in Bordeaux. The ever-vigilant Father Raymond has not left anything to Fortune or the Devil. He has sent a comprehensive report to me. As is his custom," he said with a resigned air.

"Master, we are grateful. But there is one new thing that he may not have told you."

"I do know that this is your wife, who has rather an unusual idea of her duty," he said, frowning.

Illesa dropped her eyes humbly. This small, serious man disapproved of her. Through God's mercy, that would not prevent him from helping them.

"Yes," said Richard, "but there is even something else." He drew a breath. "When I was in the tower, the Count of Artois insisted that I spy for him against my own country. He wanted me to fake an escape and pass information about the English plans to him through one of his men, a Gascon called Almaric." The Master steepled his fingers and pressed them against his lips as Richard continued. "Almaric has tracked us, and is following us at the moment. The Count promised that if I did not produce information, Almaric would kill me."

"When did he find you?" the Master asked, his forehead lined with concern.

"Last night. At the Hospital at Le Barb. We have not seen him today, but we know he keeps watch on us."

"Does he know that you are being helped by the Templars?"

"He might. Or he might place the blame at the feet of our friend, Gaspar, who dressed as a Benedictine and pronounced me dead. He suspected that Illesa was part of the plot to get me out, but he only saw her with Gaspar not with Father Raymond."

The Master was silent for a while. Outside a bell sounded, its ring scattered in the wind.

"And he expects you to go to Bayonne?"

"The French want information about the intentions of the English commanders there and entry to the city. If I do not produce it, they have also threatened to kill my squire Hugh, who is still their prisoner."

Illesa glanced quickly at Richard. He had not said anything to her of Hugh, had kept that burden to himself until now.

"There is nothing you can do for him," the Master said, leaning forward. "A quick death is a blessing as long as he is shriven. It would have been worse if he had died of his wounds or from a disease."

Richard shivered and bowed his head.

"You would not have been able to do anything for him in those circumstances," the Master said firmly. "You have been offered what seems a chance to save him, but it is false hope. He is beyond your help. Even if you gave the French information, he would die in the aftermath of the English defeat. All you can do for this boy is to pray for him. God alone can help him now."

Richard nodded. He swallowed hard before he spoke again.

"We owe your Order a large debt already, which I will gladly pay in alms when we return home to our manor, but may we beg your help in one final way?"

"I was expecting you to require our help. You need not beg. We are sworn to protect those going to Saint-Jacques, and you are going on that way although you may not yet complete it."

"We are thankful for your kindness."

The Master waved his hand in the air dismissively.

"I will consult with my cellarer. I believe there is a shipment of wine barrels leaving Mimizan soon. It has been diverted from Bordeaux to stay out of the hands of the French army. It is destined for Bayonne."

"Perhaps we can sail with this shipment?" Richard suggested.

"But Almaric will simply follow it," said Illesa.

The Master looked at her coldly. There was a long silence, and he turned back to Richard.

"You could be hidden on board. Then when you get to Bayonne, you could seek help from the English commanders," the Master said.

Richard paused and stretched out his leg.

"Maybe. But I think that Lady Burnel is right. Almaric will follow me and may accuse me to the English if I do not give him what he wants. The French would love to know that I had been executed by my own side, like Turberville," Richard said, looking at his hands folded in his lap.

"If we convince Almaric that you have left for Bayonne, he will follow you there," Illesa said. "You don't actually have to leave. He just needs to believe that you have."

Both men looked at her. The Templar Master sucked his teeth.

"Explain."

Chapter XLIV

Thursday the 1st – Friday the 2nd
December 1295
Gastes – Aquitaine

The next day the Master came to them before prime with the result of his conversation with the cellarer. The barrels of wine were at another Commandery at Gastes on the lakeshore. They would be loaded onto a barge the next day and taken down the south-east side of the lake to the canal. Then they would travel through the town to the port at Mimizan and be loaded onto a sea-going ship heading to Bayonne.

Illesa and Richard sat in the cloister and argued about the plan until tierce.

"I understand what you are proposing," Richard repeated, "but it will not work."

"It will. Almaric has no idea that we are married. As far as he knows I am just your Gascon lover. And a low-born one at that." Illesa looked at her rough and reddened hands. "When he sees me alone, he will assume that you have left me behind. That kind of betrayal is common. Just think of Theseus abandoning Ariadne after she helped him escape the labyrinth."

"That is an old tale," Richard said. "A hired killer like Almaric will know nothing of it."

"He will know many men who have done exactly the same thing." She touched the Saint Margaret badge on her cloak absentmindedly. "It will be easy to convince him that I am a crazed and desperate woman."

Richard shook his head.

"You are in a foreign land, and what you want to attempt is dangerous."

"I will be near enough to the Abbey. If anything happens, I will take refuge there."

"No," Richard said. "You are putting the Lord to the test."

Illesa looked up into the sky. The day was bright and cold. Distant gulls soared in the burnished air. She put her hand out and tapped Richard's good knee.

"You don't like it because I thought of it, like the Templar Master. He wants you to go to Bayonne and live in fear for your life for weeks, rather than admit that a woman can have a mind. If my plan works, we will be home by Christmas."

"That is ungracious of you, Illesa. I have never denied you a mind. Common sense maybe, and a reasonable fear of danger certainly. But not a mind. The reason I don't like it is because you are the one exposed to the most danger."

Illesa took the restless weasel out of her pouch and fed her a small piece of rabbit. She smiled at Richard.

"I have learned a few things from Gaspar. Always give the public the story they expect to hear, and then they will follow you like lambs follow the ewe all the way to the end that you have prepared for them. It is a very simple trick."

Richard did not return her smile.

"It is not a courtly way to escape," he said, grasping for a new argument.

"It wasn't courtly for the French to force Turberville to spy for them and then to let him be killed and execute his sons. And there is certainly nothing courtly about the Count of Artois. He has no sense of chivalry."

"Even so, it seems a cowardly way. I don't want to be as ignoble as them."

"You have been imprisoned for months and battling the French for a year. Is that not enough?"

Richard sighed.

"I am leaving Hugh to die and you to face Almaric."

Illesa took his hand.

"Sometimes you need a different kind of strategy. Think of the Greeks at the end of the Trojan War."

"They were treacherous."

"True. But they got back to their ships and sailed home."

* * *

They reached the Commandery at Gastes late that afternoon. The Master there read the letter from Poms twice before he looked up.

"Three of our Templar Knights will be on board to protect both the shipment and the pilgrims arriving at the port. One French guard, or even two, will not cause trouble for them," he said calmly, looking out of his window at the clear sky. "It will be a good day to sail tomorrow. Have you seen the Count's man? Do you know how many others he has with him?"

Richard shook his head.

"No, he has stayed out of sight, so he might be alone."

The Master left the parchment on the table and got up.

"I will send out a scout. It would be good to know where he is when we set off and if he has men with him."

The Master took Richard with him into the inner house to have his leg examined and perhaps to find him some different clothes. It seemed an embarrassment to both of them that he looked so much like a peasant.

The wine was due to leave at first light the following day to catch the tide at Mimizan that afternoon. Illesa spent some time in the Commandery Chapel, which was dedicated to Saint André like the Cathedral. Here the offerings were modest appeals to the saint to protect those who plied the sea: clay and lead models of fish, fragments of fishing nets and the stubs of many candles that had burnt out the previous day during his feast.

There was enough money for a voyage home and very little else. But Illesa paid for a candle and prayed for Gaspar and for the squire Hugh. Then she sat quietly with the weasel in the cloister and decided on how to behave and what exactly she would say to make Almaric angry enough to forget his suspicion. It was as if Gaspar himself sat in front of her, directing her practice.

* * *

By prime the next day, Illesa was sitting on a box, driving the cart, with her legs only inches from Sancha's haunch. It would take half the day to get to Mimizan at this pace. She flicked the switch at Sancha, but spoke to her gently.

After two hours ride under a clear sky, a man on a fast rouncey rode up beside her. No livery, only a crossbow slung across his back. Very young.

"Where are you going?"

"Mimizan," she replied in her best imitation of Azalais' Gascon accent.

"Your business there?"

"Why should I tell you?" She let a few tears drop onto her lap and turned away from the man.

"Lost someone?" he asked slyly.

She didn't answer.

"Perhaps he'd rather have some barrels of wine?"

"Go away. I haven't lost anyone," she shouted at the crossbowman. "Leave me alone!"

He laughed at her.

"Feeling lonely? I can help you." He tried to grab Sancha's rein, but Illesa pulled her out of his reach and began cursing him, using Azalais' considerable repertoire.

He backed his horse away.

"Bitch! No wonder he left you behind."

He galloped ahead down the narrow track along the lake, signalling with a high, long whistle. The other man, presumably Almaric, would be tracking the barge which was already nearing the end of the lake. Once she'd left the lakeshore for the canal path, the young crossbowman appeared fifty paces behind her. He must have circled back to keep her in sight.

After a while, the water in the channel began to move more swiftly downhill. Ahead Illesa could see the wheel of a watermill on her left in an even faster race channel. Beyond it the land dropped away as the barge canal approached the wide river. There were buildings on its banks, and the Abbey tower rose above them, bright in the sun. The port was too far west to be visible.

Behind the mill there was a small cottage and outside it, standing next to a bay mare, was Almaric.

He came into the path and took Sancha's rein as she trotted past, pulling her to a halt. The cart was thrown round to the left as her head was turned, and one wheel nearly went into the canal.

"Get down," he said, pulling the horse towards him.

The crossbowman cantered past them, keeping watch on the barge which was some way ahead. Illesa clambered off the cart and stood in front of Almaric, her face set in fury.

"You're the man who took my pet! If the Count wanted her so much, why did you send her back to me?"

"You know why," Almaric said calmly. "The Count of Artois does not notice details. But I saw your expression when Burnel collapsed. I knew there was a link between you." The Count's man had a quiet, monotonous voice, and his face moved little as he spoke. But his hands were quick. He grabbed her right wrist and held it tight.

"The Count doesn't care, as long as he has his new plaything. Your friend and her voice is the latest. But I asked myself, what had happened to you and that blond player who was so swift to the aid of the fallen man. Yes, I knew there was something strange. I started to ask questions. It didn't take long to track you," he said, sniffing dismissively. "The weasel has a remarkable nose. I let her go in the doorway of the hospital ward, and it took her a mere moment to find you. Careless of you to pick her up. If it had been me, I would have sent her flying against the wall."

"You are a fucking traitor, you are," Illesa shouted, letting her spit fly. "Working against your own people!"

He squeezed her wrist until it hurt.

"You are no better, sleeping with the English who steal from us all the time. But you chose the wrong knight in Sir Burnel," Almaric said, his colour rising. "He's got no fortune. He is as poor as a common trader."

"I never asked him for money," she said twisting her arm to loosen his grip.

"You just like being a whore to the English?"

"He saved my life," she said defiantly.

"So you tried to save his? That is touching."

"He was going to die in that prison if I didn't help him."

For the first time there was an expression on Almaric's face. He looked smug.

"No he wasn't. He was going to be freed and sent to work for the French."

"You are lying! Sir Richard wasn't working for the French. Those bastards killed my whole family in Podensac!"

"Well, your *noble* English knight agreed to spy on his own side," Almaric sneered. "He was being released anyway. The ridiculous escape you planned was pointless." He squeezed her wrist harder. "And I am watching him to make sure he keeps his promise to the Count of Artois. That is the only reason I haven't killed him yet."

Illesa twisted her arm but could not loosen his grip. Almaric still held on to Sancha's rein with his other hand.

"Well, you can fucking kill the bastard now, if you want. Snuck out this morning while I slept. Disappeared with those Templars in the barge. He's probably dressed as a Templar now."

Almaric glanced towards the town. He wanted to check that his young lieutenant had not lost the quarry.

"He just left me, after all I did for him," Illesa cried, twisting her arm again and trying to move nearer to Sancha. If the horse panicked, she might back the cart into the canal. "But I've got his horse and the cart, and I will find him," she said reaching for Sancha's rein. She got hold of it and jerked it out of Almaric's hand. "And I will curse him. If you don't kill him, I will call upon the sea to swallow him," she screamed, trying to pull Sancha away from the canal.

"Be quiet, woman. You are making yourself mad!" Almaric shouted, reaching for the rein. "He's my prisoner and I will deal with him." His grip on her wrist had become excruciating.

"Let go of me, you bastard," she cried, stamping on his foot.

Almaric slapped her hard across the cheek.

"You want someone to drown, do you?" he asked, holding her chin so her stinging face was close to his. "Pretend to be so sweet, playing your music, but you are just a dirty whore, and you will get what you deserve." He whipped the rein out of her hand and pulled her arm behind her back, dragging her from the cart down the path away from the cottage. Eve was awake and agitated, turning circles in her pouch.

Illesa began to scream.

Almaric put one hand over her mouth and held her tight to his chest with the other. He pulled her to the edge of the canal where it was running fast downhill into the river channel.

And he threw her in.

Illesa went under the cold water. The current was strong, and she had to kick and kick to get to the surface. She took a breath, her body already feeling numb with cold, fighting to stay up in the flowing water, knowing she would be dragged down.

Almaric was not on the bank, so if she could climb out he wouldn't be there to throw her back in. But she had already been carried a long way down the channel. Some stones caught at her feet, but the water flowed too fast for her to stand.

A tree branch hung low over the channel where it widened out into the river. She kicked and pushed to the side so she could grab hold of it. It was rough and cut her hands, but she clung to it, feeling the terrible weight of water dragging at her skirts, pulling her towards the river.

Someone was calling from the bank. A man in a brown tunic with a red cross. He held out a long pole, trying to hold it steady near the slippery branch. Another man came up behind him and steadied the pole.

She grabbed for it.

At first they pulled her away from the branch and back into the full, heavy flow of the water so that they could pull her in beside the tree, reaching out to get her hands and her clothing to heave her up on the muddy stones of the bank.

She sat there, unable to speak, shaking. Her hands were so cold that she couldn't undo the pouch at her waist.

"Help me," she croaked at the men who knelt beside her. "Help me get her out."

The first man leant over her and worked at the clasp on the pouch. He opened it and looked in.

The weasel was sodden, not moving.

Illesa took her out gently.

"Have you got a dry cloth?" she asked, teeth chattering violently.

The second man, who was not a Templar, took the weasel and put it in his apron, folding it up and rubbing gently.

"Come, get up before you die of cold out here," said the Templar. "The Count's man and his guard have gone after the barge."

"Have they taken the cart?"

"No, they have left your horse and the cart on the track. It is all still intact."

A blanket appeared from somewhere, and they wrapped her in it.

The Templar assured her that he would have the cart taken out of sight immediately. When he came back a few moments later, he led her to the mill cottage. The cart was there, standing tipped up in the yard. The weight in the secret compartment was gone. Sancha, indifferent to the drama, was tethered and drinking from a trough.

Inside the miller's hall at the table in front of the fire, Richard was holding Eve on his lap.

Illesa sat down on the bench next to him, and someone brought her a cup of warm wine.

"She is dead," Illesa said in her choked voice. She put her hand on the small wet body, but there was no movement. The paws with their strong, sharp claws were limp.

Richard nodded, stroking the soft fur with one finger.

"But you are not."

"I should have left the pouch open. She can swim. She could swim."

"You didn't know you would be thrown in the river. How could you have known?" he said, putting his arm around her shoulders. "I heard you go in, and I couldn't even get out of that bloody cart to help you. I thought you had drowned." He held her close until the shaking in her chest subsided.

She looked down at the unmoving body on the table. A flame doused. Outside, rain was falling on the river.

"How long will we stay here?" she asked.

"Until the Templar comes back from the port. He will tell us if Almaric took the bait and went aboard the ship to Bayonne."

If Almaric had, he would have a humiliating landing. And he would return empty-handed to Bordeaux to receive a punishment devised by the Count of Artois. Perhaps to be cut into bait for his wolf.

The spasms of shock and cold came again. Illesa put her head on the table and shut her eyes.

When she opened them, it was much later. A lamp had been lit and the shutters closed. Someone had covered her in a thick wool blanket and laid her on a mat by the fire.

She rolled over, feeling the dampness of her skirt around her legs. The Templar who had pulled her from the river was in the doorway.

"Almaric sails for Bayonne, Lady Burnel." He came towards her, but did not touch her. "And there is a ship in port, bound for England on the morning tide. I am here to take you to it. Richard is already mounted and ready outside."

Chapter XLV

Saturday the 24th December 1295
Langley Manor
Vespers

Christopher went in and out of the kitchen. He was very hungry, but Adam would not let him have anything. "It is still a time of fasting," he'd said. "Why should it be any different for a lad like you when grown men are hungry from working all day?"

But Christopher had been working. He had watched Pelta with her new litter of puppies and had made sure they all found a teat and drank her milk. Then he had brought in wood for Cecily and also helped her to trim the lamps. He could not stand still anywhere in the manor without someone giving him a chore.

Now the day was nearly over, and still there was no sign of the old woman bringing the pastries she had promised. If she didn't come soon it would be too dark for her old eyes, and he would have to wait for tomorrow.

The news of the other potential arrival, he did not believe. Cecily had told him last night of the latest rumour from her friend at Acton: a sighting of his father at Ludlow.

But Cecily had shaken her head as she smoothed his hair out on the pillow.

"We won't believe it, will we, Christopher? Not until we see that face for ourselves."

At the end of November, a joiner had come all the way from Shrewsbury to say that he had seen Sir Richard Burnel, very changed but certainly him, riding a roan horse on the road from Oswestry. They'd paid him two silver pennies.

Then they'd waited and watched for days, but no one came. Christopher had come across Cecily crying in the pantry.

"A different one-eyed man," Cecily had said. "They see the one eye and assume. Don't even bother to look at the rest of the face."

But today William had gone out early on the road past Acton, just in case. He'd been gone since sext, and that was one of the reasons Christopher was being asked to do so much work. Now he had to see to the three horses, which was usually William's job. He didn't mind the feeding, but brushing them and polishing the tack made his arm ache. And the stable boy teased him about it when William wasn't there.

Christopher crossed the yard to the stable block, kicking his boots against the cobbles. It would be a miserable evening if William didn't come back. They would just sit round the fire watching Joyce try to eat her toys. It would be his task to stop her from falling in the embers. Cecily would want to sing with her out-of-tune voice. She would tell him a story he already knew. She would not let him talk about his worries, but all the time she would be biting her nails and turning her head towards the door like a weathervane.

Christopher put his hand on Jezebel's side. She shivered, shook her head and the tether strap rang on the ring like a bell.

"This won't be much of a feast," he said. "I might as well be a servant, with no parents and no friends."

Jezebel stamped her hoof and whinnied. There was some noise outside. Probably William returning. Good. He could finish the horses and let Christopher get into the warm and play with Little Edward the weasel before supper.

Christopher put down the brush and ran out into the twilit yard. All he could see at first was the light from the open hall door and Cecily, standing on the threshold with a straining Joyce in her arms, letting all the heat out and laughing.

Two palfreys were coming across the yard, their riders covered in long capes, their faces just pale blurs in the darkness. Pelta came past him and ran up to the horses, barking and jumping, her tail wagging furiously. Behind them, William was striding across the moat bridge, smiling wider than Christopher had ever seen.

The smaller rider had dismounted and was coming straight towards him. She covered him completely in her wet cloak. His mother didn't say anything, but kissed his head many times.

When she let him go, she went straight to Cecily, who had brought Joyce into the yard.

William was helping Father down from his horse.

Christopher felt suddenly shy, but Pelta was nearly knocking his father down in her excitement. Christopher grabbed her collar and held her back.

His father bent down to him, his face strange and familiar. An old man's face on his father's body. But the scar below his missing eye was the same.

"Christopher." He put his arms around him, trying to lift him up. "You are too big for me, my son," he said. There were tears falling down his face.

Christopher stepped back. He had never seen his father like this. Weeping, and so odd and wretched. But there was something to show him that would make him glad.

"Pelta has puppies," Christopher said. "Come and see."

He took his father's hand and pulled him towards the barn.

Notes

I have tried to reflect the various different languages used across England and its overseas territories in the post-conquest medieval period, as well as across social strata. Rather than indicate where a language changes, I have only drawn attention to the language when either Illesa or Richard would notice the 'nationality' of the speaker due to their accent or dialect.

The language spoken amongst the nobility of England at this time was Anglo-Norman, a dialect of French. The majority of the English population spoke what we now call Middle English, so Illesa, Richard and Gaspar speak English and Anglo-Norman. In Gascony the situation was complex. France as we know it today did not exist, rather it was divided up into several Kingdoms and Duchies. The Duchy of Gascony or Aquitaine was part of the Occitan language region. But because Bordeaux bordered the area where Norman French was spoken, it is likely that the people in that area would understand both Occitan and 'Old French'. They would immediately know if the speaker was using the Langue d'Oc, and therefore from Southern France and Gascony, or the Langue d'Oïl, and therefore from Northern France. I have indicated this by referring to accents and dialect. Azalais speaks Occitan, Norman French and some English.

The body of Robert Burnel (died 1292), Chancellor and Bishop of Bath and Wells, was interred in the nave of Wells Cathedral on the 23rd November 1292. In the beginning of the 19th century, several of the medieval tombs were moved when the nave was repaved. The tombs were opened and their slabs removed. Records of the operation are meagre. However, there is a tradition at Wells Cathedral that a small lead figure of the crucified Christ was found in the tomb of Robert Burnel. Notes made by canon Roger Frankland (served 1811-26) describe what was found.

The lead Christ was at the foot of a wooden coffin with two small rings, a buckle, shoes and some filaments of silken vestments. The canon remarked that the teeth were un-decayed, but that there was a circular aperture on the back of the skull near the nape of the neck. A round stone the size of a walnut, which the canon described as a sea pebble, fell out of this hole.

Burnel's sudden death in Berwick is unexplained by the chronicles of the time, but we cannot definitively assume on this evidence that he was killed by a slingstone from the beach at Berwick. Unfortunately the canon does not identify whom the tomb belonged to, and it seems the attribution to Robert Burnel came later.

Robert Burnel's will did not survive, but we do know that his nephew, William Burnel, who was first provost and later dean of Wells Cathedral, was an executor of his will. Later William had to resign the deanery as his appointment was made 'contrary to papal regulations on such matters'. Robert Burnel's heir, Philip Burnell, was the eldest son of his brother Hugh. He married into the wealthy FitzAlan family. Despite inheriting his uncle's enormous wealth, he became deeply indebted in the brief time between Robert's death and his own on 26th June 1294.

Richard Burnel was enfeoffed with the Manor of Langley by his cousin Robert Burnel for life. Robert was also very generous with many members of his extended family, including his postulated illegitimate children, who numbered between one and four, depending on how you interpret the historical record.

There is no evidence that Richard Burnel served in Gascony with Turberville, although the two families were linked by several property purchases. Richard Burnel doesn't appear very often in the historical record, but he *is* listed as travelling to Flanders with King Edward in 1297, as part of the disorganised attempt to defeat Philip IV of France from the north. On 10th July 1297, Langley and Ruckley were both seized into the King's hands, but the chronicle states that these manors were given back to Richard and his heirs by service of a fourth part of a knight's fee 'seeing how Richard was about to cross the seas with the King'. It seems Richard was threatened with the loss of his property if he didn't serve the King overseas. I am indebted to Richard Huscroft's thesis on Chancellor Burnel (listed in the **Selected Resources**) for bringing these intriguing events to light.

The Anglo-French War of 1294–97 was a complicated and ultimately futile conflict that took place against a background of increasing financial pressure on Edward I and his subjects. The central problem was that, due to the Treaty of Paris of 1259, the King of England held Gascony as a vassal of the King of France, Philip IV (the Fair). The French King thought he had a right to overarching jurisdiction over Edward's rule in Gascony.

In 1293 there were serious clashes between French, English and Gascon sailors. Edward saw the conflict as a private war but was forced to get involved as it escalated. In May 1293 he sent a high-ranking embassy to Paris, including his brother, Edmund Earl of Lancaster, to try to arrange a truce. The French King refused all suggestions. Instead he chose to summon his vassal Edward I to *parlement* after Christmas 1293. Charles of Valois, Philip's brother, was probably responsible for hardening his attitude and was widely believed to have been responsible for the naval war.

Edward refused to attend the *parlement* and, in early 1294, Edmund made a final attempt to negotiate a settlement. The following agreement was reached: Various fortresses and towns in Gascony would be handed over to the French and twenty Gascon notables would be given as hostages. Philip would revoke the summons to *parlement*, and King Edward would marry Philip's sister, Margaret.

Edward agreed to this plan, but it was a secret agreement. To satisfy opinion in France, it was to be announced in public that Edward would surrender all of Gascony, and letters patent to this effect were issued by the English King. The private understanding was that they would not be put into effect, and that the Gascon towns taken by the French would quickly be restored to Edward. Earl Edmund was satisfied by Philip IV's statements of intent, made before witnesses. In March 1294, he went south to arrange the surrender of the Gascon towns, including the city of Bordeaux, to the French, assuring the Gascon citizens that things would soon return to normal. But Philip then announced to his court that Gascony was not to be restored to the English and that the summons to appear before *parlement* was renewed. Edward rejected the summons and therefore lost his fief of Gascony. Edward renounced his homage to Philip formally, and from then on he could challenge him on equal terms, as a king, not as his vassal.

One contemporary explanation for this disastrous appeasement policy was that Edward was so overcome with lust for the King of France's sister that he acted rashly, without counsel. This theory is unlikely, as Edward was more motivated by his Crusading vow than by any marriage plans at this point. The most likely explanation was that his brother, Edmund, was duped by the French. Edmund has a strong connection with the French court through his wife Jeanne of Navarre, and he was too trusting. He and Edward failed to recognise Philip's intention to gain control over Gascony. But Philip was famous for being a taciturn and impenetrable man.

After it was clear that war was inevitable, Edward's strategy was to conduct a holding operation in Gascony while creating alliances with northern continental princes against Philip IV. Edward intended a large force to sail to Gascony at the end of September 1294, but the nobility were reluctant to serve and conscription caused resentment. Geoffrey Clement and Walter de Penderton were sent out to raise men from South Wales and the Marches. But their methods and the injustice of the English rule led to a rebellion when the Welsh conscripts were mustered at Shrewsbury Castle on the 30th September, and Clement was killed.

Now King Edward had two wars to fight. He redirected some of the forces that had been due to embark for Gascony to Wales. A small and under-resourced fleet including pardoned criminals set out from Portsmouth to retake Gascony in early October 1294 under the King's inexperienced nephew, John of Brittany. The King intended to send a much larger force, but the events in Wales, the French attacks on the English coast and the tension in Scotland meant that the small force was not relieved until January 1296.

The force did, at first, receive good support from local Gascon lords and had initial success, but the abandonment, rioting and siege of Podensac and Rions are recorded as self-inflicted disasters by the English, caused in part by the elderly Giffard and his Welsh guards. Twelve knights were taken hostage at Rions, including Sir Thomas Turberville, who would later turn traitor and be the first person to be executed for spying in England. The English held on to Blaye and Bayonne, but the rest of the towns had been surrendered to the French by the summer of 1295.

After months of fighting, the leader of the Welsh rebellion, Madog ap Llywelyn, was brought to battle at Maes Moydog on 5th March 1295 and defeated, although he escaped from the battlefield. After this turning point, Edward toured Wales, reducing opposition. By the summer, the rebellion had been completely suppressed.

Robert, Count of Artois (1250–1302) was known to keep a pet wolf, which he allowed to hunt across his lands, eating the herds of his peasants. He was a ruthless and talented military leader, until he met his humiliating end at the Battle of the Golden Spurs, fought between the Kingdom of France and the County of Flanders (modern-day Belgium) on 11th July 1302, in which three hundred nobles of France were slaughtered by the yeomanry of Flanders. Robert of Artois was surrounded and killed on the field. According to some tales, he begged for his life, but the Flemish refused to spare him, claiming that they did not understand French.

The cope in the story is based on the Madrid Cope, which featured in the exhibition: *Opus Anglicanum – English Medieval Embroidery* at the Victoria and Albert Museum in 2016. I have tried to stay true to its amazing artistry and subject matter but have taken the liberty of adding Saint André to its representations of saints. The cope was given to the church of Santa María de los Sagrados Corporales at Daroca by Pope Benedict XIII, who reigned at Avignon. As Raymond Bertrand de Got, Archbishop of Bordeaux 1299–1305, went on to become Pope Clement V at Avignon 1305–1314, it is possible that this cope may at one time have been used in the Cathedral in Bordeaux, although there is no evidence of this.

The character of Azalais of Dax is influenced by the female poet and singer, Azalais de Porcairagues, who lived in Provence in the mid-twelfth century. In Occitania women were given more freedom than in Northern Europe. In this environment the concept of courtly love flourished in the late twelfth and early thirteenth centuries, and women, known as *trobairitz*, were composing and singing courtly poems alongside men.

Classical topics were subjects of much Old French literature, but Homer's Illiad and Odyssey were unknown. Medieval Western poets had to make do with two Latin translations of short prose narratives based on Homer, ascribed to "Dictys and Dares". The twelfth century Norman poet, Benoît de Sainte-Maure, used the source material to write *Le Roman de Troie*. The poems that were written on these topics were called the *romans d'antiquité*, and treated the heroes of the Trojan War anachronistically as knights of chivalry.

A Greek legend told by Hyginus reports that Odysseus tried to avoid fighting in the Trojan War by feigning lunacy when Palamedes came to conscript him. He yoked a donkey and an ox to his plough and began to sow his fields with salt. But Palamedes tested Odysseus' madness by putting his infant son, Telemachus, in front of the plough. Odysseus veered the plough away, showing that he was not insane, and he was forced to go to war.

Text References

In Chapter III the Welsh translates as: "You take their weapons and return to Welshpool, we will march tomorrow to the north."

In Chapter V the extracts from the Bestiary are reprinted by permission of Boydell & Brewer Ltd from *Bestiary,* Richard Barber, Boydell Press, 1992, 9780851153292

In the Prologue and Chapter XIII the extracts from The Roman de Troie are reprinted by permission of Boydell & Brewer Ltd from 'The Roman de Troie' by Benoit de Sainte-Maure: A Translation, translated by Glyn S Burgess and Douglas Kelly, D S Brewer, 2017, 9781843844693

In Chapter XX 'The Ballad of Thomas Turberville' is influenced by the translation of the original ballad, translated by Michael Ingham in *Multilingualism in the Middle Ages and Early Modern Age* pp. 249-278, listed in **Selected Resources**

In Chapter XXVII the song is influenced by a song of the *trobairitz* Castelloza born c. 1200, translated by Meg Bogin in *The Women Troubadours* p.119, listed in **Selected Resources**

In Chapter XXXIII the song is adapted from the translation of a medieval French chanson, *'Volez vous que je vous chant'*, found in Paris Bibliothèque de l'Arsenal, ms 5198, pp. 314–315, with kind permission of the translator, Professor Samuel Rosenberg of the University of Indiana. The full text of the song is printed below.

In Chapter XXXV the song 'When Violets Bloom' is adapted from a translation of a Motet from *The Montpellier Codex*, Part 4: *Texts and Translations*. Translations by Susan Stakel and Joel C. Relihan. <u>Recent Researches in the Music of the Middle Ages and Early Renaissance,</u> vol. 8. Madison, WI (USA): A-R Editions, Inc., 1985. Used with permission. www.areditions.com. The full text of the Motet is printed below.

In Chapter XLII the extract comes from Psalm 112: 9–10

Volez vous que je vous chant
Would you have me sing for you
a charming song of love?
No rustic composed it,
but rather a knight
under the shade of an olive tree
in the arms of his sweetheart.
She wore a linen shift,
a white ermine wrap,
and a tunic of silk;
she had stockings of iris
and mayflower shoes,
fitting just right.

She wore a sash of leaves
that turned green in the rain;
it was buttoned with gold.
Her purse was of love
and had pendants of flowers:
it was a love-gift.

She was riding a mule;
its shoes were of silver
and its saddle of gold;
on the crupper behind her
three rosebushes grew
to provide her with shade.

So she went down through the field;
some knights came upon her
and greeted her nicely:
"Lovely lady, where were you born?"
"From France I am, the renowned,
of highest birth.

"The nightingale is my father,
who sings on the branches
high up in the woods;
the siren is my mother,

who sings high on the shore
of the salt sea."

"Lovely lady, may such birth bode well!
You are of fine family
and high birth;
would to God our father
that you were given me
as my wedded wife!"

When violets bloom

When violets, roses and gladiolas bloom and parrots sing,
that is when prick me the loving thoughts which keep me gay. For a while I didn't sing, but now I will sing and compose a merry song on account of the love that my little sweetheart has given me for such a long time.
God, I find her so very sweet and loyal towards me,
so free of baseness that I will never leave her.
When I remember her little mouth, her beautiful blond hair, her gleaming throat more lovely and white than the lily in May, her small, firm, pointing little breasts, I am abashed with wonder.
She is so perfectly formed that the moment I found her
my whole heart was filled with joy.
But I pray to the God of Love who cares for lovers
that he keep our love good, true and perfect;
may he curse those who, out of jealousy, spy on us,
for I never will leave her unless because of the deeds of those wretched spies.

Glossary

alms – charity for the poor

anchoress – female recluse often enclosed in a small cell adjoining a church

Aquitaine – the Duchy of Gascony, including the further region of Dordogne held by the King of England as a vassal of the King of France 1152–1453

bailey – the courtyard within the walls of a castle

bailiff – justice officer under the sheriff who would collect rents

boon work – extra work done for the lord of the manor at harvest and haymaking

bordelaise/bordelaise – French term referring to an inhabitant of Bordeaux or the surrounding area

braies/breeches – undergarments for legs and loins worn by men and women

burgess – freeman of a borough

cantor – leader of chants in a choir

caparison – ornamental covering spread over a horse's saddle or harness

cerecloth – cloth coated in wax

challoner – maker and/or seller of blankets

chantry – chapel or altar endowed for the saying of prayers and singing of Masses for its founder

cog – clinker-built ship, widely-used from the twelfth century on, with a single mast and a square-rigged sail, from 15-25 metres in length, able to carry up to 200 tons

cope – long semi-circular coat or cape often with a hood. A special garment worn in religious processions

cotter – farmer of small plot of land owned by a lord

cowl – hood of the garment worn by monks

crupper – piece of tack for horses and other equids to keep a saddle, harness or other equipment from sliding forward. Usually attached around the tail

dalmatic – long, wide-sleeved tunic, a liturgical vestment in Christian churches

demesne – manorial land retained for the private use of a feudal lord

destrier – best-known war horse of the medieval era, carried knights in battles and tournaments

estampie – medieval musical form, and a dance, using repeated and rhythmical patterns

ewer – jug, usually of metal

falchion – curved broad sword

fitchet – vertical slit in the outer tunic through which the hands were passed to allow access to the gown underneath and the pouch suspended from the girdle or belt

frumenty – porridge made of wheat or barley, savoury or sweet, cooked in milk, sometimes with dried fruit and spices added

gambeson – tunic of heavy cloth or hardened leather worn as protection

Gascony/Guyenne – Duchy including the area south of Bordeaux, bordered by the Atlantic ocean to the west, the Pyrenees to the south, and the Garonne river to the north and east

hauberk – shirt reaching to mid thigh, made of mail.

hose – tight-fitting clothing for the lower body, usually worn by men

jennet – Spanish horse, bred to be small, calm and agile

jerkin – overjacket

jesses – straps attached to a hawk's legs

jongleur – courtly singer/entertainer

kirtle – woman's loose gown

Lazar house – place to quarantine people with leprosy

livre – medieval currency for accounting purposes in the Kingdom of France, equivalent to a pound of silver

maslin – bread made from mix of rye and wheat

mêlée – mock battle between sides of armed horsemen

mews – cage or building used for keeping hunting birds

mummer – actor of short entertainments, often masked

palfrey – small horse, often used by women

pluviale – cope, or other garment intended to keep off the rain

pottage – stew usually of vegetables, sometimes mixed with grain

poultice – soft, moist mass of cloth, bread, meal, herbs etc., applied hot as a medicament to the body

prie-dieu – literally 'pray god', a stand for a book which has a ledge for kneeling for private devotions

rouncey – good riding horse/charger for men-at-arms in battle

sacristan – officer of a church or religious house charged with care of the sacristy, the church, and their contents

scapular – Christian clerical garment suspended from the shoulders

shift – body garment or shirt of a washable material such as linen, cotton etc.

shrive/shriven – forgive/forgiven

simples – herbal remedies

solar – private chamber, often an upper room designed to catch the sun

sortie – (from the French for 'exit') a deployment or dispatch of a military unit from a strongpoint or a castle under siege

squire – young man, usually noble, who is training for knighthood

steerboard – long, flat board or oar that went from the stern to underwater, used to steer vessels before the invention of the rudder. Traditionally on the starboard side of a ship (the 'steering board' side)

supertunic – tunic worn over other clothing

surcote – outer coat of rich material

thwart – bench seat across width of an open boat

trebuchet – common type of siege engine which uses a swinging arm and counterweight to throw a projectile

troubadour – poet and composer, who often performed own work

trobairitz – Provençal/Occitan word for a female troubadour

vesica – pointed oval shape; the usual shape for the seal of a cleric or a woman

veil/wimple – headdress worn by women from the 12th to the 14th century

villein – peasant occupying land subject to a lord

Acknowledgements

My thanks go to:
Ann Mason, for her skill, patience and enormous generosity
James Wade http://jameswade.webs.com for the beautiful maps
Mike Ashton of MA Creative for the book cover

Writing West Midlands, my colleagues in Room 204, members of Borders Poetry Writing Group and members of Bridgnorth Writing Group

The Independent booksellers of Shropshire, the Shropshire Museum Service and my friends at Eaton Manor

Professionals who were generous with help and advice: Manda Scott, Karen Maitland, Adam Maisano, Henrietta Leyser, Christina Green, Peter Reaville, Maria Richards, Chris and Jenny Wroe, Jonathan Davidson and Liz Hyder

Friends whose support and belief kept me going and readers who commented so thoughtfully on the imperfect typescript:
Gwen Sideaway, Lou and Dave Bleackley, James and Kristin Hatt, Catherine and Stephen Nelson, Bob and Bonnie Havery, Deborah Alma, Claire Coventry, Amanda Robinson, Deborah Jackson, Heather Green, Heather and Mike Streetly, Katriona Wade, Hal and Sharon Holladay, Kate and Phil Smith, Jo Barker, Ram Aston, Lucy Heywood, Susie Stapleton, Pascale Presumey, Karen Robinson, Sarah Ibberson, Rosemary Sgroi, Ted Eames, Jo Jackson, Adrian Perks, Lisa Blower and Steve Harrison

Freya, James, John, Mum, Dad, Clair, Kirk, Jill, Braw, Nico, Clare, Alex, Marc, Christine, and all my loving family near and far

All those who have taken time to review or comment on *The Errant Hours* – whose encouragement has been invaluable

Michael Innes – who makes things both possible and enjoyable

Selected Resources

Printed:

Anglo-Welsh Wars 1050–1300, Stuart Ivinson, 2001, Bridge Books
Bestiary, Richard Barber, 1992, The Boydell Press
Edward I, Michael Prestwich, 1988, Methuen
England's Medieval Navy 1066–1509, Susan Rose, 2013, Seaforth Publishing
English Medieval Embroidery – Opus Anglicanum, Clare Browne, Glyn Davies and M A Michael eds., Yale University Press, 2016
Everyday Life in Medieval Shrewsbury, Dorothy Cromarty, 1991, Shropshire Books
Falling from Grace – Reversal of Fortune and the English Nobility 1075–1455, J S Bothwell, 2008, Manchester University Press
Guide du Bordeaux médiéval, Annick Bruder, 2005, Éditions Sud Ouest
Histoire des Maires de Bordeaux, Volume 1 of <u>Grand Journal de Bordeaux</u>, 2008, Les Dossiers d'Aquitaine
Les Chemins de Saint-Jacques dans les Landes, Francis Zapata 2002, Éditions Sud-Ouest
Life in a Medieval Village, Frances and Joseph Gies, 1990, Harper Perennial
Marie et Marion – Music from the Montpellier Codex, Anonymous 4 (CD with lyric booklet) 2014, harmonia mundi usa
Medieval English Verse, Brian Stone ed., 1964, Penguin Books
Medieval Grafitti, Matthew Champion, 2015, Ebury Press
Medieval Pets, Kathleen Walker-Meikle, 2012, The Boydell Press
Medieval Wall Paintings, Roger Rosewell, 2014, Shire Publications
Medieval Women, Henrietta Leyser, 1995, Phoenix
Multilingualism in the Middle Ages and Early Modern Age – Communication and Miscommunication in the Premodern World, Albrecht Classen ed., 2016, De Gruyter
Pilgrimage in Medieval England, Diana Webb, 2000, Hambledon and London
Saints and their Badges, Michael Lewis and Greg Payne, 2014, Greenlight Publishing
Studies in Medieval History Presented to F M Powicke, Hunt, Pantin and Southern eds., 1948, Oxford at the Clarendon Press
The Book of Beasts, TH White ed., 1954, Jonathan Cape
The Hanged Man, Robert Bartlett, 2004, Princeton University Press
The Heroides of Ovid, Harold Isbell, 1990, Penguin Classics

The Iliad of Homer, translated by Robert Fitzgerald, 1974, Oxford University Press

The Medieval Traveller, Norbert Ohler, 1989, The Boydell Press

The Mighty Dead, Adam Nicolson, 2014, William Collins

The Odyssey of Homer, translated by Robert Fagles, 1996, Penguin Books

The Pilgrimage to Compostella in the Middle Ages, Maryjane Dunn and Linda Kay Davidson eds., 1996, Routledge

The Political Career and Personal Life of Robert Burnell, Chancellor of Edward I, Richard Huscroft, 2000, Submitted thesis for Degree of Doctor of Philosophy at Kings College, University of London

The Roman de Troie by Benoît de Sainte-Maure, translated by Glyn S Burgess and Douglas Kelly, 2017, D S Brewer

The Thirteenth Century, Sir Maurice Powicke, 1962, Oxford University Press

The Time Traveller's Guide to Medieval England, Ian Mortimer, 2009, Vintage

The Welsh Wars of Edward I, J E Morris, 1901, Alden Press

The Women Troubadours, Meg Bogin, 1980, W W Norton & Company

Websites:

http://www.victoriacountyhistory.ac.uk/counties

https://www.bl.uk/manuscripts/

http://www.gallowglass.org/jadwiga/herbs/herbhandout.htm

http://rosaliegilbert.com/

https://en.wikipedia.org/wiki/Medieval_cuisine

http://www.mainlymedieval.com/blog/

http://etheses.dur.ac.uk/1509/2/1509_v2.pdf?EThOS%20(BL)